THEY

DROWN

OUR

DAUGHTERS

KATRINA MONROE

Poisoned Pen
PRESS

Published by Poisoned Pen Press, an imprint of Sourcebooks
P.O. Box 4410, Naperville, Illinois 60567–4410
(630) 961-3900
sourcebooks.com

Library of Congress Cataloging-in-Publication Data

Names: Monroe, Katrina, author.
Title: They drown our daughters / Katrina Monroe.
Description: Naperville, Illinois : Poisoned Pen Press, [2022]
Identifiers: LCCN 2022002458 (print) | LCCN 2022002459 (ebook) |
    (trade paperback) | (epub)
Subjects: LCGFT: Horror fiction. | Novels.
Classification: LCC PS3613.O53696 T47 2022 (print) | LCC PS3613.O53696
    (ebook) | DDC 813/.6--dc23/eng/20220128
LC record available at https://lccn.loc.gov/2022002458
LC ebook record available at https://lccn.loc.gov/2022002459

Printed and bound in Canada.
MBP 10 9 8 7 6 5 4 3 2

For my mother.

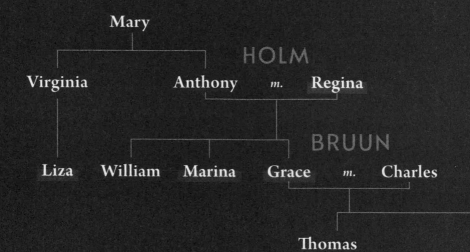

Mary

HOLM

Virginia   Anthony   *m.*   Regina

BRUUN

Liza   William   Marina   Grace   *m.*   Charles

Thomas

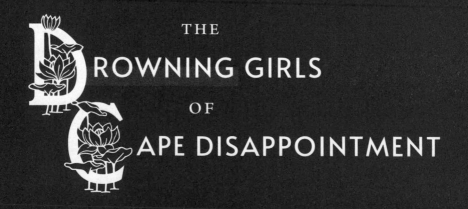

THE

DROWNING GIRLS

OF

CAPE DISAPPOINTMENT

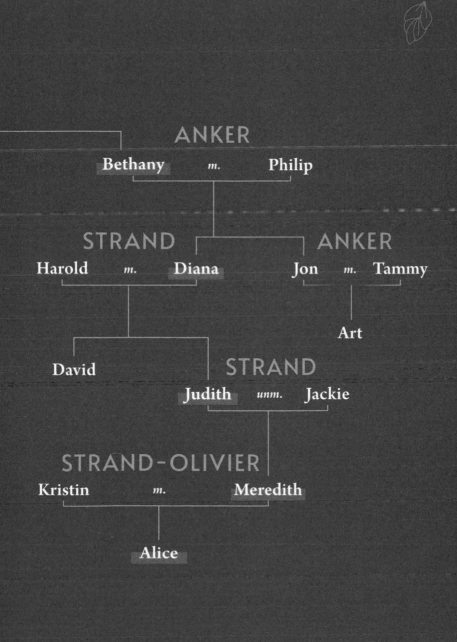

ANKER

Bethany *m.* Philip

STRAND

Harold *m.* Diana

ANKER

Jon *m.* Tammy

Art

David

STRAND

Judith *unm.* Jackie

STRAND-OLIVIER

Kristin *m.* Meredith

Alice

REGINA

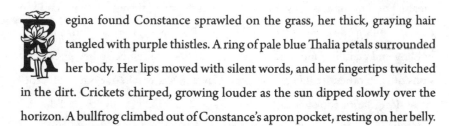egina found Constance sprawled on the grass, her thick, graying hair tangled with purple thistles. A ring of pale blue Thalia petals surrounded her body. Her lips moved with silent words, and her fingertips twitched in the dirt. Crickets chirped, growing louder as the sun dipped slowly over the horizon. A bullfrog climbed out of Constance's apron pocket, resting on her belly.

"I don't want to kill my husband," Regina said.

Constance cracked one eye, closing it just as quickly. "Admirable." Then, "It's rude to stare while a woman communes, Gina."

The bullfrog glanced up at Regina with big, wet eyes before climbing back into Constance's pocket.

"Are you talking to me or him?" Regina asked.

Constance smirked. "Either or. It suits you both, I think."

Seemed every time Regina hiked the hill at the far end of the peninsula to see Constance, the woman had a creature hidden somewhere on her body, clinging to her as though they could absorb that essential something that softened her face and brightened her spirit while the rest of them went hard and gray. It was resentment that made some of the people of Cape Disappointment call Constance a witch. If not for Regina's middle-class upbringing and her marriage to a man of means, she might have succumbed to the same fate.

Friends since childhood, it was Constance who Regina had gone to when she couldn't conceive. Under Constance's direction, she'd swallowed remedies. She'd danced the dances, naked around the phallic maypole. She'd burned sage and eaten enough pumpkin to turn her orange. She'd buried eggs in her hearth, under her pillow, under the bed, in the garden, beneath the steps of their front door, until her house was a veritable chicken coop, and nurtured a small ficus from seedling to leafy adult, until finally she conceived her daughter—Marina, her miracle child, who'd been born too small, her lungs struggling to take in a first breath. For days after, the doctors told Regina to expect the worst, that a child so delicate couldn't be expected to last the week. Regina had nursed Marina herself, holding and cuddling and touching until their bodies seemed to become extensions of each other. Regina never called Constance a witch, not out loud, especially after Marina took her first wobbly steps. That didn't mean others did not.

William and Grace followed Marina soon after, barely a year apart. Her husband gave his praise to the doctors who'd poked and prodded her to bruising, but Regina gave his money to Constance. Her friend was powerful in ways the doctors were not, ways Regina made a point of learning for herself.

"What's the point of the frog?" Regina asked.

"He grounds me. Keeps me tethered to the here and now."

"Sounds awful."

Constance smirked, nudging the bullfrog out of her pocket and into the grass. "If you've come for a character witness in the event of your husband's untimely demise, I'm afraid I won't do you much good."

"I don't want—"

"To kill him. So you said."

Sighing, Regina gathered her skirts between her legs and lay down next to Constance. Her hair smelled like bonfire and pine sap, and if Regina closed her eyes, she could imagine she was deep in the woods, away from the ocean and the lighthouse, the letter still crumpled in her fist.

A marriage drowned by apathy...

Women like her have teeth...

Tread carefully, my darling...

She tossed the ball of paper onto Constance's chest. Constance opened it and read silently.

"Who's Jeanie?" she asked when she'd finished.

"The daughter of one of Anthony's partners." A pause. "The woman he'd see in my place."

"Oh." She paused too. "You say you *don't* want to kill him?"

Regina smirked despite the tears welling in her eyes. "No." She sat up, snatching the letter back. "But I'd like to hurt him."

————————

Dinner was a silent affair. The children, along with Anthony's niece, Liza, visiting for the summer, traded kicks beneath the table. She and Marina were both fourteen, womanhood creeping up behind them with a sack and hammer. Though Anthony shot them warning glances between bites of potato, Regina hoped they clung to their childishness. Once that line was crossed, there was no going back.

Regina pushed her food around her plate, stealing glances at her husband when she dared. He had to know the letter was gone. That she'd stolen it from his desk. Would he deny his intention to leave her? His relationship with Jeanie? Or would he approach her like a stubborn ship's captain, using honeyed words and a firm hand to convince her that his was the correct decision and never mind the rain-bloated storm clouds in the distance or the leak in the hull?

She shouldn't have been surprised. He'd had other affairs, but they were quiet and brief. Despite never meeting those women, Regina believed there was an understanding between them. They could have her husband in their bedrooms, but it was Regina who was on his arm. Regina, who'd given everything to create and maintain the kind of home and lifestyle befitting someone of his station. It was Regina who would die in the largest room of the largest house on the cape. And it was Regina's children who would inherit it all when she and Anthony were gone.

It was this understanding that helped Regina look the other way, to play the part of the blissfully ignorant wife. This time was different. This time, her husband was on the verge of throwing away all that Regina had achieved—for herself and for her children.

Dinner ended without a word. Anthony planted a dry kiss on her forehead before disappearing into his office, where he would stay until he crawled into bed in the wee hours of the morning, stinking of whiskey and cigars.

"Would it really be so bad if he left?" Constance had asked.

Yes. It would.

Because he wouldn't leave. Not after he'd spent the better part of a decade culling out a private port for his business, after dumping too much money into building a lighthouse to silence the critics calling Cape Disappointment a smugglers' port. It didn't matter how much of her own blood and sweat had been mixed into the mortar that held the lighthouse together, that it was her who made sure it was lit at night to guide sailors safely home. Regina would be made to leave behind everything she'd built, to run home with her tail between her legs or move somewhere new and be a pariah.

And her children?

He'd keep them, too, if only out of spite. And then the moment Jeanie had children of her own, they'd be pushed to the side, forgotten.

Marina laid her head on Liza's shoulder, teasing a curl out from behind Liza's ear with her little finger. Across the table, Grace slipped the last of her potatoes onto William's plate, a gentle grin on her face as he heaped them all onto his fork. When it was time for dessert, Regina knew he'd pretend to eat his entire pudding in one bite only to give it all to Grace.

She imagined the day Anthony would come to her dripping of pity and false remorse and tell her their marriage was over. In her mind's eye, she saw Jeanie waltz through the front doors, plump and ripe. She saw her children sent away to schools on the other side of the country, away from their home, away from *her*.

Regina couldn't let that happen.

She caught Marina's eye across the table and smiled.

I would do anything for you, Regina thought.

Anything.

———————

Anthony finally came to bed at a little after two o'clock in the morning. Regina lay death-still until his body sank into the mattress and his snores rumbled the pillow. She could have leapt from the bed, screeching that the house was on fire and he wouldn't have moved, but she took care anyway, creeping from the bedside to the loose floorboard beneath the window. With every movement, she checked over her shoulder; Anthony was dead to the world.

When she plucked it from its hiding spot, the charm looked like something out of a nightmare, tentacled roots tied with colored string in knots so tight they cut the flesh. Caked in a mixture of black mud and a palmful of Regina's blood, it was heavy and awkward to hold. She cradled the thing as she crept from her bedroom and into her husband's office, using a stolen key to let herself in.

"The thing you have to know," Constance had told her that morning on the cliff, "is that, in the end, these things have a mind of their own. They'll take your wishes into account, but there's no telling if they'll obey."

Her eyes went directly to the desk, almost expecting to find another letter, but the surface was clear, save for a couple of books.

Constance's voice whispered in her ear as Regina moved around the office.

Somewhere he will be exposed to it but not discover it.

Dig the roots in.

It must be warm and comfortable and eager.

I don't have to remind you what will happen if it's found.

Though the days of burning a witch at the stake were long over, it would only take a word from her husband to get Regina locked in a sanatorium forever.

She circled the office three times, no closer to finding a suitable hiding place. His office was immaculate, and Anthony was particular about the placement of his things; the door had been locked from the day they were married. Finally, she settled on a cubby on the bookshelf. The books on this shelf were small and dusty. Rarely touched.

The charm was hot as sunbaked earth and seemed to writhe in her hands. Constance had warned her to be concise in her request, but now, the moment upon her, Regina didn't know what to say. She held it close to her lips and whispered, "Save me. Save my children. Save Marina—"

"Aunt Regina?"

Regina's heart fell into her stomach as she turned to see Liza, a barely there shadow in the darkness of the hall. "Go to bed," she ordered.

Liza stepped into the office. Regina tried to stuff the charm onto the shelf without her looking too closely, but Liza was young and her eyes were sharp. "Is it…dead?"

"It's nothing," Regina snapped. "Go to bed like I told you to."

"It's not nothing." Then, "My mother says you're friends with a witch. Is that true?"

Regina's voice shook. "Go to *bed*, Liza."

"Is that hers?" Liza took another bold step forward. Lifted her hand like she might reach for the thing. "What does it do?"

Regina could feel the charm start to thrum in her hands. What would it do if she held it too long? What other wishes might it pull from her heart? Finally, she managed to shove the thing between her husband's books.

"It's a…good luck charm," Regina said, on the razor edge of panic. "For a prosperous winter."

Liza's eyes went wide. "You *do* know a witch." Then, eyes narrowing, she added, "Are *you* a witch?"

"Of course not."

"I don't believe you."

"It's only for luck, child. Now go back to bed before—"

"My mother says witches are evil. That they come into your room at night and summon their demons to eat away your soul." Liza's gaze flicked between charm and Regina. "I'm telling."

In the instant it took for Liza to turn toward the door, Regina saw the future in bright, red-rimmed flashes—a stone-walled room and a thin cotton night-gown in the freezing cold, her children forced into obscurity by the memory of a mother locked far away.

A shrill voice ripped through her mind. *Stop her.*

Regina lunged for the girl, catching her by her nightgown just as she reached the end of the hall, and yanked her back. The seam of her sleeve tore, revealing flushed skin. Liza cried out in surprise. Trembling, Regina wound the material around her fist, pulling Liza back. She would sit the girl down. She would make her understand. She would bribe, threaten, whatever it took.

In her panic, she clawed Liza's arm. Liza's scream echoed in the narrow hall-way. Clapping her hand over Liza's mouth, Regina shot a worried look toward the bedrooms. It was only a matter of time before the struggle woke the children. Or worse, her husband. She had to—

Liza bit down on Regina's hand, snagging skin. Pain ripped up Regina's arm, and she pulled away too fast, making Liza stumbled backward.

She was too close to the stairs.

Their eyes met, Liza's wide with terror. Her foot slipped, and she clawed for the wall, but it was too far.

As Liza fell, Regina felt the urge to reach for the girl rise and fall like a wave.

Liza's body hit the bottom stair with a sickening crack. Though it was too dark to see properly, Regina knew she was dead. *She's just a girl*, Regina thought. *What have I done?*

What you had to, she told herself.

"Mama?" a voice whispered from farther down the hall.

Regina spun around, startled. *Marina.* She could just make out the long tendrils of her daughter's hair. She held her hand to her throat, pulse pound-ing beneath her fingertips. "Go to bed, sweetheart. You'll wake your brother and sister." *And none of you can ever know what I've done.*

"Liza's gone."

Regina forced a smile into her voice. "She's probably in the kitchen sneaking some of those cakes your father brought home. I'll send her back up." Then, when Marina didn't immediately go back into her room, "To bed, Marina. Now."

Marina's door closed with a timid click.

And Regina set to work.

———————

After wrapping Liza's body in a blanket, Regina half-dragged her almost a quarter mile, down to Dead Man's Cove. There, she lit a small fire and hoped the flames were big enough to be seen from Constance's house, high up on the hill. She'd climbed the lighthouse to douse the light—and prayed no one attempted to sail to the cape tonight—so the dancing flames were all she had to see by.

What felt like years later, Constance appeared at the mouth of the cove. Her gaze immediately fell on Liza, the blanket having fallen away from her face. "What happened?"

Regina shook her head, unable to make the tangled mess in her mind unravel. A single-minded survival instinct had made her capable of dragging a young girl's body to the cove, but in the dark and quiet, the gentle lap of water on the shore, she was slowly coming undone.

Constance took Regina's hand. "You have to tell him. He'll understand."

"I can't. He won't." She looked toward the water. "I have to get rid of her. You have to help me."

"No. Regina, I—"

"I'll tell him she ran away. She only came to us because her parents were struggling to keep her in line. They'll believe it." Regina nodded to herself. "This is the only way."

"She won't rest." Constance forced Regina to look at her. "Do you understand?"

Regina pulled away. On her knees, she wrapped the blanket tighter around Liza's body and then set to work looking for stones to fill it with. Among the stones, she nestled a small, opal-pink shell, whispering a brief "I'm sorry." It wasn't much of a eulogy, but it would have to do. When she looked up again, Constance had gone, her footsteps in the sand leading back toward her house on the hill. Regina didn't blame her. This was her mistake. She needed to fix it.

After she filled the blanket with stones and ensured it wouldn't come unwrapped, Regina undressed and waded into the water, pulling Liza's body behind her. She heard what sounded like footsteps in the sand, and for a moment, she thought maybe Constance had come back, but when she scanned the rocks at the edge of the cove, she only saw darkness. What if one of the children...? Fear prickled her skin as she stared harder at the rocks, studying the curves of the shadows.

But all was still. There was no one there.

Liza's body sank easily, but Regina continued to drag, kicking and gasping as the ground fell away and the waves threatened to pull her out to sea. Regina was a strong swimmer, but even she got disoriented in the dark. Finally, she swam for shore—if not for her fire, she might have drowned. When she looked back, a few bubbles marked the place where Liza's body sank. Then there was nothing.

At the house, she abandoned her underthings, burning them in the kitchen hearth. The last of the white fabric had charred when Grace and William surprised her.

"Does no one sleep in this house?" she asked.

"Marina left," Grace said.

William dug his finger into her shoulder. "Rat."

"It was a long time ago," Grace continued, rubbing her arm. "I saw her from the window, heading out into the dark."

Regina's chest tightened with sudden terror. *The footsteps...* "Where did she go?"

Grace shrugged.

Standing, Regina shook her head. Marina couldn't have followed her. She would have noticed. She would have *seen*.

Except, maybe she wouldn't have. She'd had tunnel vision, singularly focused on making sure Liza's body wouldn't be found. The longer she considered it, the more the possibility that Marina had been on the beach, had seen everything, became solid in her mind.

Regina went back and forth with herself. Wouldn't Marina have said something to her? Wouldn't she have tried to stop her?

Maybe not if Marina was afraid.

Regina's stomach twisted into painful knots.

Was she hiding somewhere? Terrified of her own mother?

Or worse, had she gone in the water to try to save her cousin?

Regina imagined her daughter struggling through the waves, blinking against the dark, groping, reaching, before getting caught in an undertow, dragged beneath the foam.

Regina ran from the house, cutting her feet on jagged rocks, salt air stinging her lungs. "Marina!"

Her voice echoed along the bluff. She followed the sound to the lighthouse, thinking, praying, Marina had gone to the light room, but the door was locked.

"Marina!"

Panic edged up her throat, a dozen knives carving her sins on her tongue. Her mind kept trying to reassure her against what her heart knew. She would go back to the cove. Marina would be there, wet and shaken but alive. But only if Regina hurried.

She found the still-smoking remnants of her fire, and by the faint moonlight, she could just make out the line where the water met sand. She strained to hear her daughter's voice, splashing, anything. But the cove was eerily silent.

She ran to the rocks at the edge of the cove, thinking she'd find Marina there, hiding. She'd find out exactly what Marina saw and then she'd fix it. She'd make Marina understand. But the only thing Regina found at the rocks was a pair of small footprints, dug deep in the sand. She got on her hands and knees and crawled, following the footprints down the beach, where they disappeared into the night-dark sea. A wave washed over her wrists and along her legs, and carried with it the ghost of a high-pitched giggle. Regina's body went cold. Had Marina been driven into the water to try to save Liza, or had Liza called her in to play?

The thing you have to know is that, in the end, these things have a mind of their own.

CHAPTER ONE

MEREDITH

he peninsula curved like a crooked finger, beckoning ships and people with its siren song of safe harbor. From atop the bridge, Meredith could just make out the mouth of the Columbia River, the place they called the Graveyard of the Pacific, where the remains of dozens of ships littered the brackish floor. Beyond the mouth of the river, hidden along the coast behind a bluff, was Dead Man's Cove, nestled just inside Cape Disappointment's town limit. Farther, just visible in the distance, was the lighthouse, standing sentry against the too-bright autumn sky. On the other side of the lighthouse, down the hill barely half a mile, was her mother's house.

In the backseat, her seven-year-old daughter, Alice, pressed her face to the window, half a Kit Kat congealing in her fist. Her hair was a nest of tangles, and her too-small nightgown pinched her upper arms.

She still hadn't asked where they were going, why Mama Kristin wasn't with them, and Meredith wasn't offering any answers. *Kids are resilient,* she told herself. *Alice will be fine.*

She almost believed it.

The last time Meredith had come back to Cape Disappointment, it'd been to bury her stepdad. It had been September, a little over five years ago, after Alice was born and after her courtroom marriage to Kristin. She'd had to explain to her mother, to friends, why they hadn't been invited. *We didn't want to jinx it*, she'd said, as though they could lock their marriage in a secret cabinet, safe. Hidden. Preserved. Guarded as it was, the marriage was doomed to break. How were they supposed to know it'd be them that did the breaking?

When she and Alice showed up at her front door, Meredith's mother, Judith, looked both sad and surprised to see her, ushering them through the door with the resignation of a woman with a death sentence getting her first look at the firing squad.

"You're back," she said.

"I'm back," Meredith said.

Judith sighed, walking deeper into the house with Alice at her heels. "That's that, then."

They followed Alice as she ducked in and out of rooms, a one-sided game of hide-and-seek, before finding themselves all together in the kitchen. Meredith should have felt at ease moving through her childhood home, plucking sugary-sweet memories from the air like candy, but the longer she'd been away, the more foreign the place felt. Like seeing the place through different eyes, she saw the flaws—in the house, in her mother, in herself.

"Kristin and I are separating," Meredith blurted after the silence between them had gotten too long, too awkward. She'd been battling the entire way how to tell her mother, mind bending in complicated word gymnastics as she tried to phrase it in a way that didn't make it sound like a failure, but from the moment she'd walked through the door, her head was a blank.

"Divorce isn't the end of the world," Judith said as she dug through the junk drawer in the kitchen. "Keys got to be here somewhere."

"We're not divorced. We're separated," Meredith said.

"Same thing."

"No. It isn't."

They'd only just arrived and already Meredith and her mother were fighting. A new record.

Judith sighed, still digging. She pulled out a flashlight, the warranty for a microwave she no longer had, a sandwich bag of batteries. Alice grabbed the flashlight and flicked the switch on and off, growing frustrated when nothing happened.

"It's dead, darlin'," Judith said. Then, glancing up at Meredith, "She looks good."

"Of course she does." Meredith snatched a lock of black hair and tugged. Alice yelped, then laughed. "She's mine."

Judith didn't respond. Up to her elbow in the drawer now, she closed her eyes, focusing. "Aha!" She pulled out her hand and held up a set of keys that hung on a small metal ring, behind a cartoon frog key chain. She handed them to Meredith.

"What's this?"

"Light room keys."

"And I need them because…?"

"With Alice here"—Judith snatched a glance at Alice, who still hadn't given up on the flashlight, banging it on the floor—"someone needs to keep the light on."

"I thought it was automatic."

"Mostly. It might break down."

"Okay, but I don't get why—"

"It's not that much to ask is it? You show up with Alice and a couple of suitcases expecting me to take you in...all I ask is that you keep the light on. It's important."

Meredith clenched her fist around the keys. The teeth dug into her palm. "I didn't expect anything, Mom. I just wanted..." *Somewhere safe?* "I didn't have anywhere else to go." Alice looked up at her, a frown forming that would no doubt turn to tears if this kept up. She smiled at Alice, then turned back to her mother, smile straining. "We can leave if you want. Get a hotel or something."

And eat up what little savings she had separate from their joint accounts. She was terrified to touch anything in them, worried it'd send some kind of signal to Kristin. If a hotel bill showed up on the credit card statement, what would that say to her? *Separation's great, look what fun I'm having?* Or *I'm so desperate and alone without you?*

Judith ignored her. "It's for Alice. We have to keep her safe. You know what would happen if—"

"Mom." Meredith lowered her voice. The last thing she needed was Alice to get all worked up over something hiding in the dark, waiting to get her. So far, she'd handled everything with more grace than Meredith, nodding with sage understanding as Meredith finally explained that they were going on a little vacation without Mama Kristin, and not to worry, they would be back, and did she want to get a new stuffed penguin or dinosaur? "Nothing is going to happen. Okay?"

"You don't know that."

"Mom, please. I'm begging you. Don't do this right now. I need you—"

"Mom?" Alice had abandoned the flashlight and was looking up at Meredith with a pained expression.

All the fight went out of her at the sight of her daughter, little wrinkles between her eyebrows and her mouth twisted with concern. Alice had witnessed almost every fight between Meredith and Kristin over these last few months, and she could only imagine how it had affected her. But how could she have protected Alice from them when she couldn't protect herself? The fights came out of nowhere, a series of sharp, lethal bites. She could never come up with the right things to say to fix it, so she eventually stopped saying anything at all. Then Kristin accused her of being complacent. She said Meredith wasn't trying. But what was Meredith supposed to do when her partner of ten years came to her claiming to be unhappy and then refused to say another word on the matter?

Meredith's parents had never argued much; it was always Meredith and her mother. She'd promised herself that coming out here would spare Alice the brunt of the inevitable collapse of her relationship with Kristin, but being around her mother brought out a juvenile combativeness she'd thought she'd left behind.

She hoped bringing Alice to the cape, getting them both away from everything, would, if not fix things, at least make them tolerable. It was easier to look at her problems from a distance, through the wrong end of a telescope, making them smaller, more manageable. Years away from the cape, though, had blurred the memory of this place, leaving visible only the beatific and obscuring that which had given her nightmares.

Nightmares fueled by her mother's paranoia.

"You know why we have to do this," Judith said, almost under her breath.

Meredith sighed. Twisted a bit of Alice's hair around her finger again. "Okay, Mom. I'll go up and look around. I'm sure it won't be hard to figure out."

"Thank you," Judith said.

"I want to go to the beach," Alice chirped.

"Grandma will take you."

Judith started to protest, but Meredith shot her a look.

"Mom. Don't. Please. Just take her to the beach. I'll be half an hour at the most. You guys can look for shells."

"Wouldn't you rather go get ice cream?" Judith asked Alice. "Or see the fountain?"

Alice shook her head. "Beach."

Judith knelt down to Alice's level, taking her face in her hands. "We can't go to the beach, honey. It's not safe there. Just because your mommy is okay risking your life for the sake of a few shells—"

"Stop it," Meredith ordered through clenched teeth. "Don't you dare."

"I'm trying to protect her."

"And I'm not?"

Alice pulled away from Judith, and when Meredith tried to reach out to comfort her, she flinched. This was a mistake. They shouldn't have come here.

"Please, Grandma," Alice said. "I just want to see the water."

Meredith was all ready for Judith to argue further, but even she softened under Alice's big brown eyes.

"Fine. Thirty minutes. That's all."

Alice fist-pumped, making both women laugh. Meredith tried to catch her mother's gaze, to share a smile, but Judith avoided her, letting Alice drag her out the door, toward the beach.

She could've driven, but she preferred to walk. It was less than a mile from her mother's house to the lighthouse, and it felt good to have her face and neck warmed by the sun, a rarity in this part of the country. She smelled the salt water even before she saw it. It was one of her favorite smells, next to freshly ground coffee and the Thalias her mother still grew in the bathroom sink. It was why she'd moved from one coast to the other; she'd hoped to at least have that scent of home with her. But the Atlantic Ocean had never smelled right. A little too crisp, too bright. The ocean surrounding the cape was heavy and dense. It had substance. A person could float halfway across the world on the Pacific, but Meredith had never set foot in the Atlantic because an irrational part of her worried she'd sink straight to the bottom.

She didn't intend to stop at the museum, but a memory hit like a squall and she couldn't fight the pull of it.

Tell me something interesting about yourself.

She'd met Kristin at a bar in Arlington. After a long day of job interviews, she was three sheets to the wind when Kristin approached wearing a wry smile.

Desperate to impress but unable to think of anything clever, she replied, "There's a curse on my family."

She regretted it the moment it came out. It sounded like someone making light of a tragedy. It made her sound damaged, which in a way, she was. It just wasn't something she'd wanted Kristin to know. At least, not then.

And it wasn't as if she actually believed it. Maybe when she was Alice's age, when she accepted everything her mother told her with the kind of religious faith all kids had in their parents. It wasn't just the belief in her mother, though. The curse, in a way, had made a young Meredith feel almost special. But as she got older, she started to see her mother's fear and constant warnings for what they were: trauma-induced paranoia. Yes, terrible things had happened to her family. To *her*. But that didn't mean they were cursed. By the time Meredith hit high school, she had made a conscious decision not to get wrapped up in the stories, seeing them as a kind of self-fulfilling prophecy. She wouldn't let it rule her life. Or Alice's.

And while her mother tunneled deeper into her fear and Meredith tried to claw her way out of it, her stepdad, a man with more entrepreneurial spirit than skill, had used the story of the curse to make money by creating the Cape Disappointment Mermaid Museum.

Lemons into lemonade, as he would have said.

Dozens of tourists used to claim to see the famous Cape Disappointment mermaid every year and would be asked to spend several minutes describing it to Belinda, the resident cartoonist, who would draw a rough facsimile and then charge the sap twenty dollars for the picture. They always paid—it was proof, they said, that she was real. Meredith's stepdad had been the start of it, the first to "see" the Cape Disappointment mermaid up close and survive to tell the tale. A lie, of course.

Still, it didn't take long for mermaid fever to catch. Her stepdad fed the fire, cobbling together a kind of museum that charged five dollars a head to look at old seaweed (mermaid hair), shells (mermaid gifts), and photographs of the "mermaid herself." When upkeep for the lighthouse became too expensive to maintain on his own, he managed to raise the money to build a fountain in the town square, almost half as wide as the street, with a stone mermaid perched demurely on a boulder at the center. People who visited the cape could toss in their coins and make a wish, then the money would be collected and used to keep the lighthouse lit. It worked for a while. The wishes dried up about the same time the mermaid sightings dwindled. No mermaid, no wishes, no light.

Mom hated the legend. Called it trash, even as it fed her bank account and kept her precious light lit. "Putting a pretty face on it won't change what happened," she'd said. "You can't fix it. This place is cursed."

The museum hadn't been open since her stepdad got sick. When he was too weak to get out of bed anymore, Judith had hidden the key. Probably would have burned the place down if she'd thought she could get away with it.

Silly as it was, the museum had been her stepdad's baby. And now that he was gone, it was a kind of monument to his memory. Meredith wished she knew why her mother hated it so much.

It was little more than a double-wide trailer disguised behind poorly constructed driftwood walls. Sea-glass wind chimes hung inert from the gutter, lopsided and dim. Part of her hoped the key wouldn't be on the set her mother had given her, but the door unlocked on the first try. The building shared electrical wiring with the lighthouse, just up the bluff from where the museum was built; when she hit the switch, a single fluorescent tube blinked to life.

Dust coated the vinyl floor like a carpet, and most of the plastic exhibit cases were so caked it was all but impossible to see what was inside. She took one of the novelty T-shirts from behind the desk at the front and wiped down some of the cases. No one had replaced the "mermaid hair," so the bottom of that particular display was covered in dry, cracked seaweed. In the display of mermaid "gifts," she found a dozen shells that'd lost their sheen. The comb was just a comb, and the "pearls" had molded, the cheap plastic bending with the force of the bacteria.

On the other side of the museum was the only display that had nothing to do with the mermaid. A small glass case held a laminated business card from the Holm Fishing Company, founded by her great-great-great-grandfather, and a silver hand mirror and brush supposedly owned by his wife, Regina. Part of her was surprised the mirror hadn't been stolen by now. It was real silver, probably worth a little bit of money. But the idea of the curse didn't just have its tentacles in her mother. Anyone over fifty who'd lived here most of their lives wouldn't admit to believing in anything as pagan as a curse, but they'd tell you something *wasn't right* with Meredith's family. She figured they'd all rather have their hands cut off than handle anything touched by Regina, the woman who, most of the stories claimed, the curse started with.

Meredith walked through the whole museum, wiping down displays and studying what they held, feeling an odd relief at their contents. It was the same feeling she got when she walked into her apartment in Arlington alone, in the dark, flipping on lights and looking behind doors to reassure herself that no one was there, that her fear was all in her head.

She came back to the mirror and pulled it carefully out of the display. It was heavier than it looked, but delicate, the intricate carving along the handle already beginning to wear away. An odd fear kept her from looking directly at her reflection, like maybe it wouldn't be her face she saw looking back. It made her think of sleepovers in middle school, her friends spinning deliriously in the dark on full-sugar pop and gummy bears in front of the bathroom mirror, a low chorus of *Bloody Mary* on their lips.

The story behind Regina's disappearance was a mystery, but at the end of it, she was still just a woman. Not a monster or a witch or whatever the stories deemed her.

Still, Meredith set the mirror back in the cabinet facedown and made sure to lock the display.

She dumped the T-shirt in the garbage on top of other ancient trash, then picked up the whole can, thinking she remembered seeing a dumpster somewhere outside. As she carried it, she let her mind play out a fantasy of moving back, of picking up where her stepdad left off. Alice would love the museum, and Meredith could almost picture herself behind the counter, selling cheap magnets and ceramic figurines to tourists. A brand-new start. But the fantasy fell apart just as it began to take shape. She couldn't live here again, no matter how the sound of the water just on the other side of the wall stirred her soul.

She found the dumpster at the edge of the lot. Judging by the smell, it hadn't been picked up in a while. She shoved the lid open with her elbow and held her breath as she emptied the can. Just as the last of it fell in, she felt eyes on her.

"What do you think you're doing?"

Meredith jumped, ramming her elbow into the corner of the dumpster.

"I'm talking to you!" the voice said.

Heart pumping, Meredith turned.

The lot was empty. Above her, behind the bluff that separated the lot from the street, she saw heads bobbing up and down, but none of them turned toward her. A flash of red streaked through the corner of her eye. Someone laughed—a woman—muffled but sharp.

"Hello?" Meredith called.

The first voice was back. "You know you can't be here."

Meredith ventured up a few steps toward the street and saw a box-shaped man with slicked-back black hair marching away from the bluff. It was clear he hadn't been talking to her; he was still shouting but hadn't looked back once. Several feet ahead of him, a group of people shot concerned glances over their shoulders. A girl with bright-red hair walked ahead, pointedly ignoring him. When she did finally turn, her gaze skipped over the man and landed on Meredith, staring her down as if she'd known she was there all along. She smirked, teeth flashing bright.

Startled, Meredith jumped down a step, then walked quickly back toward the museum, where she dumped the garbage can back behind the desk, knocking over a stool in the process. She left it, eager to get out of the museum and away from the bluff. Meredith didn't like the way the girl had looked at her. Like she knew her. Ridiculous, of course. Still, something about the girl pricked at her.

She brushed the feeling away. She was oversensitive, emotions still raw from her last fight with Kristin. *Get a grip*, she thought, as she slammed the museum door and shakily turned the lock.

The lighthouse stood on a small hill in the center of the peninsula. It wasn't much to look at; the navy-blue paint had worn away in chunks, and rust coated the rails of the catwalk. Small windows dotted the side to light up the stairwell, but the glass was foggy, stained with salt. It was a steep climb up the side of the small hill, all chipped concrete stairs with no rail. Meredith hunched forward and focused on each step as it came, fighting back the vertigo. She broke her arm once falling down these stairs before there were chunks missing. No matter how much her daughter begged—and Meredith knew she would—there was no way Alice was coming up here.

"Meredith!"

She turned to look for the direction of the voice and misstepped, her toe hitting the next stair. She went flying forward and caught herself on her forearms on the edge of the concrete. Pain rocketed up her arms, knocking the wind out of her.

"Oh, shit. Hold on!"

She was halfway to standing when an arm looped under hers, pulling her the rest of the way up.

"Careful, now," he said. "Are you okay?"

She smiled when she realized it was Art. Mom's cousin and probably the only family member Meredith had always gotten along with, apart from her stepdad. His hair was much grayer than the last time she'd seen him, and deep creases lined his cheeks and forehead. He was only a few years older than her mother, but he looked twice that.

"When did you get old?" she asked.

"About the same time you did."

She slapped his shoulder and winced at the pain. Her forearms were scraped up good, and blood wept from the wounds, dusty with gravel. She sucked in a breath as she tried to clear the biggest pieces.

Art nodded at the lighthouse. "Come on. I'm pretty sure there's a first aid kit in there somewhere."

They finished the climb arm in arm, though after a few more steps, it was Meredith doing the guiding. Art's knees popped with each step up, which he tried to cover with conversation. But that ended quickly; neither of them was in the best shape, and it took all of their breath to make it to the top. Finally at the door, Meredith went through three keys before finding the right one, and even that took some finesse to turn.

The door creaked open, and a dank, animal odor washed over them.

Meredith gagged.

"Something probably got in and couldn't find its way out," Art said.

"Great."

They went inside, propping the door open with a folding chair. A thin layer of dust covered the desk. The room was like a cave, swallowing whatever light managed to get through the door. On the stairs, ghosts of footprints traveled all the way up in the dust.

"Does no one ever come up here?" Meredith asked. With how adamant her mother was that she be responsible for the light, she figured someone had to have been climbing the stairs and winding the mechanism.

Art shook his head as he started opening desk drawers. "The day you went off to college, Judith locked the door and that was that." He peered into the drawers. Closed them again. "Why she suddenly decided it needed to be up and working is beyond me. Boats don't come this way anymore. Not if they can help it."

Now that Alice is here...

"She thinks it'll keep Alice 'safe,'" Meredith said, throwing air quotes around *safe.* "She used to talk about the red light warding off evil."

Art made a noncommittal noise.

"I know. But going along with it is easier than arguing with her."

He snorted. "That, I believe. Oh, here we go." He pulled a small metal box from one of the drawers and opened it on the desk.

There weren't any bandages, but there was gauze and alcohol wipes, which she was pretty sure couldn't expire. She cleaned out the dirt and managed to stop the bleeding, but the cuts stung and moving her arms made them stretch, sending up little shards of pain. The only thing distracting her from it was the smell. The sooner she found whatever had died and got rid of it, the better.

With few places an animal could get stuck, they searched the bottom floor in no time. Art managed to pop open the small window above the desk, and a cross breeze took out some of the odor. Meredith rifled through the desk but only found a twelve-year-old sports page, some junk mail, and paperwork related to the lighthouse's upkeep. Someone had gotten a stack of quotes on painting the place but apparently never followed through.

Meredith followed Art upstairs, tracing her fingers along the wall, pausing about halfway up to admire her thirteen-year-old self's handiwork. Carved in the wall at about chest level, no bigger than her palm: *Judith Strand is a BITCH.* She remembered doing it, remembered cutting herself with the kitchen knife she used to carve the words, but couldn't remember why. Could've been any number of things. Meredith and her mother could never be in the same room for more than a few minutes without biting each other's heads off. Her stepdad tried to tell her it was because they were alike; Meredith figured it was because her mother hated her. As a teenager, the lighthouse was where she came to cool off. Minor vandalism was sometimes part of the process.

The smell got worse the farther they climbed. Meredith slipped her collar over her nose, her eyes watering with the dust and the stink. The hall curved at the top of the stairs, leading to the light room. Beer bottles lined the far wall next to a pile of clothes and blanket that, until she kicked it, she thought might have been a person. The kick shuffled the pile, and a new burp of rot wafted up from it.

Meredith breathed into her elbow to keep from puking.

Art's nose twitched, but he kept his composure. As a taxidermist, he'd probably smelled worse. "I knew kids would get in here. I fuckin' told her..." Using his foot, he shifted the rest of the pile out of the way to reveal a mound of fish carcasses, some half-decomposed, others little more than skeletons.

It was a sludgy, putrefied mess that squelched as Art moved the clothing, making Meredith's stomach turn and her head spin. She bolted for the nearest window, broke a nail sliding it open, and stuck her head outside, sucking in deep breaths of fresh air. She heard Art circling the room, mumbling, sliding open the rest of the windows. Once her vision righted itself and she felt mostly confident she wouldn't throw up, she went back to the pile and noticed stubs of cheap candles and wax drippings all over the floor. A half-rotted Ouija board stuck out from beneath one of the blankets.

Old shame bubbled in her guts.

"I thought all this ended when I was in high school," she said.

"All what ended? Juvenile delinquency?" Art laughed. "Trust me, doll, you were an angel compared to the little shits I'm chasing away from my shop every Friday night."

"No. The Fish Lady crap."

Fish Lady. Fish Witch. They'd never been very creative with their taunts. Some of the kids she went to school with had taken the legends of her family, of the tragedies that plagued them, and twisted them into something they could use to taunt and demean. They told stories about her mother, that she was a witch or communed with witches. Her obsession with the danger in the ocean spawned rumors that a sacrifice of fish would grant you wishes. None of it ever made any sense to Meredith, but it didn't have to. It was a small town, and the kids were bored. Meredith and her mother were convenient targets. She knew that now, but back then it was the final nail in the coffin of what was left of their relationship.

"Just some kids being stupid," Art said, as though it wiped everything away.

Not for the first time, Meredith wondered if coming home had been a good idea.

With his face turned away from the mess, Art gathered the blankets back over the fish mess and scooped it all into a bundle, wafting the stench further. "I'll see if I can't get most of this out of here. You try to find some bleach or something."

She clapped one hand over her nose and mouth and gave him a thumbs-up with the other.

While he carried the bulk of the pile downstairs, she rifled through the cabinets beneath the light itself, a fourth-order Fresnel lens that'd somehow withstood a steady stream of teenage partiers. In the first couple of cabinets, she found a pile of books she recognized as keeper logbooks, along with a few other journals and stacks of paper. She'd been through these before, a long time ago, and remembered one of them had belonged to a relative of hers—Grace—from when she was the keeper. Her stepdad had shown it to her when she was in high school, at a time when the strain between Meredith and her mother was at an all-time peak. Meredith had accused Judith of not being her mother, a claim made out of anger but no actual proof, and Judith hadn't contradicted her. But her stepdad told her there was a lot in Grace that he saw in Meredith. Other women in the family too. He said it was impossible for her not to be blood of their blood, and offered the books as proof. All Meredith had ever taken from the logs and journals was that there was something wrong with their family, and not in the way her mother meant. They weren't cursed. They were mentally ill. Afraid. Angry.

She absently flipped through one of the books now. Dried flower petals—Thalias, she thought—rained from between the pages. Through the windows, the sound of the ocean filled her ears, and if she closed her eyes, it was like being cradled in the sound. She *had* missed this. More than she thought. Her skin *ached* for the water. Setting the book down, she glanced longingly through the window to the ocean below. She could almost feel the rush of the foam over her body.

Jump.

The thought was like a knife, in and out before she could stop it. She looked down to her feet and went cold. She'd taken a step toward the window without realizing, and even as she came back into herself, she was already leaning forward into a second step.

She shook her head, rubbing her arms against the chill. It was nothing. She'd had intrusive thoughts before. *Just brush them aside. It's fine.*

To distract herself, she continued exploring. The next cabinet was empty save for an impressive spiderweb, but in the third she found several mason jars full of murky water. At the bottoms of the jars were an inch or so of sediment—sand and tiny shells and bits of wood and seaweed. She frowned, thinking, *Kids*, but as she picked up one of the jars, the sound of the waves seemed to grow louder and it was hard to think anything at all.

There was a drain in the floor near the far window, meant to let out any rain that got in before it had time to flood and damage the lens. Meredith grabbed two of the jars from the cabinet and, opening the first, strew the water over the fish sludge to try to nudge it toward the drain. It didn't move much, but at least now the muck was diluted. She opened the second jar. A thin scum rested on top of the water, which she scooped out with her fingers. The moment her skin touched the water, the room seemed to fall away. The scent of the sea made her salivate. A sudden, desperate desire for the water made her bring the jar to her lips and, before she could stop herself, she tipped a tiny splash of water into her mouth. Grit rubbed against her teeth as she swallowed. She continued to drink even as a small voice in the back of her head ordered her to stop, drowned out by the roar of the ocean in her ears. For an agonizing minute, it was like her body wasn't her own.

Meredith finally pulled the jar away from her mouth, and it was like coming out of a fog. She breathed against the tremble in her hands as she dumped the rest of the water down the drain. *Intrusive thoughts*, she told herself. *That's it.* She knew coming back here would be hard, that she'd struggle mentally. But if she kept her head up, focused on herself and Alice, everything would be okay.

She licked her lips. Swallowed. She could still taste the water. It tasted like midnight. Like the foam that brushes the curl of a fast-moving wave. Bitter, like patience growing thin. Like desire. Like someone watching. Waiting.

CHAPTER TWO

JUDITH

J udith was halfway to the beach when she forgot where she was going. Not forgot, no—that implied something darker and deeper. It just slipped her mind. Like grappling with a fish, her thoughts slid right out if she didn't hang on tight enough. She stopped in the middle of the sidewalk, in front of a window full of flowers. She remembered Meredith had come home to stay for a while; maybe Judith had been intending to get her some flowers as a welcome? It seemed like something Meredith would appreciate, so whether it was her true intention or not, Judith went inside the flower shop. The cloud of scents was disorienting, thick as soup, in a room no bigger than her kitchen. Her nose perked up at the scent of roses; there was a full wall of different arrangements, labeled for the intended occasion: wedding, anniversary, funeral.

As she ventured farther, the walls narrowed until she was surrounded, stroked by petals and pricked by thorns. She followed the sound of running water to the back of the shop, where she found a row of black buckets, each filled with delicate Thalias, their stems bloodred and blooms a delicate violet.

A girl with coppery red hair, couldn't have been more than sixteen, hovered over the last in the row. So quickly Judith almost missed it, the girl tore one of the petals off the bloom and slipped it onto her tongue, a communion wafer.

To ward off evil spirits.

Who'd told her that? Judith held a brief image of a girl's face in her mind, with narrow eyes and a thin nose and... It faded before she could get a look at it. *A friend*, she thought. And in her heart she knew she was right, even if she couldn't remember.

She didn't like being this close to the water. It made her mind go all fuzzy. Thoughts—hers and not hers—slipped in and out like fish through a reef. When she was younger, it was easier to push through the fog. Now she was lucky if she made it through the other side at all. She needed to get home.

Judith left the shop, lips forming a silent mantra—*get home, get home*—but when she started toward the sidewalk, she discovered she wasn't sure which way home was. She'd get there eventually if she kept moving, she figured. Muscle memory. But instead of getting farther from the water, her traitorous feet brought her closer, and soon sand spilled over the sides of her shoes as she walked over the dunes and to the water's edge.

Cassie. The name came to her in a flash, and she instantly looked up the cliff, toward the rundown house she knew sat behind the trees. She started toward the cliff, stopped by a splash beside her. A woman flailed in the surf, mouth wide in a silent scream. Judith's stomach dropped.

She's here.

But then the woman's arms were only curves in the curling wave, her hair dark weeds caught in the sea foam. A memory. *Just* a memory. Heart pounding, Judith looked up, blinking hard at the bright sunlight. She glanced at the lighthouse, where a woman dove from the widow's walk. A scream died in Judith's throat as the woman became a gull diving for a food wrapper.

She pressed her fists into her eyes, but the visions continued behind her eyelids. Memories or warnings or both.

Finally she opened her eyes to see Alice standing at the edge of the water, the girl with the coppery red hair gripping her shoulders.

Oh God, Alice. How could she forget Alice? Little Alice with tears streaming down her face and snot bubbling in her cupid's bow. Judith ran toward them. She crouched and pulled Alice tight against her, each of her granddaughter's soundless sobs a blow to her chest. God, what was wrong with her?

Alice rubbed her face in Judith's hair. Her voice tickled Judith's neck. "You left. I got scared."

"Shush, honey, I know. I'm sorry. I got distracted and I just... I'm here. It's okay, now. It's okay."

The girl circled the pair of them, pausing behind Alice. From her vantage point, Judith could only see the girl's knees, raw, with dirt in the creases. A gardener's knees.

Then the girl squatted, flashing her underwear before tucking the skirt of her pineapple-patterned dress between her knees. She studied Judith, her deep blue eyes traveling the length of Judith's face, and then tapped Alice on the shoulder. "Don't forget what I told you."

Alice nodded without pulling her face out of Judith's hair.

Judith opened her mouth to thank the girl for finding Alice, for bringing her to Judith, but something in the girl's expression made her stop. Why was she looking at Judith like she knew her?

The sobbing had slowed, but Judith knew—*remembered*, damn it—Alice was a painfully shy kid. She saw how it frustrated Meredith, but it was one of Judith's favorite things about her granddaughter. Shy girls didn't get in trouble. Shy girls loved harder than girls like Meredith.

"Don't forget what?" Judith asked, but the girl ignored her. She stood without a word and started back toward the street.

Ignoring the protest in her hips and knees, Judith lifted Alice, tucking the girl's legs around her waist, a starfish. She put the red-haired girl out of her mind a little too easily. The red-haired girl didn't matter. Only Alice mattered. They were on the beach. They were going to collect shells. And tonight, the light would be on, and she would be safe. They all would be safe.

Judith carried Alice until they reached the far side of the beach, away from the noise of the street. Even with Alice wriggling to be set free, Judith clung to her a moment longer, imagining that she remembered what it felt like to carry Meredith this way. Memories slipping, slipping away, little eels in Alice's hair as she ran toward the surf. Unfair that Judith couldn't remember where she was sometimes, or what she was doing, but should someone ask, she could detail every instance of a young Meredith coming in for a hug, how Judith stiffened, her arms limp at her sides. It wasn't that she didn't love her daughter. It was that she loved her too much.

Alice took two hesitant steps into the water, her shoes discarded behind her. A wave crept up and then—splash!—Alice shrieked and giggled and danced on tiptoes. Another wave, this one bigger, stronger, which pulled at her legs. Alice stumbled forward—*Grandma!*—and fear trickled cold down Judith's back, even colder as she snatched Alice away from a third wave.

"No!" Then, when Alice's frightened eyes turned on her, softer, "No."

"But, Grandma—"

"We can't go in the water, sweetie."

"Why not?"

"Because we can't." Judith took slow, measured breaths, willing her heart to calm. Her husband had died of a heart attack only a few years ago. *You're just afraid*, she thought. *You're not dying.*

Alice crossed her arms, and her eyes flashed with a challenge. "Mom lets me swim."

An upturned crab corpse, inches from Alice's bare feet, caught Judith's eye. As she scanned the length of the beach, she noticed dozens of them. Several feet away, a pair of boys poked at one with a stick. Birds circled overhead, eyeing the buffet.

Judith nudged the crab with her toe, drawing Alice's eye. "You want to end up like him?"

Alice shook her head.

"Then we don't go in the water. Ever."

After a long moment, Alice nodded. Judith took a deep breath to settle her mind, then goaded Alice into letting Judith show her how to build the perfect moat.

Watching Alice play, Judith couldn't help but scrutinize every movement, every expression, studying her like a particularly difficult poem, written backward in Sanskrit. She was resilient too, the incident with the red-haired girl seemingly put out of her mind. As much as Meredith beat herself up about it, she was doing a fine job of raising her daughter, starting with putting an entire country between them and the cape. She only wished Meredith had stayed away for good.

Tearing herself away from Alice for a minute, she looked back up at the lighthouse. Shadows moved around inside, then Meredith stuck her head out of one of the windows, looking nauseous. Judith shouted up at her, but her voice was swallowed by the crash of the waves and Meredith disappeared back inside. It'd been one of Judith's more clever ideas, setting Meredith to work in the lighthouse. She'd stay out of trouble there.

Alice ventured dangerously close to the water, jumping back each time Judith took a step toward her. Seemed she was watching Judith just as closely as Judith was watching her.

Somewhere behind her, someone shouted. Judith turned to look and noticed a woman, presumably the mother, jabbing the shoulder of the boy who'd been jabbing one of the dead crabs. When she turned back, Alice was ankle deep in the water with something cradled in her hands.

"Alice! Get back!"

Alice looked up and smiled, her teeth a little crooked and a little too big for her mouth. "I found something."

Judith's heart hammered as she scanned the immediate shoreline. She didn't see her, but that didn't mean she wasn't there. "Come show me, then. Come on." Judith waved her over. "Come show Grandma what you've got."

Alice trotted over, kicking up sand. "It's pretty, huh?"

Seeing the spiral pink shell in her granddaughter's hands was like having ice poured down her back. It just fit in the palm of Alice's hand, every spike, every crevasse exactly the same as it'd been when Meredith found it. When Judith found it years before that. She tried to snatch it out of Alice's hands, but Alice must've seen it coming; she leapt back, nimble as a sprite.

"Give it to me," Judith ordered. "Now."

Alice clutched it to her chest. "Why?"

"Because I said so."

She sniffed. Her eyes watered. "But it's mine, though."

"Alice."

She inched backward toward the water, and it became a battle between getting the shell and keeping her out of the water. Each time Judith reached for it, Alice stepped farther away from the shore.

"Please," Judith said. "Come out of the water."

"You're gonna take it."

"I won't take it, sweetie."

"Yes, you *will*."

"Alice, please." Judith shot a look over Alice's shoulder where she thought she saw a shadow dart under the water. *Not again*, she thought.

"It's just a shell, Gramma. I want to show Mom."

The shadow grew darker. Denser. There wasn't much time. Swallowing back her fear, Judith ran into the water, flinching as the cold splashed up her legs, and grabbed Alice by the arm. She yanked hard—too hard—and managed to get her a few inches closer to the sand.

"You're hurting me," Alice whimpered.

"Just a little closer." Judith grunted as she looped her arm around Alice's back and hoisted her onto her hip. Something in her back cracked, and white-hot pain slashed down her side.

Alice must have seen something was wrong because she slid out of Judith's grip and scampered up the beach, out of Judith's reach, but out of the water too. Still, Alice held the shell behind her back, a defiant frown on her face.

"Give it to me. Now." Judith held out her hand, but Alice hid the shell behind her back. Judith breathed. In. Out. *Relax. She's safe. We're all safe.* She knelt, gently stroking Alice's arms. "Come on, sweetie. Hand it over."

"But it's mine!"

Biting back tears, Judith stood. "No. It's not. Don't you ever, ever say that."

She snatched the shell out of Alice's hands before she could react and hurled it hard enough to make her shoulder pop. She watched it fly, then drop back into the ocean where it belonged.

Don't you dare.

CHAPTER THREE

MEREDITH

fter they finished clearing what they could out of the light room, Meredith invited Art over for dinner.

"It's the least I can do," she said.

He shook his head. "Appreciate the offer, but I don't think your mom would like it much."

"So?"

He laughed once, but it quickly became a frown. "Seriously. Probably not a good idea."

"Why not?"

"It's complicated."

"What isn't with her?"

"I don't think you give her enough credit."

"Pot, meet kettle." She smirked. "Come over. Have dinner. Please."

She knew she'd won when he shrugged, all out of excuses.

They said a brief goodbye, and Meredith went straight to the house, desperate for a hot shower.

Her mother and Alice were back from the beach, probably had been for a while. Meredith doubted her mother would've lasted longer than an hour that close to the water, but she wanted Alice to spend time outside, to enjoy the place a little, even if it was only for a short time.

She found her mother in the living room, flipping through a book without really looking at the pages.

"Did you two have a good time?" Meredith asked.

"It was fine." Judith turned the page.

"Great." Meredith was rooted to the spot, unable to leave, but with nothing else to say and therefore no reason to stay put. Maybe she was just expecting something more out of her mother. She wanted to tell her what she found in the lighthouse, but she wanted her mother to ask first, to at least pretend to be interested. It was like being thirteen all over again.

She noticed the wall behind the chair, full of pictures, none of which had Meredith in them. There were several of her stepdad, posed proudly in front of the lighthouse, the garage where he worked on stuff for the museum, and others with his arm draped protectively around her mother's shoulders, her mother sunken in with a tight smile on her face. In the far corner was a picture of her parents in front of the lighthouse, a tall man with slicked-back, black hair between them, his smile all teeth and bloodred gums. She couldn't be sure, but it looked like the guy who was shouting outside the museum.

"Who's that?" she asked.

Judith grudgingly turned in her chair to follow Meredith's pointed finger. "You don't remember Vik?"

"The name sounds familiar."

"He was around more when you were little. Couldn't get enough of you."

"Huh."

Judith rolled her eyes. "It wasn't anything inappropriate, Meredith."

"I didn't say it was." But now that her mother had brought it up, she couldn't help but wonder. He gave off a creepy vibe. She couldn't imagine being drawn to him as a kid. "He still live around here?"

She nodded. "Farther inland, I think."

"You don't talk anymore?"

"He...helps me sometimes. He's a good man." She closed her book. "What's this sudden interest in my life?"

Sudden? She'd been trying to probe the past out of her mother for decades. "I saw him down by the museum today. He was freaking out over something. I don't know..."

Frowning, Judith glanced back at the photograph. "You must've been mistaken. Vik isn't the type to freak out."

"Everybody freaks out sometimes, Mom." This conversation, exhibit A. "It's not a big deal."

"This is just like you, Meredith. Telling stories to get attention."

"What are you talking about? I was just wondering—"

"Vik is a good man. He was there for me at a time when no one else was."

You said that, Meredith thought. She didn't like where this conversation was going. "What about Dad?" Having never known her birth father, her stepdad had always been Dad.

"What about him?"

What was Mom looking for? Did she want Meredith to spell it out? Wilting under her mother's steely gaze, she couldn't do it. "Nothing. I... Nothing." After a long minute, she added, "Sorry."

The tension never left Judith's shoulders, but she sat back in the chair and reopened her book. "Leave Vik alone. Understand?"

Anxious to end the conversation, Meredith nodded. "Where's Alice?"

"Upstairs somewhere." Judith flipped a page, and Meredith noticed a slight tremor. "Hiding."

Meredith's stomach dropped. *Hiding?*

It took a minute to find Alice, who'd sequestered herself in the hall closet and didn't answer Meredith when she called for her. She'd taken most of the towels down and stacked them around her body, like a half-built igloo. Meredith didn't notice she'd been crying until she clicked the hallway light on.

Ignoring the stench wafting off her own clothes, she knelt and pried Alice from the towel structure and hugged her. "What happened, sweetie?"

Sobs bubbled up from Alice's chest like hiccups. "G-gr-grandma. She *hates* me. S-she…"

That was it. Judith could torment Meredith all she liked, but Alice was off-limits to her mother's barbed tongue.

Standing, Meredith grabbed Alice's hand and half dragged, half carried Alice from the hallway into the living room. Judith looked up from the book, still holding the page, midturn.

Meredith nudged Alice forward, her tear-soaked face an accusation. "What did you do?"

Judith's gaze went from Meredith to Alice and back again. Her expression faltered into something like confusion before hardening.

Meredith turned to Alice. "What happened, baby? Tell me."

"Is that what you do at home?" Judith asked. "Put your child in the middle?" Then, "What's that god-awful smell?"

Heat slashed through Meredith's body. She ignored the dig—she'd had years of practice—and focused on her daughter. Alice's lip trembled, and she kept snatching looks at Judith, like she was afraid of getting in trouble. The thought that there might be a whisper of truth to what Judith implied rose and was squashed just as quickly. Meredith was a good mom. Better than Judith had been.

"You stink, Mom," Alice whispered.

Meredith smiled thinly. "I know. I promise I'll shower as soon as you tell me what happened."

Alice sighed and it seemed to take everything out of her. "I found a shell. It was pink and pretty and had little spikes on it. It looked like a hedgehog." She paused.

"And you love hedgehogs," Meredith said, urging her on.

Alice nodded. "They used to be called urchins, but hedgehog is cuter."

"Totally cuter," Meredith agreed.

It was enough to earn a small grin, but it quickly dipped. "Grandma took it and threw it away."

"I saved her life," Judith interjected, her voice shaking with frustration. "You should thank me."

"God damn it, Mom. Not this shit again. Please."

"You cuss in front of her too?"

Her mother had never been violent, but she had a way of verbally cutting at Meredith that stung just as badly as a slap. Sometimes it was outright criticism; other times she slung carefully crafted remarks like arrows. She had excellent aim.

"Mommy, you're hurting me." Alice pulled on her hand, which Meredith quickly released.

"Go upstairs," Meredith ordered.

Alice's lip quivered, driving a stake through Meredith's heart, before she ran for the stairs.

All her frustration—the shit in the light room, the itchy feeling she got from being in her mother's house, the little voice in the back of her head reminding her that her marriage was all but over—came pouring out. "You will not screw up my kid, okay? It's bad enough that I had to pull her out of her home, away from her friends, while Kristin and I sort out our shit. I don't need it coming from you too."

"Your shit, as you so eloquently put it, is your own doing. Everything I do, everything I have ever done, has been for your own good."

Meredith laughed. "My own good? You're out of your mind."

"It's going to happen again." Judith's voice cracked. "You know it will."

Meredith balled her hands into fists at her sides. All she wanted to do was shake her mother. Judith was so wrapped up in her made-up threats she never noticed the real ones. Alice loved her grandmother, but Judith drove a wedge between them every time she did something like this. Pretty soon that wedge would be impossible to remove, like the one between her and Meredith. Lowering her voice, she said, "Are you listening to yourself? When's the last time you went to a doctor? Or spoke to the therapist I found for you after Dad died?"

Judith's cheeks puffed and reddened. "You don't—"

"There is nothing out there. There is nothing coming to get us. There's just me and my daughter. You're the one who scared her. You're the one who made her cry." And then, because she couldn't stop, "You're the monster, Mom."

Tears pooled in Judith's eyes. Out of habit, Meredith started to apologize but quickly closed her mouth. Just because she was too exhausted to keep arguing didn't mean she had to say she was sorry. She wasn't. She'd meant everything she'd said. Maybe this time Judith would apologize first. She doubted it.

Leaving her mother in the living room, she dragged herself to the bathroom. She still needed a shower, and remembering she'd invited Art over, she probably needed to get to the grocery store. Like Meredith, her mother lived on TV dinners, frozen pizza, and bananas.

Booze, she added to her mental list, turning on the shower.

Steam filled the room, fogging up the mirror. Though her reflection was mostly obscured by the Thalias living in the sink—roots tangled down the drain and around the faucet—she noticed how purple her skin had become under her eyes, which were bloodshot. Her black hair had come away from the ponytail in Medusa-like tendrils. She released her hair, undressed (ignoring the soft pooch of her belly and the thick purple veins in her legs), and stepped under the stream.

It was hard to believe her life had ever been so uncomplicated that all it took to set her right again was a long, hot shower. Now, letting the water pummel her face and neck only pushed her deeper into her head.

She wondered what Kristin was doing now. If she was thinking about Meredith at all or if Meredith leaving had been a relief. Did she wander around their apartment and feel Meredith's absence? Or did she hardly notice? Back when they were just fighting, when *separation* wasn't a word either of them had dared use, Meredith had fantasized about taking herself out to dinner, to a movie Kristin would hate. She'd daydreamed entire weekends filled with doing things she loved, with no one there to tell her how stupid or repetitive or childish it was. She would spread out on the bed and drink coffee on the new duvet and brush cookie crumbs on the carpet. At the time, it'd sounded like heaven.

The first night after they talked about separation, Kristin stayed in a hotel. For all of her fantasizing, all Meredith could do was curl up into a ball on her side of the bed, trying to make herself as small as possible.

So she'd left. She could have gone anywhere—savings account be damned—but the pull to the cape was too strong. She *needed* to be here. She just didn't know why.

She couldn't stay, though, if her mother kept up with her make-believe monsters.

She lathered up a loofah and scrubbed at her skin. If she scrubbed hard enough, maybe it would all go away. If she scrubbed hard enough, maybe she'd dissolve, disappear down the drain and end up somewhere in the middle of the ocean where a small voice once told her she belonged.

———————

The dining room table was covered in boxes of Dad's things that neither of them had ever been able to go through, let alone get rid of. Rather than move them—Meredith's biceps twitched just with the effort of lifting the pasta pot—they settled in the living room: Alice on the couch with a TV tray in front of her and about a million paper towels laid down around her; Art in the rocking chair, heels tucked beneath the runners; Judith in Dad's chair (once a deep green, now a dusty gray), perched on the edge of the flat cushion to keep from disturbing the indent of his body, wearing one black pearl earring despite an exhaustive failure to find the other; Meredith on the other side of the couch, her plate balanced on her lap and a large glass of cheap red wine on the coffee table. She shook a saltshaker over the wine, swirled the glass, and sipped, earning a queer look from Art, but no question. There couldn't have been more than ten feet between any two of them, but it might as well have been miles. Conversation was all slurps and nods and forced smiles. To Art's credit, he pretended to be enjoying himself so much that Meredith almost believed he didn't hate being in the same room as her mother. Made it easier to believe he and her mother were cousins and, once, friends.

"Great sauce," Art said, mercifully breaking the silence.

Meredith slurped a tail of spaghetti. Chewed. "Ragú."

He nodded. "Right. Pretty sure that's what my wife used to use. Though it could've been Prego."

"Prego's good too."

"Mmhmm."

Meredith inwardly challenged her mother to bring up her lack of cooking skills, but she seemed just as worn out by the earlier argument as Meredith. Her back was hunched forward at an old-person angle, giving her the impression of a hump. As she chewed, her cheeks trembled, a premonition of jowls to come. In Meredith's head, Judith forever existed as the dark-haired, slightly wrinkled, straight-backed woman of Meredith's preteen and teenage years. The woman who forbade Meredith from going near the water when her friends held Friday night bonfires and swam until the cops kicked them out. The woman who didn't hug or kiss but jabbed and bit. But faced with this old woman, Meredith couldn't reconcile the two. This woman was soft, her bark worse than her bite. Meredith almost felt shame for what she said. She almost apologized. Instead, she shoveled the rest of her spaghetti in her mouth, so much she almost choked on it.

"Chew, then swallow," Alice said, parroting Meredith's own words.

Meredith tried to grin around her sauce-stained teeth, earning a giggle.

"Good manners, Alice," Judith said. An olive branch of sorts.

"Say thank you," Meredith said after finally swallowing.

"Thank you," Alice singsonged, then pushed her plate away. "I'm full. Can I have ice cream?"

"Sure." Meredith mopped Alice down with most of the paper towels and heaped them all onto her plate. "I'll be right back."

"I'll help." Art stood before she could protest, piling Judith's plate on top of his. "Judith? Ice cream?"

She shook her head, frowning at him, though not in her usual *I really dislike you* kind of way, but in a more *I'm not sure what's happening* kind of way. Maybe Meredith would call that doctor. From what little she knew of memory disorders, the earlier they're caught, the better.

"Mom?" Meredith asked.

Light flared in the woman's eyes. "I'm going upstairs."

"Oh. Um. Okay. Good night, then."

Judith strode from the room, her arms wrapped around her chest like she was struggling to hold her insides together.

"Night, Judith," Art called after her.

Meredith met Art's glance with raised eyebrows.

"With chocolate syrup!" Alice added, in case they'd forgotten their oh-so-important ice cream expedition.

The kitchen was a wreck, but Art went at the dishes like a soldier going into battle—rolled sleeves and a small prayer—while Meredith unearthed the ice cream.

"Thanks for that," Meredith said, nodding at the pile of dishes. The suds were bloody with spaghetti sauce.

"You know me. I like to keep my hands busy."

She did know. When the fights got really bad between Meredith and her mom during Meredith's sophomore year, she'd packed a bag and walked the three blocks to Art's house, where she watched TV, did homework, and harassed him into making her weird taxidermied creatures. She had a particular fondness for crossbred creations: an octo-carp, a crab-obster, a cat-flounder. For a graduation gift, he'd given her a replica of the Fiji Mermaid, the scales painted silver and jewels glued in place of the monkey's eyes. To this day, it was her favorite gift anyone had given her.

He continued, "You know you and Alice are welcome if things get too hard with your mom."

She nodded. "Thanks. Really." It wasn't like she hadn't considered it. Alice would have a blast going through Art's creations, same as Meredith had. He had a boat that he never took out but wouldn't begrudge Meredith and Alice a day on the water. He'd never do to Alice what her mother did. "But I need to be here. You saw Mom. Something's off."

He nodded.

"And I just want to figure some things out with us. I want us to be okay."

Because, she didn't add, if they weren't okay, then she and Alice might not be okay. If she'd learned one thing from those journals and logs her father had shown her back when she was younger, it was that the women in their family had difficult relationships with their mothers. She desperately didn't want to be that kind of mother—manipulative and angry and accusing—and being here was a way to prove to herself that she wasn't. That she was a good mom. A good daughter.

Thinking about the journals, about the women, made old thoughts surface. She used to tell herself that she and her mother might not have gotten along, but at least Judith wouldn't run away, wouldn't disappear into the water the way so many women in their family had. Mom called it a curse, and maybe, in a way, she was right. Except Meredith didn't think anything waited in the water to lure them away. It was inside them. For all her faults, Mom was fighting it. Maybe that was enough to keep her close. To stop the cycle before it got to Meredith. Before it got to Alice.

The ice cream was rock hard, so she set it on the counter to thaw. When she was sure Art wasn't looking, she slipped her phone out of her pocket. Kristin hadn't called or texted once. She had to have noticed them missing by now. Had to have read her note. But there was nothing. Nothing to check on Alice, to make sure they'd arrived okay. No wanting to talk. *I'm not happy* wasn't an explanation. It was a cop-out. Meredith still clung to the notion that, once Kristin had had some time to think, she and Alice could come home.

"Is that Mama Kristin?" Alice slid around the corner in her socks, wobbling at the stop.

Meredith stuck the phone in her pocket before Alice could ask to see it. "Yep. She said she misses you."

"Good." Not *I miss her too*. Meredith didn't know if it was a good thing or a bad thing.

She bent two spoons scooping the ice cream but managed to fill three bowls—one with enough chocolate syrup to drown a cow—and carried them back into the living room with Alice on her heels. They ate on the floor, in a circle, knees touching.

Halfway through, Alice asked, "Is it true that if you catch a mermaid, she has to give you a wish?"

Art rolled his eyes. "I can't escape."

Alice frowned.

"Art doesn't like the mermaid," Meredith said.

Alice's jaw dropped open. "That's stupid."

"Alice."

She slouched, digging a trench in her melting ice cream. "You just don't know the story. You would if you did."

"Do you know the story?" Art challenged.

"Yes! The mermaid came to visit the people and gave them gifts. Someone caught her, and she gave them a wish and they lived happily ever after. The end." She crossed her arms. "See? I know it."

Art nodded thoughtfully. "That's a great story, I'll admit."

"Where'd you hear that one?" Meredith asked.

"Grandpa's book."

Meredith frowned. Then she realized Alice was talking about the kids' book her stepdad had self-published. He'd wanted something new for the museum gift shop, so he wrote a book about the cape mermaid, complete with simplistic illustrations. He'd dedicated it to Meredith. A copy of it sat on Alice's bookshelf at home.

Alice's shoulders sank, her enthusiasm waning.

"I know we didn't bring *your* book, but I bet I could find another copy around here somewhere," Meredith said.

Alice swirled her spoon around the bowl. "It's not that."

"What is it, then?" Stones shifted in Meredith's stomach. "Did Grandma say something to you while I was in the shower?"

She shook her head.

"Then what's wrong?"

"The girl told me another story."

"What girl?"

"Red-haired girl." Alice sniffed. "It's not true, right? What she said?"

Meredith and Art shared a look. She'd never seen Alice this worried. She gently grabbed Alice's fidgeting fingers, already scratching at the cuticles so much they bled. "Whatever it was, baby, I'm sure it's not true."

"Yeah," Art added. "Nothing to worry about, kiddo."

Alice nodded, but tears dripped down her red cheeks into her ice cream bowl. "She said I'm gonna die." The dam broke, and her whole body shook with the force of her tears. "I don't wanna die."

A chill snaked down Meredith's back as she gathered Alice up in her arms, pulling her into her lap. Seeing the fear on her daughter's face flipped a switch inside her body, pulling every muscle tight. She ground her teeth to keep from yelling. "Of course not, sweetie. You're not gonna die. No one's gonna die. Everything's fine." She rocked Alice, pressing her against her chest, but Alice only cried harder. She stroked Alice's hair and planted kisses all over her, but it seemed like nothing could stop the trembling.

Whatever this red-haired girl had said to Alice had terrified her.

After a long time, when Alice had calmed a little, Meredith tried to get her to tell her more about the red-haired girl, but every question was met with a frustrated *I don't know.*

Finally, Alice got so huffy she crawled out of Meredith's lap and started for the stairs. Her daughter's emotions were fraught lately, flipping between impossible calm and at the edge of a meltdown at the drop of a hat. She blamed herself. It couldn't have been easy trying to keep a brave face on for her sake. Meredith stood to follow when she spotted her mother at the top of the stairs. She wondered how long her mother had been standing there.

"I was just going to put Alice to bed," Meredith said.

"It's getting dark," Judith said. "You should get up to the light."

"I will. After I deal with this."

"Let me." Judith's voice was firm, then softened. "I owe her an apology anyway. Let me do it."

After a moment, Meredith relented. "Okay."

"Thank you."

Meredith nodded. Then, thinking about what Alice had said, "Did you see a red-haired girl while you guys were on the beach today? Did she talk to you?"

Something flashed across Judith's face she couldn't quite read. "No."

"You're sure?"

Her expression hardened, defensive. "My memory isn't as bad as you keep implying, you know. I'm perfectly fine. Everyone is forgetful every now and again, and I don't like that you keep—"

Meredith threw her hands up in surrender. "Okay, Mom. I wasn't trying to accuse you of anything. I just..." She shook her head. "Never mind."

"Can I go tuck my granddaughter in now?"

"Sure. Just be nice, okay?"

Judith pushed Meredith's hair behind her ear, an unexpected gesture of affection, as her expression softened, an almost frighteningly quick transformation. "I'll take care of it. I'll take care of everything. I promise."

Cheeks burning, Meredith offered a small smile. "Okay. Thanks."

Judith nodded, then turned, heading back upstairs.

Art joined Meredith in the hall and patted her back. "Everything will be fine. You'll see." Then, "You've got a good kid."

"She's all right."

"Can't abide that mermaid business, though," he joked. "Gonna have to take care of that."

She offered a weak smile. "What about you? You know any red-haired girls?"

"Wish I did," Art joked, then shook his head. "Probably just some kid thinking it's funny to scare the little one."

"Probably." Then why didn't her mother say anything when she'd asked? She sighed, glancing in the direction of the stairs. "It was a bad idea to come here."

"Why *did* you? I've been trying to get you to visit for ages now. Not trying to make you feel any sort of way, but I figured you had your reasons for keeping away as long as you did."

"I did. I do." She rubbed her face. "The short answer is I don't know."

"And the long answer?"

She wanted to tell him about what happened in the lighthouse. The urge to jump. The jar of water. They were nothing, really, but a lot of nothing could turn into something. If she told, she worried she'd start to sound like her mother.

"It sounds stupid," she finally said, "but there's something about the cape that's always stuck with me. Like a bad itch or a splinter I can't get to. I do my best not to think about it, but when I do, it's *all* I think about. I came over the ridge and saw the lighthouse and heard the water and..." She struggled to put the feeling into words. It wasn't relief, not even close. "I felt...connected. In a way I don't feel anywhere else."

"That *was* a long answer."

Meredith laughed. "Yeah. Thanks."

He patted her shoulder. "It'll all work out. You'll see."

Coming from Art, she almost believed it.

Casting a quick look up in the direction of the lighthouse, Meredith held the door for Art while he left. She doubted she'd find the answers to anything up there—to why her marriage was falling apart, why her mother had never treated her like a daughter, why being at the cape did things to her...things she couldn't name—but that didn't mean she wasn't going to look. She had to believe she'd come back to the cape for a reason. She had to believe that the answers were here somewhere, because she knew now that she couldn't leave again without them.

CHAPTER FOUR

GRACE

1910

oday marked the twenty-third year of Grace's vigil. The light room was dark, the sky overcast and hazy, making it almost impossible to see far out across the ocean. Every few seconds the light made its pass, casting a red glow over everything, with a Grace-shaped shadow cut through the center. She considered moving, to let the light roam unobstructed, but she began to see her shape as a message: *I'm here. I'm waiting.*

If Grace had one wish, it would be to see a small boat on the horizon, with her mother at the helm, heading for the cape.

Soon, another shape joined hers—taller, fatter, elbows bent and hands on his hips so that he looked like a sugar pot. Her brother, William, used to sit with her on these vigils, until their father decided William was old enough to start learning the family business. Grace didn't think bookkeeping was so complicated that William couldn't at least spend a few nights a week up here with her, but it didn't matter what she thought. Their father had long dismissed her and let her do what she liked, provided it didn't embarrass him. If anyone asked, he told them Grace was in mourning. True enough, she supposed, but not the whole truth.

William took the mug out of her hands and sniffed before taking a long sip. "Your husband's looking for you."

She snatched it back. "He knows where to find me."

"That's not the point."

"What is the point, then?"

"He's neglected at home."

"Is he?" She withdrew a small flask from her pocket and filled her mug almost to the brim.

"So are the children."

Heat rose in her face, and she stifled the urge to slap him. "My children are fine."

"They miss their mother."

"They're barely out of diapers, William. How could they possibly notice I'm not there when they're sleeping?"

He sighed, leaning one shoulder against the metal scaffolding around the light. "She's gone, you know. For good."

She looked at him, taking in the narrow shoulders, perfectly pressed clothes, and the whisper of a blond mustache that made him the spitting image of their father, a man who'd written their mother off with the same efficiency as dashing off an invoice. She'd overheard him say to a friend one night, "Regina is gone, and that's the end of it." Neither William nor their father had forgiven her for leaving them to handle Liza's and Marina's disappearances on their own. Though most people felt empathy for them, some whispered dark, devilish things. That they'd run off together. They'd leaped from the bluff, a suicide pact. That they'd been snatched by the witch who lived in the house on the hill.

Yes. Their mother was gone. But that wasn't the end of it. Far from it.

Grace drank from the mug, her husband's scotch warming and emboldening her. "Do you remember anything about that night?"

William frowned. "Obviously not."

She hid her satisfaction at having struck a nerve beneath another sip. Grace remembered.

She didn't sleep much in those days—didn't sleep much now either—but as a child she was plagued by nightmares that would force her awake hours before sunrise.

She didn't know if it was a memory or something her child mind had conjured, but when she closed her eyes, she always saw the night Liza and Marina both disappeared.

In her memory—in her nightmares—Grace had perched herself at the window, counting down the minutes until morning. Her father had brought home Russian honey cake, a family favorite, and promised Grace and William the last two slices for breakfast. She remembered willing the sun to come up faster, wondering exactly how much trouble she'd get into if she sneaked down to the kitchen while everyone was asleep.

And then the nightmare shifted. The dark became darker. Stars blinked out, and the moon disappeared behind a cloud. The only thing piercing the blackness was the lighthouse, but even that went out too. In the nightmare (memory?), Grace leaned out the window as a shadow drifted across the ground, followed by her mother, nightgown soaked through and hair wild. The waves lashed the shore like thunder, and the wind blew her mother's nightgown against her, skirts flickering, a ghost in the dark. Just before she woke up, her mother looked up at her with coal-black eyes and screamed.

"Do you ever think about them?" she asked.

"No." In the dark, she couldn't tell if he was lying.

"I do. All the time." She studied his face for a reaction, but his expression remained maddeningly neutral. "Sometimes, when I'm down by the water, I can hear her. She's reaching out to us. Can't you feel it?"

A deep V formed between his eyebrows. "Don't you think—"

"No. I don't. Despite what you and Father think, I'm not insane."

"I never said that."

"You didn't have to," she snapped. "And even if it's not Mother, someone out there needs us. Needs *me*. And if, somehow, helping them means she can come home…"

"So you spend every night here, avoiding your family, listening for something that may or may not exist, for…what? To shake hands with it? What if it…" William crossed the room and gripped Grace's shoulders. "You have to understand how this sounds."

She knew exactly how it sounded, but it didn't matter. How was she supposed to explain to him what she'd felt in the few seconds of looking into the water and seeing the *need* between the waves? There was something out there, desperately clawing its way up from the depths. How was she supposed to ignore something like that?

"She wants something from me," Grace said. "And if I give it to her, maybe it'll bring Mother back."

"She?" William raised an eyebrow.

Grace nodded.

"She who?"

"I don't know."

"And if you don't give this *something* to her?" he asked sarcastically.

"I will."

William shook his head. "Don't do this to yourself, Grace. Please."

"I'm going to find out what it is, and I'm going to give it to her." *Because if I don't*, Grace thought, *she might just take it anyway.*

William left her alone in the light room, but not before lecturing her on the duties of a wife and mother. She gently reminded him that he was unmarried and that his only frame of reference was a woman who'd abandoned her remaining children for reasons unknown, but like her father and her husband, he *knew what was best* by virtue of his gender. Grace aspired to be so confident in her ignorance.

Though her blond hair and wide-set eyes had come from her father, inside Grace was all her mother—curious, determined, and single-minded. She *had* seen something in the water, even if it wasn't with her eyes. Could a person see with their soul? Hear with their heart? She believed so. To pass the time, she counted the rotations of the light as it passed over the ocean, but her eyelids had begun to droop under the weight of the scotch, and in that place between sleep and awake, Grace started to doubt herself. There was so much she didn't understand; she'd been a child when her mother disappeared. Yet...the nightmares never changed. Didn't that mean there was something to them? Had she seen her mother out there that night? Even sober she couldn't remember any more than those few minutes. She didn't remember what happened after—if they'd had the honey cake the next morning, how long it took to realize Marina and Liza were gone. She used to think she'd find the answers in the bottom of a bottle. She never had, but that didn't mean she wouldn't try.

No, she thought, setting down her glass. *There is something. There has to be.*

She revisited that night in her mind. There had been something different about it. But what?

The light passed over her, and as it passed, the shadows closed in at the corners of the light room. She looked across to the water, where the waves were as inky black as the sky, and with a shock, she realized: that night, the light had been off. How many stories had she read warning against the darkness? Even as an adult, she believed there was something different about the night. There were things that lived in the dark that didn't in the light.

Which meant, if she turned off the light now, maybe...

She frantically went over the mechanism controls until the light died under a soft hum. The floor vibrated with the force of the gears slowing until finally there was silence, the darkness so dense she could barely see her hand in front of her face. Guiding herself by the rail surrounding the lens, she went to the glass door that led to the catwalk. Outside, a warm breeze whipped her hair from its pins and tangled her skirts in the railing. Languid shadows rippled over the water, bleeding onto the beach. She leaned over the side of the narrow rail. It was a long way down.

Still, she leaned farther, as far as she dared before self-preservation ripped her back. *They're louder in the dark*, she thought, straining to see through the blackness to the water. As her eyes struggled to adjust, the wind picked up, making them water. Further blinded, she groped along the rail, trying to find her way back to the light. Though part of her wanted to wait a little longer, to try to see what she saw that night, a deeper, animal part fought to get to the light. *Danger*, her body warned. *Turn on the light.*

Movement in the corner of her eye made her stop. She turned, misstepped, and nearly went over the side. She cried out, but the sound of the waves swallowed her voice. As she righted herself, she looked down to the beach, where she swore she saw a woman walking toward the water, pale yellow nightgown all but glowing in the darkness.

Mother?

She ran from the light room and down the winding stairs, rolling her ankle on the bottom step. Pain sliced up her leg, but she kept moving. Tears burned her eyes as she navigated the steep stone steps from the lighthouse to the trail that would lead to the bottom of the bluff and, finally, the beach. Her shoes sank into the damp sand, so she kicked them off. She limped toward the shoreline where the woman had paused. Grace slowed, not wanting to scare her.

Moonlight brushed the edges of the woman's body, making her more shadow than person. Her hair was wet and oil black, and the yellow of her nightgown had faded. Her shoulders were narrow and dipped inward, her toes buried in the sand. An arm's length away, Grace reached out, but the woman—no, girl— bolted for the water. It was like the water parted for her as she waded smoothly through the waves. Her skin and hair seemed to spread like ink under the foam. Waist deep, she glanced over her shoulder, but her face was hidden in shadow.

Still, Grace heard, felt, what had pulled her to the window that night. "I'm here," she said.

Grace took her hand, but it was too soft, the bones shifting under her touch, and a rancid stench wafted up from the foam. Soon all she heard was the rush of the water, muffled, like hands clamped over her ears. She wobbled on her feet as the girl gently guided her toward the water. *I don't want to go in*, she thought, but it was far away. A whisper of a consciousness that didn't quite catch.

The girl's features were distorted, her neck just a little too long and her eyes a little too wide. Too dark. Too empty. But Grace couldn't look away. A voice in the back of her mind screamed through the fog, too strangled to hear.

I know you, she thought.

The girl's hand twitched as though she'd heard it, tightening her grip as they reached the water's edge.

Up to her ankles now. Her knees. Even as her heart pounded and the muscles in her body stretched tight to snap, it only took a gentle pull from the girl to make her walk deeper into the water.

Blood felt stilled in Grace's veins and she trembled, cold seeping through her skin. She clenched her jaw as a wave broke over her shoulders. Spray went up her nose and covered her mouth, and she tried to pull away, but a voice in her ear soothed and coddled, and soon she was floating, floating down, and she opened her mouth to breathe in—

But another voice broke through. "Grace!"

There were hands on her shoulders and tangled in her hair. Her face broke the surface and she gagged.

And when she got her feet under her, she looked into William's face, which was stone pale.

"What were you thinking?" he asked. "How could you?"

"Look!" Grace demanded. "She's there. I told you."

But when she turned, the girl was gone and the water was still.

William helped her onto the shore, peppering her with questions she couldn't answer. She leaned into him, her legs weak and trembling.

"Cold," she finally said— the only word she could make her mouth form, her mind still mostly clouded.

Sighing, William helped her wrap her arm around his neck and leaned to the side, holding most of her weight. "There's a fire going. Let's get you inside."

In the house, Grace shakily stripped out of her wet clothes, and something fell out of the pocket. A shell. Furtively making sure no one could see her, she put it up to her ear, and though she only heard the ocean, she knew the girl was there too. Whispering. Waiting.

A week passed before William and her husband left Grace alone with the children. Her son, Charlie, kept mostly to himself, but Beth followed Grace from room to room, quietly watching. She wondered if Beth heard the whispering at night the way Grace did. She kept the shell in her pocket, jabbing the sharp edges with her finger every so often to remind herself that it was real—what she'd *seen* had been real.

The nightmares grew stronger. More vivid. When she closed her eyes and saw her mother on the beach, her hands and nightgown were streaked with blood. And every time she opened her eyes in the middle of the night, she somehow felt the girl staring into the window.

Soon, she stopped sleeping altogether. Her husband had given up trying to hide the whiskey, calling it an unladylike drink, but even several glasses of the stuff couldn't lull her to sleep.

Bleary and numb, she stood by the window and stared up at the lighthouse, watching the hypnotic turn of the light.

It's too bright.

A thought too sharp to be her own.

She blinked and opened her eyes to complete darkness.

"Mom?" Beth's voice came from somewhere behind her, the girl likely startled out of her bed. "What happened?"

"The light keeps her away," Grace said.

"Keeps who away?"

As the sounds of her husband's breath and her daughter's voice faded beneath the crash of the water, she fought to keep above the fog closing around her mind. It was too hot in here, too stifling. The air was thick. She was drowning. She struggled to open the window latch with numb fingers, and when it finally flew open, she sucked in a deep breath of dead air.

"She needs me," she said, words slurring with her too-heavy tongue.

Beth whimpered. "Mom? What's happening? Who's out there?"

She spotted the girl in the darkness, waves splashing over her feet. She held her arms out, and Grace copied the gesture.

Too far.

She leaned gently out the window, arms stretched wide. An unfamiliar ache seeped through her. A need she couldn't name.

She had to get to the water. The yearning pulsed through her, hot and sharp.

Get to the water, she thought. *Get to the water and the pain will stop.*

She hooked one leg over the side of the window ledge.

Somewhere far away, Beth called out for her.

Deep inside the fog, Grace called back.

As she fell, she saw the girl's face. *Really* saw it.

And she knew.

CHAPTER FIVE

JUDITH

PRESENT DAY

ime was elastic, stretching and contracting around Judith like a cocoon. Cottony and hot. How long ago had Meredith gone to the lighthouse? Minutes? Hours? Bowls sticky with ice cream and chocolate sat in the sink; Judith dipped her finger in the milky residue and stuck it in her mouth. Three bowls for three women. But Judith hadn't had any. *That's right.* Art had been here. Though her mouth shaped an involuntary scowl, she imagined it'd probably been good to see him. She'd missed him.

Meredith *had* gone to the lighthouse, hadn't she? The memory fluttered like a broken spiderweb. Yes! There. The red light slashed through the window. Judith closed her eyes as the light washed over her. It prickled, like she could feel the energy, the hum from the mechanism.

It felt alive in here, her bare feet on the cool tile of the kitchen, skin to skin with her house. The walls whispered, spitting from the vents and hissing through the gaps in the windows where the weathering had come away. The walls groaned and the floor creaked. Old women they were, their joints degrading like sand under the tide. Judith loved this house. Loved it like a friend or an aunt who slipped her candy and fed her secrets. It had out-of-the-way nooks with cracks for hiding secret thoughts scrawled on napkins, cabinets with deep shelves to cradle the things most special to her, thick walls to protect her from Out There. This house had history. It had breath. It had a life that stretched all the way back to the woman who first watched the lighthouse, who started all of this. The woman who made this mess.

And now who was left to clean it up? Judith, that was who. Always cleaning, always sweeping under rugs.

She'd been standing so long in one place her feet began to sweat and stick to the tile. They *peeeeled* with her first steps toward the liquor cabinet. She called it *the liquor cabinet* only in her head. She kept vodka and window cleaner there, and *window cleaner cabinet* just didn't have the same ring. The first glass she spotted in the cabinet was a coffee mug like the ones her husband used to order for the museum gift shop. The handle was a lime-green mermaid tail, the mermaid's face wide and smiling on the side, surrounded by turquoise hair. On this mug, one of her eyes had been worn away, like she was winking. Judith's first instinct was to smash it. Instead, she plunked a few ice cubes in it, poured a generous amount of vodka over the ice, and then drank, her teeth grinding against the ceramic until pain shot through her jaw.

A noise upstairs startled her. She jumped, making her drink slosh over the side of the mug and drip down her hand. There was no one else home, right? So then who—

Another sound, like a voice, like water.

Still clutching the mug, Judith raced up the stairs as quickly as her knees would allow. Her heart thudded and her breath strained in her chest. Meredith's bedroom door was wide open. How many times had she told the girl to keep it closed? Judith peered inside. The room was mostly dark, but light from the hallway illuminated her daughter's sleeping form on the bed, covers tucked up around her face, leaving only the top of her head exposed. *Something's not right.*

Judith blinked hard, letting the image of her daughter blur. She kept that word on her tongue. Daughter. Daugh-ter. She tapped her tongue against the roof of her mouth, forming the word without opening her mouth. The sound was like bubbling water.

It wasn't Meredith in the bed. Meredith was in the lighthouse. Grown.

Alice. Judith reddened as the memory pushed through the haze. Her granddaughter.

Judith sat on the edge of the bed, setting her mug on the floor. Alice's slight frame dipped toward her weight, and the blanket fell away from her face. She looked so much like Meredith it made Judith's breath catch. The longer she stared, though, the more Alice's differences stuck out: freckles under her eyes, long black eyelashes, a nose that turned up at the end. Features she didn't get from Judith's family. Sparse eyebrows that arched far from the middle. Small, delicate ears. She almost nudged Alice awake just so she could see those big brown eyes. She gently brushed Alice's cheek. It'd surprised her, this fierce love Judith felt for her granddaughter. She'd never been the maternal sort, and Meredith, bless her, had always been strong but a little hard to like. But Alice was something else. Something incredible. Someone that desperately needed protecting.

After tucking the blankets tightly around Alice's body, Judith leaned over her to plant a kiss on her forehead.

As her lips brushed skin, she saw it. On the nightstand, sitting on the back corner, just out of reach of the hallway light.

The shell.

Judith's blood went cold and her skin burned. In her head, she snatched the thing off the table and hurled it out the window, but her arm wouldn't budge. It didn't matter how many times she threw it away, it would come back. It would always come back.

You can make it stop. The whisper of a memory surfaced, deep in the dark place of her mind that spoke of curses and women. Of revenge. Of an island in the Pacific where she'd left her girlhood.

She stepped around the bed, knocking her mug over in the process. The mermaid's tail broke. The smell of vodka wafted up from the floor, but she ignored it as she lifted the familiar shell and held it between her palms.

It was only a little thing, but the shell was heavy in her hands. It wasn't as bright as she remembered, the opalescent sheen faded and cracked. The sharp points had chipped. She thought about the day she'd first found it, remembered how excited she'd been by the discovery. And then it spoke to her, and everything changed. All that happened after was her fault.

Judith had known she wouldn't stay away forever.

Alice stirred; Judith had to be fast. There was only one thing she could do.

She cupped the shell to her lips and whispered, "I'm coming."

The ocean was a ghost of itself, all gray and frothy, like cotton stretched too thin. Foam curdled in long, arching lines on the beach. Her exposed skin pinched with the cold, and she bit back a shudder. The water would be worse.

No. Can't think of that now. She needed this. Alice needed this. It would all end with her. No more curse. No more voices crooning from the waves. This was the end and it was good.

The red light grazed over the water once. Twice. On the third time, she caught a strange glimmer in the distance. She'd never seen it before but knew in her heart what it meant. She started for the water, her gaze locked on the place in the darkness where she'd seen the glimmer. *I know you're here,* she thought.

The water was like icy pins in her feet, but she didn't hesitate, not for a second, even when a voice far behind her threatened to steal her attention. Water up to her ankles now. Her knees. It was harder to move with the ocean working against her. Wave after wave pushed her back precious inches.

"Mom?" The wind practically swallowed Meredith's voice. Judith wouldn't have heard it if she hadn't been listening for it. "What the hell are you doing?"

Judith shook her head. *Go back,* she thought. *Hear me.* She didn't say it out loud; she needed all her breath for this.

Water to her waist. Head down, she slogged through the waves until her feet slipped off a sand bar and she was floating. A wave threatened to undo all her work, but taking a deep breath, she slipped beneath it. The cold bit at her ears and nose. Skull pounding, she relished the quiet until she couldn't stand it anymore. When she surfaced, she heard frantic splashing behind her.

"Hold on, Mom!" Meredith shouted. "I'm coming!"

Judith knew Meredith's strength in the water. Though Judith's husband had bowed to her insistence that Meredith never be allowed in the ocean, he was no match for Meredith's powers of persuasion. He had taken her to swimming lessons at the Y for years, thinking Judith was none the wiser. But eventually word made its way to her. Meredith had joined a swim team. She was the fastest five-hundred-meter butterflyer they'd ever seen. It kept her out of the ocean and sated her need to be in the water, which was good enough for Judith. She never said a word.

There was no way Judith could outswim her, so she waited, treading water. The red light passed again, and Judith saw a wraith in the foam, head barely above the water, unbothered by the waves, like she was anchored to the spot.

It felt like only seconds had passed when Meredith's hand gripped Judith's shoulder. "Jesus, Mom, are you nuts? What are you doing out here?" She spat seawater. "Where's Alice?"

"Alice is fine." A pause. "She's going to be fine," Judith corrected.

"What does that mean?" Panic rose in Meredith's voice. "Did something happen? Is she okay?"

"She's asleep. In bed."

Relief, then Meredith's eyes widened. "She's alone?"

Judith shook her head. If she let this go on too long, she might change her mind. She couldn't let that happen. Pulling Meredith into her, she hugged her, harder than she'd ever done before, kicking like mad to keep them both afloat. Meredith froze in her grasp.

"Mom?"

"They didn't do it right," Judith said. "The others. But I'm going to do it right. Then you and Alice will be safe."

"Do wha—" Meredith dipped slightly beneath a splash, making Judith's stomach drop. She reached out and grabbed Meredith's arm. She was still there. She was okay.

Judith could give her this. She would give her this because Meredith gave her Alice. She kissed Meredith's ear. "Listen to me. This is the right thing. I know I messed up. I know you hate me."

"I don't hate—"

"No. *Listen.* I messed up, but this is going to fix everything." Water splashed up her face and into her mouth. The salt burned her chapped lips. "I couldn't be a good mom because of her. Except I can now. I can do this."

Meredith's shoulders shook under Judith's grip. Judith stroked her hair and shushed her and promised her everything would be okay.

"What is this? What's *happening*?" Meredith's frown deepened. She shot a glance toward the shore. "We need to go back. Your lips are blue."

"I'm fine, honey. I'll be fine."

Meredith tugged on her arm, but Judith easily slipped out of her grip. She forced a smile, and in that smile she tried to convey everything she'd never said to her daughter. That she was proud of the woman she'd become, that despite everything Judith had done wrong, Meredith was kind and beautiful and special. That everything would be okay.

She felt those deep, black eyes on the back of her head and waited for the fog to take her thoughts. When it didn't, she decided it was because the girl knew her intention. This would work. This would end it all.

"Do you see her?" Judith asked.

Meredith shook her head.

"Good."

"Mom." Meredith's voice broke. "Please. Let's go back."

Judith offered an apologetic smile before bringing her knees up and driving her feet into Meredith's stomach with as much strength as she could muster.

Meredith doubled over, the wind knocked out of her. She gagged and coughed her name, but by that time, Judith had started a mad swim for the girl, only her hair and black eyes visible above the waves. Meredith's coughing was swallowed by the water and the wind, and Judith was proud of herself for not giving up. So close now. A few more strokes.

But the girl was gone. Panic bubbled up her throat. She screamed until she was hoarse, and even then it didn't stop, flaying her throat. A tickle on her ankle cut off the sound. Splashing behind her meant Meredith had regained some of her breath, but she'd be slow—too late.

Judith smiled.

A familiar grip encircled her ankle and pulled.

Beneath the water, bubbles rushing along her hips and shoulders. She was flying. She was weightless. Down, down, deep into the swirling blackness.

Finally.

CHAPTER SIX

JUDITH

udith hitched up her skirt and waddled knee-deep into a tide pool. Uncle Thomas told her he'd seen a pink mollusk shell somewhere down here, and she was determined to find it. She had every color shell you could think of, all lined up on the window ledge in her bedroom—even a black one her cousin Art had thrown in a bonfire last summer because she'd beat him in a race. With a pink shell, her collection would be almost perfect.

Silvery minnows flitted back and forth in the pool, dodging her steps. A dismembered crab claw clacked against a rock. She snatched it up and stuck it in her pocket to give to Art later. He was always collecting weird stuff like that, bits and pieces, sometimes from things that were alive, sometimes from things that weren't.

She shuffled around the pool for a long time. Mud stirred up, and she dug through pebbles with her toe until her shins were numb from the cold water. Convinced she'd probably buried it with her tromping, she plunged her hand down, hissing when the salt hit a cut on her hand.

There was no pink mollusk shell.

Disappointed and soggy and in for a whacking when her mom saw what she'd done to her new shorts, Judith climbed out of the tide pool and skipped over the rocks toward the shore. She was exactly three jumps away when she saw the body.

She'd seen dead bodies on TV before, on the news late at night when Mom and Dad didn't know she was watching from the stairs. None of them had looked like this. His skin was stretched out and purple in places and his hair knotted around bits of seaweed and wood. Part of her was scared, but another part wanted to get closer. To touch it. Something wasn't right about it, the way the limbs puffed out and the face swelled. He looked like an overfilled balloon.

She hopped one rock closer, balancing on one foot.

"Oh my God. Judith! Get away from him!"

Her gaze snapped toward the beach where Uncle Thomas waved both arms at her.

"I'm fine," she said. "I didn't touch him."

"Just come around this way." He pointed to a path the long way around another tide pool. "Be careful, now."

Judith obeyed, but not without sneaking glances at the body while it bobbed with the waves. Once her feet touched the sand, Uncle Thomas pulled her into his side, burying her face in his shirt. He stroked her hair and shushed her even though she hadn't said anything. Grown-ups always thought she was more scared than she was.

He kept a tight hold on her until they were past the boathouse and climbed the hill toward the lighthouse. When she finally wrenched herself away, she was irritated to find she couldn't even see the beach, let alone the man.

"A damn shame. A right damn shame," Uncle Thomas muttered. He squeezed Judith's hand. "You okay, little one?"

Little one. Judith was twelve. Hardly little. "I said I was fine."

"Okay. Yeah. Good. You be strong. That's good. Lord knows we all need to be strong right now."

He held her hand the whole walk from the tide pool to her house. Dad would be gone at work, but she spotted Mom on the front porch hanging up the towels to dry. One look at Uncle Thomas and her face fell. Judith could tell her mom didn't know whether to be mad or worried, so she settled on confused.

"What's going on, Thomas? Judith's not causing trouble, is she?"

"No, no. Nothing like that." He let go of Judith and pulled a half-melted chocolate out of his pocket. He handed it to her with a smile. "Why don't you give your mom and me a second, okay there, doll?"

Judith shrugged. Even half-melted chocolate was chocolate. She peeled the wrapper and walked into the house but slowed down once she was out of sight. She couldn't hear everything, but she caught bits and pieces.

"—going to say to his mother?"

"—it's not like—"

"—this goddamned war."

Judith's ears burned. Her stomach got all knotted up, and she swallowed, warning her breakfast of eggs and waffles to stay put. She knew all about the war.

Four or five months ago, they'd been sitting around the table eating meatloaf that was more breadcrumb than meat—Judith, Mom, Dad, and Judith's brother, David. David pushed his meatloaf around the plate, which Mom normally would have yelled at him about. Mom had a thing about wasting food and would let leftovers sit in the fridge, refusing to make anything new until they were eaten. Dad shoveled the meatloaf in his mouth between angry bites of mashed potatoes, barely chewing. Mom had one eye on the clock in the kitchen and the other on her uneaten dinner.

Out of nowhere, Mom stood up. Her chair scraped the wood floor. "Upstairs, Judith."

Judith frowned, trying to remember if she'd done something wrong. "Why?"

"Do as your mother says." Dad slid her plate away. "Not like you're eating, are ya?"

"I was just letting it cool off!"

Mom pulled her off the chair and slapped her bottom, but not hard enough to hurt. "Let's go, young lady."

"I'll eat! I promise!"

Mom shushed her and pulled her upstairs, depositing Judith in her bedroom. She closed the door behind her, cutting off any chance Judith had of overhearing whatever it was they didn't want her to know.

Later, Mom finally opened the door again, eyes puffy and red. Downstairs, someone cried. Judith's guts rolled when she realized it was David.

Then Mom told her about the war.

"He's with the good guys, right?" Judith asked.

Mom hesitated a beat, then nodded.

"Then he'll be okay. The good guys always win."

Mom hugged her tight. "Let's hope so."

For a day, Judith had felt okay with the idea of her brother going to war. Then Art came along and ruined everything. He kept lists of the people who died and read them out loud to her when they went to the bluffs. Every day more names. Every day she held her breath until he reached the end and David's name wasn't on it.

Judith's dad kept lists too, except he didn't read them out loud. He folded them neatly and tucked them between the pages of a Bible.

"He's probably hiding," Judith said to him. "There's places to hide in the jungle."

"Sure," Dad had said. "Lots of places. Great big holes in the ground."

"Like graves."

Dad didn't correct her.

After Uncle Thomas left, Mom smothered Judith, her shirt smelling like laundry detergent and bacon grease. "That must've been scary," Mom said.

"A little," Judith admitted because if she didn't, Mom would've poked her until she did.

"Do you want to talk about it?"

Judith pulled away and squared her shoulders. "I already know it was the curse."

Mom got that stony, blank look she had whenever Judith brought it up. "There's no curse," Mom always said.

But Judith knew better. There was a reason Mom never went into the water. A reason the lighthouse light stayed on, even though no boats came to the old harbor anymore. Hadn't for as long as Judith had been alive. Maybe even longer. There was a reason why Judith didn't know her grandmother. And that reason was the curse.

"Whatever happened to him, we should be respectful," Mom said, dismissing her. "That means no spreading wild rumors or bugging the family. Got it?"

Judith nodded.

Later, Mom let her back outside, only after Judith promised not to go back to the water for a while.

"Why?" Judith asked. "I already saw."

"Just don't go. Hear me?"

But Judith did go. Not all the way down to the beach, because there were lots of grown-ups down there and most of them were cops. She snuck behind the lighthouse toward the edge of the cliff overlooking the beach. She found Carol and Art peering over the ledge, eyes wide as plates.

Carol's hair was done up in big waves and flips, like it wanted to be the ocean all on its own. She was fifteen and smarter and prettier than Judith and made sure she told her so at least once a day. Today, Judith didn't care. Today, Judith had something Carol didn't.

"I saw him." Judith crossed her arms smartly over her chest. "I saw everything."

"Liar," Carol said.

"It's true," Art said. "I heard my dad and grandpa talking."

Carol scowled.

"It was the curse that got him," Judith said.

Art laughed.

"What?"

"No such thing."

"Shows how much you know. I saw him with my own two eyes, all blue and bloated."

"That's how people always look when they drown."

"Yeah," Judith said, triumphant. "Drowned by the curse."

Art sat back on his heels and plucked at the grass. "He did it to himself."

Carol gasped, her hand fluttering to her chest in a way that looked like she'd been practicing.

"What do you mean?" Judith asked.

"His mom said his number got called. He said he was gonna run away far enough they couldn't catch him."

Judith shook her head. She knew what she saw.

"Oi!" Uncle Thomas shouted from the light room. "You kids clear out. Nothing to see here, got it?"

Carol stood and wiped the dirt off her skirt. "Serves him right."

Art and Judith both stared at her.

"You said it yourself, Art. He was going to run away. That's traitor talk."

"Oh yeah?" Art's face reddened. "How fast would you run if your number was called?"

"I wouldn't."

Neither Art nor Judith were convinced.

"No one deserves to be dead," Art said.

Judith nudged his elbow with hers. He was a jerk sometimes, but most of the time she liked her cousin. She remembered the crab claw in her pocket and handed it to him.

His eyes lit up as he turned it over in his palm. "Thanks."

Carol pretended not to be interested but couldn't stop staring at the claw. Carol was okay too. Judith just wished she'd stop acting so old.

Under Uncle Thomas's glare, they went their separate ways—Carol to her dad's shop in town, Art to the boathouse where he kept all his found things, but Judith kept along the cliff, down the far side that led to the woods and away from adult view. She watched the policemen poke around the tide pool for a little while, get tired of getting their shoes wet, and finally leave with nothing to show for their efforts except a line of police tape staked into the sand. Even that would be gone by tomorrow.

She didn't know what she was watching for after that, only that she ought to. She thought about what Art said and decided that he was probably right. If any of the whispers were true, the curse didn't want boys.

The curse belonged to *her* family.

She watched the dip and swell of the water until her stomach growled. But even then she stayed. If she'd learned anything from stories, it was that no one got anything from running off for a quick snack when they were meant to be looking for something. If it wasn't the curse, then maybe it was a giant squid that'd gotten him. Or a shark. She swallowed the hunger and stared even harder at the waves.

She could hear them good up here. Water splashed on the rocks a ways down, and the sound echoed up the side of the cliff. She got sleepy sometimes just listening to the water. A couple times she'd been sitting up on the bluffs or even down by the cove and the waves rocked in and out, and it was like her body was being rocked with it, and before she knew it, her mom was standing over her, all wide-eyed panic and bloody lips from biting them too hard.

The only reason she was allowed down by the beach anymore was because of her dad. "What's the point of living dollar by dollar to keep this place if we don't enjoy it every once in a while?" he'd said.

She was getting that sleepy feeling now but fought to keep her eyes open. The back of her head went all tingly, like her body knew she wasn't alone. A small, distant part of her wondered if today would be the day she'd finally see—

A face emerged in the sea foam, pale and sparkling like the water, eyes like holes and hair tangled in complicated knots. A girl. She was stone-still, even as the waves rocked around her. She seemed to flicker in and out as the sunlight rippled off the water, like the light could cut her. Words died in Judith's throat, and when she made to stand, the girl lunged forward in the water, slicing through an oncoming wave, gone as quickly as she'd come. Judith raced for the beach, tripping twice and bruising the side of her shin and her wrist.

Out on the water there was only foam, but Judith could feel something lingering, eyes digging holes in her body. Maybe what she saw wasn't a girl at all but something else. What did a curse look like? She kept her distance from the shoreline, careful to keep her feet out of the water yet unable for a long time to force herself to leave.

Finally she began to walk back in the direction of the tide pools—her leg hurt too much to climb the hill the way she came—when something half-buried in the sand caught her eye. She snatched it up before the wave could bury it or drag it away. It was an opalescent pink shell, curled like a goat horn, and as she brought it closer to her face to inspect all the intricate swirls of pink and white laced through it, she heard the ocean.

And beneath the ocean, another sound, almost too faint to hear.

It was a girl, and she was crying.

CHAPTER SEVEN

MEREDITH

I t had all happened so fast.

Every time Meredith ran it all through her head, her thoughts snagged on the metal music (loud and obnoxious enough to keep her awake) that'd been playing when she saw her mother on the beach, tinny and warbling from her phone like some fucked-up soundtrack. The sky had looked a mess of stars and the ocean a black, seething monster set to devour her mother, and all Meredith could do was run and swim, and in the end it didn't matter. Nothing mattered. Her mother was gone, the word like a punch in the gut, bringing stinging tears. No, not gone. She'd *left*.

Meredith's throat was raw with salt and screams, and every time she opened her mouth to speak, bile threatened to spill. In the days leading up to the funeral—miraculously arranged through the fog that settled over the house and followed Meredith at every turn—Alice became more and more afraid of the ocean, clamping her hands over her ears every time the sound of waves rushed over the bluffs. Though Art suggested it might give Alice some closure to actually see the water, to touch it, Meredith was terrified that the minute Alice was close enough, Judith's body would wash up on the shore.

The morning of the funeral brought rainstorms and a skull-banging headache. Meredith barely had her eyes open when the pain started at the back of her head, radiating forward. Moving only made it worse. Her arm was asleep, trapped beneath Alice, who was curled into a question mark around a pink shell that she hadn't let out of her sight since it happened. Taking extra care not to wake her daughter, Meredith pulled her arm out, inch by inch, until it was free. She rolled out of bed, arm burning as blood flow returned, and trudged to the bathroom. She left the door open in case Alice woke up. Alice had had a nightmare last night and made Meredith promise not to leave her side. It wasn't a difficult promise to make. Meredith's own nightmares had driven her from sleep more than once, and having Alice beside her was a comfort. As much as she'd tried to tell herself it was shock or the cold or some psychosomatic thing she didn't have a word for, Meredith had seen something in the water with her mother.

Do you see her?

What she saw wasn't a *her*. Wasn't an anyone. It *couldn't* have been. There was always shit floating around, garbage and coolers kicked off boats full of drunk college kids. Every time she thought about it, the thing in the water took a different shape, all of which she explained away. And if it did look like a girl—and Meredith wasn't going to say it was—then it was only because there'd been water in her eyes. It was blurry, and it was probably just a reflection of her mother.

A small voice in the back of her head said it didn't work that way.

She brushed the voice away. But it was dark. But she was freaked out. But… but…

A puddle had formed on the bathroom tile beneath the window. Rain leaked through where the latch wasn't locked properly. She stuck a towel under the drip rather than try to fix the latch. She assumed that was how life would work now—things would break, and she would just let them be broken. Even the Thalia in the sink had given up, drooping under the weight of its blooms. The fanlike leaves were yellow-brown and crackled when she touched them. She ripped the Thalia out of the drain, roots snapping, and threw the thing across the room. She clawed at the drain, pulling up roots and leaves and fallen petals, pelting the lot at the wall, until a shard of dried root slipped under her nail. She cried out and, shaking, pried the shard out with her teeth.

After the pain subsided, she rinsed her face without looking in the mirror. She cupped handful after handful of water into her mouth, tears dripping into the water, salting it, until her belly ached.

"Mom. Help."

Meredith wiped her face and spun around to find Alice, already in her black dress, which Art had picked out because Meredith couldn't bring herself to, a brush dangling from a snarl in her hair.

"I tried to do it, but there's too many knots." She pulled on the brush to make her point. "Ow."

"Don't hurt yourself, kiddo. Here." Meredith gently untangled the brush from the snarl and then worked the bristles through the knots in short motions until Alice's hair was smooth and shiny. "There. All done."

"Will you put it in a pony?"

"But you hate ponies."

Alice held up her wrist. A black hair tie was wrapped around it. "Yeah, but you like 'em."

Meredith carefully pulled her daughter's hair into a high ponytail. She loved how Alice's hair twisted into one perfect curl, and twirled it around her finger a few times before planting a kiss on Alice's head. "I'll be out soon."

Alice returned the kiss, then frowned. "You're not going to the beach, right?"

Something sharp poked from beneath Meredith's ribs. "Why would I go to the beach?"

Alice shrugged.

Damn you, Mom.

"I'm not going anywhere," Meredith said. "Promise."

Alice studied her face, frowning harder. "You can't promise."

"Sure I can. Just did." Meredith swallowed the hitch in her voice. "Go sit in the living room, 'k?"

Alice obeyed without another word but looked back over her shoulder twice before turning the corner to the living room.

Meredith leaned over the sink, resting her forehead on the porcelain. She had to get through this without breaking—not for herself but for Alice. She didn't know how to explain what'd happened to Judith without anger spilling over into her words. Alice deserved better. She deserved to believe her grandmother was good and not selfish and loved her deeply enough to want to stick around.

Alice deserved—Meredith deserved—not to have to say goodbye.

She'd battled with herself over asking her wife (ex-wife, soon to be ex, whatever) to come to the funeral but in the end didn't even tell Kristin that her mother had died. When Art asked, she justified it by saying it would be bad for Alice. He didn't buy it, but that was okay because she didn't either.

"You could use all the support you can get," Art argued as they sat in the car, waiting for Meredith to be ready to go inside. "Even if it's temporary."

"I've got you. It was good enough before; it'll be good enough now."

Art pulled her into him. She buried her face in his scruffy, old-man neck and tried not to cry. She'd done enough crying in the last week to last her the rest of her life. She was dried out. Hollow. A husk.

She pulled away and glanced into the back seat. Alice had Meredith's earbuds in, eyes glued to Meredith's phone. "People have been leaving notes at the house."

Art raised his eyebrow. "Notes?"

She nodded. "Stuffed in the mailbox and under the door."

"Who? What do they say?"

"No idea. None of them are signed. Some of them start out like condolences. They say they're sorry about my mom, but then they get weird." She shifted in her seat. "They say the curse killed my mother and that if I don't take Alice and leave, we'll be next."

Art was quiet for a beat. "You're sure none of them are signed?"

"I'm sure."

" 'Cause those sound a little like threats."

"I don't think they are." She shot a glance in the rearview to make sure Alice was still occupied. "I'm sure they think they're helping, but all they're doing is perpetuating the same bullshit. I almost prefer the juvenile *witch* crap to this." She rubbed her temples, focusing on the throb in her head to keep the tears at bay. "My mother killed herself. She wasn't killed by some curse or spirit or whatever they think. There is no curse. Bad things happen because people make terrible, stupid choices. That's all." She picked at a stain on her pant leg. "I wish people would just…stop."

"I get it. I do. People are…complicated. Some of these folks who've been here a long time, they've seen a lot of bad. Sometimes it's easier to say it's a curse than to say there's no reason at all."

"It's bullshit."

"I don't disagree."

Sighing, she looked back at Alice again. Alice looked up and smiled weakly. Meredith winked, and Alice returned her gaze to the phone. "Kristin used to talk about visiting Mom. She was obsessed with the idea of being close to her, like her presence could magically cure the thing that made it impossible for me and Mom to get along. I thought it was sweet at first." She paused, shaking her head. "Anyway, I fought her on it. Not just because of Mom, but because I didn't want to come back to the cape at all. Kristin said my feelings about Mom clouded my perceptions of the cape. She said it couldn't be all that bad here. When I showed her pictures, all she could say was how beautiful it was. But maybe that's the function of beauty, you know? To keep the bad hidden away." She paused. "It wasn't that I didn't want to come home. I did. Too much, I think. That's why I stayed away. Because what if it—what if Mom—didn't want me back just as much?"

For a long time, Art was quiet. She regretted saying anything until he finally spoke. "It's easy to remember the bad things. When you're just looking at all the terrible that has happened, I can see why you would think that."

"But you don't."

"No. I don't."

"Then why did she do it?" Her voice caught. "Why did she leave me?"

He scratched his chin. "It's one of those…what do you call…self-fulfilling prophecies. That summer her brother was sent overseas, Judith started to fear the water. It didn't make sense to me—she was all but born with gills—but she was convinced it would kill her someday. And then it did." He shook his head. "But it was her fear that killed her. Not some curse."

Except she wasn't afraid that night, Meredith thought. *She was relieved.*

She told herself that was just how suicide worked. When someone decided to kill themselves, of course they felt relief when it was finally happening.

"Might as well go in," she said.

Art patted her knee. "It don't look that way now, but everything *will* be okay. Eventually. You and Alice have each other. You'll get through it. Okay?"

She nodded. Took a deep breath. "Okay."

The rain hadn't let up, so they ran under pitiful umbrellas from the car to the door of the funeral home. Though they weren't the first to arrive. Meredith spotted familiar faces mingling outside the chapel: the Parrishes who owned the bakery, Vik Nielsen, the man from her mother's photograph, and others—the funeral director, a stout man with oversize glasses who'd perfected the sincere frown, led Meredith, Alice, and Art into the chapel to give them time alone before the ceremony. As she walked through the small crowd, she wondered how many of them had stuffed notes under her mother's door. How many of them looked at her now with a mix of pity and fear.

"The flowers look great," Art said.

Meredith agreed. The Thalias were Alice's idea. She'd made Meredith promise to buy an extra one to replace the one she'd ripped out of the bathroom sink.

"Where do we sit?" Alice asked.

Art pointed. "Front row."

Alice eyed the casket warily. It was closed, made of white pine with a bouquet of roses like a bloody wound on top, and empty. Before Meredith could assure her that she didn't have to sit there, Alice walked purposefully for the pew, smoothed her dress, and sat, setting her folded hands demurely in her lap.

"She's a good kid," Art said. "You did good."

"She's been like this all morning. All week, really. It's not right."

"What do you mean?"

"I'm supposed to be the one comforting her. I'm supposed to be the strong one."

"Says who?"

Meredith didn't have an answer.

"She loves you. And kids are resilient. Let her help you." Then, "You can't protect her from everything."

Without taking her eyes off Alice, she said, "Watch me."

By the time the funeral director approached the lectern, only half of the small chapel's fifty or so seats were filled. Every cough, shuffle, and half-hearted sniffle made it up to the front pew where Meredith squirmed under their watchful gazes. And they *were* watching. The word *cursed* came from somewhere in the back, making her stiffen. Alice slipped her fingers between Meredith's. Ignoring everyone and everything else, Meredith focused on her daughter's hand, her arm, the little freckles that dotted the outside of her wrist, forming an almost perfect star shape.

"Dearly beloved, we are gathered here today to mourn the loss of—"

The funeral director was cut off by a loud bang at the back of the chapel.

"Oh God. I'm so sorry. Hang on, I'll…"

Meredith turned around to see Vik righting a chair that'd fallen against a stone cherub. He kept looking up toward the front, smiling apologetically, then frowning in the direction of a redheaded girl of seventeen or eighteen who sat silently at the end of a back pew. Her pineapple-printed dress looked cut from a single piece of fabric, amateurish, with slightly uneven sleeves and dirty white flip-flops on her feet.

She kicked her leg out, blocking one of the chair legs, a childish smirk on her face.

"Move," he muttered.

The girl rolled her eyes, relenting.

"Do you know her?" Meredith whispered to Art.

He shook his head.

Alice looked too. Her eyes went wide before her gaze snapped back to the front.

Meredith focused on Vik, trying to place him in the context of her childhood. Except her mother hadn't had friends when she was young, and she definitely would have remembered this knockoff Sylvester Stallone routine.

The girl looked familiar, but Meredith couldn't place her. Except...yes. The girl she'd seen walking away from Vik down by the museum. Or maybe not. She wasn't sure. Meredith hadn't seen the girl's face then. Her mind was a mess. Her conversation with Art in the car had shown her that.

The funeral director cleared his throat, bringing her attention back to the front.

"To mourn the loss," he continued, eyebrow subtly raised, "of Judith Bethany Strand."

Alice squeezed Meredith's hand. She squeezed back. They all three of them shared *Bethany*, Meredith after her mother and Alice after Meredith. Judith was named for a grandmother she never met. Meredith liked that they shared a name. It was about the only thing they seemed to share.

After the funeral director talked for a while, Art got up to speak. Meredith listened but didn't absorb. Harried whispers in the back kept distracting her. Art spoke about forgiveness, about sharing a childhood with Judith and how he wished they could go back and rewrite some of the truth to make it better, or at least easier to remember. After Art, Carol Parrish said much the same thing, though most of it was hard to hear through her cracking voice. Others spoke, too, but by then Meredith's mind was hazy and heavy and she just wanted to get out of there, away from that empty coffin and into bed, where she could stay until she could figure out why her mother had killed herself and why she chose to do it while Meredith was watching.

It'd stopped raining by the time the ceremony ended. A parade of cars, led by Art, Meredith, and Alice, wound through town up to Judith's house, where trays of cold cut sandwiches, bowls of mayonnaise-based salads, and store-bought confections waited to be picked at in between awkward condolences. When they pulled into the driveway, Meredith noticed movement on the side of the house. At first, she figured it was someone from the funeral, though how they'd beaten her home was anyone's guess. Then the person—a teenage boy with dark hair and big teeth—peeked around the corner of the house and quickly fell back.

Meredith jumped out of the car, ignoring Art's shouting, and ran after the kid. "Hey! What the hell are you doing?"

The kid bolted from the side of the house, followed by half a dozen more, all laughing. One of them flipped Meredith the finger. Another shouted something like *Fish Witch*. That was when the smell hit her—the same she'd smelled in the lighthouse that day.

"You've got to be fucking kidding me."

She rounded the side of the house and spotted it: a pile of old fish filets, some of them still in the grocery store packaging. Art caught up with her, already out of breath from the short run.

"For Christ's sake," he muttered.

Her body went hot and cold. She couldn't be seeing this. The anger started in her belly, acidic and roiling, and moved through her, a physical ache. Her mother was dead, but even now she couldn't escape the ignorance. The stupidity. The lighthouse stunt was one thing. The place was all but abandoned, and you had to expect kids to do stupid shit. But this was her mother's funeral. Between the notes and this, it was enough to make her want to set the place on fire. To stand on the bluff and watch the entire cape burn. "I'll kill them," she said.

"Meredith…"

But she was already running, her flats smacking the asphalt. She'd watched them long enough to know they'd turned at the end of the block. She followed the same route, her heart pounding, only to meet another intersection with no way to know where they'd gone. She thought she heard laughter come from the right, but when she sprinted that way, she ended up at a dead end. Her nails dug into her palms as she screamed like some feral thing. Something wet dripped down her lip; her nose was bleeding. What was she going to do now? Spend the next hour peering into windows and around cars looking for a couple of kids? Adrenaline still pumped through her, making her hands and chest tingle, but she was just so *tired*. Tired of the stories and everything that came with it.

Casting one last look toward the houses lining the street—no open windows or guilty eyes peering out from behind bushes—she pinched her nostrils shut and walked back on trembling knees and aching feet.

Most people had gone inside by the time she got back to the house. She noticed a couple of tarps thrown over the pile of fish. Art was waiting in the front yard with Alice, whose trembling lip settled when she noticed Meredith watching. Vik stood next to them, talking to Art. Clutching the pink shell to her chest, Alice tapped Art's shoulder and pointed to Meredith.

He jogged over, worry etching a few new wrinkles across his forehead. "Jesus, what happened to you?"

Vik followed, already pulling tissues from his pocket.

He'd filled out a little—the man in her mother's photograph at least twenty pounds thinner and a decade younger—the buttons of his blue dress shirt straining against the makings of a beer belly, and there were twice as many crow's-feet around his eyes, but his slicked-back hair and a touch of concealer under his eyes made it clear he wasn't letting go of youth anytime soon. "Nosebleed?" he asked.

Meredith nodded, accepting the tissue, which she jammed up the offending nostril. "It's no big deal."

"Used to get them all the time myself. Figured it was just allergies. Weather. Something. Doctor said it was hereditary. Got so bad they had to cauterize the inside of my nostrils to keep it under control."

Meredith had been offered the same procedure in her early twenties. She'd declined purely based on the description of the procedure. No one was going to stick something up her nose and burn it to hell, thank you very much.

"Vik's son, Bobby, has been helping me around the shop," Art offered. "Bright kid. Really...enthusiastic."

"He's at my ex-wife's this week," Vik said. "Otherwise, I would've brought him. Judith used to watch him when he was a little bugger, back when I was working full-time and his mom was running around with God knows who."

"You're divorced?" Meredith asked, her own impending split clawing its way to the front of her mind. "Was it hard?"

"Not as hard as it could've been, that's for sure. She lets me see Bobby. He's a good boy."

"You okay, Mom?" Alice asked.

Vik crouched down until he was eye level with Alice. "And who's this beautiful thing?"

"My daughter," Meredith said. "Alice."

Vik offered his hand. "Lovely to meet you, Alice. Have you been through the looking glass lately?" He smiled, all teeth.

Alice grimaced.

"Shy one, eh?" he said, looking up at Meredith with mild irritation.

"Sometimes." Meredith grabbed Alice's hand and pulled her closer, adding, "She's upset, obviously. We all are."

Vik's expression blanked, then softened. "Yes. Obviously."

Alice shifted her weight, fingers clenching and unclenching in Meredith's grip. The big girl facade was cracking.

Meredith nudged her toward the house. "Why don't you have Art bring you inside for some juice and chocolate cake?"

"Cake for lunch?"

Meredith winked. "Just today."

Alice smiled and then dragged Art toward the house.

"She looks just like you," Vik said once Alice and Art had disappeared inside.

"I suppose she does." She offered a grim smile.

They shared a beat of strained silence. Meredith had been on the other side of this more than once; she didn't envy those looking for something meaningful to say in the face of death. She decided to relieve him of the responsibility. "I should go inside." She pointed to her nose. "Get cleaned up."

"Try corn."

She frowned.

"Frozen. On the nose. It'll stop the bleeding faster."

"Thanks."

She turned to head for the house, but he followed, cutting her off. He ran his fingers through his hair, and they came away shiny. He absently wiped them on his pants, which were bleach stained at the hems, probably from dragging them through the sand and ocean. He didn't look like the fishing type, so she briefly wondered how they'd gotten that way.

He flashed an apologetic smile, exposing a rotting, black canine. "Hey, listen. Can I come by tomorrow? To talk?"

Something about his smile made her stomach clench. "Uh. Sure. About what?"

He stuffed his hands in his pockets and offered a weak smile. "Just some stuff that's come up. Don't worry about it today. I'll come over. Bring the kid some more chocolate cake." His smile widened.

It reminded her of the girl in the pineapple dress. The *red-haired* girl. Could she have been the same one who'd said those awful things to Alice? Had she been with her mother the day before she died? Suddenly it seemed like the red-haired girl was important, but how? Why? There was a link there, and somehow, someway, Vik was part of it. "Did you know that girl at the funeral? The one with the red hair?"

His smile dipped, but barely. "Klutzy thing that knocked the chair over? Nah. Why?"

She feigned a shrug, but her body was buzzing. "I didn't recognize her, so I figured someone Art invited must have brought her."

"Wasn't me."

Hesitating a beat, she nodded. "Okay. Just wondering."

He looked like he was going to come in for a hug or a handshake, but the last thing she wanted was to let him touch her. She took a half step back. "Well."

"Well."

"See you."

"Yeah. See you."

Instead of heading for the house, which Meredith had expected, Vik walked to his truck, a rust-lined Silverado with tinted windows. He waved before climbing into the truck and starting the engine. She waved, too, then turned to go inside. A rock had lodged itself in her stomach, heavy, with jagged edges. Vik lied to her about the red-haired girl. She was sure of it. But why?

Later that night, Meredith held her own vigil in the lighthouse. After putting Alice to bed (with Art keeping watch in front of the television), she gathered a few tea light candles, a blanket, the last bottle of wine, and hiked through the dark, up the stairs, and into the light room where she wound the mechanism to start the light and then sat cross-legged on the floor with the bottle cupped in her hands like an offering. As she listened to the crash of the waves and the whistle of the wind through tiny gaps in the window frames, she struggled to conjure a good, happy memory with her mother, something to cling to in the future, something to tell Alice when she got older and forgot and wanted to know what Grandma had been like.

She shuffled through a dozen or more snapshot memories of her mother flinching away from a hug or watching Meredith from across the room, eyes narrowed and lips in a straight line, like she was waiting for her daughter to screw up. She remembered bedtime stories that told of monsters lurking beneath the water, just waiting for the right moment to snatch her, to eat her. She thought of the summer her mother ran away, a grocery bag full of canned goods, a roll of toilet paper, and a new package of underwear her only baggage. Dad had brought her home the next day. Mom didn't speak for over a week.

Then, when Meredith had drunk half the bottle and the small tea lights had all but extinguished themselves, she thought of the moment in the ocean that night, when her mother had hugged her—really hugged her—for the first time. She drank the last of the wine in one long pull, realizing that her happiest memory was of the night her mother died.

Still holding the empty bottle, she stood to watch the light pass over the ocean. During the first few months of their relationship, when everything was exciting and the idea of their splitting up was laughable, Kristin had tried to teach Meredith French. As she watched the waves lap the shore, she remembered that the sea (*la mer*) and the mother (*la mère*) were a single letter different. It made sense that her relationship with both were equally as complicated. Ever since she was little, she'd felt called to the water. It was like the waves and the foam were their own language and she could understand it. Kristin used to call her a dowser.

She could find the ocean with all her senses cut off. She didn't have to hear or smell or see the water to know it was near. It called to her. As a kid, it was a special kind of torture, needing to be near the water but not allowed to go in.

You're allowed now.

The thought wound itself around her head, her throat. She could walk straight into the waves and no one would stop her.

The light passed over the ocean, and a distant glimmer caught her eye.

Her stomach sank. The bottle fell out of her hand, smashing on the floor. For an instant, she thought it was her mother.

She held her breath for the light to pass again. It was too far away, and her breath had fogged the window, but she could swear she'd seen a face. A woman, with hair almost as black as the night and shoulders that glimmered in the red light, staring at her—*through* her—with eyes like black holes.

But then the light twisted around, and by the time it came back again, the woman—or whatever it was—had gone.

CHAPTER EIGHT

MEREDITH

PRESENT DAY

eredith tucked Alice's hair behind her ear. "Don't touch anything unless Art says it's okay."

"I know, Mom."

"And wash your hands really good if you eat anything."

"I know, Mom."

"And—"

Art cut her off. "We know, Mom." He laughed. "It'll be fine. Trust me."

Meredith trusted Art implicitly. But she knew the draw of Art's workshop and all the interesting tools and creepy sculptures he kept there, all irresistible to curious kid hands. When he offered to take Alice to his shop for a few hours so Meredith could have some time alone, Alice had jumped at the chance. Meredith didn't have the heart to tell either of them that the last thing she wanted was to be alone in her mother's house, surrounded by her mother's things.

After finally getting home last night, she'd climbed into bed only to toss and kick, waking several times imagining the same face from the water was staring at her from the corner of the room. It'd looked familiar in a passive way. Like she knew someone who looked like her or had seen a photo of her once. In the early hours of the morning when the dreams were most vivid, she could almost grab on to a memory but couldn't hold it long enough to make it make sense. But that wasn't possible because it hadn't been real, right? She'd seen a face because, in that heated moment just before her mother died, she'd asked about a girl. *Do you see her?* Her mind was trying to tie it all up in a neat little bow, but all it did was confuse her further. The notes hadn't helped. She should have thrown them away, but something made her keep them, tucked away in a drawer like a dirty secret. In a sick way, they were a small comfort. If it wasn't for them feeding the stories of the curse, pushing her mother to such a point of fear and self-defeat, maybe she might still be alive. In a way, *they'd* killed her mother, and that meant her mother hadn't *really* left her.

When she woke for good in the morning, she found Alice snoring on the floor with a bath towel stuffed under her head as a pillow. *It was just a dream,* she thought. *This is real.*

She stood in the doorway while Art pulled away, waving and smiling until her elbow and cheeks hurt. It was good that Alice would be distracted. Meredith had more than once caught her talking to the pink shell she carried around. All the Mom Books taught her that it was normal for kids Alice's age to have imaginary friends, including ones that lived in shells—Meredith had even had one once— but she still found her thoughts wading through the terrifying rhetoric of the doctors Kristin worked with. Repressed trauma. Ill.

No. Alice was fine. Meredith was fine. Everything was fine.

Or at least, would be. Probably.

She made herself a strong cup of coffee and took it upstairs to her mother's room. A preliminary search downstairs before the funeral had yielded nothing in the way of paperwork, which she would need to sort out her mother's affairs. The funeral home would want to be paid for a start.

The door was shut; it hadn't been opened since that night. Part of her expected to find her mother on the other side, and absurdly, she wondered if she ought to knock. Mom's room had always been off-limits. Mom needed her space, she needed quiet, and couldn't Meredith find something to do other than bother her every five minutes? Even as a kid, she'd learned nothing was important enough to bother Mom with when the door was shut. The longer she stood there, coffee cooling, the more convinced she was her mom would be waiting on her bed, book in her lap, wanting to know what Meredith could possibly want now.

A knock on the front door jolted her out of her thoughts.

Art had a key. There was no reason to knock. She'd forgotten all about Vik asking to come by until she saw him through the peephole. He couldn't seem to stand still. His gaze flicked back and forth from the window to the peephole, staring directly at it like he could feel her watching.

When she opened the door, she saw he held a casserole dish, covered in foil and smelling like something with marinara sauce, which he offered up before even saying hello. "Lasagna. My ex-mother-in-law's recipe. My wife thinks she got it in the divorce, but I copied the page out of her cookbook before she left." He tapped his temple. *Smart.* "Best thing you'll ever put in your mouth, hand to God." He peered around her, into the house. "Where's the short person?"

Somehow, she managed to balance the casserole dish on the mouth of her coffee mug with one hand. "With Art. At his workshop."

"The two of them getting along?"

"She loves him."

Vik smiled out of the corner of his mouth. "As she should. Family's important."

"Yep." They stood in awkward silence for a long minute. He kept looking past her into the house, as though waiting to be invited in. Like a vampire.

She didn't want to let him in, but she also didn't want to cause a scene. He was already here. "You want to come in?"

He slid past her into the living room, his eyes making their way over every surface before settling on the couch. He seemed to be sizing the place up. "You'll want to refrigerate that," he said when she just stood there, trying not to drop the dish.

"Right. Of course."

Leaving both the casserole and her cold coffee in the kitchen, she came back to find Vik furiously tapping on his phone.

"Girlfriend?" she asked.

"No," he snapped. Then, calmer, "Why would you ask that?"

She frowned. "Just a bad attempt at humor. I've never been good at it. Apparently grief doesn't help."

"Apparently." He flashed another smile. The black tooth unnerved her. "No girlfriend," he continued, a hard wink his own poor attempt at being funny. "Not for lack of trying." Then, "Nice place. *Really* nice."

"Yeah," Meredith said, because she didn't know what else to say.

He stood and wandered through the room, pausing at the fireplace to knock on a few bricks, nodding to himself. "I meant to say yesterday how nice the service was. She was a good egg, your mom. Deserved every bit of what you gave her."

Somehow it didn't sound like a compliment.

"Thanks." Meredith walked around him, blocking his path to the kitchen. She didn't like the way he was fingering the house.

He seemed to understand her intention and paused, tucking his hands behind his back. "Everything else going okay?"

She wanted to keep her answers short. Vague. The longer he was in the house, the more uncomfortable she felt.

"He's a good guy," Mom had said.

Kristin would have told her to give him the benefit of the doubt.

She forced her shoulders to relax. Took a breath. "Yeah. Mostly. I mean, I'm having trouble sorting some stuff out. She wasn't the most organized woman, so I'm struggling trying to find her important paperwork. Birth certificate and stuff. There's still a lot to sort through."

He nodded knowingly. "It's rough. First you bury them, then you have to dig them back up again with all the paperwork."

"Something like that."

"It was particularly rough when my father died. His business dealings were mostly…under the table. People came looking for money, and I didn't know whether they were really owed or if they were taking advantage of a kid who'd lost his only parent."

Meredith wasn't surprised. "That must have been hard."

"Mm. I was smart, though. I got it all figured out eventually. I had help, too, of a kind." His cheeks reddened. "What I remember most, though, was the anger. How he died… He didn't have to die is what I'm saying. I couldn't shake that anger for a long time. Still haven't gotten rid of it all, if I'm being honest. But I found a way to channel it, you know? I take all that shit and put it into something useful. Something good."

She had a feeling Vik had an unusual definition of *good*.

"That's…good," she said. "Good for you."

"I hope you find something like that," he continued. "Otherwise, all that crap, the anger and the grief, it'll eat you alive." He smiled, but it didn't reach his eyes. "In the meantime, I think I can help." Vik strode into the kitchen and opened the pantry.

Meredith followed, practically on his heels. Who the hell was he to act so comfortable in her mother's kitchen? "What are… I'd rather you didn't go digging around in there."

He ignored her and squatted, groaning with the effort, and pulled out empty plastic grocery bags, bunched up newspaper, and a couple of old T-shirts. The flotsam strewn across the floor, he reached in one more time and withdrew a cardboard file box.

"That's... Is that it?" she asked, frowning. She could have sworn she'd been through this pantry already. There'd been a lot of trash but nothing important.

He blew dust off the lid. "She started getting worried last year. Thought there were people trying to break in to steal her information."

That didn't sound like Judith. And how would he know? Her mother had said they were friends, but this whole situation rubbed Meredith the wrong way. It sounded cruel, but her mother didn't *have* friends. The curse, the witch stuff, alienated her.

"It happened around the same time she started forgetting things. She wouldn't admit it, but I noticed. So I offered to help her keep up with things. Bills and all that. Cheaper than hiring an accountant and, believe me, she couldn't afford to have some scumbag suit tricking her out of what little money she had just to push some paper around."

Meredith peered over his shoulder at the box. Tried to get at it, but he blocked her way. "Why didn't she come to me?"

He shrugged. "You were busy."

"Not that busy," she muttered.

"You know your mom. She was...private. Probably didn't want you to worry was all. Ah. Here we go." He pulled out a file marked *Bank*, another *Insurance*. Everything she needed was right here.

"Thanks," she said.

"Don't mention it." He sighed. "Though I doubt you'll find good news in there. There's life insurance—just about enough to cover the funeral, I'd wager—but not much else."

She sat on the floor next to him and accepted the files. She paged through but didn't find anything glaring at first. A few bank statements included a red-printed negative balance. That didn't make sense. Judith hadn't been rich by any means, but she'd been comfortable. They'd talked about a savings account for Alice for college, a kindness Meredith had had trouble accepting. "What about Dad's pension?"

"Not enough I guess."

"You guess?" Meredith shot him a look. "I thought you said you were getting the bills paid."

"I was. I did. Everything got paid on time."

She found the most recent life insurance statement, and thankfully, it looked like her mother had been up-to-date on her payments. Vik was right, though. The coverage amount was barely enough to cover the funeral. "This isn't right," she said. "When Dad died, she told me she wanted to up her insurance, just in case."

"Maybe she never got to it."

That couldn't have been right either. She remembered one phone call in particular when her mother complained about the cost of life insurance and asked if she could go to jail for lying about being a smoker.

Vik stood, taking the box with him over to the kitchen table. She joined him, still holding the insurance statement. As he pulled out the rest of the paperwork—was that a file labeled *Cape Light?*—he worked his jaw like there was something caught in his teeth.

"Wasn't there something you wanted to talk about?" Meredith finally asked.

He nodded, still working his jaw. "Yep. Yep. And I'm glad you brought it up because...this is difficult for me to say, being a friend of the family and all, but trust me when I tell you that this is all coming from a good place."

"Okay..."

"See, when the money started drying up, I had to allocate. I had to rob Peter to pay for milk and bread, see what I'm saying?"

"Vik—"

He put his hands up. "Okay. It's like this. There's pretty much no money left. I'm talking pennies. A few bucks at most. And with your mom gone, so goes your dad's pension."

She knew that much. "What's your point?"

"My point is, you're going through enough as it is—I know divorce, remember? That shit's brutal on the wallet—without having to worry about maintaining a house and the light. Sure, you could sell the house, but you're eventually going back to the East Coast, yeah? What are you gonna do for the light all the way over there? I'm proposing you sign it over to me. Let me be the keeper."

There it was. She knew there had to have been some ulterior motive for helping her mother, though she questioned the quality of the so-called help. He didn't seem the type to do anything for free, even for a "friend." Had he asked her mother to take over the light before she died? Had she turned him down? "And what do you want with the light?"

He frowned, and Meredith could tell he struggled to keep his voice even. "It's a historical gem. Same with this house. I mean, the *stories* alone... Without it, Cape Disappointment is just another seaside town with a bad shtick."

"And what? You think I'll just let the thing fall down?"

"Judith didn't do it any favors. Frankly, I was surprised to see the thing light up at all. Meredith, I know how it feels to want to cling to something because you think it'll make you closer to someone. It won't."

Meredith shook her head. He was wrong, and she told him so. "The light is mine." Not because she thought it would somehow bridge the gap between her and her mother, but because it'd always been hers. Her sanctuary. She didn't realize it until now, but no matter what happened between her and Kristin, she wasn't letting the lighthouse go. Not for anything or anyone.

Vik watched her, face all screwed up, for a long time before finally throwing his hands up. "Fine. That's fine. I was only trying to help."

"Sure."

He took one last look inside the box before rubbing his hands together. "I'll head out, then. Got some work to do."

Meredith stepped out of the way, leaving a clear path for the door.

"You enjoy that lasagna. Be sure to let me know what you think."

"Yeah. Thanks."

"And if you need any help with all this"—he gestured over the box—"you let me know, okay?"

Meredith forced a strained smile. Anything to get him out of the house. "You bet."

With a final nod, Vik made his way to the door where he let himself out, slamming the door behind him.

———————

An hour spent with the paperwork only managed to prove Vik right, at least in one aspect: Mom had been broke. Her bank statements didn't provide any clues as to why, though; the account activity section only showed a list of checks for varying amounts, most even and never more than three hundred dollars. It was hardly proof, but she suspected Vik had been stealing from her mother. Meredith's head throbbed from lack of caffeine, and she remembered her cold, abandoned coffee, cursing Vik under her breath. She stuffed everything back in the box and lugged it up to her old bedroom, casting a guilty glance toward her mother's bedroom door. Would any of this have happened if Meredith had been around?

Yes, she decided. At the same time a small voice at the back of her head whispered, *No*.

———————

To get to Art's workshop, Meredith had to go through his house. It was one of the oldest houses on the peninsula—like her mother's, a bundle of paperwork and a processing fee away from being established as a historical landmark. The lawn was brown in spots, but the garden that lined the house was bright with yellow and orange blooms, perennials and ivy growing untamed up the walls of the house and over the stairs leading up to the porch, where someone had abandoned a dark-green bicycle.

The door was unlocked, so she let herself inside. It looked like Art hadn't changed a thing since the last time she'd been here, more than a decade ago—a floral couch with wooden armrests hugged the far wall across from a small television and a bookshelf filled with some of Art's earliest projects: a duck with lopsided eyes, a flounder pinned inside a shadow box, a catfish with whiskers thickened and painted and a tiny bowler hat on its head. In the kitchen she found two paper plates on the counter, smears of peanut butter on one and bread crusts on the other. Her stomach growled, reminding her of her lack of breakfast. She dipped the crust in the peanut butter and popped it in her mouth.

She knocked on the back door that led to the workshop as she turned the knob, nudging it open. "Hello?"

"In the back," Art called.

After a careful navigation of boxes and plastic bins full of disturbing things that stared out from the sides, she found them—Art hunched over the table with giant glasses over his eyes and a pair of tweezers in his hand, Alice clad in goggles she had to hold in place with one hand while the other steadied the palm-size head of an octopus, and a boy who couldn't have been older than eighteen, with dark hair and a shirt that read *The Loch Ness Monster Is Real*. She assumed he was Vik's son, Bobby.

"What are you guys up to?"

"Shh, Mama," Alice scolded. "Art has to concentrate."

Smirking, Meredith peered over her daughter's shoulder as Art settled a glass eye into the awaiting octopus socket.

"There," he said. "Perfect."

"Perfect," Alice parroted. The goggles drooped off one eye. "Art said I can have her once she's all done."

"You come up with a name yet?" the boy who was probably Bobby asked.

Alice scratched her chin thoughtfully before exclaiming, "Octopussy!"

Meredith nearly choked on her own tongue. "Maybe that's not—"

Art shushed her, winking. "It's an excellent name."

Alice beamed.

Pushing his glasses up onto his head, he gestured to the boy. "Meredith, this is Bobby."

He offered a hand, noticed the latex glove, and waved instead. "Nice to meet you."

She smiled. "Art speaks very highly of you."

"Aw, hush, Meredith. You're making the boy blush." Art offered Alice his hand so she could jump off the stool. "After you, your highness."

Alice hopped down and ran to Meredith, wrapping her arms around her waist.

"Did you have fun?" Meredith asked.

"Mm-hmm. Bobby's gonna catch the mermaid!"

"Oh?" She caught Bobby blushing again. "That so?"

Alice answered for him. "Yep! But I made him promise not to stuff her. That's rude."

"Very rude indeed."

Bobby smirked. "Not to mention messy."

Art rolled his eyes.

"Besides," Meredith added, "I doubt you get your wish if you stuff the wish-granter."

Bobby's smile faltered slightly. "Oh. Uh. Yeah. Ha-ha."

Something in his expression reminded her of Vik, and the question was out before she could stop it. "Do you have a sister, Bobby?"

"Huh?" His face paled. "No. I mean yes."

She raised an eyebrow.

"Yes. I mean. A stepsister. Mom's new husband's daughter."

"What does she look like?"

"Um. Dark hair. Short. Why?"

So, not the red-haired girl from the funeral. She flashed a smile. "Curious."

"Okay." He looked from Art to Meredith and back again, confused.

Patting Bobby on the shoulder, Art said, "I think we're done for today. You can head home."

Bobby nodded, then pinched Alice's shoulder. "Bye, squirt."

She stuck out her tongue, making grotesque faces at his back until he reached the door where he spun around and squished his face together, waggling his tongue. Alice screamed, then laughed. As soon as he was gone, she said, "I like him."

"Me too," Art said. Then, "Hey, kiddo, how about you go wash up and see if you can find where I hid the candy?"

"Candy!" Alice took off like a rocket.

"I figure we got about two minutes before she finds my stash behind the couch cushion," Art said. "What's going on?"

"What do you mean?" Meredith asked.

"I've never known you to be curious about someone's relations, especially seconds after meeting them. You keep as many people out of your circle as possible."

She frowned. "You'll think I'm nuts."

"Probably. Tell me anyway."

She told him about the girl at the funeral, how she was almost sure Vik had lied about not knowing her. She mentioned his grab for the lighthouse, too, which made Art's lip curl. "Asshole."

Alice kicked the door open. She carried a bag of jelly beans in one hand. "That's a bad word, Uncle Art."

"Sorry, kid."

"'Pology accepted."

"You're too kind."

She grinned only for it to dip into a frown. "I saw the red-haired girl too, Mama."

"What'd I tell you about eavesdropping, Alice?"

"Sorry. But I did see her! Me and Grandma did."

"When?"

"When we went to the beach." She popped a jelly bean in her mouth. Chewed.

Meredith's heart skipped as realization dawned. "Is she the one who told you the scary stuff?"

Alice nodded sheepishly.

"What else did she say? Did she tell you her name?"

"No. But I didn't like her. She was mean." Then, screwing her face up, "She said someone was gonna get Grandma. And me."

A chill snaked down Meredith's back. She looked to Art. "Sound like anyone you know?"

He shook his head. "I'll ask around, though."

"Thanks." She scooped Alice into her arms, who promptly laid her head down and started to drool down the side of Meredith's neck. "For everything. Really."

He pulled them both in for a hug. He stunk of taxidermy chemicals, but it was a familiar stink. Comforting. "Everything will turn out okay. You'll see."

"Yeah," she said. "I hope so."

CHAPTER NINE

JUDITH

The pink shell was by far the prettiest in Judith's collection. Once she'd washed away the salt water and dried all the little nooks, it sparkled. It so outshone the rest of her shells on the window ledge that she made a special place for it on her bedside table, where it could be close to her while she slept.

Dinner that night was quieter than usual. Dad pushed the mashed potatoes around his plate even though Judith knew they were his favorite, with the cheese and green onions all mixed in. Mom sipped from her wineglass between soft, subtle sighs. Judith wanted to ask her about the dead man. About the war. But every time she got up the nerve to open her mouth, Mom's eyes glistened and she hid a tear behind the rim of her glass. Judith hadn't seen Mom this sad since David left.

Judith couldn't stand to be around all this sadness, so she shoveled the last forkfuls of food into her mouth and swallowed most of it whole before excusing herself. Mom barely acknowledged Judith's empty plate.

When her feet hit the stairs, she heard Mom start to cry, like a dam had broken.

"What if he doesn't come back?" Mom asked between gut-wrenching sobs.

"He'll come back," Dad said, but even Judith could tell he wasn't sure.

She sprinted up the stairs and locked herself in her room, where she'd hidden one of her brother's shirts underneath her pillow. She pulled it over her head and the hem fell all the way to her knees. Though she wasn't that tired, she climbed into bed and under the covers, tucking her nose beneath the collar of her brother's shirt. It still smelled like him, but barely. Boy sweat and cigarettes and musky cologne.

She wondered if he was thinking about her. She wondered if he was scared. If that man today had jumped off the bluff rather than go to war, what did he know that Judith didn't? More importantly, did David know? Would it help him? Or would it just make him afraid?

Tears soaked the pillow, cooling her cheek.

She hated crying. Hated how pressure built up in her cheeks and nose and forehead and how it became impossible to speak or think. For as long as she could remember, when the corners of her eyes prickled and her nose got all stuffy, she'd immediately start thinking of something else. Anything else. But once the tears started, she couldn't stop them.

Judith wept silently as the sun started to set, casting a bright orange-and-pink glow over her walls. She wept until it grew dark and the moon stood vigil above her house. She wept until her eyes fluttered closed and her mouth fell open and she slept.

———————

It was still dark when the voice woke her. She rubbed the crust out of her eyes and wiped a slick of drool off her chin as she sat up, listening. She was still in that place between sleep and awake, where she couldn't be sure if it was a dream, so she pinched the soft spot inside her arm, wincing at the pain. She blinked until the room came into focus, the light from the streetlamp illuminating her desk and chair and the mess of clothes on the floor. Her mattress and box spring sat directly on the floor; there was no one under her bed. She slid carefully, slowly, off the bed and went to the closet. After a deep breath, she flung open the door. No one there either. She was alone.

So where had the voice come from?

Easing the door open, she peered into the dark hallway. The rumble of the furnace and the usual creaking of the walls were the only sounds. Judith tip-toed across the hall to her parents' room. The door was shut, but she pressed her ear to the wood and listened to Dad's gentle snores for a moment before pulling away. Next, she looked in David's room. Her breath caught at the shape she saw curled up on his bed. David? But when she got closer, she realized it was her mother, snuggled deep beneath David's checkered blanket. The pillow was damp, and her hair was matted against her face. Judith leaned down to kiss Mom's forehead, like Mom always did for Judith when she was sad, when she heard the voice again.

She couldn't make out the words—they were garbled and watery—but the lilt was soft. Feminine. It came from her room.

"Hello?" she whispered, inching out of David's room and back into the hall. She carefully shut the door to make sure she didn't wake Mom.

The voice answered, a little louder this time but no clearer.

Driven by curiosity and a little fear, Judith inched back to her bedroom and flipped on the light. The room looked exactly as she'd left it. There was no one there.

Her gaze moved to the pink shell, unable to look away once it was there. She remembered the sound she'd heard the first time she'd held it up to her ear but not since. There were stories about the cape, about the lighthouse, Judith wasn't supposed to know. About the danger of the water. About drowning girls. It wasn't magic—Judith felt sure she would know—but she'd spent enough time down by the tide pools to recognize something *other*. Growing up with the waves as her lullaby, her body was more seawater than blood. "There's something special about girls who grow up by the sea," Uncle Thomas used to say. She knew when a shell was just a shell—and when it wasn't.

She sat on her bed, feet over the side, still looking at it, as though waiting for it to tremble or dance or light up. But she'd lived on the coast her whole life. She knew, if the voice really came from the shell, there was only one way to hear it properly. With a shaky hand, she picked up the shell and pressed the opening against her ear.

At first, she only heard the whooshing sound of the ocean. Art's voice invaded her thoughts—*it's not the ocean; it's all the little sounds outside it resonating through*—but she pushed that thought away. This shell was special. It came to her for a reason, which made *her* special, and she was determined to find out what that reason was.

She listened for another minute—still nothing—when she got an idea.

She moved the shell from her ear to her lips and whispered, "Hello."

When the shell touched her ear, the soft, feminine voice echoed back, "Hello."

CHAPTER TEN

BETH

eth wasn't much of a swimmer, but that didn't keep her from the beach any more than the March chill. Today, the sun was out and warming the sand; it was hard to believe it'd snowed just two weeks ago. She sat on a towel and dug her bare toes in, the cool, damp under layers sending a chill up her legs. The breeze rustled her skirt and hair, and she closed her eyes, breathing in the salty scent of the air.

Today, she was the same age her mother had been when she fell out of the second-story window. Tomorrow, she would be older. For the rest of her life, she would be older than her mother ever was. It wasn't fair. It wasn't right.

She remembered that night more vividly than she remembered anything else. Watching from the doorway, she'd seen her mother's face just before she fell. She'd been happy. And when she hit the rocks at the bottom of the garden—Beth flinched now, thinking of the way her mother's head had split open like a melon—Beth had run to the window, reaching, screaming.

It wasn't until her mother's breath stopped that the lighthouse light flicked on, spinning as though nothing had happened.

The beach was empty except for a few birds that'd come to peck at the remnants of meager weekend picnics. What the tourists brought, the tourists ate. They licked crumbs from sandwich wrappers and ate apple cores and shook the last drops of coffee into their open mouths. Everyone was hungry, even the birds. One of them pecked at a pretty pink shell that someone had stuffed with a wad of paper. Beth pried out the greasy paper only for the brave gull to snatch it out of her hands. She tucked the shell in her pocket thinking she'd put it in the baby's room, next to the crib.

While Beth watched the waves roll in, the rest of Cape Disappointment surrounded their radios for updates on the war. Everyone was worried about getting involved and what that would mean. Her in-laws still talked about the Great War like it was yesterday. Rations. A country turned poor with the cost of defending its people. Beth didn't care about any of it. She ate to survive, and money was just something that changed hands—a sentiment her husband hardly shared. He was constantly worried about where the next dollar would come from, more so lately because of her second, unexpected, pregnancy. There'd be no money for dinner out, for new clothes, for trips out of town…but Beth didn't care about any of that either. Never did. Where other people saw the world in color, she felt like she was walking through life experiencing shades of gray. Except when she looked at the ocean.

"That's because you're cursed," her brother told her once. He'd been twelve at the time. She was ten.

"Am not."

"Uncle William says you are." He blushed. "Just like Mom was."

She'd punched him then, earning a switch to the backside for her trouble. Truth was, though, she'd heard the same thing. When Uncle William came over at night between his fishing expeditions, he and her father drank until their pores leaked bourbon, loosening tongues and bringing out old grievances. Uncle William blamed her father for not keeping her mother safe. Her father blamed Uncle William for not "doing what needed to be done." Whatever that meant. Their arguments almost never devolved into physical fights but continued throughout her entire childhood, into her adulthood. It wasn't until she married that the tension seemed to settle between them. And then Beth had a daughter, Diana, and it all flared up again.

This, more than anything, drove her back to the ocean time and time again, looking for something to make sense of it all. And if the answer to everything didn't exist out there, well, then it didn't exist at all. Sparkling and blue and wild, the ocean teemed with life undiscovered. When she pressed her ear to the ground, she could almost hear their hearts beating.

Her back ached from sitting, but she wasn't ready to leave. Her sister-in-law would be waiting to taunt her for what she called Beth's obsession. When she thought Beth wasn't listening, she called her *touched. Slow.* But Beth was neither, her pensive nature foreign to her husband's family of clucking chickens, obsessed with rumor and speculation. They itched for a scandal. This, her sister-in-law said in a moment of pure meanness, was why she and her parents had allowed her brother to marry Beth in the first place. Stories of Beth's family would provide them endless entertainment.

Legs cramping as she stood, Beth stretched her arms up and back. A soft groan escaped her lips. She had to remind herself that the ocean would always be there. Every time she left, there was the knowledge that she could come back. The thought was almost enough.

Three times her father had tried to send her away.

The first was in the weeks following her mother's death. Beth had been inconsolable, blinded for days by her tears and anger at anyone who said her mother had jumped on purpose. An alcoholic and obsessed with the disappearance of her own mother, they said Grace had been a woman teetering on the edge of insanity. Her father sent Beth to a girl's school in the city, where she lasted a total of four days before she found her way back. Thinking of it now, it was a miracle she hadn't died. She remembered walking for hours in a sort of fugue state, a single thought circling her mind—she needed to get back to the water.

The second was when she was fourteen. She was out of town for barely a day when she woke in a hotel room, out of a dead sleep, clutching her throat. The nightmare lingered only long enough for her to remember a face—hollow, fish-eaten eyes and sunken skin—but the unease it planted in her remained until her father agreed to let her come home for a weekend. The relief she'd felt at seeing the water, of feeling the spray of it when she got close, was enough that she refused to leave again. She told her father, "I'll kill myself first."

The third almost stuck. She'd been pregnant with Diana, living with her new husband in his family's house, at her father's insistence. She needed women around, he'd said, not an old man and her brother. This was before the taunting, before the outward disdain. She didn't hate it. They had a small property just outside the city, close enough she could venture to the shops without much trouble but far enough away that the skies were full of stars at night.

The pregnancy hadn't been easy. She was sick every day, vomiting more than she could ingest, until she started to lose weight and her doctor became worried about the baby's survival. She couldn't explain why, but she knew if she didn't go back to the cape, she would lose her child. Just hours after arriving home, her fever lifted, and her appetite returned with a vengeance. By the time Diana was born, her husband had settled into her family's home. When her father died shortly after, leaving them the house, it was decided: they were home to stay.

Now, she walked toward the water's edge, gliding her feet through the sand, relishing the soft scratch of broken shells. As her toes touched water, she gave a sharp intake of breath. The icy water pricked her feet and ankles, and her skin pinched with goose bumps. Chills danced down her spine, and she had to clamp her jaw to keep her teeth from chattering.

She looked out over the ocean to take in the roll and crash of the waves one more time…and saw a face.

At first she blamed the cold. Like heat, it did strange things to the mind. But the face didn't flicker or waver or disappear when she cleared her eyes and focused. The face belonged to a woman, or something resembling a woman, wraithlike, with black hair that sparkled in the sun and pale, sickly skin. It was the face out of her nightmares.

Beth stumbled back toward the shore, sand sucking at her feet. It seemed to be studying her. Watching her. Looking for something *within* her. Those hollow eyes followed every movement, and it was almost like Beth could feel them on her skin, slick and cold. It sent chills down her body, skin pinching painfully.

For every step she took toward the shore, it only seemed to get farther away. She didn't dare turn her back on the girl—the *spirit*—for fear of what it might do without her keeping it rooted to the spot with her eyes. Waves pulled like greedy hands at her clothes, her legs.

"What do you want?" she shrieked. "Leave me alone!"

She slipped on a slick rock and plunged beneath. It was like the world had been pulled away, all sound and color faded except for the girl and her voice, which carried through the water. She clawed her way back to the surface, sucking in a deep breath. Her eyes burned, and sharp bolts of pain radiated up from her ankle.

But soon the pain faded, and it was like being back under the water.

"Come in," the voice crooned. Words tilted and spun. She could almost pluck them from the air.

She no longer felt her toes and worried about the cold, but the spirit crooked a gnarled finger, and Beth, instead of fighting for shore, took a step deeper. Another. Moving through the stilled ocean was like moving through sand. Her whole body tensed with the cold and smoothness of it. Her skirts wrapped around her legs, making it difficult to go any further, but she couldn't stop. Diana's face flashed through her mind, and for a second, she paused. What was she doing? She needed to get home to her daughter. Her hands found their way to her belly, and she could just feel her son moving around inside.

The spirit reached out to her then, a cry on its lips, and once again it was like she was below the waves.

Her feet shuffled, inch by inch, the water creeping up her legs until she was waist deep, but the girl seemed to move farther away. The music fell out of her voice, and her head tilted at a sickening angle. Like fingers gripping her ribs, Beth leaned into each wave, but her feet were stuck in the silt. Hot tears streaked down her face, blurring the girl into a swirling, black mass. It felt like her body, her soul, was split in two and the two sides fought against each other. With each step, she was being ripped apart.

But she didn't feel the cold anymore. Her legs were like blocks of ice attached at her hips; they tingled but then that feeling went away too. She was close. So close. Bubbling up from under the pain and the terror was a shroud of calm. This was *good*, she realized. She would never have to leave the ocean again.

———————

They took her legs at the thigh, leaving nubs of flesh that were angry and red at the ends. Her husband wept as the men spoke to Beth, only parts of which she caught between her brother's tirade. *Hypothermia. Dead flesh. Lucky.*

On that last part, she agreed. Beth was lucky. The hardest part was over.

They told her that her mind was damaged, that there were no girls in the sea.

No spirits. When her husband finally gained control of his emotions, he sent Beth to a home for people "like her."

"Until you get better," he'd said. "Get better again and we'll bring you home."

There was nothing wrong with her. She was fine. She was perfect. All she needed was to get to the water. Everyone else had it wrong. Her mother and grandmother were the only people who had seen what Beth saw. One day, her own daughter, Diana, would see too.

CHAPTER ELEVEN

MEREDITH

fter leaving Art's, Alice begged to go to the beach. "I want to ask her something," she said, eyes on her shoes. "It's important."

Meredith took Alice's hand and squeezed. "You know Grandma isn't here anymore, right? You understand?"

Alice frowned, confused, but nodded, no less determined. "Please can we go?"

Despite her fears over what they might find there, Meredith didn't have the heart to say no. So they followed the sidewalk until it reached the grassy precipice, which led to a bridge that crossed the rocky edge. They kicked off their shoes at the end of the bridge and walked barefoot through the sand. Meredith watched her daughter pause where the tide washed over the shore, little toes digging into the wetness where she sighed, content.

Meredith slowed her pace. Gaze moving between Alice and the water, the skin on the back of her neck prickled. A wave washed over the beach, and the spray speckled her shins. Alice was already on her knees, a bright smile Meredith hadn't seen in days on her face. It was a feeling Meredith recognized, one she hadn't been able to experience until she was in her teens.

The weekend of her sixteenth birthday, Meredith and her friends had snuck down to the cove with a couple of six-packs of wine coolers someone had stolen from their parents' garage. Her mother was sick that weekend, barely well enough to get out of bed, so she couldn't physically stop Meredith from going. She'd been telling Meredith for nearly her entire life that going to the water invited trouble. That it was dangerous. That there were things out there looking to get her. While other parents soothed their children's fears about monsters—under the bed, in the closet, in the bath—Meredith's mother had described in intimate detail all the beasties hungry for her flesh and thirsty for her blood. This had been her one chance to prove her wrong.

At the cove, someone started a fire with some driftwood and a stack of newspapers abandoned by the side of the road. Her girlfriend at the time, Hannah, laid out a blanket and snacks. They toasted to Meredith, to the night, to the salt spray that sizzled in the fire as the waves crashed against the rocks on either side of the beach. Her initial anxiety over the water, the secrets it held, and the possibility of getting caught faded with every minute (and every sip of the fuzzy navel wine cooler). She finished three bottles on her own, tossing the last into the fire. Everyone cheered at the crash. Emboldened by the booze and Hannah's smile, Meredith stripped to her underwear and demanded that everyone go swimming. It was her birthday, after all, which meant they all had to do her bidding—not that they needed much coercion.

Meredith hit the water first. She gasped with the cold, and her skin prickled with pleasure all the way up to her scalp. She could have melted on the spot. While the others stuck to the shoreline, splashing each other and screaming with each wave, Meredith wandered farther in, until the water reached her waist, and then she sank down, down, until the water completely enveloped her. Squeezing her eyes closed, she lay down on the ocean floor, running her fingers and toes through the sand.

See? she'd wanted to say to her mother. *There's nothing here that can hurt me.*

But then something grabbed her foot. At first, she thought it was some seaweed caught around her ankle and she tried to kick it free, but then the grip tightened and started to pull her toward the deeper water, toward the dark. Fear knocked the wind out of her, and she kicked, hard, but the thing held tight. *A hand,* she thought. *It feels like a hand.* Panic shot through her and she twisted, eyes wide and stinging as she tried to see what—who—had her. When she was finally able to kick free, she shot to the surface. Her friends stuck by the shore. Hannah waved.

"That's not funny," Meredith shouted.

Hannah frowned.

Even as she said it, Meredith knew it couldn't have been her. Hannah couldn't have reached the shore again that fast.

"I'm coming in." She said it loudly, intently, like an announcement to whatever had deemed her a trespasser. *I get it. You don't want me here. I'm leaving.*

She took two steps, and the thing grabbed her leg again. This time, it pulled her down and kept pulling. She clawed at the sand, her screams lost in the water. The blood in her veins seemed to freeze as dread moved up her body. The salt stung her eyes, paralyzed open. She couldn't tell how fast they were moving, but before she knew it, the floor seemed to fall away, dipping beneath her. Still the thing pulled. Her lungs screamed for air, but even as she kicked and thrashed, the thing's hold was iron-tight. Her vision went fuzzy at the corners. Her head pounded.

A fog seemed to come over her then and, with it, a kind of calm. A small voice told her this was what it was like to drown. Soon her lungs would force a breath in, and they'd fill with water and everything would fade. The grip on her leg moved up her body. Hands that clawed and gripped at her thighs and hips and then wrapped around her middle. Like an alligator before it spins its prey, drowning it. She felt cold, too-slick skin against her neck. A mouth.

Suddenly, miraculously, the thing let go. As the fog faded from the edges of her mind, she kicked and pumped her arms until her face broke the surface. She sucked the warm night air in deep and gagged. Her body felt weak, but she fought to tread water and breathed until the coughing slowed. She wasn't as far from shore as she thought. Her friends waved frantically from the beach. Hannah's hands were clutched to her chest, like she'd been the one on the verge of drowning.

A splash to Meredith's left had forced her to look, terrified of what she would see.

But there was nothing there. A ripple. The moon shining off the water.

Back on shore, she tore knots of seaweed from around her waist and legs, and decided that when she'd been drifting along the seafloor, she'd been caught in a tangle of it. It was the current that'd made her feel like she was being pulled. The cold skin she attributed to some kind of fish.

Sitting around the fire later, an untouched wine cooler in her hand, she'd brushed cautious fingers over the spot on the back of her neck where she'd thought, for the briefest second, she'd been kissed.

"That's far enough, sweetie," Meredith called now.

Alice flashed a thumbs-up, then returned her gaze to the water. She stood tall and still at the edge of the shore, tiptoeing back each time the water got too close. Tranquil and pensive, like a vestal virgin in sacred waters. Her hair swirled with the wind like black silk, and Meredith wanted to run her fingers through it, to marvel at this beautiful creature she'd carried.

She saw a lot of herself in Alice. She remembered being her age, or close, and spending full days up on the bluffs, staring down at the water with longing. Meredith wanted to urge her in, to have what Meredith never could.

But with the memory of her sixteenth birthday fresh in her mind, even she couldn't take that first step in. She told herself it was her mother's paranoia, burrowed deep in her head. There was nothing in the water that could hurt her. Nothing *unnatural* anyway.

Still, that first careful step felt like driving down the highway at ninety miles an hour—thrilling and terrifying. Cool water splashed up her ankle, and all at once she was overcome with a desire to sink down deep below the surface. To lay on the bottom and just…be.

Closing her eyes, she scooped the water in her palms and brought it to her face, cooling her sun-reddened cheeks. She licked her lips and shuddered. It tasted metallic. Bloody. When she opened her eyes again, Alice was looking at her, a worried look on her face.

"What's wrong?" Meredith asked.

"You're in the water. We can't be in the water."

"Sure we can." She kicked a tiny wave, aiming a splash in Alice's direction. "You got me all the way out here, now you want to go back?"

Alice nodded, fingers tangled together. It was a habit she'd had since she was a baby. When she was uncomfortable or scared, it was like she was trying to tie her fingers in knots.

"Is it because of what that girl said?" Meredith asked.

Alice didn't answer, eyes stuck on the water at Meredith's feet.

"It was just a mean trick," Meredith continued. "I promise I wouldn't let anything bad happen to you."

"Grandma said the water wasn't safe," Alice said carefully. "The girl told me Grandma and you and me were gonna die." Tears welled, but she rubbed them away. "I'm done now. Can we go? Please?"

Meredith's first instinct was to give in. She hated seeing Alice so scared, but this was exactly what she didn't want to happen. She didn't want her mother's irrational fears to taint this place for Alice the way they had for Meredith.

"Come on," she said. "Just a little step in. You don't have to go far."

But Alice was already shaking her head. She'd started to tremble, so Meredith sighed and came out of the water. Alice didn't seem to breathe until Meredith was fully up on the shore.

"There. See? Everything's fine."

Alice nodded, the trembles settling, but she still couldn't seem to look away from the waves.

Meredith knelt down beside her. Rubbed her arms. "Hey. It's okay, yeah?" She kissed Alice's cheek. "You said you wanted to ask Grandma something. Did you ask?"

Alice hesitated a beat before nodding.

"Did she say anything back?"

Alice's voice dropped to barely above a whisper. "She said the red-haired girl was right."

A chill washed over Meredith. She ripped her hand out of her daughter's, immediately regretting it when she saw the hurt look on Alice's face, but her hands had begun to shake and every brush of the wind on her ankle was a hand, a rope of hair. "I'm sorry, kiddo," she said, injecting too much cheerfulness in her voice. "It's cold. You were right. We should go back."

Despite Meredith's prodding and promises of more ice cream, Alice spent the walk back to the house in silence. Not for the first time, Meredith thought that by bringing Alice here, she'd let her down. She told herself they should leave. Go back to Arlington and try to pick up their lives where they'd left off. *But the house…* she thought, and guiltily tossed a glance over her shoulder at the ocean.

Somewhere, deep down, she wondered if there was something about this place that got into her, got into her mother, that made it too easy to let down the ones they loved. And if it came down to it, would Meredith be brave enough to walk away now that she had the taste of the ocean and the sand in her mouth? Would she be able to leave it behind for Alice's sake? For her own? Or would history just keep repeating itself?

They had just finished dinner when someone knocked gently on the front door. Meredith thought about ignoring it; sure, the lights were on and it was clear someone was home, but she wasn't in the mood for company, especially if it happened to be Vik passing by to see if she'd changed her mind about the lighthouse.

Whoever it was knocked again.

"Mom. Door," Alice said.

"I hear it, kiddo." She shut off the kitchen light and pulled Alice close. "Let's play the quiet game and see if they go away."

Alice hid a giggle behind her fists and nodded.

Another knock, this one more insistent.

"Shit," Meredith muttered.

"You lose," Alice said.

Meredith tweaked her nose. "Hush. Stay here. I'll be right back."

Through the peephole, she saw a man in a dark-gray suit, a large envelope in his hand, checking his watch. Her stomach flip-flopped.

When she opened the door, he didn't bother with a hello. "Meredith Strand?"

Her mouth went all cottony, but she forced out "Yes."

He pushed the envelope into her hands. "You've been served. Have a nice evening."

The door stayed hanging open as she turned the envelope over in her hands.

The return address was an attorney's office in Arlington. They'd only been gone a few days, but remembering that they had a life outside of the cape was jarring. Her fingertips buzzed, itching to open the envelope, but her chest felt tight, and it hurt to breathe.

"Mom?"

Without looking at Alice, she said, "Go up to your room."

She expected a fight—Alice was a curious kid—but she must've felt Meredith's anxiety because she went upstairs without another word.

Meredith tore into the envelope. The stack of papers inside was thick and official looking, with date stamps in almost every corner. She flipped to the last page and found Kristin's signature, wide and looping, with a starlike flourish at the end where ink had blotted with the force of her pen. She turned back to the first page: *Petition for the Dissolution of Marriage.*

Divorce.

Meredith's jaw clenched and tears burned her eyes. She only just pushed away a flash of white-hot rage that ordered her to rip the paper in half. This was what Kristin had been doing while ignoring her texts and phone calls. This was what Kristin had deemed *thinking about our relationship.*

What about Alice?

Fighting against the knot in her chest, Meredith flipped through the paperwork, scanning for custody, finally finding the page toward the end. *Petitioner is willing to concede all parental rights to Respondent if the following conditions are met—*

Meredith sank against the wall, unable to hold herself up. She couldn't decide if she was angrier that Kristin didn't want their child (had she ever?) or that she would dare to put in writing a list of demands before she gave Alice up.

Still clutching the paperwork in one hand, Meredith shakily scrolled through her phone to find Kristin's number. She jabbed the screen and listened to the other line ring. And ring. And ring.

"Hi, you've reached Kristin…"

The sound of Kristin's voicemail's outgoing message, passive and almost robotic, only fueled the fire in Meredith's belly.

Beep.

"How could you?" The words burst out of her mouth like the first massive wave of a tsunami. "Not even a fucking phone call? You can't even talk to me before you send this… You fucking… I can't…" Each word was fighting for its place in her mouth, so many she choked. "Right after my mother died, you *cunt.*" It didn't matter that Kristin didn't know. It didn't matter that it wasn't her fault. Meredith railed into the phone until the digital voice informed her the message had exceeded recording length. She hung up and called back, daring Kristin to pick up the phone, and when she didn't, Meredith unleashed a torrent of abuse so sharp she tasted blood. Finally, throat burning, she hung up midsentence. The phone felt like a brick in her hand; she dropped it at her feet along with the divorce papers.

Movement upstairs snatched a sob from her chest. Alice. God, what was she supposed to tell her? Alice was just as much Kristin's daughter as Meredith's. How was she supposed to tell Alice that Kristin was leaving them both? That Meredith had no idea if she could be a single mom? Kristin had been the balance, the one who taught Alice how to ride a bike, how to read, because Meredith had been too busy just trying to keep her fed and safe and alive that there hadn't been room for anything else. Meredith lived her life just trying to get through to the next day. Would that be enough?

Meredith found Alice curled up in a ball on top of the covers. A small Thalia plant from the funeral sat in a bowl on the nightstand; several petals had fallen on the pillow, like a halo around Alice's head. Her little body shivered.

"Kiddo…" She didn't know what to say. It would all be okay? Don't worry, we both love you? Was she supposed to lie? "Kristin—"

Alice turned over, her face red and blotchy with tears. "It's not that."

She'd heard. Meredith flushed with shame.

"What is it? What's wrong?"

Alice pulled the pink shell she'd been carrying around out from under her pillow. "It's my fault."

"What? No. Of course not. We—"

"No!" Alice wiped her hand across her face and sniffed. "Not her. I mean Grandma."

Meredith flinched like she'd been slapped. How could Alice think…?

Alice continued. "Grandma didn't want me to have the shell. She threw it back in the water, and I was so mad I yelled and thought bad things, but then it came back! I kept it, and I think Grandma saw and that's what made her go away." It all came out in one breath, her voice cracking at the end. "I'm sorry I didn't tell you. I wanted to! But I thought you'd be mad at me."

Meredith's insides shattered. Fighting back new tears, she took Alice's hands and kissed her fingertips and her nose and the tears on her cheeks and said, "What happened to Grandma is no one's fault, especially not yours."

Alice nodded, but it didn't look like she believed her. "She talks to me sometimes."

"Who does?"

"The girl."

"The red-haired girl?"

"No. The other girl. She lives in the water." She held up the shell. "She talks in here."

"Okay…" Alice had never had what she would have called an imaginary friend before. Was this because of Meredith's mother? Kristin would know. Kristin would be able to fix it.

But she doesn't want to. She wants to run away to live happily ever after without you. Without Alice.

Meredith rubbed her eyes, brushing the tears away before Alice could see.

"I thought if I talked to her, maybe she'd give Grandma back." She hunched over, looking smaller than ever. "I tried, but I can't do it. I don't want to go to the beach anymore. I don't want to see the water or talk to the girl." She looked up at Meredith, barely able to open her eyes for the tears streaming down. "Can we go home?"

Meredith climbed into bed with Alice, bending her legs and back to conform to Alice's shape. Shushing her, she buried her nose in Alice's hair, which, even when she was a baby, always seemed to smell like the ocean. Soon, their breaths rose and fell in sync as Alice calmed and the tears slowed.

She wanted to tell her of course they would go home. But now that Kristin had taken that step, Meredith didn't know if she *could.*

Neither of them moved for what felt like hours, until Alice fell asleep. Meredith kissed her head and rolled out of bed, feeling raw and spent, but still an undercurrent of electricity pulsed at her core, feeding the anger that throbbed there. Her only relief—and it was a twisted relief—came from the thought that Alice was too caught up in her own manufactured guilt to worry about her parents' divorce.

Back downstairs, Meredith found her phone, the notification light blinking.

One missed call from Kristin.

One new voicemail.

She deleted the voicemail without listening to it. It gave her a sense of control, something that, in this moment, she craved more than anything. It was like the universe had conspired to strip her of it, a fraction at a time, ending with the complete erosion of everything that'd grounded her. Her daughter was *breaking* in front of her eyes, and there was nothing she could do about it. She felt untethered and uneasy. And the one person who should have been here to help her, her mother, was gone. More than that, her mother had abandoned her, had left her to deal with the shambles of the house and the light and to sort through these complicated feelings that came to her in waves all on her own.

Her eyes settled on a scratch in the wood floor, and she hated that scratch. The floor. The room. She hated the walls that connected it to the ceiling and the memories—she lived in a house of dead women. The paint was poison, and the windows were enemies, and she wished she could burn it all to the ground.

Her hands seemed to work without thought, searching for Art's number and then calling.

"Can you come over?" she asked.

"Of course. Yeah. What is it? What happened?"

"I need to get out of here. Just for a couple of hours. Alice is upstairs sleeping. Please."

"I'm on my way."

The Anchor was the kind of place that'd seen a dozen or more incarnations in its lifetime, but it was the only bar on the peninsula worth a damn. When Meredith was in high school, sneaking in through the back door when a friend worked as a waitress there, the Anchor was a *Bar and Grille*. In college, it'd dropped the *Grille* and catered to metal bands and their fans. Then new owners kicked out the metalheads and embraced the nautical theme, hoping to lure in lighthouse tourists. Now, the building was sandwiched between a furniture depot and a Polish market and, without the neon sign flashing BAR, Meredith would've mistaken it for a gift shop. Tiny anchors, about the size of her palm and made of different materials and all different colors, dangled along the edge of the overhang.

Inside, there was just enough light to see the drink in front of you and not much else. She wound her way to the bar, avoiding a couple in the throes next to the one pool table and a shattered glass either no one had noticed or could be bothered with. A woman with dark hair and soft features caught her eye. Smiled. She reminded Meredith of Kristin, so the attraction was instant. She offered a smile back that was all teeth and turned away, embarrassed. She noticed Vik sitting midway along the bar. She paused, wondering if she should leave, but if she did, where else would she go? Almost like he heard her thoughts, he turned and saw her staring. He waved half-heartedly before turning back to the bar. He threw back a shot, scattered a couple of bills on the bar, and then slid off the stool like someone trying very hard to appear sober. He didn't look her way again before leaving. She sank gratefully onto a stool but had only a second's respite before she saw the sign.

Karaoke Tonite!!

The bartender, a dark-eyed man with the tattoo of an anchor on the side of his neck, pointed to the sign. "You sing?"

"Sometimes," Meredith said. "Whiskey, please."

He poured the drink and wisely left her to it. She leaned over the bar, grabbing a saltshaker, which she shook generously into the whiskey before swallowing half of it in one pull. It burned down her throat, warming her chest and loosening the knot there.

She shouldn't have been surprised. Kristin wasn't the type to have a change of heart, nor was she one for confrontation. She was incredibly independent, a quality Meredith had found attractive at first—her own independence shaky on the best of days—but soon became the wedge that drove them apart. Ironic that having Alice has been Kristin's idea.

Meredith had never been the kind of girl who thought about growing up to be a mom. Even as a young woman, when her friends and acquaintances were getting pregnant or looking forward to getting pregnant, they talked about motherhood like Meredith sometimes talked about the cape—with awe and longing.

Motherhood, to Meredith, hadn't seemed like something to look forward to. If anything, it terrified her. The only examples she'd ever had were her own mother, who at the best of times was inconvenienced by Meredith, and the stories her mother told about her own mother and grandmother. Women who lost their minds, who threw themselves into the ocean. All of them, mothers.

Kristin had insisted Meredith carry the baby. Her job was more flexible. Her body less likely to *respond badly*. Kristin's words.

Meredith's eyes kept finding the microphone, untouched despite the DJ's urging from the booth in the corner.

A third glass replaced the second. She took a sip, then wiped the condensation from the glass onto her thigh.

The room looked cocooned in a white glow. She couldn't keep still, chewing on the skin around her nails. Her toes curled in her shoes. Buzzed, she thought. Heavy and weightless all at once. Floating, but she could feel the denseness around her, like being at the bottom of the ocean.

The DJ's voice boomed from the speakers. "Tell you what, folks, the first person in front of that mic gets a free drink."

Fuck it.

Drink in her hand, she beat out a couple of giggling twentysomethings to the stage. Her nose bumped the mic, and the feedback screeched like a banshee.

"What'll it be, beautiful?" the DJ asked.

Meredith cringed, sipping from the glass to hide her expression. Finally she spoke into the mic, "Dealer's choice."

After a short silence, the walls shook with the opening bars of "Black Velvet."

She drained the watery remains of her drink, closing her eyes against the harsh yellow light. Then she put her lips against the microphone and began to sing.

It was easy to get lost in the music. She didn't even know if she was singing the right words, but it didn't matter. The rest of the bar sang over her, words tumbling around her head. It felt good. Felt like a release. When she finally opened her eyes at the end of the song, she thought she spotted the red-haired girl watching from the bar. She blinked, and it was the woman she'd seen earlier, a smile spreading across her face. While the rest of the bar clapped half-heartedly, the woman stuck her fingers in her mouth and whistled.

Back down at the bar, she set her empty glass down and raised her hand, gesturing for another.

She watched the woman approach after the song was over. She tried to ignore her, part of her hoping she'd get the hint and walk away. Another part—a stronger part—hoped she wouldn't. "What are you drinking?"

Meredith told her and she wrinkled her nose.

"Never could stand the stuff."

Any witty retort Meredith could've conjured while sober left as quickly as it formed. The woman watched the bartender slide the free drink in front of Meredith and then tapped the lips of her glass against Meredith's. "You have a beautiful voice."

"Are you flirting with me?" Meredith asked, regretting it the second it came out.

The woman laughed. "Trying to." Then, "Most people say 'thank you' when they receive a compliment."

She sounded like Kristin too. Was it really revenge, flirting with someone who reminded her of her wife? Because that was all she wanted right now. She studied the woman's slender neck and shoulders, the shadow of a tattoo peeking out from under her shirt collar. What would happen, Meredith thought, if she brought the woman into the bathroom right now, fucked her, the entire thing recorded on Kristin's voicemail?

"Thank you," she said.

"See? It's not that hard. I say something, you say something back. Pretty soon we'll have a conversation."

"A conversation would be nice."

"It would."

The woman smiled, and for the briefest second, it was Kristin's smile. Meredith wanted to rip it off with her teeth.

"Want to get out of here?"

The woman drove while Meredith hummed along to the radio, switching the stations between songs, her hand grazing the woman's thigh each time she reached for the dial. *Kristin left me*, Meredith thought when guilt threatened to chase away her buzz. *It's over. It's all over.*

They parked on the street, only a few feet from the shore. Meredith jumped out of the car before the woman had the ignition off and started for the water, still humming a nameless tune.

The woman followed.

The moon's glow glittered on the peaks of the waves just before they washed over the sand. Something inside Meredith throbbed. Beside her now, the woman kicked off her shoes and started pulling up her shirt.

"Wait," Meredith said, grabbing her elbow. "Not here."

Meredith led the woman farther down the beach, a smile burning across her face, until they reached the cove. "It's private here," Meredith said.

She couldn't remember if it was or wasn't anymore, but that wasn't the point. Meredith was in the throes of self-destruction. When she thought back to a time when she'd been most afraid, her mind came here. To the cove.

The woman stripped slowly, evocatively, and Meredith felt torn between watching her and watching the water. Its spray on her face and neck was like kisses that tingled down her spine and spread across her body. She needed more—to feel it on every inch of her skin. She slid out of her clothes as easily as a snake shed its skin only to be covered again by the woman's hands and mouth. Meredith closed her eyes, tangling her fingers in the woman's hair as she kissed down Meredith's neck and shoulders. Her chest. Her stomach.

Dizzy, she gently pulled away from the woman and started for the water.

The woman stood, clinging to Meredith's arm. Her cherry breath in Meredith's ear, "I've never done it in the water."

Water up to their waists, waves threatened to drag them farther. The woman held tight to Meredith, laughing with each splash until their lips met. Hot and cold clashed. Hands tore and grabbed and stroked and touched.

Meredith wanted to drink this moment, the water, inhale it through her pores until it filled all the holes gouged by the last few days. She wanted the air from the woman's lungs. The voice from the woman's throat. The salt from the woman's skin. The thoughts seemed to come from outside of herself but embedded into her mind as easily as if they were her own. Drunk on the whiskey and the feeling of the water on her skin, it was like she floated outside of herself. Words and feelings drifted over her, meaningless and airy.

With the water up to their shoulders now, they tumbled into each other with every wave. The woman knocked her head into Meredith's mouth. She tasted blood.

Laughing, she dragged her nails down the woman's shoulders. The woman gasped and then pressed her body harder against Meredith. For a moment, she felt nothing. An exquisite numbness. Her body felt heavy, and she imagined letting go, drifting down to the ocean floor and letting it eat her. Light and shadow played in the corners of her eyes—one shadow bigger, darker than the others— and a small voice in the back of her head tried to sound a warning, but the numbness was stronger, easily quashing the voice before Meredith could hear it properly.

Meredith dug her fingers into the woman's arms. The woman barely flinched, her face a tranquil mask.

Down, a voice in her head ordered. *Down*.

A flash of red cut through the corner of Meredith's eye. She turned, still holding the woman, and saw there, on the beach, wind whipping her hair like a comet tail, the girl from the funeral. From the bar. From the bluffs. The girl who told Alice she would die. And all at once, all Meredith wanted in the world was to face her down and ask her *why*.

Like a wave against the rocky shore, a sharp cry ripped through the dark.

Meredith pushed the woman away, gaze fixed on the red-haired girl as she swam for shore, limbs heavy and head spinning. The numbness still lingered, promising calm and tranquility at the bottom of the sea.

But she pushed harder until her fingers grazed sand. Finally in the shallows, she stood.

The red-haired girl sprinted away, toward the dark part of the street.

Shit. "Wait!"

She struggled into her clothes, leaving her shoes behind, and ran after the girl. Her calves burned until she reached the street, and then she managed to step on every broken shell and twig. Pain shot up her legs, but she didn't stop. The slap of her soles echoed along the road where she thought she saw the girl's ethereal form disappear around a corner. Meredith followed, but when she looked down the street where the girl had gone, it was empty. She started down the sidewalk but caught someone watching her from their front window. She could only imagine how she looked. Still, it was like she could feel the red-haired girl watching her from some dark corner.

When Meredith finally stopped, accepting that she'd lost the red-haired girl, she realized her mother's house was on the next block. Part of her thought she should go back and check on the woman she'd left at the cove. Adrenaline had sobered her enough to remember pain, and her mouth still tasted like her own blood. In her drunk, self-destructiveness, had she hurt the woman? No, she decided. She would have remembered that.

Besides, she no longer particularly *wanted* to go back.

She walked the rest of the way to her mother's house, flinching with each step. Cold, aching sobriety cracked across her skull. She focused on the dull throb starting at the back of her head instead of what'd happened in the water. She told herself it was nothing. The woman was fine. They were drunk. She was lonely. That was all. She wasn't actually going to—

From the street, she saw lights on in the living room. Upstairs, too, in Alice's room. As she got closer, she realized the front door was ajar. Despite the pain in her feet, she jogged the rest of the way, her heart hammering and her skin prickling, knowing in that deep-down animal way that something was wrong.

She found Art unconscious on the stairs, his face blackened and bloody. Blood bubbled from between his lips with each raspy exhale.

White-hot fear sent her flying up the stairs and into Alice's room.

The bed was empty and the room was trashed, the Thalias crushed beneath the overturned nightstand.

"No," she breathed.

Alice was gone.

CHAPTER TWELVE

JUDITH

"Who are you talking to?"

Judith slipped the shell in her pocket but didn't turn around. If she ignored him, Art might go away.

It'd been weeks since she first heard the voice in the shell, and nothing since that one word: *Hello*. It'd been so long that she started to think maybe she'd imagined it, which made her sad. Art had a habit of bugging her most when she was sad. She thought coming down here, to Dead Man's Cove, would somehow make something happen, to prove that she *was* special, that this *was* important.

She sat at the edge of the beach, perched on a rock, with her feet buried in the sand. She liked how the waves drifted up her calves and pulled away, like they wanted to pull her out to sea with them.

"I heard you," Art said. Then, "Are you ignoring me now?"

She shrugged.

"Do you want to see what I did with that crab claw?"

She shrugged again. Yeah, she wanted to see, but she wanted to talk to the voice in the shell more. David still wasn't home, and they hadn't gotten a letter from him in weeks. She worried something had happened to him and hoped the voice could help. Judith imagined the voice reaching all the way across the ocean and popping up into the air from the foam. The voice could tell her David was okay.

Art squatted next to her and pulled something out of his pocket. It was a necklace, with the crab claw cleaned and painted a beautiful gold with copper wire twisted around it. "What do you think?" he asked.

"It's pretty," she said.

He barely nodded, but his cheeks had gone pink.

"Who's it for?"

A shrug. His whole face was as red as the claw used to be. "No one."

Judith turned back to the water. The waves had slowed, and in between them she could see straight down to the floor where tiny mussels dug in the sand. She nudged one with her toe. Art tucked the necklace away. It only hurt a little that the necklace wasn't for her.

"Well. Guess I'll leave you alone, then."

"Good."

"You're okay, though, right?"

"I'm fine."

"It's just, your mom wanted me to ask because she said you've been acting weird."

If anyone was acting weird, it was Mom. She was the one who wouldn't stop talking and redecorating and cleaning everything over and over again. It was like someone had stuck one of those giant batteries in her chest.

"I said I'm fine," Judith said.

"Okay. Fine." Art kicked a small chunk of driftwood before going back the way he came.

She waited a long time, making sure he'd really left and hadn't just walked a little ways up the hill so he could watch her, and then dipped the shell in the water. She swirled it around. Filled it and emptied it a few times. Then she cradled it in her hands and held it so close to her lips she could almost taste the salt on it. "Why won't you talk to me?"

She'd just tilted it toward her ear when the voice finally, finally came through. "Talk to me."

She dropped the shell, almost losing it in an oncoming wave. Heart beating hard, she scooped it up just before the water carried it back out to sea. *The water,* she thought. *Does it maybe need the water to speak?*

"I *have* been talking to you. You don't answer." When the voice didn't respond, she said, "Is it because I could see you?"

"Can't see you," the voice murmured.

"I'm right here."

"Here."

"On the beach."

"Not the beach."

Judith hesitated. "Should I go in the water?"

"In the water."

A wave crashed against the tiny mound at the center of the cove where a shadow moved slowly behind it. "Okay," she said. "I'm coming."

Cupping the shell in one hand, she kicked off her sandals and wriggled out of her shorts and T-shirt. At first, her stomach hurt knowing that anyone could traipse down the cliff and see her in her underwear, but the longer the wind caressed her skin, the better she felt. Why did people wear clothes anyway?

She stepped into the water—it was cold, but not bitterly—pausing when it reached her ankles.

This didn't feel right.

The water didn't feel right.

It felt thick. Viscous. It clung too long to the small hairs on her legs before dripping back down again. Ice-cold currents cut across the tops of her feet, and when the breeze blew through the cove, it carried with it a stink like old food left too long in the sun. She felt the pull of the voice banging around like an echo in her head, but she resisted going any farther.

Beware mysterious figures in the dark.

David's warning tone drifted from somewhere at the back of her mind.

Before he went to war, David was going to be a writer. Sometimes he would wake her up with his middle-of-the-night tapping on the typewriter, the end of the line *ching* coming faster and faster. If she was very quiet when she sneaked out of bed, she could watch him from his doorway for a long time before he noticed, and if he'd had a good night with lots of words flowing from his brain like water, he'd read his stories to her.

One night, days before his number was called and everything changed, he read her a story about a ghost.

"But you have to promise you won't tell Mom about it," he'd said.

"Why?" she'd asked. Mom usually liked his stories just as much as her.

He'd shrugged. "She just won't like this one."

It didn't make sense, but she'd agreed anyway because if it was a story so scary it would freak Mom out, then Judith definitely wanted to hear it.

Beware mysterious figures in the dark, it began.

In David's story, a young girl had been buried in her mother's garden, her spirit trapped beneath the soil. Every spring, dozens of daisies grew on her grave. But the daisies were deformed, the petals blackened and withering, so no one wanted to pick them. Except one day, another girl came along and saw the beauty in the flowers. She picked one, not knowing the roots of that daisy grew in the girl's mouth. With the roots free, the girl was able to speak. As a thank-you, she granted the living girl a wish.

Shivering in the cold water, Judith now held the shell back to her ear. A soft whisper of air came through, like breath.

The entire surface of the water seemed to breathe, the waves rising and falling in quick, shallow bursts. It was waiting.

She was waiting.

Judith's skin prickled as she realized the voice had to belong to a spirit—a ghost. Maybe she was a girl like Judith. Like the girl in David's story. Maybe she was trapped. And Judith had given her her voice back, held gingerly in the shell.

"A wish," Judith said.

As though in response, the water hummed around her ankles. A heavy current followed a wave that reached as high as her knees, and as it flowed past, it hooked around her legs, nudging her forward. The foam fizzling on the top of each wave grew darker. One wave carried a fish the size of Judith's forearm, clearly dead, the entrails floating bloated and red beside it. A chill snaked down her body, but she kept her feet planted.

"I just want my brother safe," she said through chattering teeth. "Can he come home? Please?"

It didn't sound very much like a wish, but the ghost girl must have heard her anyway. The water stilled, and an eerie quiet fell over the cove. A gull flew overhead, mouth opening and closing, but no sound came out, and as the waves lapped the shore behind her, the only noise was a gentle rasp. Like labored breath.

Judith's heart pounded in her ears. She stepped backward, suddenly anxious to get out of the water, but the sand pulled at her feet and seaweed tangled around her ankles and between her toes, cutting the delicate skin there. She sucked in a breath, the sting instant and sharp, and automatically reached down, but she didn't see the wave moving toward her, the foam acrid and sickly brown. It pushed her backward, under the water.

The cold was like a shock. Her muscles seized, and her eyes flew open only to burn with the salt. Her feet were still trapped in the sand, so she scrambled, bent over backward, trying to right herself. Just as the wave pulled back and she could just start to claw her way back to the surface, she saw her.

The ghost girl floated just above the ocean floor, hair like knotted seaweed. She tilted her head back at a sick angle, and her eyes opened slowly, revealing black holes. The water blurred everything else, but Judith saw the gaping blackness clearly. The longer she looked, the less her body seemed to need air. The pain in her feet and back were faraway feelings.

The girl reached out with a broken fingered hand. Judith stretched toward her. *Yes,* she thought. *The girl is going to grant my wish.* If only she could reach. If only she could touch her. But another hand latched on to her arm, hard, like a vise. The girl fell away, and Judith lifted up, up, up, until finally, her face broke the surface. She tore at the hand—a warm, *alive* hand—and breathed in deep, only to gag and vomit salt water. She pulled away from the grip on her arm, but it refused to let her go.

"Judith! Calm down. You're okay. Relax! It's me." Art's voice broke through the cloud muffling her head.

She blinked away the water, the pain in her feet starting to intensify into a sharp burn.

His face purpled as he hauled her to shore.

He pulled her up to the beach, and though it was like knives ripping up her legs with every step, she scrambled for her shirt and covered her naked chest. She knew better than to let boys see her without clothes on. Even Art.

"Go away," Judith said, her voice and throat raw.

He ignored her. "You could've died! What were you thinking?"

She shook her head. She wouldn't have died. The girl didn't want her to die. She wanted to grant Judith's wish.

Sighing, he turned away so she could finish pulling on her shirt and shorts.

Panic seized her when she realized she'd dropped the shell. She'd never be able to speak to the girl again. Breathing fast, she bolted toward the water, only for Art to catch her around the waist.

"Whoa, hold on, what are you—"

"My shell! I have to get it!"

"Judith! Stop!"

She bent forward and bit his hand so hard she tasted blood. He shouted, pulling away just long enough for her to break away and stumble to the shore. She didn't have to go far. The shell was there, on the edge, where sand met water, waiting for her.

She'd bitten him so deep he needed stitches. Art's dad, Uncle Jon, was none too happy about it.

"They gave him a rabies shot," he said to Judith's mother. "Can you believe it?"

"That seems excessive," Judith's father said.

"I had to tell them an animal bit him," Uncle Jon said.

"I'm not an animal," Judith muttered. Though with her hair still matted and stinking of fish even after her mother scrubbed her beneath a scalding hot shower, she looked the part.

"Close enough," her mother said. "God, I'm so sorry, Jon."

"I'm fine," Art said, but no one was really listening.

Judith was sorry, but she was still mad at him for pulling her out of the water. What if the ghost girl wasn't going to grant Judith's wish now?

"You know better," Mom said. "You know you don't go near the water without someone with you."

"I wasn't in deep."

"That's not the point." Mom's voice shook.

"But I saw—"

"No." Mom raised her hand like she might slap Judith, lowering it only after taking a few deep breaths. "You didn't see anything. Hear me?"

"We'll pay for the medical bills," her father interjected, his face sagging under the weight of more money strain. "I'll write you a check."

Uncle Jon hesitated a painful minute before turning him down. "Don't worry about it."

Judith's father nodded, but even she could see the relief on his face.

It didn't look like she was going to get off that easy, though. Uncle Jon shooed Art out of the living room and turned to Judith. "You really could've hurt him, you know."

"He should've let go."

Wrong answer. Uncle Jon's expression twisted into something mean. "We're fishermen. You know what that means, Judy?"

She hated when he called her that. "That you fish."

"That we fish. Yes. And do you know what you need to fish?"

"A fishing pole?"

"Two. Hands." He gripped hers so tight they started to turn pink.

"Jon," her mother started.

He cut her off with a flick of his head. "If we can't fish, we don't make money. You're old enough to know about money. Without it, you don't have food or a roof. You starve. You freeze. Get what I'm saying?"

She imagined Uncle Jon and Art huddled in the boathouse, icicles hanging from their noses and tongues, blue skin and bloodshot eyes and—

"Sorry," she said.

He patted her shoulder, but it felt more like a slap. "Just be grateful my Art was there in the first place, eh? Who knows what could've happened to you?"

"Enough, Jon!" Mom said, startling them both. "There's nothing..." She paused, rubbing her face. "I'm sorry about Art. Really. But you should go now. We'll handle Judith."

———————————

Uncle Jon left after practically forcing her dad to promise he'd help on the next trip out to deep water for free. Everyone knew Dad hated going to deep water with Uncle Jon, but Judith guessed that was probably the point. She was a kid, so he couldn't make her suffer without someone stepping in, but no one would come to Dad's rescue. At dinner, she turned down a second helping so Dad could have more. Roasted chicken was his favorite.

She should've known it wouldn't help.

She wanted to try to explain, but every time she tried to tell her mom about the ghost, about the wish, she shut her down.

"There's nothing in the water, Judith. Nothing," she said, spearing a carrot with her fork.

"But I'm not the only one who thinks so." And she wasn't. In the time she spent in her room—sent there to think about what she'd done—she realized she wasn't the only one who'd seen the ghost girl. Except that wasn't what everyone called her. "There's no mermaid. Everyone just thinks that's what she is, but she's not. And if I can get to her and..." And what? Touch her? Talk to her? "She'll grant my wish. She'll bring David back."

Mom ignored her, stuffing her mouth with bite after bite, not even chewing, just shoveling food until her lips could barely close.

"Stop making up stories," Dad said carefully. "You're upsetting your mother."

"I'm not upset," Mom said, words barely audible around the food bulging her cheeks. She chewed and chewed, but swallowed most of it whole. Judith watched

it travel down her throat. It reminded her of a snake. Mom gasped. Coughed.
When she spoke again, she was quieter. Calmer. She smiled, all teeth. "Who's up
for ice cream?"

While Mom started the dishes, she shot Dad a look that usually meant Judith
needed talking to and it was him who needed to do the talking. When it came
to punishment, Judith preferred getting it from Dad. He often softened the blow
with promises of candy or trips into town once the punishment ended. This time,
though, he didn't take his time escorting her to her room. He didn't ruffle her
hair or poke her shoulder to let her know everything would be okay.

He sat on her bed and waited for her to join him.

She hadn't even gotten all the way up on the bed when he said, "I'm so disappointed in you, Judith."

Her stomach sank and she forgot all about her tingly hands. "I said I was
sorry."

"I'm not talking about Art. Lord knows that kid could use a biting every once
in a while." He sighed. Rubbed his face. "Your mother would kill me for telling
you this, but it's the only way I can make you understand." He didn't look at her
while he talked. She didn't know if she wanted him to. "We haven't heard from
David in weeks. It's not like him not to write, which forces your mom and me
to draw the worst kinds of conclusions. You going out to the cove on your own,
almost drowning... What do you think that does to her?"

"But I did it for her!"

"Judith."

He was quiet for a long time. Finally, he shook his head, his frown deep as a
frown could go. She'd never seen him this sad.

"Don't tell your mother that."

"But why?"

"Don't tell anyone, okay? You sound like…" He paused. She knew what he was going to say. She sounded like Grandma Beth. Art said she went crazy, but Judith didn't think so. She met her grandma once, the summer before she died. She didn't talk much. Judith figured she wasn't crazy, just sad. "It's all a story. Okay? Just a story. Between your mother and Jon…I thought you'd be the sensible one. I really did."

"Did Uncle Jon see her too?" Her heartbeat skyrocketed. "When?"

"A lot of people think they've seen her. It. But that doesn't mean it actually happened."

"Dad—"

He waved his hand. "The point, and I want it to be crystal clear here, Judith, is that you are never to go to that cove without your mom or me there with you. Understand?"

Hot and cold flashes worked their way down her body, and she started to rock. It was like her body had taken control of itself; if she kept moving, she couldn't fall apart. Tears spilled down her face.

If she couldn't go alone, then the girl might never come to her again.

"Dad, please—"

"There's no pushing me on this one, okay? It's for your own good."

She bit down on her lip hard, drawing blood, to keep from screaming.

Dad didn't seem to notice, patting her bed once, and then left her room without so much as a look over his shoulder.

Angry tears puddled in her lap. They didn't care about her. They didn't care about David either. If they did, they'd want her to do everything she could to make sure he came back. Liars, all of them.

It was up to Judith to get David back. To make them see that she was right.

She set the shell on her nightstand. It seemed…deader. The opal sheen had faded a little, and sediment had caked around the inside. She had to believe she hadn't lost her chance. The ghost girl was still out there. If Judith closed her eyes, she could almost feel her out in the water, waiting.

CHAPTER THIRTEEN

MEREDITH

PRESENT DAY

I don't even know what happened."

"I can't remember—"

"I'm so sorry."

"I can't... Agh, my head... No, it's fine. I'm fine. I said I'm *fine*."

"There's an ambulance on the way."

"Hit me in the back of my head. There was someone at the door, but it was dark."

"Looks like someone smashed the porch light."

At this last statement, Meredith finally looked up from the table where she'd shredded a paper towel, her fingers working, furious. "Smashed?"

The cop, one of two standing around her kitchen not doing a fucking thing, nudged a piece of plastic with the toe of his shoe.

"Don't touch it!" Meredith screeched, the words like knives down her throat. "Aren't you not supposed to touch things? How will they find her? How will they find my kid?"

"Ma'am..." This from the lady cop, all warm smiles and *there, theres*. Meredith hated her. "Your daughter needs you to be calm right now."

"You don't know fuck-all what my daughter needs. My daughter needs me to find her." Meredith stood, knocking over the chair.

Art flinched. "Meredith..."

"And don't you say a goddamned word to me," she snapped. Why was everyone so fucking calm? Why were they just standing there? Who was out looking for Alice? What if—

No. God. She couldn't go there. Not yet.

Maybe she was hiding. Maybe she heard the person beat the shit out of Art and escaped somehow. Alice was smart. No, she was *brilliant*. She was Meredith's daughter. She would've figured it out and run. Meredith had to believe that.

The lady cop righted the chair and placed one hand on Meredith's shoulder. "Ma'am. Please. Can I make you some coffee or something?"

Meredith sat but only because the strength in her legs was temporary. She was freezing, still in her damp clothes. The lady cop had tried to get her to change, but what would that help? She had to stay exactly like this. Exactly how she was when... She squeezed her eyes shut, counting breaths. If she stayed put, kept everything the same, she could stop time. Everything would pause, and she would be able to figure out what happened. To find Alice.

"Whatever," she muttered.

She heard the crunch of tires on gravel.

The first cop, *Nosehair* as Meredith referred to him in her head, pulled the curtain aside. "That'll be the detective. Looks like the ambulance isn't too far behind."

Seconds later, more blue and red lights flashed through the window.

"I said I was fine," Art said. "I don't need an ambulance."

"We just want to be sure," the lady cop said, setting a steaming mug of black coffee in front of Meredith. She felt the judgment in the gesture. *You're drunk, and your kid's gone. What kind of mother are you?*

Nosehair let the detective in, who introduced himself, giving a name that flitted in and out of Meredith's head without her catching. She didn't care what his name was.

"If you're here," she said, "who's out there looking for Alice?"

The detective's calm expression didn't even crease. "We have several deputies combing the area. You gave Officer Martinez a photograph?"

The lady cop nodded.

"Good. That's a good start." He sat across from Meredith, angling the chair so he had Art's full attention too. "Let's start from the beginning."

She bit back a nervous laugh. The beginning. Where was that exactly? Yesterday on the beach? Or earlier? When she left the cape? The first time her mother got trashed and demanded things of ten-year-old Meredith that made no sense? If they wanted, she could dig even deeper. She could tell them about the women who came before. Her grandmother Diana. Bethany, their namesake, who sacrificed her legs because she said the ocean told her to. Grace, who threw herself out of her own window to get to the water where her mother, Regina, had disappeared. What about the other girls? Regina's first daughter and a cousin or niece who disappeared from this very fucking house?

Her head suddenly felt very heavy. *We really are cursed.* A whole line of disappearing—*dead*—women. She thought of her mother and a new wave of grief washed over her. It wasn't supposed to be Alice next.

"It was supposed to be me," she said under her breath.

"Sorry. What was that?"

She sat up, wiped her eyes. "I was out." Memory and suspicion sloshed in her head like murky water. "I went to a bar in town."

The detective whipped out a notebook. "Which bar?"

She told him.

He nodded like he knew the place. "Anyone see you there?"

Heat ripped through her gut. "I left with a woman."

"Get her name?"

Face burning, Meredith shook her head.

"How about the bartender? How'd you pay? Cash? Card?"

"Credit card."

"Great. That's great. We'll alibi you right away and we can move on. What time did you get home?"

"Alibi nothin'," Art interjected. "Meredith wouldn't hurt me or her kid. I told you already it wasn't her."

"We're only doing our job, sir."

Art snorted, spraying blood. "So were the SS."

The idea that she might hurt Alice made her feel sick. If anything, the only person she'd wanted to hurt... No. She couldn't even finish the thought. She hadn't *wanted* to hurt anyone. But she did. Might have.

She gave some vague estimation of the time. She had no idea. "When I walked in the door, I found Art on the stairs. Alice's room was empty. All smashed up." Her voice caught.

The lady cop squeezed Meredith's shoulder. One more touch like that and she'd break the woman's hand.

The detective turned to Art. "Looks like you got pretty banged up. You say it wasn't Ms. Strand—and we're not saying we don't believe you—but did you actually see who did it?"

Art hesitated before shaking his head. "I was watching TV when someone knocked on the door. I got up to check it, but it was dark, and when I went to open the door, someone hit me in the back of the head. I fell forward trying to turn around, but whoever it was kept hitting me. I got as far as the stairs before I blacked out."

The detective scribbled in his notebook while Meredith's imagination played out the rest—this evil entity stalking up the stairs, pausing in front of her daughter's room, where she'd been sleeping, except she was awake now and screaming and screaming…

Tears streamed down her face while Art's shoulders shook with silent sobs.

"I tried to… I'm sorry, Meredith. It's all my fault. I'm too old, dammit. I couldn't even get to the damn stairs. I couldn't fight back. I couldn't do anything. I'm useless."

"So it sounds like we're looking for two people," the detective said, more to the cops than to Meredith and Art.

It took a second for Meredith to catch up. Two? Right. One person to knock on the door, one to beat the shit out of Art.

Art met her gaze, his left eye swollen shut. They'd really done a number on him. A gash along his cheek was crusted with black blood, and she could tell it burned as tears dripped into it. Bruises dotted his throat and chin. She took his hand, smearing blood on her own knuckles. If it hadn't been him, it would've been her.

His chin dropped to his chest. Tears dripped onto the table.

The EMTs, who'd been stopped at the door by Nosehair, were finally let through to tend to Art. They dabbed at his cuts and patched and wiped while the detective watched with the kind of narrow-eyed focus of a person not wanting to miss a giveaway.

"I'm going to look for her," Meredith said.

"Ma'am—" The lady cop again.

"Enough of the ma'am shit, okay? I can't just sit here—"

The detective cut in. "Miss Strand, I promise you we are doing everything we can to find Alice. But we need you here in case the kidnapper"—Meredith sucked in a breath at the word, like she'd been punched—"tries to get in contact with you."

"What, like for a ransom?" She laughed, but it felt like a scream. "I have nothing, okay? Less than nothing."

"They don't know that."

A thought hit her like a wall. "My phone. I don't have it."

The detective raised an eyebrow.

"I lost it on the beach when I…" Her whole body boiled with shame. She'd been an idiot while her daughter had needed her.

"We'll look for it." The detective barked an order at Nosehair, who went outside, barking more orders into his shoulder walkie-talkie.

The beach. The dunes. The *girl*.

Her heart hammered. "Hold on. What about the red-haired girl?"

"What red-haired girl?"

"She was watching us from the beach. Me and the woman from the bar. This girl with long red hair. She was wearing a white dress." The detective took notes as she spoke. "She was at my mother's funeral a few days ago too. I chased her."

"Where did she go?"

"I lost her at the end of our street."

"Why did you chase her if you didn't know her?"

"She said something to Alice."

He perked up at that. "Last night? You didn't mention—"

"No. Before. Days. I think. I don't even know if…" She didn't even know if she was the same girl. But she had to be. It was too much of a coincidence otherwise. "She told my daughter she was going to die." Then, panic seeping into her voice. "It has to be her, right? I mean, who says that kind of thing to a kid unless…"

The detective's expression was unreadable. "We'll look into it."

She told him about Vik too. The lighthouse. She didn't totally believe him capable of inflicting the kinds of injuries Art had, let alone kidnapping Alice, but it was there in her head and it was something. Maybe someone had heard about it. Maybe they wanted the lighthouse too.

Then the detective stood. Meredith's heart sank. "That's it?" she asked.

"We'll do everything we can. I promise."

For an hour after the detectives left, Meredith and Art sat at her kitchen table in silence. Meredith didn't trust herself to speak because it would destroy the fragile calm. She couldn't stand or leave the room either, because the first place her legs would take her would be Alice's bedroom. Seeing it again would only reinforce the idea that all of this—the attack, the girl on the beach, Alice—was real. It was happening now, in real life, and not just in her nightmares.

Art finally stood, his knees creaking and taking her untouched coffee with him. She heard the refrigerator open. Close. He set the half-empty bottle of vodka and two glasses in front of them. She knew that if she drank any more she'd only get sick, but her hands mechanically reached for the glass anyway, tipping the icy liquid into her mouth, which she swallowed without tasting.

Art poured two fingers for himself but didn't touch it.

"It's the curse." The words slipped out, wet and fatty.

He didn't give any indication that he'd heard.

It was a kindness, but she ignored it. The words hung there, suspended between them. All she could do was keep talking to fill the rest of the space. The unbearable silence. "Everyone around here talks about the cape like it exists for the sole purpose of either killing or blessing them. Curses or mermaids. They forget…" She sipped the vodka, willing it to stay down. "It's all about the mothers."

"Mothers?" He croaked the question.

"Don't tell me you never noticed. You know the stories as well as I do. Better, probably, being on the outside. Mothers who disappear under the water or lose their minds. Mothers who leave their children. A whole fucking line of us, just waiting here to get picked off, one way or the other." She pointed her finger at the window like a gun. "We're a carnival game for this place. And do you know why?"

He stared at her, jaw working.

"Because being a shitty mother is hereditary."

She'd spent so long cataloging her own mother's failings, she'd ignored her own. If Alice was brilliant, it wasn't because of anything Meredith had done. Ditto Alice's empathy. Her willingness to be helpful. Screw everyone else—*that* was Meredith's philosophy. She could have killed her child before she was even born. And here Kristin was, willing to set it all in Meredith's lap. Couldn't even keep her kid safe in her own house. A strangled laugh caught in her throat. Maybe that was the point. If there was one thing that would push her into the sea to die, it was knowing something terrible had happened to Alice, knowing it was her fault.

"Meredith..."

She waved him off, her movements heavy and languid. "Forget it."

He was going to tell her she was crazy. She was drunk. She was grieving. He was right. There were any number of reasons to suspect some sick person—a normal human person—of taking Alice. To discount the sound of the ocean in her head. But it'd started the moment she set foot on the cape, and it was getting worse. Being drunk and grieving allowed her to admit it. Sickest of all, part of her was *glad*. If it was the curse that took Alice, then nothing Meredith could have done would have saved her.

You brought her to the cape.

And if she hadn't, how long before Alice made her way here herself? Her mother was right. It was predestined. They could ignore it, push it to the backs of their minds the way Meredith had, but the pull, the desperate desire, would always be there. The cape was where it all ended. Where it would always end.

Art hesitated, probing the bandages on his face. The silence was almost as heavy as the hopelessness that settled in Meredith's chest. "My father died when I was young. I accused your mother of killing him."

Meredith looked up, figuring she knew the answer before asking. "Did she?"

"When people talked, I didn't correct them or tell them that past was past. I put the blame on the first person I saw and held on with both hands. I didn't care who it was or whether it made sense. I let it fester. And then, when I finally let it go, I'd passed the festering thing to Judith. She couldn't forgive me for how I'd treated her. For what I'd done to her."

"What did you do to her?"

He shook his head. His voice softened, like he was talking to himself. "It doesn't matter because now she can never forgive me, and I can never forgive her and this"—he gestured openly—"is my penance." He finally looked at her. "I'm trying to say there is no curse, but there is bad blood. Enough to drown in. It's not your fault for getting caught up in it."

She looked away, focusing on the condensation dripping off her glass. She wanted to believe him. "They'll find her."

She caught a sad smile out of the corner of her eye. "Of course they will," he said.

———————

Meredith finally changed out of her wet clothes just as the sun was coming up. Art was gone. He'd left shortly after telling her about his father, digging for forgiveness she wasn't ready to give. The detective came by shortly after—no news—but he had her phone. She opened the lock screen, surprised the thing still had power, to find her call log open.

There were several missed calls from Kristin, which the detective had obviously seen.

"She's in Arlington," Meredith said, in case he had any ideas about accusing her.

The detective offered a grim half smile. "We had to check, obviously."

"And Vik? The girl?"

"Mr. Nielsen claimed he was with his stepson, which the boy corroborated. We haven't found the girl, but we're still looking."

She nodded, scrolling through the call log. There was another voicemail from Kristin. She deleted that one too.

"If there's nothing else you can tell us…anywhere she might have gone…"

"There's nothing. We haven't been here long enough for her to have any secret places."

But she loves the water. She ached imagining her daughter, walking along the water, only to be pulled in. She shook her head to try to clear the image.

"Okay, then." The detective shuffled his feet. "We'll keep you updated the second we know anything."

She might have said thank you. She might have shut the door in his face. She hoped it was the latter.

After the detective had gone, Meredith started her own search, beginning with the beach.

What had looked alluring at night now looked taunting in the harsh light of day. The water washed cool and calm over the sand, stealing evidence of late-night walks and moonlit trysts. She jogged along the shoreline, watching for the slightest hint of a small footprint, a shoe, a hair, before the ocean could snatch it back. She called Alice's name until her throat burned and her mouth was too dry to form words. Gulls flew overhead and it sounded like they were laughing. A buoy bobbed in the distance, but for an instant it was a person—her mother?— and Meredith imagined her mother emerging from the water in the middle of the night to steal Alice away until the thought was seared into her head and no matter what she did she couldn't get rid of it. She saw her mother—her hair, drenched and tangled like seaweed down her back, and her skin, blue and bloated— holding Alice's perfect hand as she lured her to the water's edge.

"No!" The water swallowed her voice.

A couple walking their dog averted their eyes.

Meredith collapsed in a heap on the sand, trying to catch her breath. Her mother was gone. Her daughter was missing, and her wife had abandoned them. She was completely, utterly alone.

———————

She didn't want to go back to the house, and going into town would invite questions she couldn't answer, so she sought familiar refuge in the light room. She climbed the stairs slowly, listening for a familiar giggle. *You found me, Mom! Now you hide!* The light room was, of course, empty, but the disappointment settled like a boulder in her stomach. "This is the part where I find you," she said aloud. "This is the part where I yell at you for scaring me and then take you out for ice cream and never ever take my eyes off you again."

Every minute that she didn't find Alice, she lost her all over again.

She sat on the floor in the shadow between the mechanism and the wall, with her phone angled against the wall so she could see and hear it when the detective called. She noticed the cabinet doors were open and remembered the journals and jars of water she'd found before. She remembered drinking from them and the uneasy feeling it gave her. She remembered the fog that had shrouded her mind, and it made her think of being on the beach with the woman from the bar, how out of control she'd felt. As much as she wanted to dismiss it as an effect of the booze, she knew how it felt to be drunk. This wasn't the same. This had been a compulsion, impossible to ignore. Even now she felt the whisper of something at the base of her neck, a tingling sensation she shook off as she peered into the cabinet and pulled one of the journals off the shelf.

After checking that her phone volume was turned up as high as it would go, she sat with one of the journals in her lap, flipping through the pages gently as most of them had come unglued from the spine and were brown and fragile with age. She paused halfway through at a rough sketch of a girl with waiflike features and dark circles under her eyes. The girl's expression was serene, her mouth partially open, and her slender frame enveloped in shadow. The caption below read, in careful script:

Marina

Beside it, a short entry:

Father burned the photograph. I've recreated it here, though I am no artist. If Mother returns, she'll be furious.

Then, scribbled in almost as an afterthought:

When Mother returns.

Meredith ran her fingers over the drawing, as though by touch she could summon her to life. She already knew how this story ended, but she couldn't stop looking at Marina. As if this girl who was not Alice, but looked so much like her, could be the key to finding her.

Wind rushed past the light room, whipping through the cracks and up the stairwell. The ancient radio antenna on the roof leaned under the force of it with a deep groan. Each time the red light passed overhead, it bathed the room in a bloody glow.

She turned the page and read further.

I saw her again tonight. Hair black as night and eyes that glittered in the faintest light of the moon. She saw me too. I could feel the weight of her gaze. Her pull. What does she want from me?

Another page, a single line, dashed off so fast it was nearly illegible:

Why us? Why me? What does she want? Am I losing my mind?

Another:

…and it's strange that I only see her when Beth is near. Is it me she wants? Or my daughter?

A chill ran down Meredith's spine as she shut the journal, too frightened to read any more. Dangerous thoughts poked at her, reminding her of things she'd let slip away and others she'd shoved deep down into the dark. The face in the water. The ocean in her head. She focused instead on her phone. She pulled her knees up and wrapped her arms around her legs, willing it to ring, but the only sound was the restless crash of the waves against the rocks below.

CHAPTER FOURTEEN

JUDITH

he shell was gone.

Judith searched her room, thinking she'd knocked it under her nightstand or behind the dresser in the night. The rest of her bed was a shambles, her bedspread and pillow all cockeyed from tossing and turning. Nightmares, none of which she could really remember, lingered in the corners of her eyes like dust as shadows crept from beneath the bed and under the closet. She rubbed them until everything was a haze and blur.

When she didn't find the shell in her room, she went to the bathroom, thinking maybe she'd brought it with her in the middle of the night, but it wasn't there either. Not in the kitchen or in the living room or in Mom's white room where no one ever went for any reason unless they lost something.

If it was gone, that meant someone had taken it.

Shell gone and grounded from the cove, any chance she had of discovering whether the girl had even heard her wish, let alone agreed to grant it, got smaller and smaller.

While Judith tore through the kitchen, digging behind boxes of cereal and dented cans of green beans in search of the shell, Mom and Dad barreled in through the back door. Mom clutched a piece of paper to her chest.

"Open it, damn you," Dad said, but he laughed so Judith knew he wasn't mad.

"I will, I will." Mom shot a glance at Judith, frozen, wondering if she was in trouble again. "It's a letter. Your brother…I think he's okay."

"Come upstairs," Dad said. "We'll read it together."

Her brother was okay. Relief flooded her chest as she realized this *had* to be a sign that the ghost girl had heard her wish. Her brother was alive and would be home soon. She felt it in her bones.

As much as she wanted to read the letter, Judith saw an opportunity. They'd be in the room for at least an hour reading between the lines, dissecting each detail, until his words had been shredded by their gaze. Torn by her desire to listen at the door—she missed her brother too—and sneaking down to the cove, she made a promise to herself that she would find a way to read the letter. After all, it wasn't going anywhere. Mom kept them all.

"I'll read it after. It's okay," she said.

Dad called her a good girl before following Mom upstairs.

That was Judith. Good girl.

She didn't bother with shoes and ran as fast as she could along the lane, through the break in the trees, and down the sloping hill to the cove.

She would thank the ghost girl for granting her wish. She would try to learn more about her, to keep her company, like in her brother's story. A thrill trickled through her as, for the first time in what felt like forever, she began to believe the future held only good things.

As she reached the end of the trail and the cove came into full view, she saw them, but they didn't see her. How could they, with their faces pressed together like that? Inexplicable rage built up inside her as she watched Art kissing Carol, the crab claw necklace draped around Carol's neck. All the crap about being worried about her and saving her life...Art just wanted Judith out of the cove so he could use it as his own personal make-out spot.

Disgusted but unable to look away, Judith's body thrummed with anger and thoughts of revenge. She wished she'd bitten him harder, clear through to the bone. It was his fault she was banished from the cove, maybe even his fault the shell was gone. She imagined him sneaking into her room and snatching it out of her hand, throwing it back in the sea and laughing with Carol as it sank.

Bullshit. She colored just thinking the word, but she thought it again anyway. It felt good. Grown-up.

She couldn't go to the cove, not without Art ratting on her, but she didn't want to go home either. She started back toward the downslope that would bring her to the road when a plane passed overhead. One of those banner draggers. She couldn't read what was written on the tail but followed the path over a far hill, mostly overgrown with trees and brush. But there was something else there too.

There weren't many places Judith hadn't explored on the cape. Every summer, banished from the house because she was too loud, too rowdy, too much, she found dozens of places to hide and play, little, out-of-the-way spots where tourists didn't wander and just far enough from the edges of where adults were looking. There were places that were out-of-bounds, though—the highest cliffs surrounding the cove and the woods at the top of the hill behind it.

Though she'd been curious about the woods before, it was the ocean, the tide pools, that she loved. Whatever time she had to herself she spent there, the shadowy trees and whatever they hid put out of her mind.

Now, though, with the cove taken over, old curiosity won out.

It was a long hike up the hill. She should have turned around—there was no way she'd be back before her parents came out of their room—but once she got a look at what the trees hid, she couldn't turn back.

It was a house. Or what was left of a house. The roof had partially caved in, and the front door hung by a single hinge. The grass was patchy in places, overgrown and yellow in others. A hive dangled precariously from the porch ceiling, a mummified head, wasps darting in and out. Judith had seen enough horror movies to know the worst thing she could do was investigate what was clearly a witch's house.

So she only took one step closer.

Two steps because she was still far enough from the door that even the longest arm couldn't reach her.

A third and fourth… Her toe nudged the edge of the first step, daring the rest of her to keep moving. The house reminded her of the shell; if she leaned in—a little, not too close—she could hear the ocean echoing inside. And if it was like the shell, if she could hear the ocean, would she find the girl inside too?

Judith was going to be in so much trouble when she got home.

If, a small voice warned.

There was enough sunlight that she could see pretty far into the house without actually going inside. There was no furniture, only a couple of cushions stuffed in the corner. Wallpaper curled from the walls, dust covered everything, and the smell—like wet dog and vomit. Birds settled on the opening in the ceiling, raining leaves and twigs from what was left of the roof. They watched her. Dared her.

It was the scent of salt water on the air that finally pulled her inside.

Behind the curling wallpaper were drawings, most of which made her uncomfortable, but some that made her stop and stare. Shadowy, blurred drawings of a face or part of a face—no mouth or nose, but eyes dramatically turned down, black scribbled so hard Judith found shards of pencil lead in the wall.

"That's Lizzie."

Judith nearly tripped as she turned toward the voice.

The girl was tall, with dark hair chopped at her ears and a sweatshirt swallowing her thin frame. There were dark circles under her eyes, made worse by the gobs of mascara weighing down her lashes. She held a cigarette between two fingers, pinched, like she'd only just started smoking and wanted to make sure she looked the part. She looked like one of Carol's friends, all smirk and sass.

"You know her?" Judith asked.

"What's to know?" The girl took a drag off her cigarette. "She's dead."

"Then how do you know her name's Lizzie?"

"Because they're always named Lizzie."

"Who are?"

The girl rolled her eyes. "Ghosts, stupid. What are you, nine?"

A ghost? *Her* ghost? Judith glanced back at the drawing. Whoever had drawn it had done it quickly and angrily. "Where did she come from?"

"Same place all girl ghosts come from." The girl moved next to Judith, crossed her arms, and studied the drawing with her head tilted. "Somebody killed her."

"Who?"

"You ask a lot of questions."

"And you don't answer any of them."

The girl grinned, a sincere one this time. "I like you." Then, "I'm Cassie."

"Judith."

"Your mom know you're up here, Judith?"

Judith ignored her question. "Do you...live here?"

"Do I look like I live here? No, wait. Don't answer that." Cassie rubbed her arms. "It used to belong to my family. My great-gran's cousin or something. She was a witch." She bounced her eyebrows.

"Is she Lizzie?"

Cassie shook her head.

"Then why isn't she haunting *this* house?"

"Who says the ghost is haunting the house?"

Cold brushed Judith's arms. "No one, I guess." Then, "Did your great-grandma or whoever know her?"

Cassie looked at her, properly for once. "Why are you so interested?"

Judith shrugged, unable to meet her eye.

"You live in that big house down by the light, don't you?"

Judith didn't say anything. Didn't have to.

"Listen." Cassie moved between Judith and the drawing, blocking it. Her features softened, part of the bad-girl persona cracking. "Free advice? Forget about it. Last thing a girl like you needs is to invite more weirdness into your life."

"A girl like me?"

"Sweet. Young. Pure of heart and soul and blah, blah. You know what I mean." Then, "Go on. Out you go. I've got business to attend to and you'll only get in the way."

"And you're not?"

"Not what?"

"Pure of heart."

Another smile, all teeth. "No. I'm not."

"I don't believe you."

"Don't have to. Still." She sighed. "Bunch of masochists, all of you. If you were smart, you'd move away."

Leave the cape? Never. "If I come back another day, will you tell me about Lizzie?"

"Like hell." Then, as she shepherded Judith to the door. "Do what I say, okay? Convince your parents to move."

Judith paused at the door and flashed a grin to match hers. "Like hell."

The house was quiet when Judith got back. She had no idea how much time had passed, but she stupidly hoped her parents were still in their bedroom. Maybe they'd decided to take a nap or something.

But she found her mom in the kitchen, hunched over the sink and scrubbing a plate to within an inch of its life.

Judith started toward the stairs, thinking she could maybe convince her mom she'd been in her room this whole time and if she couldn't find Judith earlier, it was because she hadn't looked hard enough. Then she saw the shell on the counter.

She took a step closer, shoe squeaking on the tile.

Had *Mom* taken it from her room? Why?

Mom leaned against the sink, water splashing up and soaking her shirt as she scrubbed viciously at a bowl. She muttered to herself, but Judith couldn't hear what she was saying. Probably cursing Judith for disobeying.

As worried as Judith was about being punished, she needed the shell back. Now that she had a clue as to who the ghost girl was, she desperately wanted to try to contact her again.

"Mom? I can explain. Listen—"

Mom dropped the bowl, and it hit the side of the sink with a hard crack. Hand still soapy, she snatched the shell off the counter and stepped away. Her back was ramrod straight, the muscles in the backs of her legs jumping.

"Where did you find this?" she asked.

Judith flinched. She thought about lying; something about the way Mom asked scared her. "I can't remember."

Finally, she turned and Judith realized her mother had been crying. Her eyes were red and the skin beneath them puffy. Mascara bruises colored her temples.

Judith's stomach dropped. Her first thought: David. "I thought you said he was okay. I thought—"

Mom shushed her. As she turned the shell over in her hand, it was like she couldn't bear to look at it, eyes straining to look at Judith while her head tilted slightly down toward the shell. "David." She breathed his name. "I was happy they called him up for service. *Happy*. Because it meant he would get away before it could happen again. It meant maybe he had a chance to escape this." She held the shell out, accusing. "You brought this into my house. You brought her back into my house."

"You know Lizzie?"

Mom's eyes widened and she opened her mouth to say something, but she caught herself, clamping it shut. Her teeth made a cracking noise. She shook her head, a hint of determined calm falling over her. "There's no Lizzie."

Judith almost didn't believe it. Her mother knew. More than that, she was *scared*. Judith didn't understand—why pretend otherwise? "There is, though." Judith chanced a step forward, eyes darting between the shell and her mother. "She's the reason David is coming home. I made a wish—"

"A wish?" Mom laughed, mocking, the calm breaking again. "She doesn't *grant* wishes. How could you even think that? How could you think she could bring anything but death and suffering?"

Before Judith could say anything, Mom turned quickly away and all but ran for the door. Judith slipped on the water on the floor as she started after her, giving Mom a head start. She'd never seen Mom run so fast. Judith chased her down the path to the beach; Mom shoved a couple of tourists who'd jumped the fence to get a better look at the lighthouse out of the way. Judith had to catch her before—

But she was too late. By the time she reached the beach, panting, Mom had already thrown the shell.

Judith tried to run into the water, but Mom grabbed her arms, digging nails into her skin.

"Don't even think about it."

"You don't understand," Judith pushed. "She's *good*."

A light seemed to click on behind Mom's eyes. She straightened but didn't loosen her grip. "You're grounded. Don't you dare leave the house without permission again." Then, looking hard at Judith, "There is no *she*. Understand?"

Judith frowned. How could Mom say that? She knew about the girl. She'd said so.

She thought of the weeks leading up to David being called for service, how Mom baked and cleaned and planned, like their whole world wasn't about to change, *was* changing, forever. She thought about the time Uncle Thomas got sick—so sick he couldn't get out of bed most days—and while Dad urged Mom to visit, she refused, saying he was being stubborn, that he'd get out of bed when he wanted to.

For Mom, the sky was only blue because she'd decided to accept it.

The longer she stood there, silent, the harder Mom dug her nails in. There was nothing Judith could say that would change her mother's mind. And anyway, what did it matter? The shell was gone. She'd won.

Finally, Judith relented. "Yes, ma'am."

Mom softened, but only a little. "Good girl."

CHAPTER FIFTEEN

MEREDITH

The call came the following evening, during the one hour Meredith spent outside the lighthouse. She made herself go back to the house to eat something other than granola and to charge her phone, which was seconds from dying. She'd just plugged it in when it rang, the display showing the detective's number.

Her trembling fingers slipped so many times on the touch screen she almost missed the call.

"Hello?"

"Miss Strand, it's Detective Catano."

"Do you have her?"

A pregnant pause. "No."

"But you know where she is."

"No."

Rage boiled behind her navel. "Then why the fuck are you calling me? She's not—"

"We're still looking. Are you at home? I'd like to come by and have you look at something."

She took a breath. It could be anything. It didn't have to mean something terrible.

"Yes, I'm home. What is it?"

"I'll be there in ten. Sit tight."

———————————

She stank. She knew because she could smell herself—sweat and salt and terrible breath. She didn't care. As the detective sat next to her on the couch, a pair of gas station coffees on the table in front of them, he withdrew a plastic bag with a scrap of fabric inside. She recognized the pink-and-green pattern immediately: Alice's pajamas.

Her heart plummeted.

"We shouldn't think the worst yet," the detective said. "But this is Alice's, isn't it?"

She nodded. "Where did you find it?"

"On the beach, near the water."

The words in Grace's journal came rushing back. She shook her head.

"What is it?"

"Nothing. I… Nothing."

"If you have any ideas, anything at all, you should tell me."

She didn't have anything. Nothing he would believe. With the detective still staring at her, his face all scrutinizing concern, she rationalized the piece of Alice's pajamas away. She'd ripped it on something and the wind carried it. That was all.

"Nothing," Meredith said.

He paused a beat, then returned the bag to his pocket. She thought about taking it. She wanted to bury her nose in it to see if there was still some part of Alice woven between the fibers. There were a hundred reasons her pajamas could have torn, but Meredith couldn't think of a single one that didn't end with Alice being hurt or worse. A kaleidoscope of images flew through her mind— Alice hunched cold behind a dune, Alice twisting out of the grip of some faceless stranger as the fabric tore, Alice floating facedown in a tide pool, pajamas shredded by a bit of coral.

"This is good, though, right?" she asked, her voice strained and just this side of manic. "It's a clue."

He offered a weak smile like a tiny ember of hope. "Of course it's good. Every scrap of information is good."

She thought of Grace's journals again. Every scrap.

After the detective left, Meredith changed her clothes and washed the crust from her eyes. Information was the key to getting Alice back, and she was determined to find it. She'd start at the flower shop where Alice had seen the girl with the red hair.

The sky was overcast, but Meredith wore sunglasses, partly to conceal the red rings around her eyes and partly to avoid making eye contact with anyone with half-hearted condolences to offer. No one approached her on the walk to the shop, but she caught several startled looks out of the corners of her eyes. She walked faster, her shoes slapping the sidewalk, wishing she could be invisible.

A small bell announced her presence when she opened the flower shop door. Sitting behind the counter, an older woman with shock-white hair and beaded glasses perched on her nose lowered her book, frowned, then shook her head and clicked her tongue. Her name tag read "Kayla."

Meredith didn't recognize her, but that didn't mean the woman didn't know

Meredith. Growing up on the cape had taught her that everyone's business was everyone's business and secrets didn't exist. Before the woman could launch into her *I'm sorrys* and *You're so braves*, Meredith made a beeline for the counter and lifted her sunglasses, giving the woman the full force of a mother on a mission.

"My daughter was in here last week," Meredith said. "She saw a girl, a teenager, with bright red hair. Do you know her?"

But the woman had already started shaking her head before Meredith had finished talking. "I've been in the shop maybe twice in the last month. It's rare I see anybody in here, let alone several somebodies. In case you hadn't noticed, the economy is in the tank. No one wants overpriced flowers anymore."

"You're sure?" Meredith didn't even try to hide the desperation in her voice. "Absolutely sure?"

"I'm sorry."

"What about the other employees?"

The woman scoffed. "Those two? Unless you're a dime bag, those two wouldn't look twice. And they're the best I could find. Doesn't matter, I guess. I'm selling to the first person who makes me a decent offer." She nodded at a sign in the window. Meredith hadn't noticed it until now. *Business For Sale.* "Listen, the cops were already here. I told them same as you. If I see her, you'll know."

Meredith thanked her, making sure to mention the Thalias her shop had provided for her mother's funeral. The ones she hadn't bothered charging Meredith for. "My daughter loved them."

Just as Meredith hoped it would, the mention of the Thalias softened the woman's hard expression. "Did she keep any? From the funeral?"

It was an odd question, but Meredith was too frustrated by another dead end to think too deeply about it. "I think so."

"Good. That'll help." Then, "My evenings are pretty open. We close the shop early most nights. A few walks on the beach won't hurt me."

Meredith thanked her, and before she left, Kayla pressed a few petals into her hand. Told her to keep them in her pocket. For luck.

It couldn't hurt, she supposed.

Meredith left the shop feeling aimless, her one lead having dissolved before it even had the chance to fully take shape.

The next logical step was to find Vik. Though he'd lied about knowing the red-haired girl, Meredith felt sure about seeing them together, that she was the same girl who'd spoken with Alice. She already had a vague idea of where he lived. She thought about calling Art; if he spent a lot of time with Vik's son, it was likely he'd know. But Art was also the kind of person who would have told her to let the police handle it. Instead, she called her mother's bank. Through some creative manipulation of the woman on the phone, she was able to get copies of the last year's worth of checks her mom had written to Vik emailed to her. The endorsement on the back of one of them, beneath his signature, had a street address.

Her GPS brought her to the other side of the cape, where most of the old properties had been bought, torn up, and turned into condos that still sat vacant. Attempts to renovate and revamp the cape as a hipster haven of breweries and midcentury modern architecture had lived and died in this square mile.

As she turned onto a road only half-paved, her GPS seemed to have a fit. The image on her screen got turned around, then twisted back again, unable to find her.

What if someone brought Alice here? she thought.

Her heart skipped as she pulled to the side of the road a few houses down from where Vik's address should have been. She resisted the urge to yell Alice's name as she walked along the broken street. If someone had her here, she didn't want to alert them to her presence.

Except no one has her here, a voice whispered in the back of her head. *It's the curse that got her.*

A squirrel skittered across a skeletal-looking branch above her, making her jump.

For all her mother's warnings, she'd been maddeningly silent on what exactly the curse was. What the curse could do. Her mother might have thought she was trying to keep Meredith safe, but all her mother's secrets only managed to bring them here: her mother dead and Alice missing and Meredith completely in the dark.

But hadn't she tried to tell Meredith? And all Meredith had done was brush her off, dismiss her as paranoid. The longer Meredith was without her mother, the more she realized how much she needed her.

As she walked past abandoned house after abandoned house, something shifted inside her. This couldn't be right. It was clear no one actually lived out here anymore. Still, she continued on, glancing into windows and around fences, just in case of a miracle.

She patted the petals in her pocket. For luck.

Finally, she reached what was supposed to have been Vik's house. She checked the rusted numbers on the mailbox against the copy of the check twice, but she still couldn't believe this was it. A chain-link fence surrounded the overgrown property, a sidewalk from the street to the dented front door mostly hidden beneath weeds and brambles. The house itself looked one good storm away from collapse. The shingles on the roof were sun bleached and the skirt surrounding the bottom of the porch was rotted.

She lifted the latch on the gate and let herself through. "Hello?"

This was a stupid idea. Even if she didn't think Vik had had anything to do with Alice, she couldn't shake the unease of her last interaction with him. She'd all but accused him of stealing from her mother, and the light-switch change on his face from concerned friend to something more sinister had disturbed her.

She walked the rest of the way up to the house and stepped carefully over a broken stair before going straight to the window. She couldn't see much—the place was dark, and the sun shone too bright on the glass, making it impossible to see through the glare. Casting a quick look over her shoulder, she went to open the door but found it locked.

She tried the window again, but all she was able to make out were shapeless shadows and the light from probably another window on the other side of the house. She knocked, positioning herself just to the side of the peephole, and listened. No movement came from inside, so she knocked again. Still nothing.

Planting her foot sideways for leverage, she leaned experimentally against the door. It gave, but not much. The lock was flimsy, and she figured she could probably break it if she kicked hard enough.

Any hesitation was buried under the weight of Alice's absence. She needed answers, whatever it took.

She stepped back and, bracing herself on the porch rail, reared back and kicked the door just under the lock. The old wood cracked easily. Two more well-placed kicks and the door swung open, sweeping up a cloud of dust.

Covering her mouth and nose with her shirt collar, she went inside.

If Vik *was* living here, he hadn't been there in at least a day. A bare mattress sat tucked against the nearest wall, with a few flat pillows tossed aside. A pizza box lay open at the foot of the mattress, a single congealed slice remaining. There was a camp stove and lantern and a small box with clothes. If he was stealing from her mother—and the longer she looked around, the more convinced she was—this explained why.

It occurred to her he might have just given a random address to the bank when he'd cashed the checks, but a quick rifle through the clothes changed her mind. She recognized one of the shirts as the one he'd worn to her mother's funeral.

She thought she heard movement in one of the other rooms, and her head snapped up, her heart in her throat. "Hello?"

No one answered, but the air had gotten heavy. With every passing second, she was less and less sure she was alone in the house. What sounded like footsteps on the porch sent a bolt of fear up her back. She ran into the hallway, into what had probably been a bedroom, as quietly as she could and carefully shut the door behind her. She pressed her ear to the wood, skin crawling with the feel of dust and cobwebs on her skin, and strained to hear movement or voices, but the only thing she could hear was the pounding of her own pulse. She held her breath. Willed her heart to slow.

Eventually she pulled away, thinking it was squirrels again, or the wind. She'd look out the bedroom window—it faced the front yard—and if the coast was clear, she'd get the hell out of there.

But the boxes in the corner grabbed her attention. No, it was the writing on the side that stopped her.

For Meredith, in big, bold black marker in her mother's shaky handwriting.

Forgetting the window, she reached for the box closest to her and unfolded the flaps.

Photo albums. Some familiar—she recognized one of the oldest-looking ones as having been up on the shelf when she was a teenager—and a couple she hadn't seen before. She flipped through one of the older albums to find pictures of her and her stepdad at the museum. In one picture, Meredith wore a cheap pink wig and a pair of bathing suit bottoms with a fin sewn on the butt. But the picture was blurry, and out of nowhere she remembered that was because her mom had been laughing too hard to take the photo properly. She hugged the album to her chest as she fished through the box for another, this one newer. Inside she found pictures of Meredith and Alice, ones she didn't even know existed, probably taken during the few times she could get her mother to visit them in Arlington.

My girls, she'd written beneath one of Meredith holding a then two-year-old Alice.

Tears blurred the rest of the pictures, but Meredith couldn't stop turning the pages. Finally, she set the albums carefully back in the box and went for the second, expecting to find more of the same, but this one was mostly empty. A few knickknacks, including a ceramic bird she didn't recognize and a framed picture of two girls who couldn't have been older than sixteen or so. It took a long time to realize one of them was her mother, impossibly young and bright looking. Her hair was long and wild, and she leaned against the other girl in the picture, who pretended to scowl, but her arm was wrapped just as tightly around Judith, a mischievous glint in her eye.

Why would Vik have these? He had to have taken them from her mother's house, but when? Why?

She looked back at the side—*For Meredith*—and it dawned on her. He'd probably thought there was something valuable inside. Something he could sell or pawn. New waves of anger washed over her as she imagined him creeping into the house while she mourned.

Still clutching the framed photo, she went back to the albums. Ran her finger along the split spines. There *had* been good memories between Meredith and her mother, and she felt guilty for forgetting them. But how could a few laughs compete with a life embroiled in her mother's fear and frustration? Her obsession with a curse Meredith only now thought, maybe, was real?

She looked back at the picture of her mother as a young woman. The girls stood in what looked like a house. Behind them was an image she hadn't noticed on first glance. She squinted to make out the features of what looked like a drawing of a face. A girl, with Medusa-like hair, gaunt face, and hollow eyes.

Do you see her?

Her mother's words came rushing back.

There was something about the drawing that made Meredith think of the red-haired girl, but the image was grainy, and the harder she focused, the less clear it seemed to become.

Meredith stood, bringing the photo to the window for more light, but it didn't help. She carefully pried the back off the frame and slid the photo away from the glass. On the back corner in handwriting she didn't recognize:

Judith, Cassie, and Lizzie.

Cassie? Lizzie? The names meant nothing to Meredith. Her mind was moving in circles, making her dizzy. The only thing she knew for certain was that there was a girl at the center of all of this, and right now her gut told her she needed to find the girl with the red hair.

Find the red-haired girl, she thought, like a mantra, *and you'll find Alice.*

CHAPTER SIXTEEN

JUDITH

OCTOBER 1971–APRIL 1975

udith had just finished her breakfast and was rinsing the dishes—part of a new regimen of punishment for her forays into the cove—when she saw the mailman climb out of his truck and take off his hat. She knew something was wrong because, for one, the mailman never got out of his truck, not after the neighbor's dog hopped the fence and nearly took a chunk out of his calf. For another, the way he carried the letter, like there was a bomb attached to it, made Judith's stomach clench. When he started up the driveway, her forehead started to sweat.

Her mom came downstairs, hairpins stuck between her lips and fussing with a ponytail. She pulled the pins out. "Don't think you're getting out of this by faking sick, Judith." Then she got closer and saw the mailman. "Oh Jesus. Oh my God. Harry! Harry get down here now!"

Dad rumbled somewhere upstairs and then his heavy footsteps thumped all the way into the kitchen. "What is it? What happened?"

Mom pointed to the window.

The mailman had his head down, and he pinched the envelope by the corners with both hands. His steps were heavy. Slow.

Dad's face went white. Judith knew what he was going to say before he said it. "Judith, go upstairs."

For once, she didn't argue. She cast one last look at the mailman before shutting off the water and wiping her hands on a dish towel. She went as far as mid-stairwell and sat. She doubted they'd notice.

Silence shrouded the house until the doorbell rang. Even the chipper *ding-dong* sounded ominous.

The mailman's deep voice carried. "Harry."

"Martin."

There was a beat of silence, and Judith imagined the mailman handing her parents the letter, her mother trying to open it with shaky hands and then her father gently taking it from her to rip it open. She imagined their eyes passing over the contents while the mailman looked away, unable to stay, unable to go.

Mom sobbed once before her voice became muffled, probably by Dad's shoulder.

The wind rushed out of Judith's chest. It took all she had to make herself breathe in again.

Later, when Mom and Dad finally came out of their room, their faces gaunt and pale and splotchy and tearstained, they told her. *Missing in action*, the letter said.

"It means he's lost," Mom said.

Dad added, "It means he could still come home safe."

"He won't, though."

Dad shot a look at Mom. "Di—"

Mom turned, quick as a snake, and slapped him.

For a second, no one breathed. Then Mom turned and shakily walked out of the room.

Judith didn't care about being grounded anymore. Ground her forever, it wouldn't make a difference. Her mom might have been right. Maybe the ghost girl didn't grant wishes. Maybe by trying to speak to her, Judith had made her angry, so she refused to do anything to keep David safe. Or maybe it had nothing to do with Judith at all.

She thought of what Cassie said to her, that Lizzie—if that *was* her name—had been murdered. Could she be trapped somehow? That day at the cove, when she'd reached out for Judith, what if she'd been reaching out for help?

Cassie would know, she thought.

It'd been a month since she first met Cassie at the house on the hill, and she hadn't been back since. Mostly because her parents had kept a closer watch on her, but also because she wasn't sure she hadn't dreamed it all up. Her nightmares had gotten worse, bleeding into mornings that left her gasping for air. In her mind, she opened her eyes to find herself underwater, no idea which way was up. She'd drowned a hundred times in the last week alone.

Heart pounding—she'd never openly defied her parents before—Judith marched downstairs and out the front door.

Someone had had a party at the house on the hill recently. The remains of a bonfire sat on the lawn, which was littered with beer cans. Inside, she could smell the ghosts of pot and cigarette smoke. On the wall, someone had drawn a penis next to "Lizzie's" mouth.

The place seemed empty, but Judith didn't want to accidentally stumble upon someone sleeping somewhere in one of the house's nooks, so she made a show of stepping on every creaky board and tapping the walls as she moved from the front room to the small kitchen. The wood floor had been hacked away in places, revealing moss-covered stone underneath. Empty pizza boxes sat on the vintage stove surrounded by cheap candle stubs. Someone had tried to pry a metal fixture off the wall but abandoned the task halfway through; the iron hooks hung from stubborn iron nails.

"I swear to God."

The voice came from somewhere else in the house, echoing down the hall. It sounded like...

"If you came back for the charm bracelet, I'm keeping it as payment for this fucking mess." Cassie paused in the doorway, holding a black garbage bag. "Oh. It's you." She sniffed. "I was starting to think I got rid of you for good." She pulled another garbage bag from a roll in her pocket and handed it to Judith. "Long as you're here, you can help."

Judith took the bag without complaint. She was grateful to have something to do with her hands. To distract herself from the news about David.

When the bags were full, they carried them down the hill, where Cassie's car waited at the dead end. They dumped the bags into the hatchback.

"Not that I mind"—Cassie leaned against the open car door—"but you've been really quiet. Something wrong?"

Like a dam had been broken, she spilled everything. Almost everything. She told Cassie about her brother, that he was probably dead and her mom hated her and she'd thought she'd done a good thing, but now she wasn't sure.

Cassie nodded thoughtfully but kept her arms crossed over her chest. "It's not your job to fix everything, you know?"

Judith shrugged.

Cassie sighed. "About a month ago, my stepbrother knew the army was coming for him. He'd missed check-in, which means they find you and, if you're lucky, arrest you. It was my fault." She bit her lip. "I thought I could hide him. Stupid. Anyway, I was up here when I saw a military vehicle come down that big hill outside town. Ran to the house and told him. I figured he was gonna just lay low. Instead, he threw himself off the cliff. Washed up near your lighthouse."

"Oh."

"I'm not saying he'd be alive right now if it weren't for me. If he'd been sent off like your brother, he might not have made it either. Still." She rubbed her face. Sighed again.

"I thought—" Judith bit off the rest of her sentence.

"You thought what?" Cassie pulled a pack of cigarettes from somewhere in the car. "Lizzie got him?" She shook her head. "Lizzie doesn't want us. She wants you."

"Me?"

"All of you."

The curse. She opened her mouth to ask if it was possible, only the moment she thought it, she realized she didn't need to. It felt right. True. They were cursed. "Why us? What did *we* do?"

"Killed her. Obviously."

"But who? When?"

Cassie ignored her, focusing on lighting her cigarette.

"If we're in so much danger, why won't you tell me anything?"

"I told you to leave."

"We can't."

"Why not?"

Judith didn't have an answer. Because they couldn't. Because the thought of being anywhere else filled her with longing for the cape. As much as her mother used to complain, Judith knew she felt it too. There was a time, a little over a year ago, that Dad started looking at jobs in California. Almost had one, too, until Mom stepped in and talked him out of it. She didn't want to uproot Judith and her brother, didn't want to leave their family behind, excuse, excuse. So they stayed. They would always stay.

"Why should I believe you anyway?" Judith asked. "You could just be trying to scare me."

Cassie smirked. "I don't need to try. You're plenty scared."

Not scared enough to admit it.

Cassie paused a beat, then continued, "Do you remember what I told you? About my great-grandmother's cousin?"

Judith nodded. *A witch*, she'd said.

"There's this family story that she insisted the people she loved keep Thalias in their homes. Fresh, dried, didn't matter as long as it was a Thalia. She was crazy about it, wouldn't step foot outside her home without at least a few petals hidden somewhere in her clothes because, she said, they protected her from evil spirits. Story goes she wasn't always that way, though. That it started about a hundred years ago, the night a couple of girls disappeared from your house."

Judith swallowed, gaze darting up at the house, where she could almost feel Lizzie's black eyes boring into her. "What else does the story say?"

"That instead of continuing the tradition of herbalism and magic, our family settled down to become nice, respectable florists." Cassie opened the passenger side door and reached into the glove box. "Just think, if it weren't for your family, I might have had powers beyond your wildest imagination."

When she stood up again, she held a small velvet satchel. She considered Judith a moment before handing it over. "You probably need this more than I do."

Judith peeked inside the satchel to find a handful of dried flower petals. "Can I come up here sometimes?" Judith asked. "I won't bug you. Promise. I just…" God, she sounded like such a baby. "Please?"

Cassie took a long drag off her cigarette. Studied the embers before ashing over the top of the car door. Judith glanced through the back window and saw a couple of books, a jacket. Empty soda cans and bags of chips. Cassie wasn't wearing a ton of makeup this time, and Judith realized she couldn't have been older than sixteen.

"Fine," Cassie said finally. "But don't make a mess, and don't bother me. And never on a full moon. Those are mine."

"Okay."

"And only if you promise, the first chance you get, you get out of the cape. Hell, out of *Washington*. Got it?"

"Got it," Judith lied.

She couldn't leave, *wouldn't*, not without learning everything she could about Lizzie. She would cut herself off from the water, from Lizzie, until she learned to outsmart the curse. Until she could free herself and her family for good.

———————

Time passed in which Judith and Cassie moved in and out of the house on the hill, one girl's presence a ghost to the other—gum wrappers lazily left on the floor, replaced by an annoyed note. Soon gum wrappers turned into gifts— agates and bags of gummy bears and cigarettes—and annoyed notes turned into less-annoyed notes. Cassie might not have ever admitted it, but Judith thought of her as a friend. Her only friend.

Though Judith was tempted, she didn't visit the cove, even when Mom stopped asking where she was going every time she left the house, even when Art and Carol begrudgingly invited her to bonfires on the beach, even when Uncle Thomas—the light's current keeper—went to the hospital for a broken leg and the light stayed off for a full week and Judith could hear the ghost girl cry out to Judith in her dreams.

Now, it was nearing dusk, and Judith walked to the house on the hill wearing her brother's jean jacket. A little over four years after the *missing in action* letter,

David was now *missing, presumed dead.* Her parents hadn't given up, but Judith was careful not to get sucked into their what-ifs and maybes. A little hope was a scary thing.

One of the first things Judith did when she started coming to the house on the hill regularly was rehang the front door. She'd helped her dad with handyman projects a dozen times, so it only took a couple of tries to get it right. She tried the door now, but it was locked. Weird, because they didn't have a key, so unless you locked it from the inside, you couldn't.

She went around to the back, where a door into the kitchen didn't even have a handle, let alone a lock, and let herself in. The smell of incense hit her like a wall, and smoke lingered along the ceiling. She ran to the front room, thinking something had caught fire, but she found Cassie and a guy sitting on the floor, candle nubs flickering, while Cassie waved a burning bundle over their heads.

The guy caught Judith's eye and smirked.

Judith's face burned.

Cassie must have caught him looking; she turned and scoffed. "Full moon, Strand! It's, like, my only rule."

Judith arranged her face to look like she was as bewildered as Cassie, but in truth, Judith knew Cassie would be here tonight. She'd just hoped she'd beat Cassie to the house. She didn't want to be alone, even if that meant bugging Cassie.

"Sorry," Judith said. Then, "I can go…"

"Nah, let her stay," the guy said. "More the merrier, right?"

"Fuck off, Jackie." Cassie sighed. "Doesn't matter. My chill's all messed up." She turned back to Judith. "We're ending the war."

"Oh?"

"See?" Cassie said to Jackie. "She doesn't believe. She shouldn't be here."

"I didn't say that," Judith said.

"Didn't have to."

"Give her a break," Jackie said. Then, looking at Judith, "We've all lost someone, right? We figure it can't hurt to conjure a little peace."

"Yeah," Cassie interjected. "Except this was our last shot before I leave."

Judith frowned. "You're leaving?"

"Yeah. Had it with this place."

"Where are you going? When?"

"Not sure yet. But this is my last full moon at the cape. I decided."

"Okay." It was hard to hide her disappointment. As much as Cassie feigned disliking Judith, they'd grown relatively close—as close as they could, given the circumstances. And truth be told, she'd miss Cassie. Having this house and Cassie's perpetual frustration to occupy her mind, she hadn't thought about the curse. Much. "Sorry to bug you. I'll leave you to it, then."

Cassie huffed, but was that a little regret on her face?

Jackie patted the floor next to him. "Stay."

But Judith shook her head. "It's my turn to cook," she lied. "Better get back."

As she moved past them toward the front door, she glimpsed the drawing of the girl on the wall. The crude doodles had long been scrubbed away, leaving the girl blurred at the edges.

Judith and Cassie never talked about Lizzie, ignoring her and her presence— something they both seemed to feel—as a kind of survival tactic. Judith still carried the Thalia petals, though. Whether they worked or not, she couldn't be sure, but having them on her made her *feel* safer, even if she didn't totally believe in their power the way Cassie did.

Once, Judith suggested they paint over the drawing of Lizzie. Cassie dismissed it right away. "You want to piss her off more?" she'd said.

It was the *more* that drove Judith to finally try to find out what she could about Lizzie. Whatever her mother might have known, she was keeping her secrets, so the only thing she could think to do was go through Cassie's stuff. It didn't make her feel good, breaching her only friend's trust, but Judith needed answers.

The one thing Cassie could be counted on to bring to the house was her journal. She was a diligent writer, scribbling everything from poetry to shopping lists to snippets of thought that broke off midsentence. But Judith also knew that, stuck between the pages were articles and pictures, pieces of history and art and politics Cassie cared so deeply about she wanted them on her at all times.

The story about Lizzie was folded neatly at the back of the journal, tucked between a couple of crinkly, dry Thalia petals. The article looked like it'd been cut out of a book, only a couple of inches long with a picture of Judith's house as it would have looked a hundred years ago in the center.

Lizzie's actual name was Liza, and she had been fourteen when she disappeared. No one ever found her body or heard from her after she supposedly ran away from her aunt and uncle's house. *Judith's* house.

Now, when Judith looked at the drawing in the old house, she thought *Liza*, and it was like the darkness in Liza's eyes deepened.

Liza was lost, Judith thought. Scared maybe. Trapped someplace she didn't know how to escape. As much as the idea of facing her chilled Judith straight to her bones, she wondered if maybe she could help Liza somehow. If she did, maybe the curse that hung over her family like a guillotine would finally end. But what if she was wrong? She'd already done damage by attracting Liza's attention. If she was wrong about this...

She needed air.

She left the house not realizing Jackie had followed. So wrapped up in her thoughts, she didn't hear his footsteps behind her, so when he called her name, she practically jumped out of her skin.

Her face burned as he laughed.

"Sorry," he said. "I didn't mean to scare you."

"You didn't," she said too quickly. She looked past him, expecting to see Cassie too.

He must have noticed. "She's communing." He shrugged. "A lot of sitting around and doing nothing if you ask me, but don't tell her I said that. She hits hard."

When he smiled again, Judith's heart thumped. It was easy to forget Jackie was attractive. He didn't look all that different from the guys at her high school, but when he smiled at her, sometimes it felt like he was smiling just for her.

"I won't," she said finally.

A beat passed. Judith tried to come up with an excuse to walk away, but her brain seemed to glitch.

"I was just making sure you're okay," he said. "You look like something's bothering you." Then, "Do you want to talk about it?"

Before Judith could answer, he gently touched the small of her back and guided her toward an overturned tree where they sat. Judith was hyperaware of the miniscule distance between their thighs.

For a long time, neither of them said anything. Judith studied the tops of her shoes, the chip of blue nail polish on her thumbnail. She was overcome with a feeling of wanting to tell him everything and at the same time too terrified to say a word.

"I didn't really mean it," he said, "about the communing? I was just hoping it would make you laugh."

"Oh," Judith said, then laughed too loud. Jesus. What was wrong with her?

Then he smiled, and it didn't matter. "I may not believe everything Cassie does, but I do believe in intention. I think what we do isn't as important as our motives for doing it. Karma and all that."

Judith frowned. "I don't think that's true. I think we can do horrible things with the best intentions, but it doesn't make the horrible things less horrible."

"Maybe. But it makes them easier to live with." He gently nudged her, grinning when she nudged him back. "Besides, the important thing right now—the important thing always—is finding the courage to help, to give, when we're needed. I'm not saying it was right that your brother, or anyone, was pulled into this pointless war, but when the time came, he had courage. Now, it's our turn. Sometimes that's communing the way Cassie does. Sometimes it's standing in front of a building in the cold for hours with a sign. Sometimes it's putting ourselves in danger for the sake of others."

"Is that what you do? Put yourself in danger?"

"Did I mention that Cassie hits hard?"

Judith snorted. "Seriously, though. Do you?"

He seemed to think hard about it before answering. "Not as much as I should."

"But why is it up to you? Why can't someone else do it?"

"If we're all asking that question, then who's left?"

"So you…help, then. No matter what that means."

"I think so. Yeah."

She nodded. He was right, of course. Just not in the way he thought.

"Listen, I get that you might not want to talk about your brother or whatever it is that's bothering you, and that's okay," he said. "But I wanted to make sure you knew that I'm around. I'll listen if you want to talk. Or just sit in the quiet with you if you need."

"Thanks," she said. "Really."

"And," he added, leaning softly into her, "I would like to see you again. If that's okay."

A smile pulled at her lips. "You will." Feeling brave, she planted a small kiss on his cheek before quickly standing and walking toward the path.

Jackie was right. She had to have the courage to help Liza. For Judith's sake and for her family's.

Once the thought was planted, there was nothing she could do to shake it free. She left the old house and walked in the direction of the water.

She reached the bottom of the bluff just as storm clouds started to roll in on the far edge of the horizon. She could see Uncle Thomas in the light room. He caught her looking and waved. At the pier, she spotted Art and Uncle Jon prepping a boat. The wind had picked up, snatching at her brother's denim jacket, and she could smell rain in the air. Already the waves were choppy. Their small fishing boat rocked and swayed as they carefully stepped onto the deck. Art clung to the mast, his long hair whipping into his face.

The season had been pretty lean for Art's family. It made sense they'd want to make use of whatever daylight was left, but the storm looked ugly. They'd be lucky to have twenty minutes.

Judith considered coming back another day—the rowboat she planned to take out didn't stand much of a chance if the storm rolled in too quickly—but if she chickened out now, before she'd even had a chance to properly think about how stupid the idea was, there was no way she'd try again. It was now or never.

She waited until Art and her uncle were well on their way out before creeping along close to the rocks—mostly out of sight of the lighthouse—and then bolted across the way to the boathouse. She was pleased to find it unlocked. They would have been in a hurry and probably figured they were the only ones dumb enough to be out on the water today.

She dragged the rowboat out of the boathouse and around the pier to the sand. If she'd tried to put the rowboat in the water off the pier itself, the waves likely would have carried it away before she had the chance to get in it. Still, the slog was difficult. The boat weighed more than it looked—it was old and sturdy, with a heavy bottom and high sides—but the ground was dry here, and once she got a momentum going, the boat slid through the sand like it was water.

I'm coming, Liza.

At the edge of the shore, Judith gently nudged the bow of the rowboat into the waves, which lapped at the sides, splashing up her legs. She stiffened, the water so cold it felt sharp. But it also focused her. She climbed into the boat and scrambled to get the oars into the oarlocks before the waves pushed her back too close to the shore. Her arms burned with the effort to pull herself into deeper water. But she got into a rhythm and soon the shoreline fell away. Every few seconds, she shot a wary look up at the clouds. They covered the sky like a shroud, thick and dark and suffocating. The red light from the lighthouse slashed across the water, making the foam on the tops of the waves morph, and every time she blinked, she thought she saw Liza's hollow eyes watching her.

A loud clap of thunder made her jump, knocking one of the oars out of the oarlock. As she struggled to get it back into place while the boat rocked her off balance, the red light flickered and died.

For a long moment, Judith didn't move. The clouds had darkened, and without the glow from the lighthouse, the water was inky black. Somewhere behind her she heard her uncle's shouts. She didn't hear the words, but she did hear the motor start up. They'd probably spotted her. She didn't have much time.

Kneeling unsteadily at the bottom of the boat, she gripped the side, stomach rolling each time a wave crested, dipping the bow and then pulling it up again. Icy water splashed over her, into her eyes and mouth. Her nails dug into the wood, and she cursed herself for not bringing a life jacket.

"Liza!" she called, her voice snatched by the wind.

Thunder rolled over and then a web of lightning struck in the distance. Her uncle's motor sounded closer.

She felt ridiculous. Judith didn't know anything about ghosts or communing the way Cassie did. Cassie would have known what to do.

Cassie would have said to stay away, she thought.

But Judith *did* know what it felt like to be lost.

She leaned over the side, squinting at the shadows as salt stung her eyes. "I just want to help. Please. Tell me what you need."

Something struck the bottom of the boat just under where she knelt.

She jumped back from the side, knocking her elbow on one of the oars.

"Judith!"

She turned and spotted Uncle Jon and Art coming up on her side fast. Uncle Jon killed the engine, and the waves carried them the rest of the way. Art scrambled to the back of their boat, where he shouldered a length of rope.

Uncle Jon looked up at the sky and scowled before turning back to Judith. "What the hell is wrong with you, girl?" he shouted over the wind.

"I'm fine!" she called back.

He shook his head. "Catch the rope. Tie it around the bowsprit, and we'll tow you back."

Art rubbed water from his eyes and then held the twist of rope, indicating he was going to toss it. Judith waved him away, then eyed the oars. She was going to have to try to row away from them.

But Uncle Jon seemed to realize what she was doing. "Art!"

Something like fear flashed across Art's face before he shouldered the rope again and then launched it at Judith. The rope smacked across her lap, and before she could nudge it away, Art climbed over the side, where a short, rusty ladder shortened the distance between them just enough he could fall into her rowboat. He whacked his head on the edge but shook it off, seemingly unharmed.

"Get out," Judith ordered.

"My dad's pissed," Art said as he crawled past her toward the bow, dragging the rope.

Lightning flashed again, closer and brighter. In the dying light of it, Judith saw Liza. She wasn't far, her face just visible above the waves. More shadow than girl, the glow of each lightning strike seemed to pierce through her. She beckoned, reaching toward Judith with gray, skeletal fingers stretched wide.

Art finished tying off the rope and shot Uncle Jon a thumbs-up. They hadn't seen her.

This might be her only chance.

Heart in her throat, Judith took a deep breath and dove over the side.

The shock was instant. The cold was like a weight on her chest, and it took too long to propel herself to the surface. Gasping, she treaded water with limbs gone tingly. Soon she wouldn't be able to feel them anymore. She frantically turned, searching for Liza, but the waves were too rough. She could barely keep her eyes open long enough to spot the lighthouse, to keep herself oriented.

Already she heard her uncle's boat engine start up again, so she started to swim.

It was almost impossible to move through the choppy waves. Every few precious inches she put between herself and her uncle were lost with swell after swell. If she had any chance of losing them, she would have to go under. But the water was ice-cold, and she would only be able to open her eyes for brief bursts. With the chop and the wind, she could get disoriented and pulled farther out to sea, making her unable to swim back.

But she *felt* Liza out here. It was like an invisible rope, tugging her body and mind away from the shore. She remembered her mother's fear at the idea of Liza, Cassie's warnings... For an instant, she wondered if she had it all wrong. But then she remembered the way Liza reached out to her, and renewed determination tamped down her fear. She focused on Liza's name, repeating it over and over in her head as she took two, three deep breaths. Finally she pushed into an oncoming wave and let it take her under, down into the dark.

She didn't know how far below the surface she was. She kept her eyes squeezed shut, but she could hear the splash above her. The cold made it hard to focus on keeping herself calm. If she panicked, she wouldn't be able to hold her breath. The jean jacket didn't help. It was like a weight around her, but she refused to let go of it.

Come on, she thought. *I'm here.*

She decided to risk opening her eyes. The sting was immediate, but she fought the urge to close them. It was too dark to see farther than a few feet, and even that was questionable. She looked up and didn't see the hull of either boat.

Already her chest began to ache. It'd been a while since she'd had to hold her breath for any amount of time, so her body fought against it. She couldn't do this for much longer.

She swam toward what she hoped was shore, flicking her eyes open every few seconds. The last time she opened them, she thought she saw something white rippling in the wave above her. Her arms and legs were tired, but she fought against the current pulling her and looked up.

A girl hovered above her, limp body splayed just beneath the rolling waves. Her face was lifeless and pale. She wore a nightgown, torn at the edges, and her hair spread ink-like from her head.

Liza.

Judith had never seen her this way. So real. So delicate. It made her think that she'd been right. All Liza needed was someone to see her.

Judith stretched her arms upward as though to embrace her, mimicking the gesture Liza had made before. Liza drifted down toward her, her pale face growing grayer the closer she became. Her eyes flicked open, startling Judith, but Judith held still as best she could. She wouldn't be afraid. She wouldn't run away.

Then Liza's face darkened, black circles around her eyes engulfing them, leaving a cavernous nothing.

Liza reached for her, and the moment her skin touched Judith's, her body became heavy. Lethargic. Her eyes burned with tears and salt as a feeling of despair overcame her. Liza wrapped her arms tight around Judith, and they began to drift down.

Unable to move, Judith felt her lungs hitch and contract. The urge to cough was overwhelming, but Liza only clung tighter. She pressed her lips to Judith's ear as if in a whisper, and the edges of Judith's vision darkened. She began to pull back into her body, like her mind was reconnecting to the rest of her, and she realized with frightening clarity: Liza was drowning her.

Somewhere deep within her, she found the strength to wedge her hands between them. She pushed, but Liza was stronger. Judith clawed at Liza's chest, feeling the flesh give. Her stomach rolled.

Soon the gray light of the surface fell away, Liza's body an anchor on Judith. Even if she somehow was able to escape Liza's grip, she didn't know if she had the strength, the *air*, to swim back to the surface, let alone to shore. If Liza didn't kill her, the storm would.

A small voice told her to give up. It was useless. She was going to die no matter what she did. But just as she started to twitch, and the urge to breathe in the water was almost too great to push away, someone else pulled at her arm.

Uncle Jon held on to her wrist, shoving a line of rope into her hand. She understood immediately and gripped it. She watched him look hard at Liza, saw his face twist in confusion. He tried to pry Liza away, and it was like a bolt of energy shot through her. Liza turned to look at him, releasing Judith just long enough for her to pull the rope tighter. She twisted it around her arm for a better grip and kicked with what little strength she had, putting more distance between her and Liza. Art must have been above them in the boat, waiting for some kind of signal to start pulling them up because she shot upward, out of Liza's grasp.

Uncle Jon reached for Judith, his eyes wide with panic. She put her hand out, but she was moving too fast. Their fingers brushed, but she couldn't get a grip in time. The last thing she saw before breaking the surface was Liza wrapping herself around Uncle Jon. His mouth opened in surprise as they plummeted into the dark.

Finally above the water, she choked, struggling to breathe. Art hauled her over the side of the boat, then leaned over again, looking for her uncle.

"Where's my dad?" he asked.

Judith couldn't answer. Her throat burned, and every time she opened her mouth, a coughing fit took over. She was lightheaded, barely able to sit upright.

In the distance, she spotted the lighthouse. They were farther out than she thought. Another boat approached, flying across the waves as rain poured down. She crawled into the small enclosed steering room at the bow and leaned her head against the base of the console. Her pulse thumped in her head and fingertips, just louder than the voices outside.

She wanted to tell them there was no point, but she was too weak. She turned away from the window. She couldn't bear to watch Art scream into the wind. On the floor was a tangle of net, recently pulled from the water. Seaweed and snags of fins were caught in the barbs. And in the middle, bright as a beacon, was her shell.

She reached for it, snatching her hand back when her skin grazed a sharp edge.

She was wrong. This wasn't about a girl in need. It wasn't about being courageous enough to help when no one would. It wasn't about peace.

Finding the shell had nothing to do with a wish or even reaching out to Liza. She didn't want Judith's help. She wanted her dead. The shell wasn't a gift—it was a threat.

It was one thing for Liza to threaten Judith's life. Now Uncle Jon was dead, and if this shell was any indication that the death and destruction Judith's mother had predicted wasn't over, then someone needed to do something about it.

No, Judith thought. *Not someone.*

Me.

CHAPTER SEVENTEEN

MEREDITH

PRESENT DAY

he small crowd that would be the search party gathered around Art's porch a little before six. Most carried flashlights, and some wore reflective vests, so new the folds from their packaging were still visible along the front. Meredith recognized almost everyone—including the florist, lingering toward the back, with coffee in hand—but Vik and Bobby were conspicuously absent. A man, presumably a reporter, pointed a camera at a couple standing stoically at the edge of the group. Meredith stood next to Art, a picture taken the day before Alice went missing open on her phone. Part of her expected to see Kristin drive up in a shiny rental, all apologies and humiliation for her role in the complete collapse of their family. Meredith hadn't caught much in the way of media coverage of her daughter's disappearance—she shut off the TV anytime someone mentioned Alice's name—but part of her hoped Kristin would see it so Meredith could place the blame firmly on her shoulders. If Kristin hadn't ended their relationship, Meredith wouldn't have come back here. They would've been safe. The thing about small towns, though, especially Cape Disappointment, was that it was selfish with its tragedies. The same people who would talk behind her back, who would leave fish heads at her mother's funeral, would scoff at any national news networks trying to get the scoop on one of their own. Like an older sibling protecting a younger one, no one was allowed to beat on the people of the cape except the people of the cape.

"Try not to cluster," Art said to the restless crowd. "We want to cover as much ground as possible before dark."

At Meredith's feet, a stack of papers printed with hers and Art's phone numbers fluttered with the breeze, held in place by a rock

"She's probably scared. Hungry. Don't go running toward her if you see her. Call us and keep her where you can see her."

"What if she runs?" someone asked.

"Let her," Art said.

The man didn't seem satisfied with that answer; Meredith prayed he wouldn't be the one to find Alice.

Even though it was Art doing the talking, she felt their eyes on her. Studying her. Judging her. What kind of parent allows their child to disappear? *That kind,* they'd say, pointing at her. *Look at her. There's something not right about her. What do you want to bet she did it? Of course she did. It's always the mother.*

When Art finished, the crowd dispersed, slowly at first, then all at once. The stoic couple ventured farther back into the neighborhood where streetlights were weak and teenagers liked to meet for fires. The reporter followed the group headed by the man who thought Alice would run, his voice carrying across the street: "Bet you next month's salary I find her in one of those empty condos along the shore. That's where I would go."

With Art following, Meredith headed for the water.

Once she reached the sand, she slipped off her shoes, carrying them under one arm. She walked along the shoreline where water brushed over her feet, cold and tingly. Too scared to look across the water, too scared not to, a dark feeling settled in the pit of her stomach as she considered that she might see her daughter's body carried to shore on a wave.

They passed the cove and continued toward the rockiest part of the shore accessible on foot. Art leaned on her shoulder as they negotiated the jagged cuts and curves before finally sliding down the other side onto dry sand mixed with the crushed remains of billions of shells.

"You should put your shoes back on," Art said.

Meredith waved him off. Other than the girl, there was only one thing every story of the curse had in common: the water. Had Alice been pulled to it the way the others had? The way Meredith felt now, a tug just behind her ribs? If— when—they found Alice, this was where she'd be.

Midway down the beach, they came upon an ancient-looking boathouse. The windows were foggy with salt and age, but the door was unlocked.

Art nudged the door open, a strange smirk on his face. "I haven't seen this place in years."

"You know it?"

"Your mom and I used to keep stuff in here we didn't want our parents to see. My first taxidermy projects. Her jars. Pretty sure it belonged to a great uncle or someone once."

Meredith's pulse skipped. "Jars?"

There was just enough sunlight to illuminate the room. Her heart sank. No Alice. Taking up most of the ground in the center was a small rowboat, the oars tucked inside. Along the walls were half a dozen shelves, all filled with mason jars like Meredith had seen in the light room. Water and silt and seaweed trembled inside them as Art tripped on a piece of fabric, falling into the wall.

"You okay?" she asked.

He nodded and then bent over to see what he'd tripped on. He held up a scrap of vivid pink cloth, ragged along the edge. A fish was embroidered into the corner. "Looks like a baby blanket. Yours maybe?"

"Maybe." She didn't recognize it.

She turned back to the jars and pulled one off the shelf. The lid was too tight, so she tried another. This one opened fairly easily, releasing a sickly sweet odor, like rotting fruit. She opened two more, and both emitted the same scent. It was animal—sweat and pheromones. Like her skin after a long day or a hard run.

"Do you smell that?" she asked, holding the jar beneath his nose.

He shook his head.

"Strange."

She replaced the jar but was reluctant to leave. If these were her mother's, what was she doing with them? Had she read Grace's journal too?

"Come on," Art said. "We're running out of daylight."

They returned to the shoreline, where Meredith walked with her eyes half-closed, taking deep breaths, trying to pick out that particular scent. For a moment, she thought she had it and she followed it into the water, stopping when the waves reached her knees. She felt Art's hard gaze on her back, and she hoped he wouldn't ask because she wouldn't have an answer. She was acting on instinct, going where her gut told her to go. If this was the curse—and she was less and less convinced it could be anything else—she would need to stay with the water. If she was out there, if *she* had taken Alice, maybe somehow Meredith could convince her to give Alice back.

Meredith took another step forward and nearly tripped. Something sharp jabbed into the arch of her foot. At first she thought *stingray*, but as she probed the object with her toe, she realized it wasn't alive. She plunged her hand beneath the water, feeling around until she finally pulled it up.

A shell.

No.

Alice's shell.

"Alice?" Meredith fell to her knees and frantically crawled along the ground, running her fingers over every surface. "Alice!"

"What is it?" Art kicked up water as he ran toward her. "Is it Alice?"

Meredith held up the shell. "I found this. It's hers. She's here somewhere."

His face fell. "It's a shell, Meredith. It could be any—"

"No!" She continued to crawl, waves crashing against her body, over her head, up her nose, and in her mouth. "It's hers. She wouldn't let it go for anything, unless—" She bit off the last of the thought.

She crawled farther out, struggling against the current to stay close to the floor as it knocked her back. Her fingers slipped through a cluster of seaweed, and her heart thudded until she realized it wasn't Alice's hair.

Come on, Alice, she urged. *I'm here. Come find me.*

She only managed to crawl another foot before Art grabbed her under the arms like an infant and pulled her out of the water. Meredith writhed, struggling to break his grip. Grunting, he wrapped his arms around her waist and dragged her back to shore while she thrashed.

They collapsed together on the sand, his grip solid even as his breath came in ragged spurts. "Meredith. Stop. She's. Not…not here."

Hot tears fell down her face. "You don't know that! I found the shell. She left it here for me. I know it."

"Hush. Breathe."

"No!" Sobs wracked her body. "You have to let me go after her! She needs me!"

"Yes. She does. But not like this, okay? Please. We will find her. I swear to you we will. But you can't disappear like the rest of them."

She fell quiet, and when she looked up at him, he couldn't quite meet her eyes. "The rest of who?"

He shook his head, his voice barely above a whisper. "Come on. We still have a lot of beach to cover."

"Who, Art?" She knew exactly who. She only wanted him to say their names. To confirm what she already knew.

He helped her to stand, eyes lingering on the shell still held tight in her hand. "This place does things to people. I don't know why or what it is, but it makes people fall apart. You were smart. You left. Now you're back and I see it digging its claws into you, and I can't let you do to yourself what your mother did, not when you've got Alice."

"I would never do that to her."

"Judith might have said the same thing if someone bothered to ask." Before she could respond, he added, "Judith wasn't a bad person. She was troubled."

"Troubled." A rueful laugh burst from her mouth. "That's what all of you say when we tell you something you don't want to believe. They were all troubled. I'm troubled. Alice is troubled."

A chill seeped into her bones, and she started to shiver. Art slipped off his windbreaker and wrapped it around her. He was a good man, and he cared about Alice, about all of them, but Meredith was glad she hadn't told him about the boxes she'd found at Vik's house. He'd only dismiss her and focus on the theft. Not what she'd found or what it meant.

She supposed it was easy for him to look the other way despite everything he knew. Maybe it was because she was a woman that Meredith was used to looking over her shoulder, expecting some faceless monster to creep out of the dark and devour her. Back in Arlington she was careful about parking under a streetlamp at night and never accepted a drink from the hand of a stranger. She carried pepper spray and kept a stun gun in her nightstand. Precautions against a known, expected threat. It was easy to miss in the moment, but in hindsight she realized that ever since she came back, her awareness, her expectation of the worst, had been dialed to eleven. All the precautions in the world did nothing against the curse. Her mother had proven that.

Thick clouds moved in, casting a gray pallor over everything. The sun gone, cold seeped deeper into her bones. A patch of seaweed brushed against her ankle with a small, silvery fish caught in the mass, bloated, with one bulging eye.

She looked away, unable to stop the image of Alice's body taking its place.

To push the thought away, she focused on the red-haired girl. When she told Alice that they were all going to die, had it been a threat? Or was it the mechanism that put the machinations of the curse in motion? She'd spent all morning after being at Vik's digging through the journals in the light room, her mother's things, even a few of her own diaries from when she was a kid, miraculously shoved at the back of her childhood closet. There had to be a link between all of them—her mother, her grandmother, and so on, and not just their familial tie. There was a beginning somewhere. Whoever, whatever the red-haired girl was, she'd known who Alice was. Even if Alice had broken their stranger-danger rule and told, her last name was hyphenated—Alice Strand-Olivier—a name not obviously tied to the curse or the stories. Which meant the red-haired girl had sought her out. Had maybe been watching them since they'd arrived at the cape.

Art put an arm around her, startling her.

"Sorry," he said. "You looked like you needed it."

"I'm okay," she said. "I think I just need…" And just as if her thoughts had summoned her, she glanced up over his shoulder and saw the red-haired girl standing on top of the rocks, hair whipping in the wind.

Art pulled back and frowned. "What?"

Meredith took a shaky step forward. "It's her. She's—"

The girl jumped down the other side of the rocks, out of sight.

Still gripping the shell, Meredith broke away from Art and ran after the girl. She would *not* lose her this time.

"Meredith!" The wind snatched his voice as she put more and more distance between them.

There was no way he could keep up with her. No way he could stop her.

She scaled the rocks, ignoring the pain in her bare feet and clambered over the edge, rolling onto the sand. The girl was there, in the distance, but close enough that Meredith could still catch her. There was no use yelling; Meredith needed her breath, so she sprinted across the sand. Her calves burned with the effort, and she gritted her teeth as her muscles threatened to lock. The girl turned away from the sand and started for the waves, her feet kicking up water. Meredith allowed herself a brief moment to catch her breath. The girl wouldn't be able to swim far.

But when she hit the water, it was like it parted for her. She easily cut through the waves, and soon she was out beyond the buoys, slicing across the water faster than Meredith thought was possible.

Meredith's body trembled with the cold and the ache. She was a strong swimmer, but she was no match for the red-haired girl. She refused to give up, though. She doubled back to the boathouse. Her heart hammering in her chest, Meredith ducked inside and dragged the old rowboat through the door and out onto the sand, toward the water. That she'd never been in a boat, never rowed, hadn't been farther than knee-deep in the surf since her sixteenth birthday didn't cross her mind.

The girl had put some distance between them already, but Meredith wasn't about to let her out of her sight. She pushed the boat out onto the water as far as she could before she was too deep to hold the boat in place. She scrambled over the side and gripped the edges as it rocked beneath her. Shooting a glance over her shoulder—the girl had stopped, but only long enough to make eye contact before she dove again—Meredith slid the oars into their oarlocks and started to row.

Somehow, the ancient thing held as wave after wave slammed into her, threatening to pull her back to shore. Her muscles burned with each rotation, and she locked her feet against the second bench to gain some leverage. The girl could only swim so far before she'd have to give up, and when she did, Meredith would be there. She would get her in the boat, and she would refuse to bring her back to shore until she told Meredith where to find Alice. She'd demand the girl take her to her daughter, and the girl would have no choice.

Meredith focused on her plan, ignoring how far out into the restless sea she was going. She swallowed the rock of fear lodged in her throat, gaze darting across the water, ready to jump at the first sight of the girl's bright red hair.

Soon, she thought. *I'll have my daughter soon.*

CHAPTER EIGHTEEN

DIANA

1948

iana was ten years old when she was finally allowed to see her mother. Part of her was excited, but a bigger, noisier part was nervous. For most of her life, her mother had existed as a signature on a birthday card. An old photograph bent at the corners from constant handling. *She's very far away,* people told her, *but she loves you very much.* If not for her aunts, she might have believed that all mothers lived very far away from their children.

As she pulled on her tights and straightened the lace on her dress, she wondered: Would her mother like her? Would she think they looked alike? Would she come home with them?

By the time she and her dad were in the car, Diana was full to the top of her head with questions. Dad had to scold her a bunch of times to stop bouncing in her seat, but she couldn't help it. The questions were alive inside her, buzzing and bunched and bumping against her insides, making her stomach flutter.

They finally stopped in front of the biggest building Diana had ever seen. Big pots of flowers lined the long driveway all the way up to the front door. When they got out of the car, a woman in a crisp white hat and apron appeared in the doorway. She nodded at Dad and then smiled at Diana. There was lipstick on her teeth.

"She's had a busy morning," the woman said, "so don't be surprised if she's a little tired."

A look passed between the woman and her dad that Diana couldn't read.

"Perhaps we should come back another time," Dad said.

Diana's heart fell all the way to her feet. "No! You said—"

The woman waved their words away. "You've already made the trip."

Dad nodded. "Yes. I suppose you're right." He smiled tightly at Diana. "Shall we?"

The woman stepped aside, and Dad took Diana's hand, leading her through the big door and down a long hallway. The floors and walls and ceiling were so white they glowed. More of the same flowers from outside were stuck in vases on tables that sat between bony-looking chairs. More ladies in white hats and aprons click-clacked along the hall, carrying trays. All of them nodded at Dad, but he must not have seen them. He stared straight ahead, his grip on Diana's hand tightening.

They passed several open doors, and Diana peered into all of them, anticipation rising and crashing each time Dad breezed past, not even slowing. She started to think this was some kind of joke, that he'd walk her around in a circle, then take her back to the car saying *Now, wasn't that fun?*

But finally he slowed his pace and then stopped just short of another door. This one was shut, and a man in a white shirt and slacks sat on a stool beside it, a book spread open on his lap.

Seeing them, the man closed his book and stood. He smiled as he shook Dad's hand. "Afternoon, Mr. Anker."

"Afternoon, Jim." Dad smoothed down his tie. "Good day?"

The man called Jim glanced down at Diana. His mustache twitched like a caterpillar. "Afternoon, miss." He turned back to Dad. "Better than some, worse than others."

Dad took a deep breath and sighed. "Okay. Thank you."

Jim nodded and then leaned across to open the door. "Give me a holler if you need anything."

"We'll be fine, I'm sure."

Yeah, Diana thought. *We don't need your mustache getting in the way.*

She was practically vibrating by now, tugging on her dad's hand until he finally stepped toward the door. She could feel her heart in her back and her throat, little drums.

Inside the room was much darker than the bright, glowy hallway, and it took a minute for Diana's eyes to adjust. There wasn't much—another of the bony-looking chairs with a white robe draped over the back, a bookshelf only partially filled with a browning plant on top. On one of the lower shelves, Diana spotted a pink shell. It looked out of place against the grays and browns of the rest of the room, and she was overcome with the urge to touch it.

"Bethany? Darling?"

Diana quickly turned in the direction her dad looked, to a small bed—smaller than hers at home—with white bars at the foot and head. A lump of blankets sat in the middle. But the closer she looked, she realized the lump of blankets was moving.

Dad took another step closer to the bed, releasing Diana's hand. "I've brought Diana to see you. Isn't that wonderful?"

He looked back toward Diana and waved her forward.

The woman in the bed looked nothing like the picture Diana kept beneath her pillow. Her mother was tall, with a round face and bright eyes and cheeks that pinched when she smiled. The body of the woman in the bed barely filled the length of the mattress. Her skin was pale, almost gray, and it didn't even look like she *could* smile. She slowly turned her head, and when her eyes settled on Diana, they only seemed to get dimmer.

Dad nudged Diana until she croaked a timid, "Hello."

"There," Dad said, too chipper, "isn't this lovely?"

Her mother shifted her shoulders, then turned away again.

For more than an hour, Diana sat on the edge of the bed, silent, staring mostly at her folded hands while Dad talked to her mother. He talked to her about the house, telling her about the roof that needed replacing and a new settee he'd bought for their bedroom.

"It's quite comfortable," he said. "I can just picture you lounging beside the window with one of your books."

Diana stole a look at the bookshelf. She doubted her mother had picked up any of them. Again, her gaze drifted to the shell, snapping away only when a knock on the door made her jump.

Jim and his mustache slipped through the door. "Sorry to disturb you, Mr. Anker. Miss. It's time for Mrs. Anker's bath."

Dad's cheeks flushed. "Of course. We'll just, uh…"

He nudged Diana off the bed and tried to shuffle her toward the door but was blocked by a woman pushing a wheelchair.

Dad gripped Diana's shoulder so tightly she yelped. He shushed her and pulled her away, toward the bookshelf. Jim and the woman got on either side of the bed before the woman pulled down the mound of blankets on top of Diana's mother, and then they bent down and tucked their arms under her shoulders.

"On three," Jim said.

He counted—one, two, three—and then they heaved her mother up and twisted her toward the wheelchair. Diana's breath caught. Dad clapped his hand over her mouth before she could cry out. Her mother's legs were gone.

"It's okay," Dad murmured. "She's okay."

But her mother wasn't okay. As Jim and the woman pushed her off the bed and into the wheelchair, her mother's head lolled like a doll's. The woman gently pushed her back against the chair and tucked her hair away from her face.

The woman pushed the chair toward the door, pausing just on the edge of the doorway. "Next week, Mr. Anker?"

"Next week," Dad said, flashing her a tired smile.

Diana and her dad stood tight against the bookshelf until the sound of the wheelchair's squeaky wheel disappeared somewhere down the hallway. He stroked Diana's hair and sighed.

"Today was a low day," Dad said. "Your mother will be better next time."

Diana nodded, but she wasn't even sure that woman was her mother. How could she be?

As he started to pull her toward the door, the glint of the shell flicked in the corner of her eye. Without thinking, she snatched it off the shelf and held it in the folds of her dress until she got in the car, where she carefully hid it in the elastic of her tights, the bulge on her hip barely visible through all the ruffles.

The entire drive home, she wondered if her mother would notice the shell missing. If she would ever notice anything at all.

In the days after, when anyone asked how her mother was doing, Dad answered, "Well. Very well. I'm sure we'll have her home any day now." The first few times she heard it, Diana questioned whether what she'd seen had been real, or if she'd dreamed up a whole nightmare mother, and her real mother—the mother in the picture—would be home soon. Then she realized: her dad was lying.

Weeks went by where, every Wednesday, Dad asked Diana if she wanted to visit her mother again, and every Wednesday, Diana said no. What began as a childish defiance that this broken woman was her mother soon became something entirely different. She carried the stolen shell with her everywhere—to school, to church, to cousins' houses for birthdays—and soon it became a prop in her own lies about her mother.

My mother brought it back from her vacation in Hawaii.

My mother sent it to me from Brazil, where she's living with tigers and teaching them how to fetch.

As she got older, the lies became less fantastic. She conjured memories from her imagination to share with friends and lovers—

We found it on the beach during a picnic when I was little. She wanted to make it into a necklace, but it was too heavy.

My father gave it to her on their anniversary because he said it reminded him of the pink of her lips.

—and she began to understand those first lies her father told. Telling her own lies, burying the truth, was less painful than reliving the fear, the shame, she'd felt after finally seeing her mother. Told enough times, the lies became real, and every time she looked at the shell, in a place of honor on her bedside table, the weight of her shame lessened until she barely felt it at all.

Her mother died when Diana was six months pregnant, more than ten years after the first and only time she visited.

"Pneumonia," her dad told her over the phone.

In that one word she could hear the lie, but after years of practice, she pushed the suspicion away and instead asked questions about arrangements and burial, and offered to come to the house on the cape to help, which he gladly accepted.

When she packed for the trip, she tucked the pink shell in alongside her clothes and toiletries, eventually moving it from her suitcase to her handbag, where she could run her fingers over its sharp edges and conjure new memories to one day tell her child.

It wasn't until she saw the lighthouse that she finally let herself mourn for her mother—her real mother—a woman she didn't know and now never would.

———————————

Coming home was like letting out a breath she didn't realize she'd been holding. The house on the cape was exactly as she'd left it when she went away to college, down to her old bedroom furniture. Her dad met her at the door and fawned over her "condition," his worry palpable in every word. Her aunts—his sisters— had already arrived and were staying in one of the guest bedrooms, he told her, prepared to be at her beck and call should need be.

Exhausted from the trip, Diana decided to go to bed before dinner. In her old room, she opened the window and breathed in the salty air. Apart from her parents' room, hers had the best view of the lighthouse. She was sad to see the red light wasn't on tonight; she'd been looking forward to watching its hypnotic turn, something that had always helped her sleep even on her worst days. With the gentle breeze and the melodic crash of the waves drifting through the room, she fell asleep quickly, still in her clothes, her suitcase open, the contents half-strewn on the end of the bed.

She woke what felt like seconds later, her mind groggy and stuck somewhere between sleep and awake. The room was pitch-black. Her eyes ached as they struggled to adjust to the darkness, and when the last of her dreams fell away, an uneasy feeling crept into its place. She lay stone still and held her breath. Listened. She couldn't see a damn thing, but she felt someone in the room with her. She strained to see into the shadowy corners of the room, but everything was shapeless and dense.

The bedroom door was shut—that much she could see—but she couldn't remember closing it. Maybe one of her aunts had after peeking in on her...

A hissing sound made the hair on the back of her neck stand on end. It was like laughter, but...not. Worse, it was coming from somewhere in the room. Slightly muffled but close. She wanted to hold her belly, to cradle her child, but she didn't dare move, imagining someone hiding under her bed or in her closet, waiting for their moment to strike.

Stop it, she told herself. *You're being ridiculous.*

It was probably just the trees rustling outside. Or a bird stuck in the eaves. It always happened in the late summer—birds would build their nests in the gutters and along the slope of the roof, only to get stuck in the nooks and cracks. As a child, she'd watched her dad pull several dead starlings from the gaps, their legs stiff and brittle as twigs.

Finally, heart skipping, she forced herself to sit up, almost daring the thing in the shadows to come for her. From this angle, she could see a light under her door. She flew out of bed and flung the door open, bathing her room with the soft glow of the hallway lamp. Nothing looked out of place, but she couldn't be sure.

Too wired now to go back to bed, she started toward the stairs. Her stomach growled, and the baby inside her stretched.

"Okay," she cooed. "Okay. Let's see what's left in the kitchen."

At the edge of the landing, she heard voices. Something about their hushed tone made her pause.

"—warned him."

"—could have been spared all this scandal."

It was her aunts. She peered around the side of the wall, where the corner of the sitting room was just visible. Her aunts sat opposite each other, brandy glasses sitting on the edge of a game of checkers they hadn't touched.

Scandal?

Diana leaned against the wall, listening.

"You don't believe all that tosh about a curse, do you?" Aunt Maggie asked.

Aunt Kate sipped from her glass. "Of course not. It's like we've always said. The family is damaged, and Beth was the worst of them."

"God rest her soul," Maggie muttered, an afterthought.

Kate continued, "To find her in the bath like that—"

"Horrendous."

"—drowned." Kate's tone suggested horrified reverence, but the way her eyes lit up, it was like she almost enjoyed it. "Philip should sue."

Diana had stopped breathing. She gripped the corner of the wall so tight she left scratches in the wallpaper. Drowned?

Maggie shook her head. "He's been through enough. The last thing he needs is to publicize his wife's suicide. Besides, there's Diana to think of. Poor thing has had a go of it, hasn't she?"

A sharp ache started in the back of Diana's head and radiated forward. *This is a dream*, she told herself. *I'm still asleep and this is a horrible dream.*

Kate made a noncommittal noise. Nudged a red checker forward a square.

"A baby will be good for her. For all of them. Something precious to focus their efforts on."

"If you say so," Kate said.

Maggie frowned. "What is that supposed to mean?"

"Nothing." She smiled. Swirled her drink. "I'm sure everything will be just peachy."

"Convincing."

Kate chuckled, then her smile slowly fell. "I just wonder if..." She shook her head. "Phil can talk around it all he likes, but there's something wrong with his wife's family. Beth's suicide is tragic, but it's hardly an isolated incident." She leaned across the table. "Did you know she was in the room when her mother threw herself out the bedroom window? Just upstairs. Philip sleeps in that room. The same bed maybe."

"You're just being macabre."

"It's true!"

Maggie shushed her, and they glanced up at the stairwell. Diana dipped back behind the wall, heart pounding.

"It's true," Kate repeated, softer. "And then there's her grandmother. People say she disappeared, but who knows?"

"Diana is perfectly stable."

"Is she?" Kate tutted. "You don't remember all those stories she told about her mother? I'm still fielding questions about Beth's supposed sojourns to Brazil."

Diana's face burned.

Kate continued, "I'm just saying there's a pattern."

A curse, Diana thought.

She couldn't listen to any more. Leaning on the wall for support, she walked back to her bedroom, not bothering to hide her footsteps. Let them hear. She hoped they were ashamed.

Back in her bedroom, the hissing sound returned. She opened up the closet and looked under the bed. She looked in desk drawers and glanced down at the rocks beneath the window, swallowing hard as Kate's comment about her grandmother replayed itself. Finally she followed the sound to her suitcase. She pulled out her clothes, scattering them on the floor, the sound growing louder and less like a muffled hissing and more a rush, like a hard wind.

The sound was coming from her shell.

It was cold in her hands, sending chills up her body. Still, she held it up to her ear, and as the roar of the ocean washed over her, a voice drifted beneath the current. *Soon*, it promised her. *Soon it will be your turn.*

———————

In the end, Diana decided not to attend her mother's funeral. It hurt her father when she told him, but she couldn't stand the thought of sitting beside her aunts, knowing what they'd said about her. About her family. Worse, she couldn't shake the feeling that it might be true.

Besides, she'd already mourned for her mother. A long time ago, in that small, gray room.

Instead, she went down to the beach, kicked her shoes off, and dug her toes in the sand. The cool feel of it was a relief to her swollen, achy feet. She wished she could bury herself in it. She blamed the stress of travel, of her aunts' gossip, but ever since she arrived at the cape, it was like a thousand tiny weights had been tied around her arms and legs and neck, slowly at first, then all at once.

And the voice.

Diana heard it constantly now, not just from her mother's shell, but from the gaps under the doors and in the heating grates, following her from room to room. She'd hoped coming down here, where the roar of the water might be enough to drown out the voice, would give her some relief, but it was like the voice was louder here. Clearer. A girl, whose demands shifted from despair to anger and back, like whiplash. She was in pain, and she wanted Diana to share in it.

The sun beat down from a cloudless sky, and soon the sand was almost too hot to walk on. Sweat pooled in the small of her back and between her legs. The skin of her belly tingled, stretched and itchy, and it was like she could feel her blood pumping through her, the veins in her hands ropy and purple.

The water would make it better, she thought.

But had it been her thought? Or was it another intrusion?

She rubbed the back of her neck, flinching at the beginnings of a sunburn.

There were no intrusions, she decided. No voice. No girl. It was just her. Her mother's daughter.

Just need to cool off a little, she thought.

It didn't occur to her to take off her clothes, and by the time the thought crossed her mind, she flicked it away, a pest. Water splashed up her body, soaked her dress, her skin, her hair, and it was like the blood stopped in her veins. Her mind and her muscles melted, and everything stilled. She sank under the surface, the silence a balm. She could stay under here forever.

But then the feeling from her bedroom returned. There was someone here with her. She opened her eyes, but the sting of the water was too much. Panic fluttered in her chest as she struggled to get her feet beneath her. The silt was loose, and her feet slipped over and over. She got turned over, and disoriented, she clawed blindly at anything she could get her hands on until finally her face broke the surface and she sucked in a deep breath.

The invisible weights were too much, though, and she dipped back beneath the waves just as she started to catch her breath. This time she took no comfort in the silence. It was heavy. Thick. And then she felt fingers scratching down her legs and across her feet. They reached up her dress to her belly and squeezed.

Her body reacted on instinct, twisting out of the reach of the probing hands. She clawed and kicked, and when she finally reached shallow water, she crawled her way back to shore, body weak and shaking. As she dragged herself farther up the beach, something sharp stabbed into her thigh. She rolled over, sand coating her face and inside her mouth, and dug the thing out.

Her mother's shell.

Angry tears burned her eyes.

I will not become this, she thought. *I will not give in to the voices that tell me the only solace is at the bottom of the ocean. My children will not tell stories to forget me.*

Wincing at the pain in her thigh and belly, she pushed herself to standing and warily stepped toward the water. With the little strength she had, Diana threw the shell as far into the water as she could. As she followed it through the air, instead of relief, she only felt heavy. An anchor tied around her neck.

She would carry it forever, if that was what it took, but this was where it all stopped. Whatever curse had happened upon her family would end with Diana.

CHAPTER NINETEEN

JUDITH

he questions came at Judith like lightning strikes, each one hotter and more biting than the last.

"What happened?"

"What did you see?"

"What is wrong with you?"

"What were you thinking?"

"Why did you kill him?"

This last one from Art, his eyes ringed with red and purple like he'd been punched.

"I didn't," Judith swore.

"Good as done. If you hadn't been out on the water like some idiot, he never would have had to save you."

Uncle Thomas had ordered them both into dry clothes, but Judith's hair still dripped down the back of her neck and into her face, making her shiver with the cold and wet.

"Why did you even come out there?" Art paced in front of her while she stood against the wall, wishing she could fall through it. His hands clenched and unclenched at his sides. He licked his lips. Huffed like a bull seeing red. He stopped, then came at her in two long strides. His hands swallowed her throat. "I'll kill you."

"Hey!" Dad bounded into the room and ripped Art away. "Keep your hands off my daughter."

"She killed him!" Tears fell in rivers down his face, and he bared his teeth like a rabid dog.

Judith shook her head. It wasn't her fault. It was *Liza*. She'd wanted Judith, but Uncle Jon had gotten in the way.

Carol came in, arms wrapped around her middle. "Art?"

Art pulled out of Dad's grip and went to her, but when she tried to touch him, he shrugged her off too.

"Both of you need to go," Dad said.

Art looked like he was about to argue, but Carol slipped her arm around his waist and steered him out.

When the door closed behind them, the air seemed to go out of her father. He looked at her and shook his head. "Your mother…"

Mom was back at the lighthouse with Uncle Thomas. Uncle Jon's body hadn't surfaced yet, but it was only a matter of time. Mom and Uncle Thomas watched from the lighthouse as the police boat zipped over the choppy waves, searching.

Judith sank along the wall until she sat on the floor and pulled her knees into her chest. Her mother had lost so much; for that, Judith was sorry.

Dad groaned as he lowered himself down next to her. "What happened out there?"

Judith shrugged.

"You could've been killed."

"I know that."

"Then explain it to me, Judith. Why were you out there?"

She cradled her head in her hands. Every time she closed her eyes, she saw Liza change. She saw Uncle Jon's startled face, saw his body seize. "I thought I could handle her."

Dad frowned. Shot a look at the door. "Thought you could handle *who*?"

She started to rock in a gentle forward-and-back motion but didn't notice she was doing it until Dad put a hand on her shoulder, stopping her. He opened his mouth to speak but closed it again, changing his mind. He took a deep breath. Nodded. "Okay. Okay." Then, "Are you sure you've told the truth? All of it?"

Something in the air had changed. The way he looked at her now, more scrutiny than empathy, raised her hackles. "Yes," she said, harsher than she'd meant.

He grabbed her hands. "You're a good kid. I know that. It was an accident. People will understand that eventually, but you have to stop lying."

"I'm not lying! How could you ever think that?"

"Honey, please—"

"It was her, Dad. You know about her. Mom knows about her. Everyone knows, and everyone's keeping secrets, and if people would stop lying to *me* for once, maybe I could figure this out. I could even stop it!"

Dad pulled back like he'd been slapped. Judith ripped her hands out of his grip and stood, nearly tripping on his outstretched legs. Liza was waiting out there for her. If Judith closed her eyes—yes—she could hear her voice. She would come after Judith again. But would she be ready? Would she ever be ready?

She ran for the door, but Dad lurched to his feet before she could reach it. He grabbed at her arm but slipped, fingers tightening around her shirtsleeve. Panic surged in her chest, and suddenly it was like she could see something dark crawling out of the ocean. An image so sharp in her mind that it felt real. Each time she blinked, the image lingered a beat longer, like it was bleeding through her mind, through her eyes, into reality. Soon, the image fattened and sharpened, and each time she closed her eyes, she knew that when she opened them, it would be more real. It would take her.

The arms came for her, and she screamed until her throat burned.

Uncle Jon's body washed up on shore the following morning. The bones in his sternum and upper arms were shattered. *Crushed* was the word the police used. *Crushed, like in a trash compactor.*

Judith didn't go to the funeral, not because she didn't want to, but because a rock through the kitchen window warned her against it. They all knew it was Art, but no one wanted to be the one to admit it. Mom went alone, while Dad busied himself with odd jobs around the house, not once looking up at Judith. She wandered through every room, deciding that as long as she was on her feet, she wouldn't fall asleep.

Nightmares from the past couple of nights followed her into her waking hours, breathing down the back of her neck and scratching the undersides of her arms and legs. But the longer she stayed awake, the fainter the nightmares became.

Last night, after the funeral, she'd overheard her parents fighting. Mom wanted to move. Dad told her it was impossible and how would it look if they just up and left after what happened to Jon? Mom said that if they'd moved when she wanted to, none of this would've happened. She told Dad he was just like his father. She told him taking Judith to a psychiatrist was a stupid idea and the next time he had another stupid idea to keep it to himself. Judith shut her door when she heard a glass break. There was a beat of heavy silence that seemed to hold the potential fate of the world, and then the screaming started up again.

This morning, Judith lay in her bed, eyes achy and stomach in knots. She hadn't slept in two days, and every cell in her body was exhausted, but every time she closed her eyes, she saw Liza's face. Heard her voice. Mom walked past her room, hesitated, then continued to the bathroom. Mom wasn't speaking to her, but Judith didn't blame her. Because, really, it *was* Judith's fault. It was like Liza had been sleeping, and by reaching out to her, Judith had stirred her awake, had released this ravenous want, a hunger Liza would kill to sate, no matter who got in her way. And what Liza seemed to want was Judith.

There was only one thing she could do.

With Mom in the shower and Dad avoiding everyone somewhere in the shed, Judith slipped out the front door, a hastily packed bag over her shoulder, without anyone noticing.

She didn't have a car, and she didn't know how often, if at all, buses came into town. She could have called a cab maybe, but her stash of summer job cash wasn't as big as she'd hoped and the thought of spending any of it on a cab ride to God knew where made her feel seasick.

She supposed she could hitchhike, but that was a last resort.

Walking to the house on the hill, Judith couldn't shake the feeling she was being watched. As she approached the top of the hill and the brush grew denser, every flicker of movement, every crunch and caw and rumble threatened to undo her until finally she reached the door and let herself inside, slamming the lock behind her.

"Hello?" she called. "Cassie?"

It was pointless. Judith could feel the emptiness of the place. Dropping her bag by the door, she went through to the kitchen to see if Cassie had left anything, any hint that Judith was too late, that Cassie had already gone.

They rarely talked outside the house—the old walls and dark ceilings a kind of sanctuary where they could crack each other open, a couple of exposed nerves—but sometimes they missed each other, their sojourns to the house mostly unplanned, so they left notes or gifts for each other in the oven, hidden from would-be partiers who broke in on the weekends. Inside, she found a folded note concealing something heavy. Another stone, maybe. Cassie was also leaving her gifts she said would protect Judith from evil. Judith had amassed quite the collection of crystals and herbs, something to replace the shells she'd gotten rid of.

She unfolded the note and found a tiny ceramic bird, pale blue and barely larger than her thumbnail. The note itself was short:

Nice to meet you. I hope I meet you again.
Jackie

Judith smiled, tucking the note and the bird in her pocket. *Maybe,* she thought.

Then she remembered why she'd come here in the first place and sank beneath the weight of it. She couldn't let anything distract her.

There was no way to know if Cassie would come by the house tonight, so she decided to try to find out where she lived. It was stupid that Cassie kept so much of her life outside of the house to herself, and Judith told her so, but Cassie was adamant.

"Just because I try to help keep your bad juju under control doesn't mean I want any on me," she'd said. "Besides, think of what Constance would think."

Constance, Cassie's Thalia-obsessed relative. Judith never told Cassie the things she'd found out about Constance, that when Regina Holm went missing, Constance was the first person the police spoke to. They'd been friends, a fact that pleased Judith deeply but would have ventured too far into *big feelings* territory for Cassie.

But she wasn't the locked box of information she thought she was. Cassie had once let slip that she could see the fountain from her bedroom. It was a start.

The fountain was at the apex of Main Street, an area with few apartments and even fewer houses, most of which were hidden behind trees or too far from the road to be able to see it. Judith studied the windows in the apartments above the storefronts, but most of them were covered by curtains or blinds or just too dark to see into.

So she did the only thing she could think of.

"Cassie!"

The echo scattered a group of pigeons that had gathered near the foot of the fountain, their angry caws drowning her out.

A woman in the florist's peered out the window and shook her head.

Was that a no, like, *no, Cassie doesn't live here anymore*? Or was she just irritated? Judith supposed it was possible Cassie had already left, but she had to believe they were better friends than that. She had to believe Cassie wouldn't have abandoned her.

Judith tried again. "CA-SSAN-DRA!"

One of the windows above the florist flew open, and Cassie stuck her head out, her face a mix of confusion and anger. "What the fuck are you doing?"

"Can you come down? I need to talk to you."

"This is borderline stalker behavior. You see that, right?" She shook her head. "How did you even know where I live?"

"I didn't."

"So you just shouted and hoped I'd come running?"

Judith nodded.

Huffing, Cassie fought with the curtains, tying them back. "Five minutes." Then she disappeared back into the room.

When she finally emerged from a slim doorway next to the florist's entrance, Cassie glanced back at the shop window before approaching Judith. Her mouth was twisted into a scowl, but there was concern in her eyes. It almost broke Judith. She bit the inside of her cheek to keep the tears at bay.

"Your family own it?" Judith said, trying to work her way up to asking the impossible.

"No, we just live above a flower shop because we love constantly getting headaches from all the pollen drifting through the vents." Then, "Sorry. It's just… What are you doing here?"

Judith hesitated, wondering how much she should tell her. If dumping her fears, her sadness, on Cassie would all but guarantee she would never speak to her again.

"Is it about your uncle?"

Judith bit the inside of her cheek, a poor attempt to keep herself from crying. She nodded.

Cassie glanced at her backpack. "Going somewhere?"

"I'm taking your advice."

Cassie raised an eyebrow. They'd known each other long enough that she probably sensed the unsaid *but*.

Judith continued, "I want to go with you to California."

Cassie laughed. "Shit in one hand, want in the oth—"

"Please." One word was enough to break the dam. Tears fell down her cheeks, soaking her collar. "I can't be here anymore. I'm begging you. If she doesn't get me, she's going to get my family. If something else happens and it's my fault…" Her breath hitched around a sob. "Cassie, please."

Another glance over her shoulder. It only just occurred to Judith that Cassie might not have said anything to her family about leaving—or that all the talk about leaving was just more of Cassie's bluster. What would Judith do if it was all a lie? She shifted her weight, painfully aware of how pitiful she looked, of her few insignificant belongings in her bag. Of a pull in the back of her neck, like a hand, forcing her to turn to her house by the ocean.

Cassie's shoulders sagged, all of the fight gone out of her. For the first time, Judith saw softness in her expression. "I wasn't gonna leave until next week." She paused, scratching her neck. "But tonight's as good a time as any." Then, "Give me a couple of hours."

"Okay."

"If I get pulled over because someone reports you kidnapped, I'll tell them I don't know you. You held a gun to my head and swore to kill my cats if I didn't take you to Disneyland."

Judith couldn't help but smirk. "Deal."

Cassie sighed. "Meet me back here, okay? We'll head out before dark."

Could she wait that long? Or would the hand on her neck push her off the bluff to keep her anchored here?

"Two hours," Judith said.

Lips pursed, Cassie nodded. "Okay. Two hours."

While she waited, Judith used a precious few dollars to buy a coffee and a box of donuts to get them through the first few hours of the drive. She didn't know where or if they would stop, if they would alternate, or if Cassie would insist on driving the whole way, but she wanted to be prepared.

Exactly two hours later, Cassie pulled her car up to the fountain. The back seat was full of stuff—boxes and garbage bags filled to bursting with clothes and bedding.

"There isn't much more room in the trunk," Cassie said. "I had to improvise."

Judith's backpack fit neatly on the car floor between her legs. Was this *really* all she was bringing? What was she going to do once she got there? Could she get a job? Where would she live?

"Ready?" Cassie asked.

"Are you?" Judith shot back.

Cassie turned on the radio and put the car in gear. "Let's get the hell out of here, then."

Judith closed her eyes until she felt the familiar hum of tires on metal, until they'd reached the bridge that would bring them out of Cape Disappointment and onto the highway. When she finally opened them, the sun was dipping behind them and a trail of headlights flicked across the dash.

Now they would all be safe. Now it would be over.

CHAPTER TWENTY

MEREDITH

PRESENT DAY

s the adrenaline peaked and the fog clouding all thought except a single-minded hunger to get her hands on the red-haired girl subsided, Meredith paused to look around, only to realize she was lost. The shoreline had disappeared as insidiously as the red-haired girl. One moment it was there, the only thing orienting Meredith in the vast blueness, and then it was gone. Her first instinct was to turn around and start paddling back the way she'd come, but a fog had settled over the water, the gray of the horizon bleeding into the gray of the fog. She couldn't tell which way "back" was. How far out had she gone? She managed to keep the panic at bay until she realized she'd gone so far she couldn't see the lighthouse anymore. Not that it mattered. She'd stopped setting the light. Without her mother's constant nagging, and with more immediate things to worry about, it'd slipped her mind.

"Hello? Girl?" she shouted, her voice lost in the water. She had to be out here somewhere too. There were no other boats around. Nothing. "I don't know what kind of sick joke you're playing, but it's over now, okay?" Silence. "Hello?"

She couldn't have rowed that far, could she? It'd only seemed like seconds, but the way her arms burned from exertion told her otherwise.

Frustrated tears squeezed out of the corners of Meredith's eyes. She noticed the baby blanket in the corner of the boat and wiped her face. The ghost of a scent—of sourness and softness and vanilla, of her mother—startled her. She didn't even recognize it, which wasn't all that weird, but she thought she'd seen all her baby stuff that survived the Great Toddler Purge. Her stepdad had been diligent about keeping things—stuffed animals with their button eyes missing, photos, clothes, blankets—insisting that one day she'd want them for herself. If he'd known about this blanket, it would've found its way into a waterproof bin in the closet.

It was barely big enough to wrap around her shoulders, but the longer she sat bobbing in the middle of this pathetic rowboat, the colder she got, so she pulled it tight around her body, and after pulling the oars in so they wouldn't fall overboard, she tucked her hands into her shirt.

For someone who spent her entire life next to the ocean, she knew surprisingly little about it. She tried to reason that the waves would eventually tug her back to shore, but the waves seemed to come and go from every direction at once. Sometimes it felt like she'd been sitting in the same spot forever, and at others, she could swear she'd been pulled a hundred feet in one direction. She tried to watch the clouds, but they were moving too. There was no way to tell one direction from the other. It took everything she had not to break down. She'd get hungry soon. And thirsty. Worse, it would get dark. She tried not to think about it, but the more she argued with herself, the more she obsessed over her dry tongue and scratchy throat. Her empty stomach.

Someone will find me, she thought.

Time passed, and in the soft pink light of the gloaming, mysterious things bumped the bottom of the boat. Huge, dark shapes curled under the water, which she saw out of the corner of her eye and refused to look at directly. Like the monsters under her bed, if she didn't acknowledge them, they didn't exist—or so she told herself. The boat rocked angrily, and freezing water splashed over the side, soaking her clothes.

She told herself she had to move. Sitting like this would only pull her farther out to sea. But if she tried to row anymore, she'd just exhaust herself further. She'd get thirsty and hungry faster. She took deep, measured breaths. Getting hysterical wouldn't help anyone, least of all Alice.

But there was a good chance she was going to die out here. The thought filled her with such heavy sadness. She thought of her daughter out there somewhere, waiting for Meredith to come and rescue her. She'd failed. As a mother. As a person. Maybe her mother had been right about her all these years: Meredith was useless. Worthless.

Exhaustion hit her like a train, driving her into the bottom of the boat, her feet tucked under one of the benches and her face shielded under the other. It was like lying in a coffin. She covered her face with the blanket, and eventually, she fell asleep.

What felt like seconds later, the boat jerked. Seawater soaked the blanket, and as she woke up choking on it, she was sure she would drown. Her muscles cramped as she extracted herself from under the benches only to soar with relief when she saw, against the clinging rays of dusk, the motorboat. Someone had looped a rope around the prow of her boat and slowly tugged her along.

Then she focused on the driver.

A girl with a deep brown braid turned and waved. "Morning!" She laughed at herself and turned her focus back to the steering wheel.

Gripping the sides of the rowboat—the girl pulled it so fast Meredith worried it would fall apart beneath her—she swore with each dip and sail over the roughening waves. Wind and spray pummeled her face, which she tried to shield with her shoulder without taking her eyes off the girl for too long. The girl wore the same dress as the one the red-haired girl had worn the day of the funeral—it was dry, Meredith noticed—and her hair came away from her braid a little bit at a time. The girl had one bare foot perched on the motor-boat's chair, removing it only when she made a sharp turn that nearly capsized Meredith's tiny rowboat.

"Sorry 'bout that," the girl shouted over the roar of the engine. "I almost always miss that turn."

They were in the middle of the ocean. What turn? Every bit of blue looked the same as the other bit, and it constantly changed. Navigating this would've been like trying to drive through a one-way grid whose streets constantly switched direction.

Meredith thought about jumping from her boat to the girl's but dismissed the idea just as fast. For now, she was at the girl's mercy.

We have to stop sometime, Meredith thought, considering the engine's finite fuel supply.

Another sharp turn and the girl picked up speed. Meredith wrapped her legs tight around the bench and prepared for the inevitable.

A spot of green in the distance grew and grew as the girl sped toward it. Land. Meredith let out a long-held breath, but her anxiety compounded, realizing they weren't heading for the peninsula.

Maybe she'll help me, she thought, eyeing the girl in the boat.

She immediately dismissed the idea. It wasn't a coincidence that this girl was wearing the same kind of dress the red-haired girl had, just as it wasn't a coincidence that she'd happened across Meredith out in the middle of nowhere.

They headed toward a tiny island, small enough you'd miss it if you weren't looking for it. Meredith went to work on a plan. Once they stopped, she would overpower the girl and steal the boat. It was a fairly new model, she figured, and would probably have some kind of navigation. If nothing else, it would have a radio. She could call for help, be home before the sun went down.

But what if people were waiting for the girl? What if they had weapons?

What if they had Alice? She couldn't leave without her.

Once they finally reached the island, the girl negotiated the boat next to a dock that looked like it'd been hastily cobbled together with driftwood. Meredith's rowboat dangled behind like a buoy, too far away to reach the dock but close enough that she could swim it if she wanted to (she didn't). The girl cut the engine and climbed out onto the dock. Her feet made wet *slap-slap* noises on the wood.

The beach where they'd docked was maybe a thousand feet across before it curved out of sight. Trees and bushes obscured the rest of the island, but in the near distance, peeking out above the trees, Meredith spotted a shoddy likeness of the Cape Disappointment lighthouse made of the same wood as the dock. Sheets of plastic rippled in the wind where windows should have been. A pair of brightly colored dresses dried on the rail, one of which she recognized as being the one the red-haired girl had been wearing when Meredith had chased her into the water.

The girl paused at the end of the dock where it fell off into the wilderness and stared curiously at Meredith. "You coming or what?" she shouted.

Meredith didn't say anything, only watched as the girl disappeared into the trees.

Once the girl slipped out of sight, Meredith shakily slid the oars into their rowlocks and rowed, heart pounding, to the dock. Her arms shook as she pulled herself up and rolled onto the wood. Something sharp jabbed her in the calf, but she ignored it and bolted for the girl's boat. The keys were gone, so there was no chance of stealing it. Looking around for some kind of weapon, she spotted a phone on the floor of the boat.

Please, please, please… She jabbed the power button only to realize what she'd already suspected. Dead. She pocketed it anyway.

Back at her rowboat, she grabbed one of the oars and hefted it, with some difficulty, over her shoulder as she made her way slowly down the dock. She'd spent too long with her legs tucked up under her and her neck bent at an odd angle, so her whole body ached and her muscles screamed in protest when she moved. Trees rustled with the breeze, conjuring up all sorts of mental monsters that made her skin prickle and her stomach turn. But she kept moving, one foot in front of the other, her hands going numb with how tightly she gripped the oar.

She followed a winding road made of broken shells and pieces of concrete. The oar was heavy, but she didn't dare drop it an inch. The trees on either side of the road with their thick crowns and low branches were perfect places to hide. She imagined the girls waiting in the branches for just the right moment to pounce. Were they part of some kidnapping ring? Pirates? Everything she saw only brought more questions. Soon she came upon a split in the road. The right fork would most likely bring her to the makeshift lighthouse—she could still see it above the trees—so she followed the left, heart skipping with each rustle in the brush.

Once the saltwater haze cleared, she smelled a heady mixture of shit and sweetness. It was a farm smell, something she was only vaguely familiar with thanks to elementary school field trips. Animals and crops. Caramel apples. It made her think of Alice and their one and only trip to the zoo, where an irritated chimpanzee had thrown dirt at her over the high fencing. With renewed purpose, she pushed on until the road abruptly stopped. A small house sat in the middle of a clearing, its walls more expertly assembled than the dock and a screen door that banged with a sudden, sharp breeze. A section of grassy area had been gated off where a dirty gray goat grazed lazily. A pair of fat chickens pecked at the ground nearby, clucking contentedly to themselves. On the opposite side of the house, a generator whirred.

Meredith had found her way to Grandmother's house. Now, where was the wolf?

The screen door banged open, and the dark-haired girl stepped out wearing yet another dress, this one long-sleeved with grass stains along the hem and wrists. Her hair was wrapped up tight on the top of her head.

As Meredith took an angry step forward, a second girl stuck her head beneath the first girl's arm. Red hair shone. The girl *was* real. Somehow, the fact didn't comfort her.

"She's here, Mama," the dark-haired girl called over her shoulder before smiling at Meredith.

Mama. That meant there were at least three of them. Meredith didn't like her chances; the oar on her shoulder suddenly felt less substantial.

The red-haired girl eyed the oar. "Nuh-uh."

Before Meredith could react, the red-haired girl lunged, grabbing for the oar, but Meredith hung on even as the wood scraped through her palms like sandpaper. The motion propelled her forward, and her foot caught on a dip between the wood slats of the porch. She dropped the oar to try to catch herself, but as the red-haired girl jerked it away, Meredith's arms extended, and her chin hit the floor with a crunch she felt all the way to her feet. The taste of blood filled her mouth. The red-haired girl smacked her in the back of the head with the wide part of the oar, driving Meredith's face in the wood again.

"Stop!" the other girl screeched.

"Amenable my ass," the red-haired girl muttered. "I don't care what Mom says, we need to protect ourselves."

Pain engulfed Meredith's head and neck, made worse when the red-haired girl straddled her back, crushing her lungs. Meredith gasped, tried to reach behind her to scratch or gouge, but getting hit in the head had made her sluggish. The red-haired girl easily grabbed Meredith's wrists and wrenched them up, backward, so hard the backs of Meredith's arms nearly met her head.

With the last of her strength, Meredith bucked, kicking her legs, not caring what they hit, but the red-haired girl only laughed.

"Ride 'em, pony," she said.

She held Meredith's hands together with her elbow, only releasing them after she'd wrapped them four or five times with rope that scratched Meredith's skin. Finally, the red-haired girl climbed off her and tugged the rope. Meredith cried out as pain shot up her arms and down her back.

"Hush now. You don't want to scare the poor thing."

Alice?

The thought of her daughter filled her with a second wind. She quickly rolled toward the rail, and though she managed to get the rope out of the red-haired girl's hands, she'd also tangled herself in it. Before she could get her feet under her, the red-haired girl had hold of the rope again.

Meredith fell against the rail, half leaning over the stairs, chest heaving.

The red-haired girl didn't even look out of breath. "You done?"

Meredith hesitated. If she got herself killed out here, any chance of getting Alice out of here—if she was here—would be gone.

She nodded.

"Good." The red-haired girl looped her arm through Meredith's and gingerly helped her stand. Meredith hoped she'd take the rope off too. The red-haired girl watched her glance at the rope. "No way. This is staying on."

"Get in here!" a voice boomed from inside. "You're letting in the bugs."

Each girl looped an arm through Meredith's and pulled her, limping, inside.

Candlelit lanterns provided most of the dim light of the room. A single bright bulb flashed from atop a lamp stand, flickering with the whir and dribble of the generator. The floor was an unpolished wood, covered in most places by oriental rugs with frayed edges. Blankets in a dozen colors and patterns covered almost every surface, draped over furniture that looked snatched out of the 1970s with its dark wood frames and itchy floral cushions, tossed haphazardly in corners and piled on shelves, all embroidered with intricate designs.

The piles avalanched from the front room into a small kitchen, where an older woman with sunbaked skin and gray-speckled hair stood over a pair of steaming mugs. Wrinkles dug trenches in her cheeks and forehead, and her jowls jiggled with a slight tremor that affected her head and hands. She squeezed a bottle of honey over one of the mugs and then looked up at Meredith as she stirred. "Do you take honey? I personally can't stand tea without it."

"I'm not thirsty," Meredith said.

The woman grinned like a cat that'd cornered a mouse. "Of course you are, dear. Water, water everywhere and nary a drop to drink, yes? You were out there for hours, poor thing." She gestured to the couch, barely visible beneath the blankets. "Sit."

"Hours?" Meredith asked. Brighter light poured in through the windows, and she realized she'd slept all night. It was dawn, not dusk. "You were watching me?"

"I didn't have to. My girl may have lost you in the fog, but you weren't hard to find once it lifted. We kept an eye on you from my lighthouse. I was hoping something interesting would happen. Imagine my disappointment when all you did was sleep."

With their arms still hooked around Meredith's, the girls escorted her to the couch and refused to relinquish their grip until she'd sat.

The woman shuffled along behind and sat the two mugs on a coffee table after nudging the blankets there onto the floor. A dollop of honey dripped down the side of the one put in front of her, which the dark-haired girl swiped up with a flick of her finger.

The red-haired girl slapped her hand.

"Girls!" the old woman snapped. "We have company." She sipped from her own mug and shuddered before turning to Meredith. "You'll have to forgive Calamity and Tempest. Spirited girls."

"I don't have to do anything, least of all forgive." She turned to the red-haired girl. "You've been stalking me. Why?"

The old woman chuckled. "A room full of spirited girls. In my day, that kind of behavior would not have been tolerated." She pointed a slender finger at the red-haired girl. "Tempest was watching you because, like me, she's curious." She sipped from her mug. "And because I told her to."

"Why?"

The dark-haired girl, Calamity, said, "Because of Alice."

Tempest pinched her sister's arm and Calamity yelped.

"Girls." The old woman used the word as an incantation, like if she said it enough they'd become quiet, demure things instead of the storms their names suggested.

"Alice?" Meredith started to stand only for Tempest to shove her back into the couch. "Where is she? Is she okay?"

"She's fine," the old woman said. "Still sleeping most likely." She wrinkled her nose in distaste. "Lazy."

White-hot fury shot up Meredith's body. She pulled on the rope, hoping the red-haired girl, Tempest, wasn't paying attention. But she held tight, yanking her back for her trouble. "If you've done anything to her, I swear to God—"

"I told you. She's fine."

"Supersweet," Calamity added. "She drew me." She pointed to a childish rendering in crayon of a dark-haired girl with stick arms and legs. Meredith recognized the sunglasses-wearing sun Alice put in almost every picture she drew.

Her skin prickled, eyes fixed on the old woman and her maddening smile. "Why?"

"We'll talk all about that. There's plenty of time." She put the mug to her lips but stopped short. "Oh! I'm so rude. Forgive me. We haven't been properly introduced." She extended her hand, then dropped it, chuckling as her eyes moved over the ropes. "Call me Gina."

"People will come looking for me," Meredith said more convincingly than she felt.

"What people? Your mother?" Her tight smile fell away, and her expression darkened. "Not likely." She stood and squeezed Meredith's shoulders just hard enough to be forceful, on the razor edge of pain. "I want you to know that I'm truly sorry about Judith. We had our differences, of course, but that doesn't mean I wanted to see her dead."

Meredith didn't rise to the bait, no matter how tempting. "I want my daughter."

"You should get cleaned up." She sniffed. "Smells like you might have pissed yourself."

She nodded at Tempest, who yanked the rope, forcing Meredith to her feet, and pulled her toward the back of the house with Calamity trudging behind. Meredith counted three doors off the hallway; which one hid Alice? Tempest opened the first and pushed Meredith inside. "If you gotta do your business, the outhouse is by the garden. I'll take you over after." Meredith realized the bathroom wasn't really a bathroom at all, just a room with a wash basin, a few towels, and more blankets. No window either. Tempest slipped one of Meredith's hands free, expertly tightening the rope around the other. "Two minutes," Tempest said, shutting the door just enough so the rope could slip through. She pulled tight on it, as though to remind Meredith of what she could do.

A small mirror hung from the wall above the basin, cloudy at the edges. Meredith looked like hell, her eyes bloodshot and the fear and confusion boiling inside her written in the lines on her face. An ugly bruise had developed on her chin, and a deep scratch traced a line down her cheek, patchy with dried blood. Keenly aware of the shadows of the sisters' feet just outside the door, she splashed a little of the tepid water on her face. It didn't make her feel any better, just damp.

She tried to come up with a plan, but without knowing where in the house they were keeping Alice, she was at a loss. Or was Alice even in the house? She thought of the lighthouse. Could they be keeping her there? She decided it was best to play along, to conserve what little strength she had for when she found Alice and it came time to fight.

"Time's up!" Tempest pounded on the door. "Out, out. Let's go."

The door flew open before Meredith had a chance to touch it.

"Feel better?" Calamity asked.

Tempest shushed her. "Come on. Mom wants us to show you around."

"The garden?" Calamity asked.

Tempest tweaked Calamity's ear. "Shut up." Then she turned to Meredith. "You're not allowed in the garden."

Meredith had no interest in any garden or anything else on the island. "I want to see Alice. I need to know she's okay."

"Mom already told you the little brat's fine," Tempest said. Again, she tied Meredith's hands behind her back, the knot tighter than before. She led her down the hall and through the kitchen, where Gina hummed over a simmering pot that smelled like onions.

Gina flashed a sharp look at Meredith, all teeth and warning. "If you pull a stunt like you did on my porch," she tossed lazily over her shoulder, "Alice will pay for it."

Calamity practically exploded out the door, skipping into a cartwheel the second her bare feet touched the grass. Tempest scowled and pulled the rope, crunching the bones in Meredith's wrists.

Meredith winced, every nerve on fire as she considered Gina's threat. "Watch it."

"You watch it," Tempest snapped, rewinding the length of rope around her forearm.

Now that she was able to study her up close, Meredith realized why Tempest had so easily overpowered her. Meredith had retained some of her strength from her swimming days, but Tempest was built like a boxer, ropy muscles hidden beneath a thin cotton dress.

Maybe it was Tempest who'd beat the hell out of Art. He was an old man and would have been no match against someone with as much strength and aggression as Tempest. Meredith imagined Calamity at the front door, all goofy smiles and *aw, shucks* while Tempest snuck up behind him, fists raised. Was it Calamity or Tempest who'd carried Alice out of the house? Had they tied her up the way they tied Meredith? Were there bruises all down her body from being thrown around like an animal?

"This is our goat!" Calamity leaped over the fence with all the grace of a newborn colt and stumbled into a broken trot. "His name's Graybeard." Meredith was surprised, and a little disappointed, that the goat didn't immediately kick her. She ground her teeth, growing more and more frustrated with her own body. She tried putting more weight on her left ankle, but pain rocketed up her leg. She sucked in a breath.

"I didn't pick it," Tempest said defensively.

They couldn't have been more than a year apart in age, but Tempest looked at Calamity like a petulant child that needed beating. It seemed to go beyond sibling jealousy. If they'd grown up on this island alone, it was a wonder they hadn't killed each other yet.

"The chickens are Grace and William," Calamity added, still nuzzling the goat. "After Mama's other kids."

Grace and William. The names made an instant connection in Meredith's head. Grace and William Bruun. But Calamity said they were Gina's other children. The woman was old, but not great-great-great-grandmother old. Meredith judged her to be in her eighties, if she was being generous. It was impossible—some kind of weird coincidence.

"Shut up, Cally." Tempest poked a sharp finger in Meredith's shoulder. "Let's go."

They followed the trail around the house, with Tempest pointing out the water pump and the outhouse (and reminding Calamity that it was her turn to till the hole). While the girls bickered, Meredith peered into the woods surrounding the house, looking for trails or clues to the island's size. It was an impossible task, and she gave up quickly. The trees were dense, and she didn't hear many birds, which meant it was too far from larger land to consider as a permanent home. There was an entire archipelago off the mainland, and at first, she considered she might be on one of those islands, but they could be seen from the lighthouse, green mounds in the distance. Wherever they were hiding her daughter, they weren't going to make her easy to find.

She got an idea.

During one of the sisters' brief silences, Meredith asked, "Can I see the lighthouse?"

Even if Alice wasn't hidden in the lighthouse, she could at least try to get her bearings from the top. Knowledge was power. The more she knew about the island, the better chance she and Alice had to escape it.

Calamity brightened. "The lighthouse! Yeah!"

But Tempest was a harder nut. "Mom wouldn't like that."

Meredith looked hard at the girl. "So?" she said, taking a chance.

Tempest's jaw worked, like she was chewing over the idea. Finally, she nodded. "Okay. But if Mom gets mad, I'm telling her it was your idea."

So Tempest wasn't as blindly devoted to her mother's whims as she pretended to be. Meredith thought she could maybe use that to her advantage. "Fair enough."

They walked in a straight line, with Meredith sandwiched between Calamity at the front—whistling and swinging her arms higher and higher with each step—and Tempest scowling at her back. It was hard not to take sides. Calamity was as disastrous as her name implied, but when she wasn't throwing rocks or taunting her from the water, Calamity was kind of sweet. Meredith imagined that was what pissed Tempest off the most. Meredith didn't have personal experience with big-sister syndrome, but she saw it in the kids she taught at the Y. Of the two of them, Tempest was in charge. She was the one Meredith needed to make friends with if she was going to find Alice and get off this island anytime soon. The problem, though, was that Tempest seemed to have to fight harder for Gina's affection, which meant her desire for it was fiercer. That didn't mean she was immune to rebellion. In fact, if she had a chance of turning either of them against Gina, if it came to that, Meredith set her bets on Tempest.

The trail to the lighthouse was more worn than the rest. Twin divots ran along the edges, probably from a wheelbarrow. Meredith tried to reconcile the image of an old woman and two girls carting wood and other materials back and forth and then building the thing itself. That kind of thing took time. Strength. Effort. They'd had help.

Up close, the lighthouse looked only slightly more stable than it had from the boat. The same concrete blocks that made up the trails formed the base, but these were reinforced with heavy wooden beams. Farther up, though, more wood than bricks had been used in the construction. It was shorter than the cape's lighthouse, but not by much. It was a miracle a storm hadn't taken it out by now.

Calamity went straight for the door without waiting for Tempest's approval. Meredith noticed there wasn't a lock. Inside, the place was empty. Hard-packed dirt mixed with crumbled concrete made up the floor, and the stairs wound upward without a rail. Meredith leaned against the wall, stomach flip-flopping with each step as they ascended. Calamity, of course, bounded up like her feet were made of springs.

"Does she ever slow down?" Meredith asked.

Tempest snorted. "No."

"That's got to be hard."

"It's hard on my mom."

"But not on you." Meredith glanced over her shoulder. "You've got her handled."

Tempest seemed to be forcing eye contact. Her jaw worked hard enough to pop. "I know what you're doing."

Meredith's face went hot. "I'm not doing anything."

"You think I'm stupid, that you can just manipulate me to get me to do what you want, but it ain't gonna happen."

"Is that what you told my daughter when she begged you not to take her?"

"What makes you think she could talk?"

Calamity stuck her head out from the light room. "Slow pokes! Come on!"

Tempest shot Meredith one last glare before shoving her onward. Distracted by Tempest's comment and what it could mean, Meredith overstepped and slipped on the stair. With her hands tied she couldn't break her own fall, and for a terrifying instant, she was falling backward, only a few feet from smashing her head open on the concrete. Tempest snatched her by the shirt and pulled her upright, her look of fear almost identical to what Meredith felt.

"Careful," Tempest snapped.

She held tighter to Meredith for the rest of the climb.

The light room wasn't more than ten feet across, and the plastic sheets gave off a hot, chemical stink. The lens at the center of the room was ancient; Meredith could tell by the style and size—too small to light farther than forty or fifty feet out. A sheet, badly dyed red, hung over the lamp. Were they trying to recreate the cape's red light? Why? As far as Meredith knew it was unique to the cape, mostly because the red light didn't do much *lighting* at all. It might have warned passing ships of land, but if they got too close, there was nothing to illuminate the treacherous rocks below. But it wasn't the light Meredith was interested in. She needed to see outside. To try to figure out where they were and how to get home, her escape plan constantly evolving in the back of her mind.

Her breath caught as Tempest led her around the perimeter. Blue, so much blue, and no land to speak of anywhere.

Calamity slipped her arm around Meredith's shoulders. She barely felt it. "Isn't it beautiful?"

She felt sick. Her stomach rolled, and she had to turn away to keep from vomiting. There was nowhere to go. She was trapped. Breathing deeply through her nose, eyes squeezed shut, she leaned against the pedestal holding the lens. She tried to comfort herself with the idea that it was a small island. If she had to search it from edge to edge to find Alice, she could. Once the spinning slowed, she opened her eyes and noticed a framed photograph, perched on a shelf behind the lens. It was a simple frame, but the shelf was decorated with dried roses. A strip of cloth was bound by black ribbon and nestled beside the photo.

She recognized the woman in it. She'd seen the photo before, in a box of her mother's things. A young Regina Holm stood dutifully, proudly, next to a girl with pinned up dark hair, seated with a blanket draped over her legs.

Calamity had followed her to the lens and peered over her shoulder.

"Are you related to her?" Meredith asked, pointing at the photograph.

Tempest snorted. "Are you stupid?"

Calamity laughed. "Silly. That's Mama."

CHAPTER TWENTY-ONE

DIANA

1975

Her daughter was gone. She felt it the same way she'd felt it the morning the letter arrived telling them David was missing. Just because the cord was cut didn't mean a mother quit feeling her children. Harry told her she was being ridiculous, that Judith was a teenager. It was normal for teenagers these days to take off without telling anyone, that they always came back in a day or two. She was being insane. Hysterical.

If she was hysterical, then Harry was a coward, head buried perpetually in the sand.

But who was she to talk?

As a parent, there had been many things Diana had done wrong. Too many. She didn't count the little things, like making Judith cry it out when they were trying to get her to sleep on her own as a baby. She counted the stuff that mattered. Those were the things she'd messed up the most. Like when David's number was pulled. She should've hidden him. Sent him to Canada. To Mexico. To the moon. Like when Judith started talking about the voice in the water and Diana said nothing. Told Judith *she* was insane. Hysterical.

She should have said something then. Done something. Instead she'd pushed her daughter away, hoping, praying, that the curse would pass her by. She should have known they couldn't hide forever.

Whatever happened next, Diana deserved it.

One in the morning and Diana couldn't sleep. The red light from the lighthouse brushed her bedroom windowsill. Rose petals and blood. She'd never understood the red. She supposed her ancestors thought red was softer on the eyes. After all, it was them who had to sleep with the light's constant touch. She turned over, away from the window, but Harry's face was too close, breathing her air, touching her body. Suddenly she couldn't stand to be in the room with him, with the red light, with the shadows. Everything was all too loud, all too quiet.

She climbed out of bed, not bothering with a robe or shoes. It was that damned light. If she shut it off, maybe she would get some sleep. There was no reason to keep it on now her children were gone, out of the realm of her protection.

It was a cool night. She hugged her arms around herself, suddenly wondering if, wherever Judith was, she had a sweater. She'd seen Judith walking around wearing David's old jean jacket. It suited her. They would have been good friends, Diana's kids, if they'd been allowed to be the grown versions of themselves together. She should have known better. She'd been selfish, thinking she could have her life, their lives. And now she was being punished for it.

David. Jon. Now Judith.

The stone steps were cold under her bare feet, sand and salt rubbing between her toes. A sudden memory came of her mother, that day in the gray room. How different might her life have been if she'd changed her mind and continued to visit? How many fewer lies would she have told? How much sooner would she have seen the girl's wraithlike face in the waves and discovered the danger plaguing her, her child, was so much more than she thought?

At the top of the stairs, Diana let herself into the light room. The red light brushed over her brighter, louder here, and she flinched away from it. A shadow streaked across the corner of her vision, and for a moment, she forgot why she came up.

She peered through the window, watching the waves lap the beach and the rocks. She hated the way the red light made it all look so sinister. She remembered when she was little, when the beach was just the beach and shells didn't speak and she could open her bedroom window without fear.

When she spoke, her breath fogged the glass. "Do you even know what you've done?"

God, the light. All she could see was red.

At the control panel, she flicked a switch and the mechanism died with a groan, shadows of the red light lingering in the corners of her eyes.

There, she thought. *That's better.*

But she didn't head down the stairs, back to her bed to lay in the dark.

She went to the window, to the catwalk.

The air was dense, tinged with a scent like sour wine. It was like a shroud had been draped over the stars, their muted light dissipating in the hungry dark. She could hardly see the water, the waves rippling shadows, but the rush and pull was hypnotic, and she felt herself leaning slightly over the rail to better hear it.

From this height, she felt like she could reach out and touch the edge of the world. She used to dream about sailing the ocean, skirting the edge of the horizon and peering over the side to see water fall into space. Silly, but the thought used to make her smile. There'd been so much she was going to do. So much she was going to see. But the cape, and her children, had kept her rooted.

Now?

Now the ocean was an oversized tub of water with ugly things lurking beneath. The edge of the world was farther, more impossible to reach. And her kids? What would she do now that there was nothing—almost nothing—to root her? She was an untethered balloon, full of hot air and fit to burst.

She closed her eyes and rocked to the sound of the waves until a small voice broke through, a tickle in her ear.

I'm scared, Mommy.

It was like the wind had broken open her daughter's voice and tried it on, but it was too big, flopping and slapping. Like being covered in a blanket, everything seemed to fall away and her body felt heavy. Like that moment just before falling into a deep, restful sleep. *That's it,* she thought. *I'm asleep. I must be dreaming.*

"Don't be scared," Diana said. "I'm here."

The voice had sounded so far away, farther than the edge of the horizon. She needed to get higher. She needed to see her.

She climbed up on the rail, gripping steel lines to keep steady.

"Should we sing a song?" The metal rail digging in her feet and the sand shifting below, Diana started to hum. She wasn't a good singer, but she'd always sung to her kids. The usual childish melodies but also whatever was popular on the radio. She sang to them to soothe their ouchies and comfort them when they discovered how unfair the world could be. She sang so they would know she would always be there for them.

Not-Judith sang too, but it was the wrong song with wrong words, and Diana hummed louder, shaking her head when she got caught up in the other melody. The wind picked up, pushing her precariously forward, but she held tight to the lines even as they wobbled.

This isn't real, she thought suddenly. *It's all in my head. I'm not here. I'm in my bed and the wind is my husband's breath and my daughter is asleep in the other room, and somewhere, someway, my son is sleeping too.*

Like magic words, as soon as she thought them, the singing stopped and the breeze stilled. Diana closed her eyes and smiled. *There,* she thought. *That's better.*

She stepped forward.

And fell.

CHAPTER TWENTY-TWO

JUDITH

APRIL 1975

The drive was quiet, their mouths sticky with donut glaze. Judith didn't explain what'd changed her mind about leaving Cape Disappointment, and Cassie didn't ask her to. Judith didn't know where exactly in California they were going or what waited for them there, and for the first hundred or so miles, it didn't matter. *Away* was all she'd asked, and Cassie had delivered. Judith hadn't heard the ocean in hours—so why did she feel worse?

Even before the curse found her, the ocean had left its mark on Judith. A moon-shaped scar on her knee from the time she fell in a tide pool, catching the edge of a sharp rock. A chip in her front tooth from the time she tried boogie boarding and caught a dip in the sand. After hours of being kept away from it, she began to feel the ache of the distance in her scars, behind her eyes, in her teeth. Liza's voice, the irresistible pull of her, however, was conspicuously absent. Would distance be enough?

They crossed the Oregon state line at about midnight, after Cassie's car overheated, and they spent the better part of an hour lugging gallons of water from a gas station to pour into the radiator.

"Sorry," Cassie said. Her first word in forever.

Judith shrugged, then tossed the empty jug in the back seat. As long as they kept moving.

She fell asleep almost immediately after they got back on the road, her head wrapped in her brother's jean jacket and wedged between the seat and the window. For the first time in weeks, she didn't dream.

Cassie woke her up a short time later with an elbow to her ribs. "I'm exhausted. We need to stop."

Judith rubbed her eyes, trying to focus on the dashboard clock. How far from the cape were they? How long had she been asleep? A feeling deep in her bones urged her to keep moving. "I could drive."

"Nuh-uh. Only one person can handle Sheila." Cassie gave the dash an affectionate slap. "Besides, you need rest too."

"I was sleeping. I'm fine."

Cassie's face went blank. "You are definitely not fine." Then, "You talk in your sleep, you know."

Judith tried to keep the worry off her face. "What did I say?"

But Cassie was already halfway out of the car. "Come on. We'll stay here, get some sleep, and finish the drive tomorrow."

The motel room was small, but there were two beds and a TV, and Judith had to admit she needed the break. She couldn't remember the last time she'd spent more than an hour in a car, and her knees creaked as she stretched out on the bed.

Cassie ordered them a pizza using the same credit card she'd used to book the room (slipping it back into her pocket before anyone, Judith included, could get a close look at it), and they ate in relative silence by the soft glow of the television. Judith kept stealing glances at Cassie, wanting to know why she'd agreed to take Judith along when it was clearly already costing double what she'd probably planned on spending on the move. They hadn't talked about where, or if, Judith would stay with Cassie. If she'd be left to her own devices once they'd gotten to California. Judith couldn't even remember if Cassie had ever mentioned a city. Would they pick one on the map or stop when the mood moved them?

As soon as the pizza was gone, Cassie curled up on top of the covers and fell asleep.

Judith watched TV on mute, not wanting to disturb Cassie but unable to go back to sleep. The motel room smelled like old food and cigarettes, and her stomach ached from the greasy pizza, and every time she closed her eyes, she saw the ocean.

Maybe she'd made a mistake.

No.

This was the right thing to do. She leaned her head against the headboard and tried to think of anything else. Impulsively, she pulled the bird figure from her pocket and smiled. She liked Jackie. A lot. Enough to lose her virginity to him and not tell anyone—Cassie included—about it. Part of her wished she'd been brave enough to ask him to come with her.

She blinked away tears and tucked the flat pillows around her body. She'd just started to drift when a sharp, electrical zip startled her. The television screen flashed bright, then died, leaving a static crackle in the air.

A loaded silence filled the room, and it occurred to Judith that neither of them had bothered to check the bathroom or the one closet when they came in. *Stop it*, she thought. *You're weirded out because you're in a new place. You're being paranoid.*

Still, she strained to hear movement or breathing but couldn't hear anything above Cassie's soft snores. Without the light from the television, the room was dark, casting malevolent shadows over the walls.

The wallpaper looked ancient, coming away from the top of the wall in places. It reminded her of the wallpaper at the house on the hill, and *yes*, the longer she looked at it, the more she realized how similar they were. Nearly identical, with vines that trembled the harder she looked at them. She wanted to reach for the lamp, to mess with it until the bulb flickered to life, but her arms were frozen to her sides. She stared wide-eyed at the corners, where shadows dripped like water down the walls.

She stood, barely in control of her body, and walked across the room and put her hand on the wall. It was cool to the touch. Damp.

Climbing on the nearby desk, she picked at the loose bit of wallpaper. It came away easily. She climbed down, still clinging to the paper, peeling it away inch by inch. Water dribbled from the edges, and the smell of salty sea air permeated so dense it made her eyes burn. With her heart in her throat, she pulled the last of the paper away, releasing a deluge of rot.

Liza, with her coal-black eyes and faded face, was waiting for her.

"Judith!"

Judith clawed at the air, Liza fading with every blink. She finally fully opened her eyes, buried under pillows. Her hand ached, and when she opened it, she saw the bird figure had cut into her palm.

"Judith." Cassie yanked the pillows away from Judith's face. "You okay?"

Judith nodded. "Bad dream."

"I can see that." Then, brightening, "Look."

She tossed a newspaper on Judith's lap. *The Oregonian.* The headline read "Saigon surrenders to Viet Cong, ending 30-year war in Indochina."

"We did it. We ended the war." She smiled wider than Judith had ever seen. "And Mom thought it was a waste of time. Can't wait to rub that in her face."

The war was over. Did that mean the search for her brother—his body— would be over too? Would they never find him? Would Judith and her parents never know what happened?

Judith nodded at the desk. "You think that phone works?"

"Maybe. You change your mind?"

"No. I just…I think I should call my mom."

Judith felt like garbage disappearing without telling anyone. Mom was probably worried, probably terrified. What kind of daughter was she, taking off like that, knowing everything they'd been through with David, whatever her intentions?

After some complicated bashing and mashing of numbers to get an outside dial, Judith called her house, but no one picked up. She hung up and tried again.

"Hello?" It was her dad, his voice harried. Probably run in from the shed.

"Dad? It's me."

"Jesus Christ, Judith. Where the hell are you?"

"I just wanted to make sure you guys knew I was okay. Did you see the paper?"

"Paper? Judith—wherever you are, you have to come home, okay?"

She could already feel her resolve waning. It might have been her imagination, but she swore she could hear the water through the phone. "Can I talk to Mom? I need to tell her something."

The scrape of wood on tile. Dad had sat down. Her stomach clenched.

"Dad? What is it?"

"Mom's in the hospital. I woke up in the middle of the night and she was gone and my first thought…" He sniffed. She could almost see him shaking his head, putting his mind to rights before continuing. "She was barely breathing when I found her." Then, "Please, Judith. Just come home."

———

Judith was sitting on the bed, backpack at her side, when Cassie came back from checking them out of the motel.

"I didn't tell him about the phone call," she said absently, "so we'd better scoot before he tries to charge me for it." Finally, she looked at Judith, and her face fell. "What happened?"

"I have to go back. My mom…"

"Okay…"

"It didn't help." Judith shoved her fists into her eyes. *I left, so Lizzie went after Mom to get to me.* "It's never going to stop, is it? She's never going to leave us alone."

Sighing, Cassie sat next to Judith. "You're sure there's nothing I can say that will change your mind? To make you stay away?"

Judith shook her head.

Cassie rubbed her face. She looked hard at Judith, and then her expression fell. Resigned. "Her name was Liza Downing. I'm pretty sure."

I know, Judith thought. "You lied. You told me her name was Lizzie. Why?"

"Liza. Lizzie. Same, same. I told you. They're all the same." She pointed at Judith. "And I didn't lie. I wouldn't lie to you."

"You didn't tell me, though. Why are you just telling me now?"

"Words have power. I figured if I could warn you away without a ton of specifics, you might have a shot."

Judith shook her head. "It wasn't your job to make me leave. I didn't *want* to leave."

"Look around you. You're the one who asked to come along, right? I didn't drag you."

"I know that."

"So then why are you biting my head off?"

"Because it obviously didn't make a difference. I just want to *understand.*"

Cassie looked her up and down and seemed to come to a decision. "Fine. On your head be it, then." She patted her pockets, probably looking for a cigarette, then cursed when she came up empty. "Remember how I said the house belonged to a relative?"

"The witch."

"Yeah. She was also your great-great-grandmother's best friend. Or the closest thing to a best friend, I guess. I can't promise the feeling was mutual. I only have her journal to go by."

Judith hesitated a beat. "I know."

Cassie frowned. "How?"

"Your journal." She looked down, shrinking under Cassie's gaze. "I'm sorry. I just…I needed to know what was happening. I needed to know how to stop it, and you weren't giving me anything. No one was."

"Because I don't know if you *can*." She hesitated, and it was like leaning over a precipice. "A few days before we met, I read about something that happened with Constance and Regina—your family's Regina—and a niece named Liza. Constance doesn't go into a lot of detail, but Liza was killed. Regina claimed it was an accident, but the way Constance wrote about it, it didn't seem like she bought it. Regina dumped Liza's body into the ocean only to disappear herself a few days later."

Judith's whole body went cold. "And you think—"

"I don't think anything. But Constance thought the way it all happened, how Regina was so quick to make it all go away…it was unsettling. That was the word she used. Liza would be *unsettled*."

"But why me? Why my family?"

"Regina's dead. Who else is she supposed to torment?"

"That's not funny."

"I didn't mean it to be."

"Why didn't you tell me all of this before?" Judith stood over her, fuming. "My mom could have died!"

Cassie's face reddened. "I told you. I was protecting you. For a long time no one told me anything either. Not about Constance or the real actual power she had. I could read between the lines of her journal—she'd participated in whatever charm or magic came before Liza's death. What if it was her conjuring that turned Liza into…something else? I thought if I kept to myself, kept Liza to myself, history wouldn't repeat itself." She reached for Judith's hand, but Judith pulled away. "Your dad buys flowers for your mom from us every year. My mom and her are practically friends. I mean—"

"Who cares about flowers? This is my life! My family!" She started pacing, her heart pounding in her throat.

"It's my family too! True or not, they came for Constance that night. The same people who'd gone to her for help decided she was the villain in a story they wrote as they went along. Regina was the wife of a wealthy business owner. It was *his* daughter, *his* niece that went missing. He wouldn't even consider the possibility that the two were connected, claiming he'd found some kind of cursed object in his things." Cassie stood. "Times haven't changed all that much, you know. Mom doesn't *just* sell flowers to the old ladies whose husbands like to ogle other women on the beach. If the women in your family start dropping dead again, who do you think the torch-and-pitchfork crowd are gonna go after? You? Or the descendants of a witch they all like to pretend didn't scare the shit out of them?"

"When I saw that drawing, you should have told me right then."

"Told you what?" Cassie shoved Judith back. "That I caught your crazy mother trying to claw through the wall with a pencil? Please."

Judith stepped backward, backpack hitting the television. Her mother?

"You're lying."

"I told you. I wouldn't lie to you."

"But that doesn't…"

Didn't what? Make sense?

If she stopped to think about it, she knew that wasn't true. She thought of that day in the kitchen, when her mother slipped up, all but told Judith she believed Liza was out there. She'd been terrified.

But then she'd taken it all back. She'd lied. Denied all of it to Judith's face even though the proof was there. Even though she'd *seen*. Even though Liza killed Uncle Jon. Was trying to kill Judith. She'd been keeping all of it to herself. Ignoring it. Ignoring the voice. The pull. How long could she keep that up before—

Your mom's in the hospital.

"I have to go home," Judith said.

"And I suppose you expect me to drive you." Cassie shook her head. "Forget it. I told you, you needed to get out of there, and now you know I wasn't bullshitting you. You go back, you're all but guaranteeing you'll die."

"Maybe. But if she's coming after my family and I'm the last, then maybe that's exactly why I should go back."

She left Cassie standing speechless in the room and headed toward what she hoped was the main road, then hiked a few hundred feet, far enough she couldn't see the motel anymore. Stomach and heart steeled, she stuck her thumb out at every passing car.

One way or another, she thought, *this ends with me.*

———

It might have been the flaming rage on her face that kept roaming hands from her thighs, but she managed to hitchhike from McMinnville to Ilwaco, just outside Cape Disappointment, without incident. Halfway there she thought she saw Cassie's car following behind, but deep down Judith knew she was on her own.

In Ilwaco, though, the only people willing to slow down for her outstretched thumb were men who stared too hard at her before hitting the brakes. She didn't have far to go, so she went into a diner and called for a cab. She didn't have the money to pay for the fare, but she'd worry about that when she got to the hospital.

They pulled up at the entrance to the ER, and Judith bolted, tossing a promise over her shoulder to be right back. The cab driver cussed her out, but she was barely listening. The smell of antiseptic seeped through the hospital doors, turning her stomach. *Mom's going to be okay*, she thought, and hesitated a beat before going inside.

At the desk, she gave her mother's name and waited an agonizing second for the bored-looking nurse to give her a room number. Through the double doors, she dodged medicine carts and strung-out patients dragging IV racks and scowling orderlies she kept bumping into because she was too busy worrying.

The door to her mother's room was open, but she didn't immediately go in, too afraid of what she would see. She listened to the efficient beep and whirr of medical equipment for what felt like a long time, until her legs were numb from the knees down.

A doctor paused in front of her, clipboard held tight against her chest. She frowned at Judith. "Can I help you?"

Judith's mouth was dry. She tried to swallow and coughed. "My mom," she croaked.

The doctor nodded. "You can go in if you like."

"Okay," Judith said, but didn't move.

On this side of the curtain, she could pretend her mother's injuries were minor, that she could come home today if she wanted. Once she went inside, though...

"That you, Judith?"

Drawn in by her dad's voice, Judith finally walked through the door and pushed aside the curtain.

Dad sat on a chair beside the bed where her mother lay, barely recognizable beneath the gauze and tubes and tape holding everything in place. Judith held her breath as her eyes moved over her mother's body. Most of the blood had been wiped away from her face, but there were still some flecks of it in her hair and on her earlobe. One eye was swollen, a purple egg. Her skin was ashen, and if not for the gentle rise and fall of her chest, Judith would have thought she was dead.

Dad reached across the bed for Judith's hand, but Judith couldn't look away from her mother. Shame and guilt moved through her, a black sludge that clung to her heart and stomach and lungs. She could barely breathe.

She didn't need to ask what happened. The details didn't matter. What mattered was that she was wrong. If Judith tried to run away, Liza would punish her family for it.

"She hasn't woken up yet," Dad said. "But maybe having you here will help. If she hears your voice, maybe…"

Judith shook her head. Took a step away. Liza had gotten stronger since that first time Judith saw her in the water. More powerful. More tangible. Even now Judith could feel her, like a nerve in the back of her head. Did her mother hear her too? Was Liza whispering to her through the haze of unconsciousness? Was it Liza that was keeping her there, drowning in her own mind?

If Judith was dead, would it all go away?

"I can't…" she started, voice breaking.

Dad stood and came around the bed, arms extended, but Judith pulled away.

His shoulders slumped, and he looked fifty years older. "We can get through this. Your mother is strong. She'll pull through. You'll see."

Judith badly wanted to believe it but knew, in the end, it didn't matter. Her mother could wake up tomorrow. Her injuries could heal and she could walk out of the hospital stronger than before, but Liza would be waiting for her. She would be waiting for all of them unless Judith could do something about it.

"I'll be back," she lied as she took Dad's keys from his coat pocket.

He wouldn't need the car anytime soon, she figured. It would take an act of God to pull him from her mother's side.

She drove in a haze, and when the first hint of salty air drifted through the vents, her body lit up, muscles tightening and breath coming in shaky bursts. She kept a death grip on the wheel as she passed the turnoff for home and started up the rocky, unpaved road for the house on the hill.

Over time, Judith had watched Cassie scatter what she'd called "protective charms" around the old house—herb bundles stuffed in nonfunctioning air vents and tied to rafters, bottles of fragrant oil tucked between cushions, red Christmas lights strung over doorways—and though Judith didn't know exactly what they did, or if they even worked, she figured it was better than nothing.

She left the car running and gathered as many of the charms as she could find. She considered leaving a note for Cassie—an apology, an explanation, something—but if anyone would understand what Judith was trying to do, it was her. Besides, she didn't think Cassie would ever come back to the cape and, in fact, hoped she wouldn't. Because if what Judith had planned didn't work, she wanted her friend as far from Liza's grasp as possible.

She brought the charms to her parents' house and scattered them as close to the way Cassie had as she could. She tucked the red Christmas lights behind the curtain rod that hung over her parents' bedroom window, the one with the clearest view of the water, and placed satchels of dried Thalia petals under their pillows.

A small voice told her it wouldn't be enough.

It *had* to be enough.

Casting one last look around, she ran her hands along the walls, as though drawing strength from the memories they held. She tried to focus her mind on all the things she'd done and seen, instead of all the things she wouldn't. She didn't want to die, but she also couldn't face another day, another moment, of seeing the people around her suffer for her mistakes.

She left her dad's car at the house and, careful not to look back, walked stoically up to the house on the hill.

She didn't mean to fall asleep. Judith paced the main room for what felt like hours, flinching at every creak, every groan of the wind through the cracks in the walls, waiting for Liza to come for her. By removing the charms, Judith had hoped to lure Liza to her. To face her on her home turf. But as time passed and the exhaustion of the drive, of seeing her mother in the hospital, weighed her down, Judith settled on the couch, eventually curling up beneath an old blanket that smelled a little of damp and mold.

A loud bang startled her awake. She sat up too quickly, the world a half a beat behind her eyes, and it took a heart-pounding moment for her to locate the source of the noise. The front door smacked the wall, the wind pulling it forward and slamming it back again. The air felt electric charged and made the back of her neck tingle. She hadn't bothered with candles, so the only light came from the sinking sun through the back windows, which cast long-fingered shadows across the room. A salty stink permeated, making her nose and eyes burn.

She stood, and the blanket dropped to her feet.

This is it, she thought, and found that she felt strangely calm.

She could feel the rush of the waves, rumbling through the floor to her feet and up her legs, settling in her belly. With each step, her stomach sloshed and clenched. She expected to hear Liza whispering in her ear, but her voice was conspicuously absent.

Judith pursed her lips and focused on putting one foot in front of the other. Liza may have known Judith was coming, may have been waiting patiently while Judith approached the door like a lamb to slaughter, but this time it was Judith who was in charge. This was her choice, and that made all the difference.

Near the door now, she heard movement just outside. She hesitated, biting back the tremble in her body, and carefully peered out.

Cassie was on her knees a few feet away, streaks of dirt along her legs and on her cheek. She was up against the house, teeth gritted, digging a trench with her hands. As she moved along the side of the house, she dragged a brown bag with her. In every inch she dug, she dropped a few petals from the bag, and then covered them with the soil.

Any relief Judith felt at seeing Cassie was immediately shrouded in worry. No one could be here with her. No one could get in the way.

Judith stormed toward Cassie and kicked the brown bag out of her reach. "What are you doing here?"

Cassie didn't look at her. She pulled the bag back toward her and resumed digging. "Trying to stop you from doing something incredibly stupid." She put a hand up just as Judith started to argue. She shook her head. "I almost stayed in California. Took all of an hour after you left to pack my shit and follow you back. Anyone else, I might have just let it go, but I care about you, Judes. You're my friend. My *best* friend." She wiped her nose with the back of her hand, leaving a smudge of mud. "If I'd known you were going to dismantle months of charm work I might have tied you to the roof of my car and"—she huffed—"driven you to the fucking moon."

Judith took her words in. Swallowed them to drown in the ocean in her belly. "You need to go."

"What I need is a pair of gloves. Some tools. But some people are apparently in a hurry to die, so I guess I'm working with what I've got." She shoved a mound of dirt over a trail of petals and then clawed the ground next to it. "You gonna help or just watch?"

From this vantage, Judith could just see the waves crashing on the rocks by the cove. The water was gray, the foam sickly green. Hazy clouds filled a sky pricked by the bare branches of skeletal trees. She rubbed her arms, trying not to think of how cold it would be. She hoped it would be fast.

She leaned over Cassie's back, wrapping her in a too-tight hug. "You're my best friend too."

Cassie stiffened. "Don't do this."

Judith planted a quick kiss on the top of her head. Cassie grabbed her arms, but the mud between her fingers made it easy for Judith to slip out of her grasp. She took off toward the trail, Cassie shouting after her, eyes fixed on the water. Wind whipped her face and hair, the chill numbing her nose and lips. She was moving too fast through the gravel. She slipped, arms windmilling as she fought to keep herself upright. But she couldn't stop, couldn't slow down, because Cassie wasn't far behind.

As Judith got closer to the beach, the water grew more restless. Waves crashed into the shore, cutting divots in the sand. Gulls circled and dove for fish that had been churned up to the surface, only to drown as the water overtook them.

Whatever bravery she'd found while in the house quickly dissipated. Tears stung her eyes and her heart pounded as she fought against a growing panic, and as the stench of death overwhelmed her, carried by the spray of the waves, she could feel Liza, needlelike, in the back of her head, her voice grating, dragging, excited.

She stopped at the edge of the sand, almost too terrified to take the first step. But then Cassie's voice behind her pushed her forward. She had to do this. For her mother. For Uncle Jon. For everyone. She was the last of Regina's line, the last *daughter*, and with her gone, all this would end. The people she loved would be safe.

She ran for the water, feeling anchored and weightless, relief and dread, all at once. The waves hit her body, and it was like being plunged in an ice bath. Her teeth immediately started to chatter, and her muscles stiffened. But she could feel Liza near, an ice-cold current that surrounded her feet.

A splash behind her made her turn. Cassie lunged at her, wrapping her forearm painfully around Judith's throat. Gasping, Cassie pulled her toward the shore, kicking Judith's legs every time she got enough purchase in the sand to fight back.

"You're not. Doing. This. To me," Cassie shouted with each wave that crashed into them.

Judith scratched at Cassie's arm, but it was like she couldn't feel it, even when Judith drew blood.

Water swirled around them, but Cassie fought hard, finally pulling them both out and onto the sand. She collapsed with Judith on top of her. She trembled, out of breath, and her grip loosened just enough that Judith was able to roll away, but all the adrenaline that'd kept her blood pumping in the icy water was quickly waning. She struggled to her feet, mouth gritty with sand and eyes burning from the salt. With a determined growl, Cassie clasped Judith's ankle.

"Let go," Judith begged.

Cassie's voice was ragged. "Never."

Looking at Cassie, at her torn clothes and bloody scratches down her arm, for an instant, Judith allowed herself to consider the idea that she didn't have to die. If someone was willing to fight this hard for her, didn't they deserve the same from her?

It was an instant she would regret for the rest of her life.

Liza rose from the shallow water in a tangle of seaweed, her skin the gray of the waves, and foam dripping from her black lips. She crawled toward them, impossibly fast, carried by the water as it violently lapped the shore. Frozen, Judith braced herself. Held her breath. But as the wind carried the stink of Liza's breath to Judith's face, Cassie launched herself forward. Still gripping Judith's leg, she pulled, forcing Judith to fall backward, just out of Liza's reach.

Cassie moved toward Liza, arms extended. Judith noticed her fingers and palms of her hands were a deep purple, as though dyed by the Thalia petals she'd been burying. Face pale with terror, Cassie all but collided with Liza and pressed her hands to Liza's face. Liza's mouth fell open wide in a silent scream, but it hardly slowed her down. As Cassie chanted, her words lost in the crash of the waves, Liza ensnared her in her arms.

Judith scrambled toward them, reaching, but before she could get close enough, the waves carried Liza and Cassie away.

Ignoring the pain shooting through her body, Judith ran into the water and dove. She scraped her chin on shell-packed silt but barely felt it. Her heart pounded against her ribs, and the harsh cold was like needles in her ears.

But she wouldn't give up.

She dove and resurfaced over and over, forcing herself deeper, farther each time.

It was supposed to be me.

Sobs rocked her body even as the foam settled and the waves calmed. Soon, the water was still.

Cassie was gone.

No. Judith fought against the ache in her shoulders, each stroke a little harder than the last. If she kept moving, she would find her. *Hold on, Cassie.*

But the rest of her had gone numb. Each movement was mechanical. She felt nothing. She was weightless. She had no body. She was *tired.* So, so tired.

Struggling just to keep afloat, she let the waves carry her out. She drifted in and out of consciousness, eyes only shooting open when water whipped up her nose or in her mouth. Her clothes weighed her down, so she used what strength she had left to slither out of them. Her sweater drifted on the waves like a ghost.

Too cold to move. To think.

A shadow crept slowly beneath her, brushing her feet. Her calves.

I'm here, she thought as the water closed overhead. *Take me. Just give Cassie back. Please.*

Judith drifted down, down, down until...hands on her torso, hot and coarse. They pried her out of the water, but she was too cold, too tired to protest. To fight. They dragged her over the side of a boat.

"Well, well, what a pretty little minnow you are."

And then blackness.

CHAPTER TWENTY-THREE

MEREDITH

It was the eyes that finally convinced her. Regina's eyes in the photograph, piercing and impenetrable, were exactly like the eyes of the woman calling herself Gina. It was impossible, though. Gina didn't look older than eighty; Regina Holm would be well over a hundred. Dust.

Was this woman some kind of lost descendant? Someone obsessed with the curse and the lighthouse? Was that where Alice fit in? Was she trying to recreate something from the past? She thought about the story of the missing girls—Tempest and Calamity looked to be about the right age. Her stomach turned as she imagined some sick play where Gina drowned the two of them for the sake of history. But what about Alice? Meredith's head was spinning trying to make sense of it.

She nodded at the girl in the picture. "Marina, right?"

"Yep." Calamity licked her thumb and wiped a smudge from the frame. "Pretty, isn't she?"

"Sure."

"Almost as pretty as Alice."

Hearing her daughter's name out of her captor's mouth caused physical pain. She thought about breaking the frame, using the glass as a weapon, but even if she managed to get her hands free, Tempest would have her on the ground before she had a chance to touch the thing.

"We should get back," Tempest said.

Meredith turned to the other girl. "Calamity, right?"

Calamity started, thrown by the attention. "Uh-huh."

Meredith had to fight back the urge to scream at her. Calamity looked sixteen or so, but her mannerisms, her behavior, were like a toddler. "You like Alice, huh?"

Calamity smiled. Her front two teeth were crooked. "She's funny."

Eyes burning, Meredith blinked back the tears. "She sure is. Do you know what she named a stuffed octopus her uncle made for her?"

Calamity shook her head, eyes wide.

"Octopussy!"

Calamity threw her head back in a deep belly laugh. Meredith could tell it was forced. She didn't get the joke, but it didn't matter. Calamity wanted to please, and laughing would please Meredith.

Meredith laughed along before adding, "She hasn't gotten to see him all finished, though."

"How come?"

"Because she's here." Meredith spoke slowly. "She's not supposed to be here. You know that?"

Calamity nodded weakly, her fingers tangled together in front of her.

"Enough." Tempest grabbed Meredith's arm, nails digging into the soft part. "Let's go."

Calamity walked behind them on the way back to the little house where

Meredith met Gina. Meredith shot occasional looks over her shoulder only to have Tempest yank her back around.

"What is your problem?" Meredith spat.

Tempest scowled. "You."

"Oh yeah? Let me go then. No more problem."

"Shut *up.*" Tempest pulled Meredith close enough she could smell her stale breath. "Or the next time Alice sees mommy, she'll be a streak in the dirt."

Spittle had gathered at the corner of Tempest's mouth. Meredith almost believed the threat. Almost was enough to keep her mouth shut. For now.

Finally back at the house, Tempest opened the door and Meredith spotted Alice immediately, in the kitchen, standing on a chair, her hands covered in pancake batter. Gina stood over her, arms on either side, caging her in. Directing her. Alice wore clothes Meredith didn't recognize, horribly outdated and too big, falling off a shoulder. The sleeve of her shirt kept dipping into the batter.

Meredith wanted to run to her, to snatch her up and disappear into the woods until she could figure out how to get off the island without the women chasing her, but she knew the second she stepped away from Tempest, Alice could be in danger. There was a large knife sitting on a clean cutting board between them.

Alice finally looked up and smiled with her whole face. Her eyes practically bulged. "Mommy!"

Gina whispered something in Alice's ear, and she shrank, nodding.

"What did you say to her?" Meredith demanded.

"Just teaching the girl some manners. It's rude to yell indoors, isn't it, sweetheart?"

Alice nodded feebly.

Meredith's whole body burned, but she forced herself to remain calm. Tempest was aggressive, but she was predictable. Gina was volatile. Unpredictable. She couldn't risk setting her off. Couldn't risk her hurting Alice. "Everything's going to be okay, kiddo."

Gina's laugh was like silverware clinking on a plate. "Well, of course it's all going to be okay." She poked Alice's side. "She's a big silly, isn't she?"

Alice's shoulders tensed, like she didn't know who to acknowledge. Meredith forced a weak smile to try to put her at ease.

"While Alice and I finish up here, why don't you set the table, Calamity? Tempest and Meredith can have a seat."

Tempest escorted Meredith to a little table with mismatching chairs where they sat, Tempest only releasing Meredith's arm when Calamity laid a fork in front of her.

"You can get rid of the ties," Gina said. "I don't think we'll have a problem." She raised an eyebrow at Meredith, her long fingers digging into Alice's shoulders so hard she winced. "Right?"

Meredith hesitated a beat, letting the threat sink in. She was getting use of her hands back. It was a start. She nodded.

"That's what I thought. Tempest?"

Tempest wasn't gentle about removing the ropes, dragging the barely loosened tie over Meredith's hands. Her wrists popped, and the burn from the rope stung.

Ignoring the pain, she grabbed a fork and held it on its end, the tines upright like a trident.

Alice came to the table carrying a plate of pancakes with Gina on her heels. She set the plate down in front of Meredith, and when her hand came down, Meredith grabbed it and pulled it to her lips. She needed to feel her skin, to know this was real. She was here. Alive.

Gina pulled Alice away and gestured for her to sit next to Gina, on the opposite side of the table. Meredith lifted her leg beneath the table, tapping her toe against Alice's. Calamity sat on Meredith's other side and twirled a strand of Alice's hair around her finger. Alice forced a smile that looked more like a grimace. She was a smart girl, keeping her head down, giving them what they wanted until Meredith could get them out of there.

"Getting along like sisters," Gina observed. "Isn't it sweet?"

Looking at Gina, all Meredith could think about was the photograph. Even as her mind screamed impossible, here was the proof directly in front of her. There was no denying the eyes, the shape of the mouth, the stiff posture. This was no descendant. The resemblance was too perfect. Gina sipped from the steaming mug she brought to the table, meeting Meredith's gaze over the rim. She winked.

"How did you do it?" Meredith asked.

"Well." Gina leaned conspiratorially over the table. "You start with eggs and flour and milk. A pinch of salt. Sugar, of course—"

"Not the pancakes."

Gina raised an eyebrow.

"We went to the lighthouse," Tempest admitted. "She saw the picture."

Gina forked a pancake onto Alice's plate, which she doused in syrup. "I see."

Beside Meredith, Tempest squirmed. For all her bluster, she seemed afraid of getting in trouble with Gina. It made Meredith all the more anxious to get Alice off the island.

Gina continued, "Good picture, isn't it? My favorite, actually." She looked at Meredith with an expression Meredith couldn't quite read. "As for how, I don't know the answer to that. But I have a theory."

Meredith waited for Gina to explain, but she didn't seem in a hurry to tell Meredith anything Gina didn't think she needed to know.

Meredith looked at Alice, who was watching her, face all screwed up with concern. She could only imagine how she looked to her, bruised and beaten.

"Eat, kiddo," Meredith said. "I bet you're hungry." Even though Meredith's stomach was in knots, she forced herself to swallow a bite of the rubbery pancake. It was all the encouragement Alice needed to fall on hers like a starving puppy.

Looking at Gina, Meredith said, "What do you want?"

Ignoring her, Gina stroked Alice's hair. "She reminds me of my daughter. My first daughter. Marina."

Tempest scowled into her plate.

"She was a beautiful girl, with long, dark hair just like this. I used to braid it and twist it into all kinds of beautiful shapes. I bet I could do something lovely with this." She twirled Alice's hair around her finger, then held it in place to admire the effect. "Alice is a bit more energetic than Marina was, but that fades with time and training."

Plastic plates. Plastic cups. Meredith had a fork, but it was unlikely she'd stab it anywhere that'd do any damage before Tempest was on her. "You're not doing anything with Alice, understand?"

"Mom…" Alice wriggled out of Gina's embrace but didn't dare try to leave the table. Whatever Gina had done to her over the last two days had stuck.

"It's okay." Meredith tried to smile. "I'm okay."

She tried to cut another piece of the pancake—just be calm, be normal, keep Alice from panicking until Tempest was just distracted enough—but it was like her arm was made of concrete. Her whole body slowed, her blood turned to sludge, and when she looked up at Gina, it was like her eyes were half a second slower than the rest of her. Her heart fluttered in her chest.

She wobbled a little in her seat. Tempest chuckled.

Gina spread a thick pat of butter on her pancake, glancing up at Meredith with a mix of curiosity and something else. Fear? No. Frustration. "A mild sedative. You'll be fine."

Mild? Meredith rubbed her eyes, but it only made everything swim faster, more out of focus. Bile rose in the back of her throat. She swallowed it down, a hard lump.

"You drugged me."

"To be safe."

"*Safe*," Meredith scoffed.

"The rope was obviously scaring Alice, but I need you compliant."

"I don't..." Meredith murmured. She chewed the inside of her cheek hoping the pain would focus her, but she barely felt it. She couldn't think. It reminded her of the way she'd felt that first day in the lighthouse, outside of her body, out of control. She struggled to keep her words from slurring. "You done this before. To me."

Gina frowned. "No. I haven't."

Meredith nodded. "Yes. In the lighthouse." Realization dawned. "In the water. In the jar." She groaned as a dull thump started in the back of her head. *God, get it together. Just breathe.* What the hell had Gina given her?

"Mommy?" Alice's voice crept toward that pitch that meant she was going to cry. Meredith ached once, hard, like the period at the end of a sentence.

Gina shushed her. "Mommy's fine. She's just sleepy." She stroked Alice's hair, careful eyes still on Meredith. Something seemed to occur to her, and she paused, hand still on Alice's head. "Was it like everything fell away except the sound of the ocean?"

Meredith nodded.

The corner of her mouth twitched. "That wasn't me. That was Liza."

The name rang a faint bell, but it slipped away. "I don't know who that is."

"Of course you do." Gina's eyes flashed. "You've seen her. We all have."

The face in the water. The voice in her dreams. Calamity and Alice wore near twin frowns. Tempest chewed the inside of her cheek.

The temperature in the room dropped.

"Who is she?"

Gina's smile dipped slightly. "We'll get to that." She pushed her plate away. "In all your research—don't look at me like that; Tempest saw Grace's journals in your living room—in all that time, what did you learn?"

Tempest *had* been there that night. Who else? Regina? Calamity? Or someone else? She became fixated on this "someone else" she decided had to exist. Were they here now? What would they do to her? To Alice? Between the drugs and getting the shit kicked out of her, it was a miracle she was upright. She needed to know who the other people were. To know what she was up against.

"Who helped you build the lighthouse?" Meredith asked.

"My dad." Calamity beamed. "He's good at building stuff."

"Quiet, Cally. You're distracting me." Gina focused her intense gaze on Meredith. "I want to know what you know so I can fill in the gaps." She grinned. "I'm getting old, you know. Can't be wasting time retelling stories you've already heard."

"I know you did something to her, and now she wants our daughters. *My* daughter."

Because that was what she'd told herself, left alone with her fear and the water for company. But she'd been wrong, hadn't she? Here was proof. A real person had abducted Alice.

Still, some intrinsic animal instinct had felt the danger each time she walked the shoreline. Still felt it, a red beacon flashing across her mind.

"Crass, but yes. That's correct." Gina tapped the side of her mug with a long red fingernail. Tempest stood and took the mug into the kitchen, where she poured hot water from a pot on the stove into it. She withdrew a blue velvet bag from the cabinet and, from that, pulled a clump of dry petals. Something in Meredith's mind clicked.

"Thalia petals?" Meredith asked.

"For warding off evil," Alice said smartly, a near-perfect parrot of Judith. She caught Meredith's eye and offered a brave smile.

"Smart girl," Gina said.

Thalias at Judith's funeral. Thalias in the house. Thalias in her pocket. Meredith had thought her mother's paranoia would hurt Alice. Maybe it had protected her after all.

After steeping the bundle for several seconds, Tempest scooped most of it out and then topped off the concoction with a heavy glob of honey. She brought it to the table. Meredith didn't realize Gina's muscles were tense until she had the mug in hand and her shoulders dropped and her jaw unclenched.

"I had a friend once," Gina said. "She could do things. Manipulate the natural world in a way no one else could. She taught me about Thalias. About protection."

"You're saying Thalias can protect you? From Liza?" Saying her name felt like a curse.

"Of course not." She sipped her tea. "I'm saying they...help."

As the drugs moved through her system, Meredith's own thoughts became harder to follow. She struggled to cling to reason. For every excuse she conjured for Gina, for the curse, a *but* followed.

None of it explained why Gina had taken Alice.

Meredith stared down at the congealed pancake in front of her, sticky syrup cloudy with the remains of the sedative. "What do you want?"

"A daughter," Gina said simply. "*My* daughter."

Meredith didn't like the way she looked at Alice when she said it.

Gina sighed and continued. "The first thing you need to understand is that none of this—as much as you're all willing to pin the blame on me—is my fault. Liza was nosy and spoiled, and what happened to her was an accident. Pure and simple."

Meredith wondered how many times Gina had told herself the same thing.

"I did what any sane woman would have done. She was my late husband's favorite niece. Preferred her even to his own children, though God knows why." She leaned across the table, unblinking. "He was having an affair. It was clear he was going to leave me—the only question was when. I didn't have much time, and this would have been just the excuse he needed to be rid of me, saving himself the problem of divorce."

"Sounds like you killed her," Meredith said.

"It was an accident! She slipped and broke her neck. It was her own stupidity." Gina huffed. "I cleaned up the mess. That's all. They assumed she ran away. I gave them hope and saved them heartache."

"By dumping her in the ocean, right?"

Scowling, Gina tore the crust from a piece of toast. "No wonder your wife is leaving you. You're so negative."

The shot hit home. "You don't know anything about my life."

"I know more than you think." Gina tossed the crust on the table. "And you're missing the point completely."

"I doubt that."

"The point is that something was taken from me too. Marina was, and still is, the brightest star in my sky. Liza—or whatever twisted thing is left of her—took my daughter, and until recently, I thought I'd never see her again. You ask why I would choose to stay alive when I could just as easily hurl myself off the lighthouse and end my suffering." Her face darkened. "I've spent the last century trapped on this godforsaken island, most of it alone. Before Liza took everything from me, I spent my whole life catering to others. I existed to nurture, to please. I gave everything I had to my husband and children, leaving nothing for myself. By the time I'd come out the other side of the dark hole that was mourning Marina, I had no idea who I was. I thought I could at least count on time to end my misery, but for better or worse, I'm still here. Still suffering. For years I accepted that my life had no purpose. I had nothing to give myself to. But now..." She wrapped her arm around Alice. "Now I have purpose."

On either side of Meredith, Tempest and Calamity squirmed.

Gina continued, "I can see by the way you look at Alice, you know how it feels."

"Because she's *my* child."

"See, that's where you're wrong."

Meredith watched Gina lean closer to Alice, pulling her toward her, angry red nails digging into Alice's delicate skin. Meredith started to stand on shaky legs, but Tempest was quickly on her feet. She brandished the knife from the kitchen, had probably slipped it into the room when she brought in the tea. Her hand twitched, and she ground her teeth. With every breath, she leaned a hair closer to Meredith.

Meredith slowly sat back down, never taking her eyes off the knife. "I'm dying to know what you mean by that." The anger felt good. Cleared her head a little.

Gina kissed the top of Alice's head. "Can't you see it? The resemblance? It's clear her upbringing has dampened her potential, but with the proper mothering, I have no doubt she'll prosper." When Meredith didn't immediately respond, she said, "Alice is my Marina come back to me. I can feel her here. A mother knows."

"You're insane if you think I'm going to just give you my child."

"You're going to give her to me, and you're going to walk away. Start a new life somewhere. Or don't. Throw yourself off a cliff for all I care. Either way, you'll be free of the cape, and I will have my daughter back." She grabbed Meredith's hand across the table and squeezed, crushing her knuckles. "Your choice."

CHAPTER TWENTY-FOUR

MEREDITH

ina whisked Alice from the table, disappearing her into the bowels of the house, claiming Alice needed a nap. "Delicate girls need their rest."

Alice was anything but delicate; still, she looked exhausted. Meredith doubted Alice had slept at all while under Gina's thumb. She hoped that in knowing Meredith was here, Alice might get some sleep. If their escape came down to a run or a swim (Alice was just as good as Meredith), she'd need it.

"She won't hurt her," Calamity said once Gina had gone. "She loves Alice."

"She threatened to kill me," Meredith said.

"Yeah," Tempest added, "she'd kill you. Didn't say anything about hurting the brat."

Calamity flinched. "She's not a brat. I like her." She looked at Meredith. "I really do."

Meredith lifted her legs, one then the other, testing herself. How long would these drugs last? "If you like her, then you need to bring her to me and help us get out of here." She turned to Tempest, who was fingering the knife. "It's clear you're not happy about me or Alice being here, so why go along with it? Why do something you know deep down is wrong?"

"Mama needs us," Calamity said weakly. "She needs Marina back."

Tempest remained silent.

Gina returned, wiping her hands on her skirt. She paused at the threshold, taking in the scene. "Don't stop talking on my account."

Meredith tried to stand. Her legs seemed to comply, but her head spun, forcing her back down. "Where's Alice?"

"Sleeping," Gina said. "Finally."

"I won't give you what you want."

Gina seemed nonplussed. "Of course you will."

"She's my *child*, not a thing to be given away."

Tell that to Kristin, a small voice goaded. *Tell that to the mirror.*

How many nights did she stare into it and wish she hadn't agreed to become a mom? How many booze-fueled escape plans did she hatch only to bury them under playdates and chocolate chip pancakes in the sober light of day?

"Trust me. It'll be better for the both of you." She smiled sadly. "I could just… keep her. Pump you full of that sedative and dump you out in the middle of the ocean."

Meredith's breath caught.

"But that's not the way I want our relationship to start. Alice has to trust me. To do that, she has to hate you." She paused a beat. "If you give her up, Alice lives a perfectly happy life here with me, you move on, and everyone gets what they want." She smirked. "Almost everyone."

"You have your own children," Meredith said. "You can't—"

Gina brushed her off with a wave. "Not relevant."

Tempest didn't look away from the table, her back ramrod straight.

"Doesn't seem like the thing you ought to say in front of your children."

"Sweetheart." Gina strode toward Meredith, taking her hand. Gina's was cold and papery. An old woman's hand. "Considering our situation, I don't think you're in a position to dole out parental advice. After all, you're the one who was fucking some woman on the beach when you should have been protecting your child."

Meredith stiffened.

"So you see, in a way, I've done you a favor, showing you your faults. A good mother does that, you know." She paused. "Judith..." Stroking Meredith's arm, she sighed. "Judith wasn't made for motherhood. I saw that from the beginning. Too selfish. Too much going on in that head of hers. And her obsession with that poor dead girl... It was sad to witness. Truly."

Who was she to say anything about Meredith's mother? How did she know her? "Mom did the best she could."

Gina helped Meredith to her feet. The room spun but slowly settled. She wobbled a little to give the impression the sedatives were still in full force, but she must have not ingested as much as they'd thought. *A little longer,* she thought. Arm in arm, Gina escorted Meredith to the living room. "Sit," she ordered.

The knife flashed in the corner of her eye. Meredith sat.

How long before Gina stopped trying to convince her to give up Alice and decided to kill her instead?

"As I was saying," Gina continued. "Motherhood. Judith wasn't meant to be a mother, but that didn't stop her from stealing a child." She leaned over Meredith's shoulder and grinned. "That's you, dear."

Meredith shook her head. "No."

"She was impulsive, so it shouldn't have surprised me. It was the betrayal that hurt most."

"Are you trying to say I'm your—"

Gina laughed. "Oh goodness, no. Absolutely not. I mean, look at you. Those eyes." She mimed a shudder. "But Judith and I had an...understanding. She betrayed me."

"I don't get it. My mom—"

"You are blood of her blood. Yes. But technically, you belonged to the both of us."

"What does that even mean?"

"Judith and I made a deal. Once she gave birth, you would save us from Liza once and for all." Gina crossed her legs. Leaned forward. "But as I said, she betrayed our deal. Stole you away, leaving me here. Alone."

"She didn't even like me," Meredith murmured.

"Of course she didn't like you. Saving you meant putting her own life at risk. Others' lives." Gina ran her fingers through Meredith's hair, scraping her nails along Meredith's scalp. "I can't imagine how she felt at the end. How she must have resented you."

"She died," Meredith shot back, almost believing it, "because she cared. Because she wanted Alice to be safe."

"But she wasn't safe, was she? Not until now. *You* never were."

How many nights had she lain awake, the ocean in her head whispering to her? How many times had she toed the surf and felt a pull on her heart? She remembered the night after Alice was born, a night she'd pushed to the depths of her memory. Alice still in her plastic bassinet and fresh stitches between Meredith's legs, she climbed to the roof, like she could hear the sound of the waves all the way from Arlington. It was the only time she ever seriously considered leaving Alice behind. If she dove into the deepest, darkest parts of herself, Meredith knew Gina was right. In that deepest, darkest part, she'd always known. There was no escape.

But that didn't mean she was going to give Alice up. Alice was *hers*, goddamn it.

"You can't have her. I don't care what comes after you or me."

Fingers still in Meredith's hair, Gina tugged Meredith's head back, making her neck pop. "Judith gave up. I won't."

"Why even ask? Why not just kill me now?"

"Because Alice and I need time to get back to the mainland. Liza is out there somewhere, looking. Waiting. She'll find her way here eventually, and when she does, she can have you, and then Alice and I will live happily ever after."

"And your other daughters?"

Gina's lips set in a tight line. "Insurance."

"Mama?" Calamity stood in front of Meredith, head bowed. "Graybeard needs to get milked."

"So milk him," Gina snapped.

"Last time I did it alone, he kicked me."

"So take Tempest with you."

"She'll just let him do it." Sheepishly, her eyes found Meredith's. "Can Meredith come with me?"

Sighing, Gina released her hold on Meredith's hair. Meredith's head throbbed, and she felt her heartbeat in her throat.

"Fine," Gina said, rounding the couch to look Meredith in the eye. "I suggest you use this time to pray to whatever god you believe in. From what I understand, drowning is very unpleasant."

She didn't blink, matching Gina stare for stare. As far as Meredith was concerned, the only people walking away from anything would be herself and Alice.

———————

While Calamity milked the goat—spraying her shoes more than the bucket—Meredith leaned against a gate post. She could hold herself up now, and when she turned her head, the nausea wasn't totally overwhelming. She watched Tempest closely, looking for any sign that she could tell the effects were starting to wear off, but Tempest looked almost bored, peeling the skin off an overripe orange. Meredith wondered if the sedative was a tool Gina had used before. If she'd used it on Tempest.

"I take it you're not going to help," Meredith said.

"Tempest never helps," Calamity said.

"Shut up, Cally," Tempest said half-heartedly. She peered briefly up at Meredith. "You too." She flashed the kitchen knife to make her point.

The more Tempest brandished the knife, the more convinced Meredith became she'd never use it. She couldn't risk it, though. Not while they were keeping Alice away from her. Still, it was clear the relationship between Tempest and Gina was on shaky ground. Maybe she could play that to her advantage. "Must feel like shit knowing your mother doesn't care about you."

Tempest didn't look at her. "Shut up."

"What do you think she'll do after she gets rid of me? Think she wants you sticking around, ruining her *happily ever after*?"

"Stop," Calamity whimpered.

Meredith ignored her. "Well? What do you think? How long before it's your bodies she's dumping in the water?"

Tempest threw the orange, missing Meredith by a mile. She stood, shaking. "I heard her say she was thinking of burying Alice in a box in the garden to weaken her lungs. To make her more like Marina." Tempest smirked. "I bet it'd hurt."

"I'm sure you'd love that," Meredith said, despite the image Tempest's words conjured. She swallowed it back. "You don't want Alice here any more than I do."

"You don't know anything."

"Mama would never do that," Calamity said, wrapping her arms around her middle. "She wouldn't hurt her."

"Stop defending her, Cally!"

Being with them only a few hours, Meredith knew Calamity would never stop defending her mother, just as Tempest would never stop doing what her mother wanted, regardless of how she felt. Meredith recognized herself in both of them. She'd spent her entire childhood behaving like Calamity, loving regardless of how much love she got in return. Meredith had been lucky; she'd had her stepdad to fill in the gaps. But he couldn't always be around, a buffer between Meredith and her mother, and that was when the Tempest inside her came to the forefront.

"You shouldn't say things like that about Mama," Calamity said. "It's not right."

"Not right?" Tempest laughed. "Please. Honestly, Cally, you can be so stupid sometimes."

"I'm not stupid."

Face red and mouth stretched into a maniacal kind of grin, Tempest turned to Meredith. "She wasn't always like this, you know. Cally. She was smart. She could read the ocean better than even Mom could. But the more time me and Cally spent on the water, the more the shadows came around, the harder it was to stay away. We had each other, though, so the days when we had no choice because we needed food or supplies, we went together, to keep an eye on each other. One day, Mom was double-checking everything we'd traded. Sometimes we got stiffed, and by the time we got back to the island, it was too late, too much of a waste of gas to turn around and try to make it right. I looked away for one second, and when I looked back, I saw Cally wobble in the boat, her face all slack like she'd been hit. Mom stood there by the dock, stone-faced and ugly." Tempest's voice cracked. "Didn't move when Cally walked herself right off the boat. She'd heard a voice like Mom's telling her to drown herself. I know. I've heard it.

"Mom didn't bother trying to save her. She said once Liza was done with

Cally, there'd be quiet for a while. She was going to let Cally die." Tempest shook her head. "I went in after her, but it took so long to find her, she was half-drowned. I got her breathing, but she didn't wake up for two days. When she did, she was like this." She pointed to Calamity, on the ground now, rocking with her knees in her chest. "So, yeah, you're right. I don't want you here. But it's not because of Alice. It's because every time I look at you, I remember that thing is out there somewhere just itching to pick us off. And if getting Marina back, in one form or another, means Mom will leave us be so I can take Cally and run away, I'm willing to do whatever it takes to make it happen."

"Is that why you come to the cape?" Meredith asked. "To get away from her?"

Tempest looked away. "I don't have a choice. It's the Thalias. She needs them. They don't grow good here. Too much sand."

"Why not just let her die? Refuse to go?"

"She's my mother."

Meredith reached out to her, tried to touch her. "I get it. I do."

"Don't," Tempest said, flinching. "You're not me, and I'm not you. I should've killed you the second I saw you. Tossed you over the side of the boat."

"You didn't, though."

Tempest sneered. "Want to try again?"

Meredith shook her head. Turning her back on Tempest—the memory of the knife tracing chills up her back—Meredith crouched next to Calamity, swallowing the nausea and the bile, and gently stroked her hair, shushing her. It was thin and brittle but a beautiful chestnut color that reminded her of Alice's when she was first born. It had darkened as she got older.

"Don't touch her," Tempest said, but didn't move to try to stop her.

"It's okay," Meredith murmured in Calamity's ear. Her own eyes burned and her heart ached. Whether it was for Calamity, Tempest, or herself and Alice, she didn't know. As she and Calamity rocked in unison, Meredith struggled to reconcile the impossibility of everything she'd learned with all that she felt. With all that she knew, deep down, to be true. She wouldn't leave Alice no matter what Gina said. But how was she supposed to get them off this island and safely across the water, back to the cape? Three generations of women, all trapped together on the same small island. Three daughters, exposed and vulnerable. By being here, they were drawing Liza to them.

On Calamity's other side, Tempest kissed her sister's cheek before prying Meredith's arms away. "She's fine now. Leave her alone."

They weren't far from the beach; even if she couldn't see the water, she still heard a boat's engine getting louder.

Calamity's eyes brightened. She sniffed and wiped the tears off her cheeks. "Dad's home!"

Despite Tempest's protests, Calamity dragged Meredith to the dock to meet the boat, which was still quite a ways out. The boat's engine roared like a hurricane, spewing smoke from the exhaust.

"Something happened," Tempest said, frowning. She carried her worry in her fingers, twisting and pinching them while she waited at the edge of the dock.

Clouds had gathered while they worked, threatening a storm. Meredith could smell it on the wind, the damp of the impending rain and static. She worried about the little house—would it be safe? Would Alice be scared? Fear prickled the skin on the back of her neck. What if it was more than a storm? What if Liza had already found them?

Calamity pulled her toward the end of the dock, whimpering under her breath. The stench of the exhaust was getting worse, laced with something rotten underneath. The water was eerily still and gray. But seeing it pulled at something in the back of her throat. The taste of salt filled her mouth. She tried to swallow, gagging. She shot a look at Tempest. Her lips were pursed, and her hands were fists at her sides. Did she feel it too?

Another step and Meredith reeled back from whatever sharp thing she stepped on. Calamity didn't notice, too worried about the approaching boat. Meredith looked down and her breath caught. It was Alice's shell.

She snatched it up before the other two looked back and stuffed it in her pocket where it practically vibrated. She'd had it with her when she chased Tempest off the cape, but lost it somewhere between getting in the boat and being towed here. It was impossible for the shell to just happen to be on Regina's dock, waiting for her. Someone had put it there. A message? A threat? She eyed the water warily, heart skipping with each splash and bubble.

The boat finally reached the dock, and at first, she thought it was the drugs, that she was hallucinating or something. But a part of her felt vindicated. And worried. And very, very angry.

"Daddy!" Calamity said.

Vik.

The realization trickled through her body like ice water in her veins. It wasn't Calamity and Tempest who had assaulted Art and abducted Alice. It was Vik.

He wore a self-satisfied smirk, as unsurprised to see Meredith as she was to see him. He yelled something over his shoulder she didn't hear, and before she could process the implication—someone *else* was in the boat with him—a mop of brown hair came into view. Her heart sank as she realized it was Bobby tying the rope that would anchor them to the dock. Bobby, who'd spent so much time with Art, with Alice. The world seemed to close in around her. All she could see was red.

All that bullshit about helping her mother, wanting to help her. The fucking *lasagna.* How long had they been planning this? How many times had he looked at Alice with hunger behind his eyes? She blinked away angry tears thinking of how her mother had scolded her, insisting Vik was *a good man*.

Vik only broke eye contact to help Bobby tie up the boat before looking back at Meredith. He winked. A pulse of adrenaline ripped through her. Her whole body hummed with the desire to wrap her hands around his throat.

Calamity hopped over the side and into Vik's arms. He lifted her into an embrace, kissing the top of her head. Even Tempest seemed pleased to see him. She waved enthusiastically; her grip loosened on Meredith's arm.

It was just enough.

Wincing against the pain in her legs and pushing through the tilt of the earth as she moved, Meredith slipped out of Tempest's grip as easily as a fish through wet hands and bounded over the side of the boat. It sent the whole thing rocking; Bobby had to steady himself on the chair. Calamity squealed while Vik slipped, falling backward. Just before he could right himself, Meredith swung, grazing his cheekbone. White-hot pain flew up her arm— she'd never thrown a punch before—even as she wound back for a second. Vik was big, but he was fast too. He snatched her arm out of the air and twisted it behind her back, forcing her up on her toes. She screamed, clawing over her shoulder with the other hand, snagging beard and nostril and lip.

"Jesus Christ, calm down!" Vik ordered.

She snarled, seeing red. "You almost killed Art! You took my child!"

"Bobby!" Vik barked. "Get that rope over here."

Sheepishly, Bobby circled behind, stepping around Calamity, who'd frozen in place. When Bobby struggled to get the rope around Meredith's legs, which she kicked high enough to make contact with his head twice, Tempest climbed aboard and finished the job, knotting the rope around Meredith's ankles. Her skin burned as she struggled to pry her legs free. Vik had her other arm around her back now too; if he let go, she'd fall face-first into the console. Clamping her wrists together with one hand, he used the other arm to heave her over his shoulder. Tempest stepped around and tied Meredith's hands with the other end of the rope as seamlessly as if the whole thing had been choreographed. Vik's shoulder dug into Meredith's stomach, making it hard to breathe, let alone yell. She wheezed against his back. It was damp with sweat and stank of old garlic.

He grunted as he shifted her weight. "Heavier than you look."

She managed a weak "fuck you" before he drove a fist into her side. Breath rushed out of her body, and she gagged trying to inhale.

"Quiet," he said. "You're upsetting Cally."

Eyes bleary and nose dripping, she writhed on his shoulder while he carried her across the dock, depleting the last of her adrenaline-fueled burst of energy but stopping only when another carefully directed punch knocked the breath from her lungs for several seconds. She tried to catch Bobby's eye, walking well behind the others, his expression downcast, but he refused to look at her.

Regina waited in the doorway, hands perched on sharp hips. She planted a kiss on Vik's cheek as he crossed the threshold.

"Look what I caught." He barked a laugh. "Where should I put it?"

"End of the hall," Regina said.

With each second, Meredith got a fraction of her breath back, and she used whatever she had to yell Alice's name. Regina slapped her, making her bite her tongue. She tasted coppery blood and spat down Vik's neck.

At the end of the short hallway, Vik slid Meredith down, gripping her just under her ass. The feel of his thumb caressing her backside sent waves of revulsion through her. She leaned over to bite him, but Tempest caught her jaw and pulled up, making something pop. Vik heaved Meredith into Tempest's arms, who held on tight while Vik struggled with the lock.

Meredith tried to twist out of Tempest's grip, but the girl was angry and strong and dug her nails into Meredith's wrists each time she fought. Her skin burned and her throat throbbed, the ghost of Tempest's hand still hovering there. The rank stench of mold and decay washed over Meredith, and she tasted vomit.

"Don't you dare," Tempest said through clenched teeth.

The room was dark, and as Tempest shoved her inside, she felt the dampness of the walls, the floor, like she was breathing water. Once her eyes adjusted, she took in the room, from the chipped and stained tile floor to the water-bloated yellow wallpaper and a claw-footed porcelain bathtub at the center. Covering every other inch of floor were buckets with large, half-dead Thalias in them looking like creatures crawling from the water. In the tub, chains extended from the clawed feet and over the side. A scream locked in her throat, Meredith deadlegged, dragging Tempest down with her. Her knee hit the tile with a sickening crunch, but she kicked out, aiming for Tempest's stomach. Tempest still had Meredith's arms in a death grip and twisted up. Meredith cried out as Tempest and Vik yanked her back to standing only to dump her over the side, into the tub where a foot of icy water pricked her skin like a thousand needles. There were handcuffs attached to the chains, and Tempest made quick work of snapping them onto Meredith's wrists. Her legs they kept bound with the rope, even after they clamped shackles around her ankles.

When it was all done, Meredith fell back against the cold porcelain. Tempest staggered toward the door. Meredith struggled to pull her hands through the cuffs, but they were too tight and scraped at her already raw skin. She heard Bobby consoling Calamity just outside the door and considered yelling, but the thought of Alice hearing, of scaring her, forced her mouth shut. How long were they going to keep her here? What if she died here? Would they lock Alice in these chains next?

"You're bleeding," Regina said.

Vik's cheek wept blood from where Meredith had scratched him. She could still feel his skin beneath her nails.

Vik forced a jovial chuckle. "You always said you liked a man with battle scars."

He cast a menacing look in Meredith's direction before ushering Regina and Tempest from the room.

"Tempest," Meredith pleaded. "You can't—"

The door slammed, cutting her off.

Alone now, she finally let the tears fall, salty and hot, down her face and neck.

This is the end, she thought. *This is where I die.*

CHAPTER TWENTY-FIVE

JUDITH

APRIL 1975

An argument raged somewhere above her between the frantic bleating of a goat. When the salt water cleared from her nose, she smelled animal shit and cigarette smoke. Someone nudged her in the side. She curled protectively, tucking her head and knees in.

"Jesus. Like a fuckin' grub."

"She's not a grub."

"Hush, boy."

"Both of you hush."

This last voice belonged to a woman. Judith wanted to open her eyes and see, but she was scared of what she would find.

The woman crouched over Judith. She felt the woman's breath on her neck and shoulders. She shivered.

"She's blue," one of the men said.

"Of course she's blue, you dolt. She's half-frozen. Get her inside."

"Nuh-uh. I ain't touchin' her until you pay up."

"Pay?" The woman laughed. "Surely you're joking. I pay you for fish, not stolen girls."

"I didn't steal her. Like I said. She was swimming out in the open. Besides, I know her family." He sniffed. "Could solve your little problem, if you know what I mean."

"Then why not leave her there?"

"Don't do nothin' for free."

The woman sighed. "She's just a girl. Take her back."

"Not my problem," the first man said. "I want my money."

"Dad, just let it go."

"Don't you tell me how to run my business, Vik." *Slap.* "I want to get paid."

Judith rolled over on her front, her legs dead weights, and dragged herself, inch by inch through the sand. She heard the water but couldn't see it. If she just kept going, she'd get there.

"Cassie," she muttered. "Liza, take me instead."

"Shit. Grab her," the older man ordered.

The young one gently pulled on her shoulders, stopping her.

The woman wheeled around on her. Crouched so low they were face to face, almost licking the sand. "What did you say?"

Judith shook her head. Everything had gone numb.

The woman studied her for a long minute before straightening. "I'll give you a hundred dollars."

"A hundred?" the man shouted, outraged. "Cheap bitch."

The woman snapped. "Either you accept my generous offer—seventy-five now—or I'll have you arrested for trafficking a young woman."

"You wouldn't."

"She's a pretty little thing. No doubt someone's missing her."

"What if I reported you for keeping her?" The man's voice was thick and gravelly "Huh? What then? How are you planning to explain yourself, eh?"

Judith's entire body shivered. She bit down to keep her teeth from chattering, nearly taking off a bit of her tongue.

"Hypothermia's gonna get her if we don't get her inside," the younger man, Vik, said. "Dad, just take it, okay? She's going to die."

"You have a smart boy," the woman said.

The young man blushed. "Thanks, miss."

"Ah, don't you get taken in, Son." The older man sighed. "Fine. Hundred. None of this seventy-five shit you're talkin'. And no discount on the next mackerel haul."

The woman nodded. Judith blinked, and the boy had her in his arms, his face and neck scarlet. The woman followed behind while the older man stood on the beach, counting a wad of cash.

They brought her inside a small house with little furniture and rose-vine wallpaper that peeled at the corners. The boy called Vik set her on the couch and cocooned her in blanket after blanket until she was wrapped too tightly to move. The woman disappeared somewhere deeper in the house, then returned with hot-water bottles, which she stuck under Judith's neck and at the bottom of the cocoon near her feet.

"You feel that, dear?" the woman asked.

Judith shook her head.

The woman cursed.

"Is she going to be okay?" Vik asked.

Judith buried herself deeper in the blankets. She didn't want to hear the answer.

"There's some more hot water going over the fire. Pour some in a cup and bring it over. We have to warm her from the inside."

Judith imagined the woman stuffing embers down her throat, her body catching fire from within. She moaned and her head pounded.

They poured cup after scalding cup of hot water down her throat, and though her tongue and the roof of her mouth felt flayed, warmth spread from her chest outward. Her toes tingled, and soon she felt the relieving heat of the hot-water bottle.

"Color looks better," Vik said.

"Boy!" the older man called. "Get yer ass out here!"

Vik cast one last look at her and smiled. Judith felt her nakedness under the blankets and wanted to scrape the image of her body out of his head.

The woman patted his shoulder. "Thanks for your help."

His face flushed.

She kissed his cheek. "Better run along now."

He took off just as the older man had started to yell again.

The woman looked at Judith, long dark-brown tendrils falling into her face. She had lines like Judith's mother. Worry lines. Life lines. But her eyes sparkled.

"What shall we do with you?" she asked.

Judith tried to sit up, but the blankets bound her like a straightjacket. Her mind shot to the fate that waited for her if she went back to the Cape, so she kept her mouth shut.

"My name's Regina. Most people call me Gina, though," she said. "You got a name?"

Judith shook her head.

"Come now. I'm only trying to help."

"Judith," she said reluctantly.

"Ah, that's a pretty name. Named for your mother, maybe?"

"No."

Regina shrugged. "Neither am I. We're our own women, the two of us. I can tell." She adjusted the blankets around Judith's face, allowing her to sit up a little. "How's that feel? You getting warm?"

Judith nodded.

"Good. You keep snug, and I'll see if I can't find you some clothes."

Regina—Gina—patted Judith's head and walked toward the back of the house. With her body warm and her head a little clearer, Judith was able to take in her surroundings. It reminded her of the driftwood shacks she and Art used to build, back before Carol. Before everything got bad.

"Here we are." Gina shook out a dress that looked like something Judith's grandmother might have worn. "It's a little old, yes, but it'll keep you covered. I have some underthings for you here too. They're clean. Promise."

She draped everything over the back of the couch and then sat facing her on a chair made of driftwood and a plastic crate. "So. Let's talk."

"I'm kind of tired," Judith said, hoping the woman wouldn't pry. What if she sent her back to the cape? If she went back now, Liza would follow. Her mother—if she was still alive—would be at risk.

"I'm sure you are. A girl only ends up naked in the middle of the ocean if she's had a very good time or a very bad time." She chuckled at her own joke. "So, which was it?"

Judith hesitated a moment, eyes drifting over the little house. She spotted a small dining table and a sink beneath a water pump. There were baskets of what looked like herbs and root vegetables hanging along the far wall. She noticed only one window, and it was covered in a thick drape.

"Where are we?" Judith asked.

"My house," Gina said.

"Okay, but where?"

"An island a few miles from anywhere else." Then, "You haven't answered my question."

"It was bad," Judith said finally. Tears stung her eyes as she saw Cassie being taken over and over again. She'd tried to save Judith and died for her trouble. "My friend...drowned."

Gina gently wiped Judith's eyes with her thumbs. She sat back and seemed to study Judith for what felt like a long time. "Is there more to that story?"

Judith shook her head, afraid that if Gina knew what'd happened, she would send her away, either with that horrible man or someone else, probably worse. Sitting here on Gina's couch, with the warmth of the water bottles breathing life into her body, she realized she didn't want to die. But she also couldn't be responsible for more death. She couldn't go back to the cape. Ever.

"Liza..." Gina continued. "You said *Liza*. Who is that?"

"No one."

"Judith." Gina took her face in her hands. "Let's make a promise not to lie to each other, okay? It's been a long time since I've had someone here worth talking to. I like you, but I won't stand for lying. So." She gestured for Judith to speak. "Liza."

There was something in Gina's expression. An instinctual familiarity. Maybe it was just because she was an older woman or because of the way she'd handled the man who'd brought Judith in the first place. She didn't decide to trust her until she noticed the Thalias—a small silver bucket in the corner, the blooms sprouting bright and blue. It made her think of Cassie, of those last moments when she'd tried to save Judith. Everything inside Judith ached for her friend.

"She's killed people I love. Tried to kill others. I thought..." She bit her lip. "I thought I could stop her, but I only made it worse." Then, breaking, "I don't know what to do."

Gina's expression was unreadable. She stood and silently walked to the window, where she pulled the curtain aside just enough to peek through. Her shoulders relaxed as she shut it again and turned back to Judith.

"I'll tell you what you do," she said finally. "You survive. No matter the cost."

———

Just like she knew it would, the shell washed ashore the next day. Judith found it while gathering wood for the dinner fire. Her legs were still wobbly, and her pinky toe remained a worrying shade of blue, but getting off the couch and outside put her in a good mood. In the night, she'd heard burbley, grumbley noises like monsters clawing at the walls. By the time she'd fallen asleep, the sun had already cast its pinky orange hues across the sky.

She pocketed the shell, its weight a strange comfort. She should have been scared, but if Liza had found her here, that meant she would linger around the island, away from the cape. Away from her family.

That night, during dinner, Judith picked at the overboiled potatoes and oily fish. She stole occasional glances up at Gina, shooting her gaze back to her food when she was caught. Gina had told her she knew about Liza—that, in a way, she was hiding from her too. While Judith was grateful to have someone who understood, her mind kept drifting back to the moment the man had brought her here.

"Something wrong?" Gina asked.

Judith shook her head. Smiled tightly.

"I'll admit I'm not the best cook, but—"

"No. It's fine. Really." Then, "Thank you." She forked a potato into her mouth and chewed, swallowing the mealy mess in one lump.

"If you're worried about Liza, I told you I have…safeguards. Things I've learned from others, things I've taught myself. I'll teach you, too, if you like."

Judith nodded absently. Gina was talking about it as if Judith would be here for a while. What was she expecting from her? What would Judith have to give in exchange? She set down her fork. Cleared her throat. Gina looked up expectantly. "You…bought me."

Gina's eyebrows shot up, then her expression softened, a smile playing at her lips. "Is that what this is about?"

Judith didn't say anything.

"I didn't *buy* you. Aaron may be a brute, but he's easily managed. If I hadn't paid him, he would have taken you back with him, maybe taken your worth out another way."

Judith's stomach clenched.

"I saved your life."

Had she? "Thank you."

"And you don't owe me a thing if that's what you're thinking. You're not a prisoner." She pushed her food around her plate. Sighed. "I've been alone for a long time."

"I'm sorry."

"Don't be sorry. You're here. You're keeping me company. I couldn't ask for more." She smiled. "And now that we're friends, maybe you'll tell me a little more about you. Where are you from?"

"Cape Disappointment," Judith said. "It's—"

"I know where it is." A wistful look crossed Gina's face. "Is the lighthouse still there?"

Judith nodded. "My great-uncle is the keeper."

"Really? And who before that?"

"My great-grandmother, I think."

"What was her name?"

"Grace Bruun."

"Is that her maiden name?"

Judith had to think. "No. Holm, I think."

Gina sank inward, her face a mix of joy and despair. "It's obviously fate."

"What is?"

"That you should end up on my little island. We're *family*, Judith. Grace was my second child." Her smile widened, all teeth as she pulled Judith into a hug. "Now that I look at you closely, it's obvious. You have Grace's eyes. So serious and inquisitive. That mind of hers was doomed to get her in trouble. Oh!" She pulled back, as though hit. "This means she had children too. What were their names? What were they like? Did you meet them? No. Wait. Don't tell me. I don't want to know." She paled. "They're all dead now, I suppose."

Judith said that they were, and Gina sank back into her chair, shaken.

"She'll come here," she whispered. "She'll come for sure."

"But that's not possible. You're—" Judith started.

"Alive?" Gina asked. "Yes. I'm alive."

Barely, she seemed to say.

"Regina Holm," Judith murmured, the pieces aligning in her head.

"The very same."

"The story I always heard was that you disappeared after..."

"After the murder?" Gina frowned.

Judith hesitated, then nodded. What had she gotten herself into?

"I didn't kill anyone. If anything, I'm a victim. Marina, my daughter—Liza stole her from me. Murdered her right under my nose. I lost everything..." Gina dug her nails into the arm of the chair, her eyes fire. "I have nothing left." Her eyes moved slowly over Judith. "Almost nothing."

After dinner, Gina donned a light jacket and told Judith to stay inside. "I'll be back soon."

"Where are you going?"

Gina smiled, but it didn't reach her eyes. "To tend my garden. I find the Thalias more cooperative when I prune them at night."

"Should I come with you?" She felt childish asking, but she didn't want to be alone in the house. From the way Gina talked about it, the island was small, and she imagined Liza bringing the entire ocean down on them, drowning everything to get to her.

"I'd prefer if you didn't," Gina said, harsher than she'd been since Judith arrived. "My garden is…private."

Judith nodded. "Okay."

"You'll be fine. Just…keep yourself busy. I find an idle mind is more susceptible to intrusion. I have books. A deck of cards." She stood, flashing Judith another too-wide smile. "Stay here."

There was a hint of warning in the words.

You're not a prisoner, she'd said.

Then why did Judith suddenly feel like the room was a little bit smaller?

Judith watched Gina leave. Listened to her footsteps fade as Gina disappeared into the darkness.

A private garden on an isolated island where, Gina said, she'd been alone for years. Judith tried not to let her mind wander too far into what she could possibly keep there because, if she thought too hard about it, she'd suspect it wasn't Thalias.

———————

Gina had only been gone a few minutes when the snarling, clawing noises started again.

Judith pasted herself against the wall, heart thudding in her chest. The sound was coming from somewhere in the back of the house. An animal, maybe. But Gina hadn't mentioned any pets. She imagined a huge dog, its jowls dripping foam, locked up in a room. Maybe it was just scared. Maybe it was hungry.

"Nice doggy," Judith murmured as she crossed the living room and inched down the hall. The snarling had become a wet, gloppy noise, like someone gargling soup. Though her feet were bare and they touched the floor with all the force of a fly on a flower petal, her steps sounded thunder-loud. The first door she knew was a makeshift bathroom, with a bowl and pitcher for washing. The second door dangled open; she peered inside and saw a small table next to a bed with the blankets thrown back. Gina's room. That left the third door. As soon as she was in front of it, the noises stopped.

Her heart hammered, and it felt like her stomach had climbed into her throat. The doorknob felt hot under her hand. She pressed her ear to the door. She heard the ocean.

The knob turned easily, but she hesitated an agonizing minute before pushing the door open. The room was too dark to see properly, and she was too scared to give her eyes the time to adjust. When she wasn't immediately attacked by a hungry dog, she pushed the door open further, resisted by an inch of water covering the floor in front of her.

Metal chinked somewhere in the room. A splash. A purr.

"Hello?" Judith took a step into the room. The water on the floor was ice-cold. "Is someone in there?"

Haunting laughter reverberated off the walls. Judith's skin prickled.

There! In the corner of the room, a tiny glowing green light. No. Judith squinted into the dark. Not a light. An eye.

Judith ran, slamming the door behind her.

CHAPTER TWENTY-SIX

MEREDITH

PRESENT DAY

eredith spent the night tugging and shaking and pulling against the chains, burning her wrists raw. Though the drugs seemed to have mostly worn off, they left her feeling twitchy and worn-out at the same time. Blood dripped down her hands, turning the fetid water a disturbing shade of pink. Sometime around sunrise, she closed her eyes and let exhaustion take her.

She dreamed she was on the beach with her mother, taunting a tiny digging clam by gouging the sand around it and then watching it wriggle helplessly down, only to do it all over again until there was a foot-deep hole between her feet. Her mother was at the edge of the water, hair long and her face unlined like she was when Meredith was little. She ran her fingers through the surf, bringing them discreetly to her lips and frowning.

"She's here," her mother murmured.

Meredith tried to ask who, but her voice wouldn't cooperate. She opened her mouth wide, straining the corners of her lips, but nothing came out.

The sky turned cloudless gray, and the sun blackened as if settling into an eclipse. Her mother shivered, and steam puffed from between her lips, but Meredith didn't feel the cold. In fact, she'd started to sweat. She stripped out of her clothes, only to find more clothes beneath. Four layers peeled away before she felt the subtle breeze on her skin. But by the time she stepped toward the water, it and her mother were gone. All that was left was a desert crackling beneath the black sun. Cracks appeared in the sand, revealing fault lines that split several inches apart. Sea foam bubbled up from the cracks, merging into a large, single mound. The mound trembled and grew until it was woman-shaped, and when the bubbles fell away, her mother's face emerged, lips pulled tight in a grimace. Her eyes had changed, though, from brown to piercing green, and her hair was dark and thick and oily. The air around her shimmered, like the surface of the ocean.

When Meredith woke, Tempest was there, leaning over the tub. She flinched when Meredith sat up. Meredith's head swam, but she fought not to show it. Tempest, for all her blustering, seemed scared of Meredith, and she wanted to keep it that way.

"Hungry?" Tempest tossed a can of sardines into the tub. When Meredith didn't immediately grab it, she frowned. "Mom won't be happy to hear you're ungrateful."

Meredith was tired of people threatening her. She stretched as far as the chains would allow, listening to her bones creak. Her legs were especially sore; she couldn't feel her feet. "I hope you're feeding Alice better than this."

Tempest rolled her eyes. "Princess Alice has requested pancakes. Again."

"And what Alice wants, Gina provides," Meredith finished.

"It's just for now," Tempest said unconvincingly. "She'll get over it later. She needs us."

"I don't think she will."

Tempest crossed her arms.

"You don't think she will either. That's why you're still standing there." She flicked the can. "Feeding time's over."

Tempest scowled. "I told her we should've just tied you to the dock. Let nature take its course."

"But this was already prepared." Meredith shook the chains. "Just for me, or do you keep chains on hand for all your important guests?"

Expression darkening, Tempest leaned back. "It's harder to resist than you think. Out here, I mean. All we hear is the ocean. It talks all the time. She gets in our heads. Just like she'll get in yours."

"Your mother…chains you up?"

"My mother *loves* me." The ferocity in the statement surprised them both. Tempest stepped back, crossing her arms.

The door eased open, making her jump. Vik walked in carrying a plate of cold lasagna, smiling at Meredith. Fire flared in her gut.

"Pancakes are ready," he told Tempest. "Your mother wants you at the table."

When he patted her head, she curled into it like a kitten.

He waited until she left, closing the door behind her, to turn his attention to Meredith. "Bite?" He nodded to his plate. "I couldn't help but notice you hadn't touched it after I spent all that time lovingly crafting an authentic Italian dish. I figured I'd give you a chance to try it before, well, you don't get another one."

"Regina already threatened to kill me," Meredith said. "Hearing it from you is redundant."

"Who's threatening? I'm talking lasagna. Although…" He made a show of peering into the bathtub at the floating sardine can. "It looks like you're all set there."

"What do you want?"

"Oh, just a chat." He sat on an overturned bucket and took a bite. Chewed.

"Last time we talked, you hustled me out of there real quick. Pretty rude if you ask me."

Meredith shook her chains in response.

He shrugged. "A necessary precaution. There's children on this island. Gotta protect them."

"From me?"

"Depends. Are you getting any stupid ideas?"

She was thinking of all the places she'd like to stab that fork he was holding and told him so.

"That'd be a yes, then." He wiped his mouth on his sleeve. "Give me some credit, Meredith. Given my position, you'd do the same thing. Or," he amended, "maybe you wouldn't."

"What's that supposed to mean?"

"Judith and I talked a lot while you were gone. While I was looking after her on my own. You should know it was Regina who asked me to, by the way. I know you think she's heartless, but really, she's got the biggest heart I've ever known." He grinned. "Anyway, when Judith and I talked, it was pretty much always you that came up, especially after Alice was born. She told me about that time she fell off the changing table and broke her little arm." He clicked his tongue. "Not exactly the most vigilant parent, are you?"

Meredith tried to fight the memory, but it clawed its way to the front of her mind—Alice screaming, that gut-churning wail, the doctor's looks, the questions. "It was an accident," she said weakly.

"Could've been, but accidents like that are avoidable, right? I mean, if you're paying attention."

"Like Regina was paying attention when Marina was taken?" she shot back.

His grin faded. "That was different."

"How? How is that different? How is that different from you coming into my house and taking my daughter and nearly killing Art in the process? How are you any better than—" She cut herself off.

"Than her?" He smiled, but it didn't reach his eyes. "There's a difference between revenge and putting things to rights. Regina lost her daughter that night. Not a day went by she didn't hate herself for it. Then lo and behold, here she is. Sort of. It's only fair Regina get her back."

Hot tears threatened to fall as she snorted. "Fair. You can't tell me you believe that bullshit. Alice is Alice. That's it."

"Like I said. Regina's got a big heart in her. She's trying to make this easy on you."

The laughter started in the pit of her stomach. Once she really got rolling, she couldn't stop until it dissolved into a coughing fit. Water splashed over the side of the tub, speckling Vik's pants. "*Easy,*" she wheezed. "You're as deluded as she is."

He finished his lasagna in two large bites, setting the plate and fork behind the bucket, well out of Meredith's reach. The shell jabbed her hip, still hidden away. She wondered how quickly she could get it out of her pocket and stab the pointy end in his eye. With her legs still numb and her wrists shaky, likely not quick enough.

When he swallowed, he picked his tooth with a nail and then said, "What I believe is that time can twist things. Hear tell on the cape, Regina Holm murdered a girl and the spirit or ghost or whatever of that girl stole Regina's daughter right out from under her. Eye for an eye. But I've known Regina a long time. And like I said, she's got a big heart. Whatever happened in the past is staying there."

"Except it's not staying there, is it? My mother is dead."

"Not Regina's fault." He sighed. "You don't get it. That's fine. But you don't deserve that beautiful little girl in there. Regina does." He grinned. "Soon everything will be put back the way it was. Gina in her house, the keeper of her lighthouse, with her daughter at her side."

"Fuck you."

"Ah, don't be like that. You think you have something to offer? Last I heard, the police were wanting to talk with a young woman about your height and look. I guess some poor lady got left near the shore, near-drowned the night we took Alice."

She shrank back.

"She's alive," he added. "No thanks to you."

"I didn't do anything to her."

"Maybe not. But I can only imagine what would've happened if you hadn't been interrupted."

Would Meredith have killed the woman? There was something about the water along the cape that did something to her. It got inside her, drowning out everything except the voice. In that moment, when she was with the woman, Meredith had imagined she knew how to manifest a deepest desire, how to pluck it from the air like a dandelion fluff, just as fragile but just as tangible. In that moment, she could've given herself anything if she'd only held on a moment longer... But was that her? Or Liza playing with her mind?

Vik continued, "It's not really your fault, of course. You can't help what you are or where you came from or what it means. All you can do is minimize the damage." He gestured to the chains to illustrate his point. "You won't hear me say this to Gina, but it really was the best thing for everyone when Judith brought you home. If it wasn't for that, you wouldn't have had Alice."

She wished he would stop saying her daughter's name. Hearing it only worsened the dread in her chest, only made clearer how impossible it was to think both of them would get off this island alive.

Vik continued, "I saw her once. The spirit." He pulled down the collar of his shirt, revealing a half-moon-shaped scar, raised and angry red at the edges. "I nearly died. Would've if it weren't for Regina."

"She should've let you," Meredith snapped.

He clapped once, laughing. "See? There it is. This is what I'm talking about. Regina would never say something like that. She cares about people."

"She cares about herself."

"No, see, you're not understanding. What happened to her wasn't fair. All she wants is her child. What more selfless thing could a woman ask for?" He smiled to himself. "Regina has a great capacity for love. Every day I aspire to earn it."

"How romantic."

"It's why I can't blame her for what happened after. Judith gone. You…"

"Me."

A moment of strained silence passed.

"You're not going to do it." It wasn't a question.

Meredith noticed shadows in the space beneath the door. Someone was listening.

"No," she said. "I'm not."

Vik didn't seem at all upset by this. In fact, he looked almost relieved. "I figured that's what you'd say. And truthfully, I'm happy. Liza—or whatever's left of her—seems to dissipate for a time after one of your line drowns, unless something stirs her up again. With you gone, it'll give us time. Regina and I will start a new family with Alice as our child. Your giving her up would only have made it easier on Alice. Easier to mourn a mother who don't want you, don't you think?"

The shadows shuffled.

"And what about Calamity?" Meredith asked, raising her voice slightly. "Tempest?"

Vik studied her for a beat. "What about them?"

"They're your children too."

"No. They're not."

"Calamity called you *Dad*."

He shrugged. "I'm sure you've noticed Calamity isn't all there. If calling me *Dad* makes it easier on her so she's less trouble for Regina, it doesn't bother me none."

"But they're Regina's children. How could she…" She stopped. "They're not hers, are they?"

"We tried," he said, the ghost of a smirk on his face, "but it wasn't meant to be. Regina needed help around the island, for days when I couldn't be here. So I went out onto the mainland and I found some young girls with unwary mothers of their own."

Meredith let what he was saying sink in. Alice wasn't the first child they'd stolen. Did Calamity know? Did Tempest? She quickly glanced at the door. They probably knew now.

"You think you're just going to move into my mother's house and set yourselves up? You think people won't be watching? You think Art won't—"

"Art won't be a problem." His eyes darkened. "My boy Bobby's working on that right now."

Suddenly, something smacked against the door.

"Mom!"

Alice.

Meredith's muscles burned as she lunged forward. Her ankles twisted in the ropes, and the handcuffs dug into already bloody skin. Her stomach rolled with the pain. The chains rattled and snapped tight, stopped just in front of Vik's face. She managed to scratch him, barely missing his eye.

"Alice! Alice, I'm here! It's—"

Vik punched her in the solar plexus, and she crumpled, unable to breathe, but she could hear Alice fighting on the other side of the door.

"No! I want my mom!"

Unfazed, Vik carried the plate and fork to the door, pausing with his hand on the knob. "I'll give Alice a kiss for you."

He opened the door, and Meredith's screams carried out into the hallway before being cut off with a slam and the click of the lock.

———————

Hours passed in which Meredith strained to hear Alice's voice. Muscles locked, she stayed as still as possible, not even willing to let the sound of sloshing water get in the way of hearing it. Just when Meredith started to think they'd tied Alice up somewhere else in the house, tiny footsteps approached the door. Meredith held her breath as someone jostled the knob.

"Mom?" Alice's voice came from under the door, barely more than a whisper. "It's locked. I can't get in."

Torn between a painful desire to see her daughter's face, to talk to her, to reassure her, and fearing what Vik would do to Alice if he found her there, she said, "It's okay, baby. I'm okay."

"I told them you wouldn't do it."

Tears pricked her eyes, though she managed to keep the tremble out of her voice. "Alice. Listen to me. I need you to be a big girl, okay? I need you to find a phone. I know Vik has one."

"Mom—"

"Shh. Listen. Find the phone, and then I want you to run and hide. Can you do that for me?"

She was met with silence. For a terrifying second, she thought Vik or Gina had already found her. Had heard everything.

"Alice?"

"I'm here."

"Okay. Okay, good." Meredith bit down hard on her lip. She couldn't ask Alice to do this. She was probably terrified. Maybe Vik was right. Maybe she was a terrible mother. "Forget what I said, baby. Just be a good girl, okay? Mama will get us out of this. I promise."

"I know." Then, "I found this."

Something small and metal slid under the door, coming to rest beside the tub. It was an earring, a large black pearl with waves of silver surrounding it.

"It's Grandma's, isn't it?" Alice asked.

She couldn't be sure in the dark, but it did look like the match to the earring her mother had been looking for the night she died.

"I think so," Meredith said.

"She was here. The woman in the water."

Meredith nodded, even though Alice couldn't see it.

"She's sad," Alice said. "I can hear her at night."

"Alice..."

"It's okay, Mama. It'll be okay. She told me."

Meredith's heart skipped. She thought of the shell on the dock. The pull at the back of her throat. *No*, she thought. *Not Alice.* "*Who* told you?"

Alice's voice grew muffled, like she'd stood. "Cally's coming. I have to go. I love you."

Don't go. "I love you too, sweetie."

And then Alice was gone.

Thirst clawed at her mouth, and she needed to pee badly. One exasperated the other, and the only water at her disposal was the stuff she'd been soaking in. She scooped a palmful and held it tentatively to her lips.

The second it touched her tongue, she gagged, but she fought it down anyway. She couldn't let herself get too weak again. They wanted to sacrifice her to Liza, so they'd have to unchain her eventually. When they did, she'd be ready.

She wondered what lies they were telling her daughter. Alice, who believed Meredith could do no wrong. Trusted she would take care of her. Would she believe them when they told her she was horrible? That she was better off with them? Would they somehow convince her that Meredith was evil? That she deserved a mother better, more than what Meredith could offer? Meredith had to trust that they couldn't. Alice was strong and stubborn in the same ways Meredith had always been. The way her own mother had been.

It occurred to her to wonder: Was it Liza her mother had been trying to protect her from? Or Regina?

All Meredith ever wanted was to love and be loved by her mother. With Alice, she'd gotten a second chance to know that feeling of connection between mother and daughter, of being able to see herself in another person and know that she was not alone.

I want my mom.

The feeling was so overwhelming she felt it in her skin. Her teeth. She'd never wanted her mother so badly, to hold her and tell her everything was going to be okay, to stand there and take it as she screamed and fought because none of this would have happened if she'd just left Meredith to die. The secrets, the pain… Why had her mother kept it from her? Why had she risked them both?

She would kill to have her mother back here, to look her in the eye and demand—

Oh God.

"I want my mom," Meredith whispered to herself. *No. I need her.* Like an emptiness inside her nothing else could fill. Meredith felt the desperation in the pit of her belly, and the longer she focused on that feeling, the more she realized it was familiar. She'd felt it in the lighthouse that day she nearly jumped. She'd felt it in the fog that Liza draped over her, pulling her toward the water. "What if…"

She's sad, Alice had said.

Meredith was so stupid. She'd already known, but it didn't seem to matter until now. It was never about their daughters. It was about them. *Us.*

It's about the mothers.

The curse wasn't about revenge.

Regina, a woman who couldn't seem to die, driven by her desire to be with the daughter she lost. A girl who called from the water for the mothers of their family.

I told them you wouldn't do it.

It was Alice, who believed so deeply in Meredith's love for her, that helped Meredith see. It was Meredith's own desperate desire for her mother overwhelming her now, in her darkest moments. *When we're lost,* she thought, *like the girl in the water is lost, when we're sad and angry, who comforts us? Who is it we want most?*

It wasn't Liza stalking the water, beckoning the women to drown.

It was *Marina.* And she just wanted her mother.

Every joint screaming, she twisted sideways and wriggled the shell from her pocket. It was impossibly hot, and as she held it, the numbness in her hands was gradually eased. Meredith had never prayed, but what she was about to do—what Judith and others had done—felt more like prayer than anything.

Meredith brought the shell closer to the lips, so that it swallowed her whole voice. "Are you her?"

Silence.

"You're her," she said more forcefully. Then, before she could stop herself, "Marina."

The sound that came from the shell curled Meredith's insides, a wild, agonized cry. It was pain and confusion and grief.

"Your mother's here," she said. "Come get her."

CHAPTER TWENTY-SEVEN

JUDITH

Y ou're focusing too much on the physical part of it," Gina said, handing Judith another glass of their limited fresh water. Judith swallowed all of it in one go. Her throat was on fire, and her tongue was shriveled like a piece of dried beef. "It's not the taste that you want; it's the feelings attached to it. The memories. Each movement of the water carries a memory with it, which dictates where it goes, how it flows, what it seeks."

"Muscle memory," Judith said, voice raspy.

"Something like that." She dipped a jar over the side of the pier and handed it to Judith. "Try again."

She drank. She gagged. Still nothing. She was starting to think it was all made up, something to amuse a woman who'd been alone and bored for too long. There were times Judith caught Gina looking at her with a curious expression. It made Judith feel like an animal behind glass. And now with these lessons…was she learning to protect herself? Or were they just party tricks?

"Why are you even showing me this?" Judith asked, her tongue barely able to form the words. "What if I can't?"

"You can. And you will." Gina sighed. "You need to protect yourself."

"I still don't understand—"

"There's a reason she hasn't gotten to me. I live on an island no bigger than the cape, alone, and somehow I've managed to keep alive. That thing you thought you saw? The terrifying green eye? It was in your head. She put it there to scare you, to drive you mad, away from the house and into the water so she could drown you. There are few things in the world stronger than a desire for revenge. You have to trust me."

But Judith didn't trust her. Not completely. She'd mentioned once that she wanted to visit the cape. Just for a day. An hour. She needed to know that her mother was alive. But Gina refused.

"You can't," she'd said. "You'll endanger us both."

She didn't understand how leaving the island would put Gina in danger, but she knew better than to argue. Arguing with Gina only made the days with her more difficult. And the nights... Sometimes she wondered if, after an argument, it was Gina who made the walls creak, who whispered under her door in the darkness. Who terrified her into keeping her feet firmly on dry ground.

It went on for days. Weeks. Judith drank her weight in seawater, and it still wasn't enough. It clicked one late evening while they sat on the pier. Gina had an old newspaper on her lap and sketched a design in the margins for a lighthouse. It would help, she'd said. *Liza doesn't like the light.*

But today, Gina wouldn't speak to Judith until she was able to read the water. A jar sat in her lap, sloshing with each rough rock of the waves. The air was biting, and the tips of her fingers and nose were numb. There'd be a storm soon.

She studied the water in the jar. The way that it moved, the sediment that swirled snow globe–like even as she sat perfectly still. Like it felt the thrash of the waves, called to them, even from the jar. She could see the connection like a web, sticky and flexible. Even as her stomach clenched, she cupped some water from the jar and tipped it into her mouth. As she held it there, in her mind's eye she felt the sudden shudder of an ocean wracked by wind and an unexplained desire to dive deeper and deeper, to where the sea was calm and cool and comforting. She saw a shadow lurking beneath the water, tendrils of impossible smoke drifting closer. Closer. Her tongue burned, and when she couldn't stand it anymore, she spat over the side.

Gina laughed. "Finally."

Judith frowned and the cracks in her lips tore.

When they weren't studying the water from the safety of the pier, they moved around each other like planets in their own orbit. As much as Gina tried to encourage her to make the island and her little house Judith's home, Judith was never comfortable, never off her guard. "Reading" the water, as Gina called it, helped some. There was something about feeling the ebb and flow of the water that was like a door to Liza in a way. A grounding line. She could feel her here in a way she hadn't been able to on the cape, and when there was a surge, like an undertow in her mind when Liza tried to reach inside her head and pull Judith toward her, Judith could, mostly, fight it. But a door could open both ways. Had Gina given Judith a view into Liza, or had Gina shown Liza how to find her?

Judith woke up one morning in June feeling…off. She wasn't in pain or sick, but her body felt alien. Wrong. She walked carefully through the house, studying her own steps, the twist and jerk of her skin, the sudden pop in her ankle. She went straight for the outhouse. When she finished, she realized she hadn't bled since leaving the cape. She thought of the nights she spent in the house on the hill with Jackie and her insides convulsed.

I'm pregnant, she thought.

What do I do?

What happens now?

I want my mom.

It'd always been there, this ache of wanting to see her. To make sure she was okay. To see if she missed Judith. If she was looking for her, or if she'd accepted that she was lost. That Liza had claimed another of their family's daughters. But now it was like a sharp pain. How could she do this without her mom?

Back in the kitchen, Gina whistled as she poured hot water into a mug. She caught Judith out of the corner of her eye and smiled. "I know it's still early, but I was thinking we might decorate for Christmas this year. I never do, so the trimmings will be sparse, but I thought because we're together, it might be a nice thing for…" She turned and, seeing Judith full on, frowned. "What's wrong?"

Judith's hand went to her belly, but she couldn't bring herself to touch it. It was like being dared to touch a live wire or a white-hot burner.

"Tummy troubles?" Gina asked. "Here. Have some tea."

Her stomach lurched. "I don't want tea."

"Hmm."

Gina pulled Judith into the kitchen and fussed over her, placing the back of her hand on her forehead, then her cheek, then her lips. Her sharp fingers prodded Judith's throat and underarms. She barely touched Judith's belly before Judith yelped and pulled away.

"Oh." Gina's eyes traveled the length of Judith's body, her arms crossed. "I see."

"I'm fine," Judith said, more to convince herself than Gina. "Just... Oh God."

She ran to the front of the house, barely two steps off the porch before she vomited.

Gina patted her back, muttering *there, theres*, still patting and muttering and staring into the water when Judith stopped.

Gina's eyebrow twitched, like something had just occurred to her.

Judith stood and wiped her mouth on her sleeve. She still felt nauseous.

"It's normal." Gina kicked some sand over Judith's sick. "It'll pass." Then, "What do you want to do?"

At first, Judith didn't know what she meant. She wanted to lie down for a hundred years and never eat again. Then she realized.

"You want me to—"

"I don't want you to do anything you don't want to do." Her eyes told another story.

Judith was sixteen. What was she going to do with a baby? What would her mom say?

She knew there were ways around it. Cassie told her about a boy she slept with her first (and only) semester in college.

"It was like I was trying to see how many mistakes I could make in six months," Cassie had said. "Getting knocked up took the cake, though."

Abortion had been legal for all of a few months, and hospitals were still hesitant to perform the procedure. Her mom took her to a clinic in Oregon that'd been conducting abortions, under the table, since the fifties.

"I won't lie," Cassie had said. "It sucked. And I was in pain for a while. But it's what was best for me."

Cassie had always been able to make the hard choices. Judith missed her.

It seemed like every decision she had made over the last year had gone from bad to worse. She wasn't fit to be a mother and wasn't even sure she wanted to be one at all.

"I don't know," Judith finally said. "I need to think about it."

"Take some time, but"—she placed a firm hand on Judith's belly—"not too long."

Judith couldn't sleep. Part of her wanted to find a way home, to fall at her mother's feet and tell her she messed up and beg her to fix it, but there was also that voice in the back of her head, warning her of what would happen if she went back.

Every gassy stomach rumble made her hyperaware of her body, too scared to move too much or too fast in case it triggered another deluge. The only thing she could keep down was hot water with a little mint.

She was so hungry.

Gina asleep in her room, Judith carefully moved around what passed for a kitchen—there were no appliances, and the sink was really just a bucket attached to a pump. An old trader's outpost, Gina had told her. A lucky find. She'd made improvements over the years. Added more space. Cut out a window. Occasionally fishermen would find the woman on the island, and she would barter for labor. Judith never asked what she bartered—seemed the only things the island offered were inedible flora, water birds, and sickly looking turtles.

A pantry held their rationed supplies for the week. The rest of their stores

Gina kept somewhere away from the house. *Safe*, she'd said when Judith asked her where exactly.

"Another mouth to feed," Gina had said as she prepared a meager dinner of sardines and tomatoes from the garden, none of which Judith ate. "But I'm sure we could make it work."

Judith grabbed a sleeve of crackers she was pretty sure were out of date and settled back on the blanket that had been serving as her bed. She gnawed on them, a chipmunk, until a growling, gurgling sound drifted from the back of the house. Her skin pinched and her heart dropped.

It's not real, she reminded herself.

A breeze fingered her hair, the back of her neck. The rush and fall of the ocean echoed in her ears, a lullaby.

But the windows were closed.

I should open them.

Still carrying the crackers, she walked to the closest window, suddenly tired. She couldn't find the latch, and there was something dark outside, darker than the night, sucking the light from the moon and stars. She wondered if she could drink the moon faster than the dark thing outside.

The window opened, and she leaned her face out into the cool night air. She could climb out and onto the roof, and then she could reach the moon and drink the light and—

Her stomach wrenched and she tasted bile. Still leaning out the window, she gagged, nothing but soggy crackers left to bring up. Slowly, the fog over her mind cleared, and she realized what she'd been about to do.

As soon as she caught her breath, she fell back inside, slamming the window shut. The dark thing was gone.

But it'd almost had her.

For the first time since realizing she was pregnant, Judith touched her stomach. It didn't feel any different, not really, but she gently prodded, seeking out something substantial.

"You saved me," she whispered.

———————

It was late July or early August—it was hard to keep track of time on the island—when Judith started to show. The clothes Gina gave her weren't exactly tight, but with the sun unforgiving and so few windows to allow a breeze through the house, by midmorning, her clothes were sweat soaked and clingy. Most days, she found a shady spot and spread out on a blanket, naked. More than anything, though, she wanted the coolness of the water.

She didn't dare.

Because if she thought about it too hard, if she let her gaze linger too long on the waves, she felt a pull deep in her belly that was getting harder to ignore.

This morning she woke up early, the first time in months she hadn't felt queasy, and went for a walk. By the time she got back, she'd made a decision.

"I'm keeping it."

Though Gina hadn't tried to push her into a decision one way or the other, Judith felt the stares across the room, heard the muttering from her bedroom.

Gina was bent over a pair of underwear, stitching the elastic back to the cotton. She didn't look up. "Okay."

"Just okay?"

"I told you it was your decision."

"Yeah, but—"

"Judith." Gina looked up from her stitching, her expression hard. "Enough." Then, "If you want to see this through to the end, you're going to have to grow up."

Judith straightened, more of a task as her body thinned and her belly grew. "I am grown up."

Turning back to her work, Gina said, "Not yet."

A few weeks later, while Judith was bathing, she felt the baby move. She froze, thinking she might have imagined it, but then it happened again, and she held her breath until the fluttering stopped.

Until now, she'd only thought of being pregnant in the vaguest of terms. Her belly would grow, and she would be sick, and at some point in the future there would be a baby. But as she sat in the tub, water chilling on her skin, she realized she knew nothing about pregnancy. What to expect. What to do. Her chest tightened, and she had to coach herself to breathe. How was she going to get through this?

She didn't care if Liza was out there waiting to drag her to the bottom of the ocean. She needed to get home. To her mom. She'd find a way to protect her. But the only way she was going to get there was if she took Gina's ancient rowboat. Gina had claimed it was the one she came to the island in, that it was barely fit for firewood, but Judith assumed it was another of Gina's half-truths.

That evening, she ate dinner across from Gina, helped her clean up, and then curled up on her mat to wait for Gina to fall asleep.

Night came, and Judith waited until she could hear Gina's gentle snores drifting from the hall, and then she waited a little longer. She didn't leave a note. Gina would understand. And if she didn't, then Judith would rather Gina believed she'd drowned.

The boat was grounded on the beach near the beginnings of a dock. She'd never seen Gina take it out, but that didn't mean she hadn't. Though it was difficult to see in the dark, Judith ran her hands along the bottom side of the skiff and didn't feel any holes or soft places where the wood had rotted. Inside, leaning against the seat, were the oars. They looked in bad shape, but they would have to do.

As she started to push the skiff toward the water, movement in the corner of her eye made her pause.

No. Don't think about it. Just keep moving.

But her hands shook, making it hard to keep a grip on the skiff. Her feet slipped in the sand, and she bit her lip to keep from crying out when sharp shells cut her feet. An ache started in the back of her head, like a hand closing over it, nails digging in. Her vision swam, and it was hard to keep her eyes open. She just wanted to lie down.

But Gina had taught her how to put up walls, how to find the red light through the mist. Judith had Gina's Thalia tea running through her, a protective charm she wished she could have shared with Cassie. And then it was Cassie's face in her mind, her mother's... She clung to them, focused on them when Liza's voice threatened to break through.

Gritting her teeth, she dragged her nails along her arms, her legs, her face, the pain breaking through the fog just enough to keep her moving. One step at a time. Closer. She could feel the spray of the water as waves lashed the shore. Liza was angry—or excited.

The bow touched the water, and as the rest of the skiff moved onto the damp sand, it became easier to push. She was almost there. She would row until she reached the cape. Until her arms fell off.

She had one foot in the boat when something yanked her back by the hair. She was too shocked to move. Her foot got caught under the seat and trying to wriggle it free only lodged it deeper into the shallow opening.

"Ungrateful. I can't believe..." Gina huffed angrily in Judith's ear.

"My ankle! It's—"

One hand still tangled in Judith's hair, she wrapped the other around Judith's middle and pulled. There was a sickening crack, and her foot, now throbbing and swelling, came free.

Water rushed at them, waves bigger and stronger than they'd been only seconds before.

"Keep moving," Gina ordered. "Get away from the water."

Nausea broke over her, wave after wave. It was like being tossed in a storm. She struggled to get her good foot beneath her as Gina tried to drag her away from the boat.

But the water reached farther up the beach now, and as it washed over their feet, she felt Gina's grip start to loosen. Liza was in her head. Another moment and Judith would be able to slip free, but what did that matter if Liza was just beyond the shallows, waiting for her?

Gina's nails dug into Judith's skin as her whole body trembled. Every movement was muscle memory, her body fighting against her mind. Judith pushed them farther away from the lapping waves, up the beach, until finally they were far enough that the water couldn't reach. Still, Gina's breath came in hard, fast bursts, and she clung to Judith like a life raft.

A few moments passed, and Gina groaned. Her breathing slowed, and Judith could no longer feel Gina's heart pounding against her back.

Wheezing, Gina said, "Don't ever do that again."

"I want to go home," Judith said. "Please, I just want to go home."

Gina wrenched Judith's head back. "You are home."

For several weeks, Judith couldn't walk. Gina made a splint of small pieces of wood and an old shirt with too many holes to be salvageable, but Judith could tell it wouldn't heal right. Winter settled in at the tail end of November, and she still couldn't put much pressure on it.

"You're lucky it was just your ankle," Gina had said. Then, when the words had sunk in, "I was so afraid I would lose you."

Judith didn't want to believe Gina had broken her ankle on purpose, but she was careful not to test it when Gina was around. Instead of sleeping, she hobbled around the house, belly out to here, working up the nerve to try to leave again. She was running out of time.

———————

December brought freezing cold and storms that shook the little house. The windows fogged, and smoke from the wood-burning stove lingered like a haze on the ceiling. Their food supply was running low, so they'd been cutting their rations. They hadn't seen any fishermen in over a month—Vik was the last to visit, trading a cooler of pollock, some beef jerky, and a bag of too-soft lemons for an hour in the garden with Gina.

The pollock was almost gone, ditto the jerky, and they'd finished off the lemons in a week, Judith sucking the juice until her lips pickled.

"Winter is tough," Gina said, "but we'll get by."

Except it'd been days since Judith last felt the baby move, and there were mornings when she woke up feeling a shroud over her body, overcome by an impossible sense of dread. There was no point in asking Gina because she was all *don't worry* and *everything's fine*. Judith's mom would have been honest. She would have taken her to the doctor when blood dotted her underwear. She would have bought her vitamins and books and hugged her when she was scared, which was all the time. With each day that went by, Judith became more convinced this had been a mistake, that she'd put herself and her child in danger and she couldn't get them out of it alive. And maybe that was the answer. Most of the time, she couldn't tell if, when she imagined drowning, it was her own dark thoughts or Liza peering in.

———————————

Her water broke in the early morning. She'd been better on her feet over the last few days and got up early to take a few laps around the house, testing her ankle. She had a sudden feeling of having pissed herself, then worried because she hadn't felt it and what that meant for the baby and started toward the outhouse only to stop in the doorway as pain and pressure circled her middle like a vise.

Not yet, she begged.

But for the next couple of hours, the pressure got worse and the pain clawed her back and her legs. Sweat pooled under her arms and dotted her forehead.

She couldn't do this. She needed help. She needed—

"Gina!"

Gina came running from her bedroom, pulling a sweater over her head. "What happened?" She took one look at Judith lying on the floor, clutching her middle, and nodded. "Right. Okay. Relax. Everything is going to be fine."

A contraction hit, and Judith howled, her nails dragging scratches in the floor.

Outside, waves crashed.

Gina made quick work of getting Judith out of her clothes and then sliding a sheet beneath her. The cold pinched at her skin, but as another contraction came, so did the heat.

"Breathe," Gina ordered.

Judith was breathing. Breathing did nothing. It was like her body was caving in and ripping itself open at the same time. She tore at the sheet and rolled her head on the ground, tears streaming into her ears.

For a moment, Gina disappeared and then returned with a bowl of water, a rag, and their sharpest knife, the one they used for butchering the few rabbits they found on the island. She lined them up next to Judith and dipped the rag in the water.

"What do you need the knife for?" Judith asked.

"Just in case," Gina said without looking up. "Spread your legs."

Judith obeyed, her hips popping with the movement. She barely caught her breath before pain shot up her back and the vise clamped down harder on her belly. Gina probed between her legs, and Judith bit back a sob.

"Not quite," Gina said. "It might be a while."

She balanced her hands on Judith's knees. One of them was covered in blood.

"I'm gonna die," Judith said.

Gina frowned. "Listen to me. I have a plan. If you want to live, if you want to go back home, you have to do exactly what I say."

Buoyed at the idea of seeing her mom, Judith nodded.

"I can feel her out there. You can too. I see it on your face."

In my head, the waves rolling, rolling, calling, calling.

"I'm fine," Judith said.

Gina's fingers dug into Judith's knees. "I said listen." Then, "If we can…distract her, we might be able to make the crossing. I know how it feels to want to go home, Judith. Do you think I've enjoyed myself? Living hand to mouth, always knowing, always seeing her? I want to go home too. I want to live." Her voice broke. "I gave and gave only to have my life taken away from me. I deserve my life back. And you're going to help me."

Judith's heart hammered. "How?"

"You're not suited to be a mother. You understand that, right?"

While a shameful part of her agreed, another flared. "You don't know that."

"I do, Judith. If it wasn't for me, you'd never have survived your little dip that day. How do you expect to care for a baby when you can't care for yourself?"

"That wasn't my fault. Vik and his father—"

"Enough. This baby is coming. You need to listen to me. I know what's best for you. For us. And what's best for us is to give Liza this child. She'll calm for a time, and we'll be able to pass."

When Judith didn't immediately agree, Gina leaned over her, a scowl etched on her face. "I took you in. I fed you. You owe me."

"I don't owe you my child."

Gina's scowl deepened. "How dare—"

Biting through another contraction, Judith snatched the knife off the floor, and as Gina fell on top of her trying to get it, Judith swung, slicing through Gina's cheek. Blood wept down her face and onto Judith's belly. Screaming, Gina thrashed, but Judith was able to shove her away. Breathing hard, Judith scrambled to sit up, to stand, but the pain was extraordinary. She was able to get to her knees before Gina came at her. Judith didn't think. She stabbed blindly, feeling a second's resistance before the knife plunged into Gina's side.

Gina fell back, gasping. "Y-you..."

Not knowing how badly Gina was hurt, Judith stood and hobbled to the door. Blood and fluid dripped down her legs, and with each crush of the pain, her knees nearly buckled. She had to get off this island.

The cold was like a wall outside, and she immediately began to tremble. Blankets covered patches of the garden; she grabbed the thickest one and wrapped it around her shoulders, but it was stiff in places with ice.

There was no way she was going to make it.

She had to try.

The skiff wasn't far from where it'd originally been kept. After breaking her ankle, Gina must not have been worried that Judith would try to leave again.

As Judith staggered across the sand, gripping the chilly blanket to her body, she heard a wail come from the house. Would Gina come after her? Would Judith be fast enough?

Wind whipped her hair as she pushed the boat toward the water. As wave after wave of pain gripped her, she dug her fingers into the wood, driving splinters under her skin. Tears blurred her vision, twisting shadows in the corners of her eyes.

Then her toes touched water, and it was like lightning shot up her legs. She could do this. She was *going* to do this.

But her legs shuddered, and she felt a drop in her belly, and the contractions that came after were harder, longer. She could barely breathe. Somehow, she lifted both legs into the boat and used the oars to push herself away from the shore. The waves were strong, and she struggled to row into open water. Fog swirled around her, and she didn't know which way she was going, whether she'd even reach the cape. If she could keep Liza out of her head long enough to get there.

She spread her legs, bracing her feet on either side of the boat. She tried not to look at the blood.

She couldn't do this.

The fog was too dense. Darkness rubbed her head and back.

Between her legs felt like fire. She gripped the oars so hard her fingers locked.

Gina shouted from what sounded like far away, a high-pitched shriek that sounded more frightened than angry. Judith chanced a look over the side of the boat, and her breath caught as a shadow swirled beneath her.

A small voice told her to push.

Her screams echoed across the water.

CHAPTER TWENTY-EIGHT

MEREDITH

PRESENT DAY

 eredith only knew it was night when Tempest walked into the room in a nightgown. Against the darkness of the room and the glow coming from somewhere else in the house lighting her thin form from behind, Tempest looked like a ghost. Meredith had been dozing on and off. At some point the shell fell out of her hands; she could feel it behind her thigh.

Tempest shut the door behind her softly and sat on the same bucket Vik had. She carried a small flashlight, which she sat on its end next to her, providing just enough light for Meredith to see her face and Tempest to see Meredith's. Tempest's hair was down, reaching nearly to her waist in thick waves. *Mermaid hair*, Meredith thought and bit back a rueful grin. Dark shadows surrounded Tempest's bright, attentive eyes. She didn't look away this time.

"That was you listening outside the door earlier, wasn't it?" Meredith asked.

Tempest didn't answer, but her gaze flicked briefly downward.

"What's Alice doing?"

"She's teaching Cally how to do cat's cradle."

"She's good at that."

The knife seemed to come from nowhere. Tempest flashed it in the beam of light before setting it in her lap. "Mom and Vik decided they're done waiting."

Meredith felt her heartbeat in her throat.

Tempest continued, "They figure Alice is still young enough it'll only take a little time to forget you. Tomorrow you go in the water, and they ride off into the sunset."

No, Meredith thought. She wouldn't let it happen. "Why are you telling me this?"

Sighing, Tempest stroked the knife handle. "Dad's a…" She stopped. Sniffed. "*Vik* is a good talker. He knows lots of words, and some days it seems like he's trying to use them all."

Meredith sat up as far as she could, the chains straining at her arms, and waited for Tempest to continue.

"He's the kind of person who knows things," Tempest said, "and wants you to know he knows things. He used to get so excited when Cally and I had questions. He'd answer anything, didn't matter how silly or strange or"—she wrinkled her nose and looked just like Regina—"inappropriate."

Tempest looked up, like she needed some kind of response. Meredith offered a small smile, worried to break whatever spell was unfolding.

"Want to hear a story he told us once?"

The shell had started to burn her thigh. She nudged it gently away before saying, "Sure."

"I was about ten or so. This was before Cally…before it happened. She was drawing some pictures for a story she'd written about a girl who talks to ocean creatures and lives in sea foam. She demanded he tell her about the girl in the water."

Meredith's heart thudded. Calamity and Alice were a lot alike. Good girls. Deserving girls.

"I could tell by looking at him he was worried about something. He does this thing where he squints really hard when he's thinking of a lie. But quick as anything he told her that one night a little girl who was too curious for her own good wanted to know what was at the bottom of the ocean, so she got up in the middle of the night and walked across the sand until she got to the water, and then she kept walking. She walked until she could hear the kelp whispering to the clams, until there was more water above her head than were stars in the sky, until—"

"Until she drowned," Meredith said.

Tempest nodded. "But Cally wasn't happy with that answer. She asked more questions. Demanded more answers."

"Curious girl."

"She didn't get it. She just kept going until he told her if she didn't watch out she'd get dragged into the sea same as the little girl." She paused. "I know what Mom says. And I believe her. Mostly. I read books Bobby brought from school."

Meredith frowned. "Bobby didn't have to live on the island, did he?"

Tempest shook her head. "Cally and me were trapped here, though. No school or friends or anything for us. He thinks we're stupid, that we can't do anything, but who do you think does everything while he's gone?" Her cheeks flashed scarlet. "Anyway, I read his history books and made him find things for me on the internet—don't look at me like that, yes, I know what the internet is—and I put my own story together, that she came after our family and that we were safe here while she was drawn to the cape, to you and your mom. Though I suppose Cally and I were always safe, right? Because she wouldn't want us—not unless we got in the way. Because we're not blood. But I also know that when there's no one left, when she comes looking for blood, Mom wouldn't hesitate to feed me and Cally to her if it meant she could live a little longer."

"With Marina," Meredith said.

Tempest nodded.

"You know Alice isn't her."

"It doesn't matter. Mom believes it."

Tempest was right. There were few forces in the world stronger or uglier than false belief.

Ignoring the pain in her wrists, Meredith twisted her body so the shell was nudged up the side of the tub.

"What's that?"

"Take it. Listen."

Eyeing Meredith, wary, she quickly snapped up the shell and held it to her ear. Her usually harsh expression softened, and she sank down onto the floor. The damp soaked through her nightgown.

"Is it her?" she asked. "It's like the ocean is crying."

"It's never been about revenge. It's not Liza out there. Liza died that day and stayed dead." Meredith hugged the side of the tub. "You know how it feels to need your mom, to beg for attention any way you know how and not get it. You know what it is to be scared and know the only thing that'll make it better is—"

"Mom," Tempest said. "It's Marina, isn't it? She's coming for her."

In the time Meredith had been chained in this dark room, all she could think about was Alice. How afraid she was. How fear blinds and angers and makes you desperate. Marina didn't tempt the women—the mothers—of her family into the water because she wanted revenge. She did it because she felt something inside them, a small piece of her mother, and she clung to it. Pulled it to her and used it as a lullaby until she woke again, lonely and afraid.

"We need to tell her," Tempest said. "If we tell her it's Marina out there, maybe it'll end this. She'll go to her and—"

Meredith was already shaking her head. "She wouldn't believe us, least of all me. I'd say anything to get her to give Alice back. If anything, I think it would only piss her off."

After a long moment, Tempest nodded. "You're probably right." She curled forward and wrapped her arms around her middle. "I kind of always knew. About being taken."

"How?"

Tempest shrugged. "Just a feeling. Dreams. I kept seeing this woman who looked like me, same red hair, but she was taller and smiled more." She smirked. "I've never told anyone about that. Not even Cally." Her eyes darkened. "And there's this place, deeper on the island. She calls it her garden, but there's only weeds and brambles and foul-smelling things that grow there. I checked it out once when I was little. Found a bunch of big flat rocks, like the ones on the beach, but they had names written on them with little crosses underneath."

Meredith's body went cold. It made a sick sort of sense. Of course there would have been others before Tempest and Calamity. How old was Vik? How long had he been *supplying help* to Gina?

"Does Cally know? About where you came from?"

Tempest nodded.

"Is she okay?"

"I don't think so. She loves Mo—Gina."

"But you love Cally more, don't you?"

A rueful smile crept onto Tempest's face. "Like a sister."

"You know what's going to happen tomorrow. Gina has her whole new life laid out, and when I'm dead and she's whisking Alice off to the cape, you'll be left behind. Or worse."

Tempest nodded, but Meredith could see the battle on her face. Even with everything Gina had done, with everything she was going to do, she was still the only mother Tempest had known.

Meredith continued, "Come back to the cape with me and Alice. Both of you." Then, seeing the battle almost won, "Maybe I can help you find the woman in your dreams."

Tempest looked hard at her. "Swear?"

"I *swear.*"

Tempest stood so fast it made Meredith jump. She took the knife and sawed through the ropes binding Meredith's feet. From somewhere in the folds of her nightgown, she produced a key, which she used to unlock the shackles on Meredith's wrists.

Even when they were off and the cool, damp air hit her raw skin, Meredith didn't move. "Where are you going?"

"Stay put until I come back," Tempest said, gathering up the shell and flashlight. "And stay quiet."

Meredith waited an eternity after Tempest left to try to stand. The same burning sensation that'd attacked her legs earlier was worse now; as she lifted them out of the water, it was like she'd been thrown on top of a pyre. She bit her lip so hard it bled to keep from screaming. Hot tears streamed down her face, dripping like rain into the bathtub. Her arms trembled with the effort of lifting herself out of the water, and her grip kept slipping on fresh blood that dribbled from broken open wounds. Finally out of the tub, she stood on shaky legs wondering how the hell she was going to run.

Thunder rumbled in the distance, and she whispered a little prayer that the rain held off.

Soon the burning in her legs and arms became a fiery tingle, like being bitten by a hundred ants. Not pleasant, but at least tolerable. She looked around for a weapon in case whatever Tempest planned turned into a fight. The chains were stuck to the legs of the bathtub, which was too heavy to try to lift, to free them. The bucket was plastic, pretty much useless. She grabbed it anyway when the door creaked open.

Tempest stuck her head in, flashlight shining from her waist, and raised an eyebrow. "What are you planning to do with that?"

"Whatever I have to."

Tempest rolled her eyes and elbowed the door open farther, letting the light in from the hall. Alice tumbled in, her eyes frantic and her hands reaching. They fell into each other like a wave against the shore; Meredith covered her with as much of her body as she could, kissing her head and face and trying so hard not to cry.

"We have to go," Alice said, pulling away.

"Hold on, kiddo." Meredith stepped around her, shielding her and looked at Tempest. "What's happening?"

She scoffed as if it were obvious. "I drugged Mom's tea. She should be good and drowsy by now."

"What about Vik?"

"Him too."

She thought of the effect it'd had on her. Maybe it was the adrenaline, but the effects hadn't been all that debilitating for long. Maybe Tempest had given them more than Gina had given her. Maybe less. Meredith had no choice but to trust her. Clutching Alice's hand, she followed Tempest into the hallway.

The house was quiet, and most of the lights were off. Candles flickered on the tables, casting eerie shadows on the walls. Outside, the thunder came louder, more often. Lightning flashed, and through the window, Meredith caught a glimpse of the already churning water.

Calamity was sitting on the couch, her knees drawn up to her chin. Tempest kneeled in front of her and whispered something Meredith didn't hear.

"We need to go," Meredith whispered. "Now."

"A *minute*," Tempest shot back.

Meredith nodded, pulling Alice tight against her, the substance and warmth of her body, of knowing that she was alive and unhurt, was like a salve.

"Are you okay, Mom?" she asked.

"I'm just fine, kiddo."

"You're bleeding."

Where the rope had rubbed her legs, her skin had split. Blood dripped down her ankle.

"Just a scratch," Meredith said. "I'll be okay."

Finally, Tempest pulled Calamity off the couch and motioned for Meredith and Alice to follow.

They walked alongside the gravel trail, all of them barefoot. Meredith gritted her teeth through the stab and pinch of broken shells, eventually lifting Alice onto her hip even though the pain of Alice's weight on what was probably a bruised rib was excruciating.

Alice must have felt her wincing. "I can walk, Mom."

"No." Meredith gripped her tighter. "I'm never letting you go again."

Calamity's whimpering slowed and eventually stopped, soothed by Tempest's careful whispers and tight hold on her shoulders. Meredith knew how much Calamity wanted to give her mother whatever she wanted; it must have been killing her to do this. Tempest, however, walked with a sureness in her step that Meredith hadn't seen in her before. It reminded her of how she felt the day she decided to leave the cape. It was a huge undertaking, and she'd known then that any shot she'd had of making Judith love her the way she wanted was gone. Looking at Tempest, she felt something between pride and pity.

She smelled the rain in the air and tried not to think about what would happen if it started to pour. They needed to hurry.

They reached the dock, and Tempest slipped into the rowboat that'd brought Meredith to the island in the first place.

"We'll never get out of here fast enough. We need the motor," Meredith whispered, nodding to the motorboat on the other side of the dock.

"We can't. I tried to get the key off Vik, but I couldn't find it." She eyed the boat. "I could go back. Maybe if I looked—"

"No. There's no time." She nodded at the sky, the roiling clouds just visible as the moon peeked through. "I don't think the rain's gonna hold off. We need to get moving."

As she spoke, the first drops hit the back of her neck.

Meredith was too weak to row, so Tempest took the oars while Meredith and Calamity climbed in. They were packed tightly, with Alice sitting on the floor of the boat between Meredith's legs, and the slightest movement sent the whole boat rocking. Meredith's heart was in her throat, and she couldn't stop looking over her shoulder, expecting to see Regina and Vik running after them. She didn't feel the cold of the rain until they'd put a good distance between themselves and the island, then she couldn't stop shivering.

The rain picked up. Meredith hunched over Alice, covering her with as much of her body as she could to keep her dry. Alice wrapped herself around Meredith's legs, rubbing her hands up and down to try to warm them.

"You're like ice, Mom," she said, worried.

Meredith squeezed her shoulder, stealing glances at the water, growing more restless by the second. Waves bumped hard against the boat, like fists.

Every splash, every groan of the old wood as it was tossed around, made Meredith's heart jump into her throat. Would Marina come after them?

She wanted to believe she'd reached Marina somehow, that by seeing her, recognizing her, she might have saved them, but Marina was scared. Overwhelmed. Meredith could feel it every time she breathed, a coppery taste in the air.

"How do you know where you're going?" Meredith asked Tempest.

"I just know," Tempest said.

Calamity moved to stick her hand overboard.

"No!" Tempest barked. "I'm not lost. It's fine."

Calamity pulled back. Alice tapped her knee. Calamity tapped Alice's back.

Lightning flashed, too close. Static pulled at the hairs on Meredith's arms. Water pooled at the bottom of the boat, and she couldn't tell if it was the rain or a leak. If Marina didn't kill them, she worried the storm might.

She shot a look at Tempest, who nodded, understanding.

Hurry.

At the sound of a boat motor, they all tensed.

Calamity covered her ears, and Alice hid beneath the bench Meredith was sitting on. Tempest grunted and grit her teeth and rowed faster.

Meredith clutched the side of the boat and squinted through the rain, but all she saw was darkness. Calamity inched closer, and Alice hugged her leg. Tempest fought with the oars, which kept getting popped out of place when the waves pitched up. The grim determination on her face had cracked, and Meredith could tell she was fighting back tears.

"Let me take over," she said.

Tempest nodded, and as the boat rocked precariously, Meredith held on to the oars to keep them in place while Tempest crawled under her legs toward the other bench. She hoped the dark was enough to keep them hidden, but as the sound of the boat motor grew louder, she realized it didn't matter. Regina wouldn't stop until she got what she wanted.

Every muscle in Meredith's body screamed as she plunged the oars into the water and pulled with her whole weight. The waves fought back, a million hands clinging. That Tempest had gotten them this far was incredible.

Alice had climbed out from beneath the bench, the water up to her ankles in the bottom of the boat now, and into Calamity's lap.

Tempest held them both. "I'm sorry," she said. "I thought I gave her enough. I thought—"

"Just hold on," Meredith said.

But she was rowing blindly now, didn't even know if she was moving away from the island or was being dragged back toward it. She glanced over her shoulder as lightning streaked across the sky, lighting up the world for an instant. Squinting against the rain and the sea spray, she saw Regina at the wheel of the motorboat, hair flying wild behind her. She was gaining, quickly.

They couldn't outrow her.

As Meredith's mind frantically tried to work through a plan, she noticed a change in the water. Waves still smacked at the boat, but they hung a beat too long before slipping away. While the sea had been dark before, now it was black, eating the faint light from Regina's boat as it approached.

Marina.

Regina swung up beside them, cutting the engine as she got close. As she drifted past, she threw a small anchor toward them. It missed hitting Calamity's head by a hair, landing in front of her feet.

Tempest scrambled to throw it out, but Regina gunned the engine, and it yanked out of her hands. It dragged along the bottom of the rowboat, catching on the bench between Meredith's legs. It caught her skin, and white-hot pain shot up her body.

She was going to drag them back to the island.

As the rope grew taut, the rowboat rocked hard, and Calamity fell back, losing her grip on Alice.

The splash was like a knife to Meredith's chest.

"Mom!"

Regina cut the engine just as their boat drifted alongside. Every wave pushed them farther from Alice.

Meredith clawed helplessly at the rope, which had twisted around her ankle.

"I got her!" Tempest started to climb over the side when Gina leaned down and snatched her back by the hair.

"How dare you?" Gina spat. "After everything I did for you. I am your *mother*."

On the other side of the boat, Calamity crouched into a ball, tears and snot dripping. "Stop, please, everyone stop!"

Tempest arched her back and clawed at Gina's face. "You're no one's mother."

Meredith finally kicked the rope free and fought to get her legs beneath her, but with all the movement, the boat was seconds from capsizing. She gripped the side and saw Alice struggling to tread water.

"Alice!"

Gina's gaze snapped to the water. "Marina!"

Behind Alice, the waves swelled and broke, cresting in unison, becoming a wall of black water.

Marina was here.

Tempest managed to twist out of Gina's grip and shoved her back. Gina landed hard on her back and gasped, the wind knocked out of her. Meredith wasn't going to get another chance. She hurled herself over the side and swam toward Alice, the water pulling her farther and farther away. The salt water burned her cuts, and her shoulders screamed in protest, but Meredith didn't stop until she reached Alice, pulling her daughter toward her. She couldn't keep them both afloat, so she held her breath and ducked beneath the water, gripping Alice's legs. She kicked, propelling them toward the boat. When she came up for air, she saw Tempest leaning over Calamity, blood dripping from her mouth. Gina was waiting with her hand outstretched.

"Come on," she said. "That's it, my darling."

Alice shied away, but Gina was quick. She grabbed her and pulled her up, over the side of the boat, then landed two quick kicks to Meredith's face as she tried to climb in after her. Meredith's head swam, her vision blurry. She could hardly move, but she couldn't let Gina get away with Alice.

Alice thrashed, using all of her little girl might to punch and kick and bite, but Gina had her wrapped in a tight embrace. Meredith gripped the side and pulled with all her weight. The movement knocked them both over. Tempest grabbed Alice and shoved her between her and Calamity, whose eyes were covered, her shoulders shaking.

Gina was face-to-face with Meredith, her eyes bloodshot. An angry scar on her cheek seemed to throb.

Meredith adjusted her grip on the side, preparing to climb over, when something that felt like nails grazed her calf. She froze, her fingers digging into the rail. She looked at Alice, but Alice stared at the place beside Meredith, mouth gaping.

The water seemed to cradle Marina, her skeletal limbs limp and shifting with the waves. The sickly pale skin of her face sunk inward, her cheeks in shreds, eaten away by time and salt, and her eyes were empty black holes. Whatever was left of the young girl seemed long gone, replaced by a wraith puppeted by the lingering fear and despair Marina had left behind. But this close to her, Meredith's body trembled with the force of Marina's anger. Her sadness. *Her memory.*

Shadows bled from Marina's body into the water, like oil, and seeped toward Meredith, too fast. The instant the inky black touched her skin, the world seemed to fall away, lingering, foggy at the edge of her vision. Like a dream, she saw the water beside the cape. A flash of white in the distance. A girl was swimming slowly and painfully through the chop. Marina. She dove beneath the waves, and though she couldn't see it, Meredith's hands prickled with the sensation of tugging and untying. A sharp prick on her thumb, and an image flashed of the pink shell. She tasted blood. Finally, in the dream, Marina surfaced. Meredith felt the pain in her chest, the panic as her lungs worked for air that never seemed to come. An undertow swept in from beneath, taking Marina's legs out from under her and forcing her back under. When she kicked her way back up, only for a second, she saw—and Meredith saw—Regina on the beach, her back to the water as she ran toward the bluff. Meredith's throat went raw as she listened to Marina scream for her mother with all the strength she had left. But the Regina on the beach didn't hear. Didn't turn around. And soon, Marina was pulled farther out to sea where she drowned, her mother's name on her tongue.

As the fog receded, Marina reached out, groping, an agonized expression on her face. It was almost like she was lost. With both Meredith and Gina there, both mothers of the same bloodline, did Marina not recognize the difference?

Meredith called out to her. "Marina."

Marina tilted her head toward Meredith, listening.

"Mommy's waiting on the boat for you."

A chill snaked through Meredith as Marina lingered, leaning closer to her, fingers moving along the surface, feeling.

"Go on," Meredith urged, voice trembling. "She misses you."

Gina stumbled back. A silent scream etched onto her face, she fumbled for the key to restart the engine, but Tempest was faster. She fell on the console, and as Gina clawed at her, she slid the key out of the ignition.

Attention finally pulled to the boat, to Gina, Marina effortlessly pulled herself out of the water, sliding over the side with a horrible squelching sound. Her lips moved, but no words came out. Alice, transfixed, mimicked the movement. As Meredith studied her daughter's face, she realized what it was—*Ma ma ma ma.*

Mama.

Gina slowly moved away from Marina, but there was only so far she could go before she tumbled over the side. She looked frantically around, settling on Calamity.

Meredith saw in the twist of Gina's mouth what she planned to do. "Don't!" she yelled. Then, to Tempest, "Get Cally!"

But Gina was too fast. She ripped Calamity up by the shoulders and shoved her toward Marina. Marina batted her away, impossibly strong, and when Calamity fell, her head hit the side of the boat with a sickening crack. She toppled over the side on top of Meredith.

Still clinging to the side, Meredith looped her arm beneath Calamity's, struggling to keep her face above-water. Rain pelted them both, mixing with the blood that ran from Calamity's forehead. She wasn't breathing.

Trapped behind Gina, Tempest shouted, but Meredith couldn't hear. Her pulse pounded hard in her ears.

Someone cried, "Mama," and arm trembling on the verge of giving out, Meredith pulled herself and Calamity up enough to see Marina touch Gina's face.

Gina's mouth went slack. Her eyes widened, out of focus.

As a clap of thunder made the water shiver, Marina wrapped her body tightly around Gina's, an embrace that seemed to crack her bones, and together they fell over the side. Waves crashed against the boat, knocking Meredith off the side. Refusing to let go of Calamity, she started to sink.

Hands plunged into the water above her, snagging her by her hair, her collar, and pulled. Meredith sucked in a breath of air as her face broke the surface. Tempest reached for Calamity, and together they were able to push her into the boat. Meredith barely made it over the side, hitting the bottom with a painful thunk. Alice fell on her, shaking and crying.

Meredith held her with what was left of her strength while Tempest cradled Calamity's head in her lap, tears streaming down her face.

For a long time, nobody spoke. The rain finally stopped, but the clouds lingered. Meredith patted Alice's head and turned to Tempest. "We need to get back to the cape. We can get her to a doctor."

Tempest nodded, but she probably knew what Meredith did—Calamity was gone. She handed Meredith the key she'd stolen from the ignition.

With Alice clinging to her side, Meredith turned the key, warm relief washing over her when the motor roared to life.

"It's over," Alice said, but Meredith heard the question in it.

Meredith rubbed her back. "Yes. It's over, sweetie."

Each movement was murder on her body, but she pushed past the pain and focused on getting home. She so desperately wanted to believe this was the end. Marina found her mother. This was supposed to be it. The happily ever after.

Alice's hands around her middle brought Meredith back into her body. At the other end of the boat, Tempest clutched Calamity to her chest, her lips trembling and her eyes shining.

As the sun began to rise, Meredith studied the horizon until she saw the familiar spire of the lighthouse. With it in her sights, she gunned the throttle, and for the first time in a long time, she breathed in deep the salty sea air without fear.

CHAPTER TWENTY-NINE

MEREDITH

PRESENT DAY

our days after Meredith's rowboat finally touched the beach, the police found Vik buried beneath the remains of the house on the island. The storm had obliterated it. Meredith's only regret was that he was probably asleep when it happened, thanks to the sedatives.

Her greatest concern, though, was Art. Vik had said he'd sent Bobby back to *take care of him*, but when Meredith finally found him, Art was alive.

"Not for lack of trying," Art had said.

He told her Bobby had set his workroom on fire with the taxidermy chemicals while Art was working, that his shop was all but destroyed, but Art had made it out without getting too hurt. A few cuts from the broken glass. Smoke inhalation. The police caught up with Bobby shortly after. Loyal to Vik, just like Vik said, Bobby never breathed a word about the island.

She wondered if that would change once he found out Vik was dead. If the police would find the garden Tempest told her about and maybe bring closure to who knew how many families whose children had gone missing.

Meredith set to work almost immediately keeping her promise to Tempest. She gathered as much information as she could about missing children's cases from around the time Tempest thought she might have been taken. Meredith wanted to help Tempest go through it all, to see if anything jumped out at her, but it didn't take long for Tempest to get overwhelmed.

Tempest might have been able to handle it better if she'd had Calamity with her, but under the weight of her sister's death, Tempest was slowly sinking inward. Though Art had gotten some response out of her showing her how to paint the bright scales of a flounder he was mounting, she just as easily retreated into Judith's bedroom, where Meredith insisted she sleep.

Kristin was there too, for a day.

"I'm sorry," Art had said. "I called her."

"I know," Meredith had said. "We talked. I'm still angry with her. I don't know if I'll ever not be angry, but I am grateful she was here."

Part of her hoped for a tearful reconciliation, a demand that she and Alice come home, that she was so sorry—but Meredith was almost glad when it never came. She needed to start over. Completely. She couldn't do that with Kristin.

They had eaten dinner in the house. Alice and Kristin played war with old playing cards until Alice practically fell over, exhausted.

"You don't have to stay here," Kristin said after Meredith put Alice to sleep on the couch. "You could come back to Arlington. It's still your home too."

"That's not what the papers say."

Kristin, to her credit, didn't take the bait. Meredith might have been in the mood for a fight, but Kristin knew her better. Meredith was wrung out and bitter and so, so tired.

"I still want to see her," Kristin said. "Maybe we can work out a weekends thing."

"Yeah," Meredith said. "Maybe."

"I didn't mean it, you know. I don't *want* to give her up. I just thought…"

"You thought it would appease me."

"I was *scared*, okay? This is scary for me too." She sighed. "This marriage isn't right for us—for me—but I still care about you. I still love Alice. I just want what's best for all of us."

"I know," Meredith finally said, and meant it.

Her flight back wasn't until the next day, but Kristin left before midnight. She was staying in town. They could have breakfast before she went to the airport. Meredith told Kristin she'd call her.

She didn't.

The next morning, Meredith went upstairs to pry Tempest out of bed. The police wanted to talk with them again, and Meredith didn't want Tempest telling them about Marina. With Regina and Vik both dead, there was a chance Tempest was going to be taken in by the state. Meredith didn't want her ending up locked away somewhere. If Tempest was up for it, Meredith was going to ask if she'd want to stay here with them.

But the bed was made—never slept in—and on the mirror above the dresser, Tempest had scribbled a note in Mom's kohl eyeliner: *I'll be okay. Don't look for me.* Then, tacked on like an afterthought: *Thanks.*

They hadn't said much to each other since that night beyond Meredith offering coffee in the mornings and dinner at night. She'd wanted to explain herself, though she didn't know exactly what needed explaining. She wanted to say a million things she didn't have words for, to relay big, complicated emotions, forgiveness being the biggest and most complicated. She understood why Tempest had done what she had. She understood what it was to need something from someone and to be willing to do just about anything to get it.

Whatever it was Tempest needed now, Meredith hoped she'd find it.

For the first couple of nights, Alice and Meredith slept in Meredith's old room together. Meredith, scared to take her eyes off Alice for longer than a few seconds, didn't sleep much. Sometimes she woke up alone, panicked, only to find Alice sprawled out in her mother's bed, face buried in the pillows.

Even in the harsh daylight, she was plagued by mental images that left her feeling out of touch with reality. In the time it took to blink, she was met with Marina's empty-eyed gaze, and it was like a shot of cold water. She waited for the relief to settle over her, the knowledge they'd come through the other side of something horrible, but as quickly as it'd come that first day back, it faded.

Art told her it was a trauma response. She was still waiting for the other shoe to drop. "Took a long time for me to get back into a boat after my dad passed," he said. "Still a struggle, to be honest, but every day it got a little easier."

For Meredith, it only seemed to get worse.

She thought about sending Alice back to Arlington while she figured out what to do with the house, the lighthouse. *Safe*, she thought. *Have to keep Alice safe.* But when she tried to talk to Alice about it, Alice begged her not to send her away.

"Don't you want to go home?" Meredith asked. "Sleep in your own bed? Play with your friends?"

"I don't have any friends," Alice said. "Art is my friend." Then, "Why can't I stay here?"

In the end, Meredith gave in. She told herself she was being ridiculous, that the nightmares would eventually stop, even as she started slipping half a sleeping pill in her mouth at night just so she could get a few hours of rest before the anxiety ripped her back into consciousness.

Yes, they could move. And yes, it was probably the right thing to do. But it wouldn't matter. Alice would find her way back, just as Meredith had. Art was right. She just needed to give the uneasy feeling in the pit of her stomach time to pass.

A few weeks passed and Meredith and Alice fell into a sort of routine. Meredith looked for work nearby while Art and Alice produced the colorful taxidermy creations of Alice's dreams (and in some cases, of Meredith's nightmares; Alice insisted the bug-eyed gull sleep in Meredith's room). Alice was happy, and Meredith thought she might get there too, in time. It was hard still, sleeping in her mother's room, hearing her voice in her dreams. And the water. Sometimes she thought she heard it calling her. She hadn't intended to turn on the red light when they'd returned, but in the end relented, hoping it would relieve the lingering feeling of unease.

Tonight, determined to get a decent night's sleep, she drank too much wine and finally climbed upstairs when she found herself drifting off on the couch in front of the television. She peeked in on Alice—fast asleep, Octopussy hugged tight—and then collapsed in bed. She was asleep before her head hit the pillow.

What felt like seconds later, a loud crash jolted her awake. Heart pounding, she blinked away another nightmare, her mind taking too long to shed the fear and the feel of water on her face, in her nose, in her lungs. Movement in the corner of her eye, she groped the bedside table until she found the lamp's switch. She squinted as her eyes adjusted to the sudden light. On the floor were the shattered remains of a water glass, the curtain flailing above it. She must have left the window open. The wind in the curtain knocked the glass over.

Everything is fine. Relax.

She climbed out of bed and carefully stepped over the glass toward the window. She thought about leaving the glass until morning, but then she thought about Alice—her perpetual early riser—bounding in here to drag Meredith out of bed and down to the beach before her interview, and knew she'd have to clean it up. She'd never get back to sleep now.

She started to close the window when something down on the beach caught her eye. It was hard to see in the dark, but as the red light passed over the sand, Meredith spotted Alice, her blanket trailing from her shoulders like a cape. She was heading for the water.

No. *Please.*

Meredith ran through the broken glass, feeling nothing but white-hot panic. This was supposed to be over. It was *over*, goddamn it.

She hesitated a fraction of a second at Alice's room, thinking, praying, she'd hallucinated it, a hangover from her nightmares, but Alice's bed was empty. Cursing, Meredith ran down the stairs and out the already swinging front door. She would not lose Alice again. Not this way. Not now. Not after everything.

She hit the sand, and the momentum nearly sent her sprawling. The sand was loose and soft and swallowed her feet with each step. Her legs burned and she screamed her throat raw: "Alice!"

But Alice either didn't hear her or there was something in her head blocking Meredith out.

By the time she reached Alice—finally, finally—Alice had stopped moving, but her eyes wouldn't leave the water, tears streaming down her face.

Meredith grabbed her by the shoulders and shook her, her own body trembling. Her mouth was cotton. "What the hell are you doing? You scared the shit out of me. You could have—"

Alice wailed and it cut through Meredith like a knife.

"Baby, tell me what's wrong. What's happening? Did you have a nightmare or…?"

Alice shook her head. "I'm sad because she's sad, and I'm scared because she's

scared. She's alone forever, Mom, and it hurts so bad and I can't breathe and…
and…" Alice fell against Meredith, her words dissolving into hiccups.

"No." Meredith refused to look at the water. To see the shadows twisting in the corners of her vision. "She's got her mom with her, remember? She's not alone, sweetie. She's not."

So then why could Meredith hear her cries in her head? Why did she have to dig her feet in the sand to keep from crawling toward her?

You're no one's mother.

Tempest's last words to Regina flashed through Meredith's mind.

"Mom?"

Alice's voice sounded so far away. Alice—Meredith thought she would be safe. She was Meredith's whole heart. Had Marina been Regina's whole heart? Or had Regina been so twisted by a nonexistent revenge, a desperation to live, that whatever heart she had left had been corrupted into something Marina couldn't recognize?

They could leave tonight. They could run away, to the other side of the earth. They could hide and forget the cape and the pine forests and the endless ocean and the magic. But they wouldn't stay away forever. Alice couldn't stay away. In the end, Marina's heartbreak would draw her back, the way it drew them all. It had to end with Meredith. Meredith, who never wanted to be a mother but who had enough love in her in the end to be mother to them all. All the drowning girls who had died and who had yet to be born.

She knew what she had to do. It was what her mother had tried to do, what a whole line of mothers had tried to do but maybe didn't understand *why* they were doing it. And that was the problem. It was why Marina had come back. Would always come back.

It had to be Meredith because Meredith knew who Marina was, had seen her death, her pain, and had *ached* for her. And it had to be Meredith's choice.

Blinking away tears, Meredith knelt in front of Alice. Forced her to look at her. "Sweetie, you have to do something for me, okay?"

Alice nodded, but her gaze kept flicking over Meredith's shoulder, her little body trembling.

"Do you remember how to get to Art's house?"

She nodded again. Alice often ran ahead of her on the days they went.

"Good. I need you to go there now."

Alice stiffened, panic etched on her face. "No!"

"Alice, it's important. You're going to be okay. Everything's going to be okay. I promise."

But Alice shrank under the weight of her tears. "No it won't! You're going to go away, and I don't want you to go away. I can't do it I can't go I won't..."

Meredith wrapped her arms tight around her daughter, muffling her protests, grateful that Alice couldn't see her own tears. She couldn't do this. She wouldn't.

She had to.

Behind her, the water raged.

She kissed Alice's head and then pulled away, prying Alice's hands off her clothes. "I love you," Meredith said between gritted teeth. "I *love* you. Do you understand?"

"Yes."

"Good. Don't forget it. Ever."

Alice's voice cracked. "I won't."

"Go to Art's. Run. And don't look back, okay? Just keep running until you get there." Alice took a shaky step back, but when she didn't turn, didn't run, Meredith ordered, "Now!"

Half stumbling, Alice took off through the sand, toward Art's. Meredith watched until she crossed the dune, until she could hear Alice's feet hitting the boards of the bridge.

And then Meredith turned to the water.

She shivered as the water rushed over her feet. The red light brushed the waves, and Meredith saw her—Marina, floating in and out of the ocean tide. Slight. Ethereal. Meredith moved toward her, thinking all the time of Alice, hoping she would understand one day. That she wasn't leaving her, that she would never leave her, that she loved her and would save her if it meant Meredith drowned over and over again.

Water up to Meredith's waist, Marina was close enough to touch. She looked so young, so frail, her expression frozen in despair and longing. As each wave crashed against Meredith, the spray carried the sound of sorrow.

"Hush now." Meredith cradled her arms beneath Marina, bringing her close. Her body was like ice. "I've got you."

Marina leaned into Meredith's chest, and as the ground dropped away, she sighed.

As they drifted lower, lower, Marina clung to Meredith. And as Meredith's chest burned and everything in her body begged her to let go, to swim, to save herself, she thought of Alice and stilled. She brushed Marina's hair from her face.

It's okay. Sleep now. Mama's here.

CHAPTER THIRTY

ALICE

It was the best sandcastle yet, with towers and a bridge and a moat filled with real water and flags made of toothpicks and gum wrappers stuck on top of the parapets.

That was the word of the day. *Parapet.*

Alice had been choosing words at random out of the dictionary for her daughters—Merry and Charlotte—to learn, their brains ever absorbing, clamoring for more words, more information. More stories.

"Papet!" Charlotte pointed at the lighthouse, her whole body vibrating with excitement.

"Wrong, dummy," Merry said. She was eleven, a whole six years older than her sister and made sure Charlotte knew it. "That's the lighthouse."

"Papet," Charlotte insisted, armed crossed.

Alice picked her up, wiped the sand off her belly and shoulders. "Merry's right."

Merry preened.

"And Charlotte's right." Alice tickled Charlotte under her arms and behind her knees, the girl writhing like a fish. Alice looked at Merry. "Your sister's not a dummy."

It was an easy mistake. They'd looked at a ton of pictures of crumbling castles this morning, and the lighthouse, with its warped catwalk and eroding stone, was falling apart. For a while, Art had been caring for the light, making minor repairs, patching broken cement, but he'd died when Alice was in college. She hadn't touched it since, content to let the thing rot. Though she would never give up the house—her house, where the last good memories of her mother lived—the lighthouse only ever reminded her of everything she'd lost. They'd condemn it eventually. Tear it down. She hoped she was here to see it.

Merry rolled her eyes, and Alice pretended not to notice. So smart, with a fierce independent streak, Alice sometimes wondered if she'd blessed or cursed her oldest by naming Merry after her mother.

She set Charlotte down, who went immediately for the water, which sparkled under the bright afternoon light. Alice resisted the urge to stop her. Charlotte knew not to go too deep, and both Alice's kids were confident swimmers. Still, it was hard to let them go. She believed that the curse—or whatever it was— that'd plagued her family was over. From that night, there was something different about the cape, like a shroud had been lifted. The sun felt warmer. The water more welcoming. But the pull was still there. She saw it in her daughters, too, last glances at the water when it was time to go, an anxious feeling in the pits of their stomachs when they visited Mama Kristin's family in Virginia, a melting relief when they returned.

Alice decided it wasn't some lingering vestiges of the curse that tied her, body and soul, to the cape. It was the knowledge that there was salt water in her veins. It was a love for this place so deeply entrenched in the blood of the women who had come before her that it passed down, an inevitable trait no different from their dark hair and hard smiles. And it was this realization that had allowed her to forgive her mother for leaving. Because of her, Alice could watch her children play, laughing in the surf, unafraid. Because of her, Alice and her children, and her children's children, could have this place, this feeling, forever.

"Mom!" Charlotte waved from the water. "Look! I'm a mermaid!"

Merry looked up from the sandcastle. "Me too, me too!" She bolted for the water, tackling her sister and then laughing when they both came up with seaweed tangled in their hair.

Behind Alice, a horn honked.

She turned to see her husband waiting in the car, waving. She wasn't supposed to let the girls get wet. They were heading to dinner in Ilwaco with a friend of his who was thinking of investing in their little florist shop. It'd been in his family for more than a hundred years. Almost sold it to a developer ten or so years ago, but he talked his aunt into letting him take over. He had quite the green thumb.

"Girls!" Alice waved them in. "Time to go!"

A chorus of groans followed them up the beach, where they reluctantly toweled off. Merry let out a wicked giggle, then snatched her sister's towel and made Charlotte chase her all the way back to the water.

"Oh no," Charlotte cried, dramatically falling back in. "My towel is wet. Guess I have to just stay here."

"Yeah," Merry said. "We'll grow fins and eat seaweed."

Alice smirked. "You? Eat a vegetable? Never."

Merry nodded solemnly. It was a sacrifice she was willing to make if it meant she didn't have to leave.

"Come on," Alice said. "Out you come. For real this time."

"Can we come back later?" Charlotte asked.

"After dinner?"

"Or tomorrow morning?"

"Please," they said in unison.

"We'll see," Alice said. "Here. Use my towel."

They batted at each other, giggling, and then squished together, shoulder to shoulder, with the towel wrapped around them. A two-headed girl-beast. An ache of sadness pressed on her chest that her mother would never be able to meet them, these two beautiful, wicked, wonderful girls she'd made.

"Thank you. Now go on up to the car," Alice said.

"Aren't you coming?" Merry asked, concern in the corners of her eyes.

Alice tweaked her nose. "One last swim."

Merry studied her a moment longer before letting a smile crack through. "Okay."

As the girls ran up the bridge to the car, Alice ran toward the water. Her breath caught with the chill, but she dove in, relishing the feel of the waves on every inch of her body. She swam harder, farther, until her chest ached, and she finally came up for air. She waved to her daughters standing on the bridge, and then closed her eyes and lay back, floating, and licking the salt from her lips. She let the water carry her back to shore, hearing the whisper of her mother, and all the women before her, in every wave.

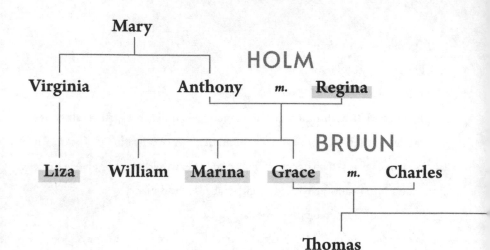

Mary

HOLM

Virginia Anthony *m.* Regina

BRUUN

Liza William Marina Grace *m.* Charles

Thomas

THE

ᴅROWNING GIRLS

OF

ᴄAPE DISAPPOINTMENT

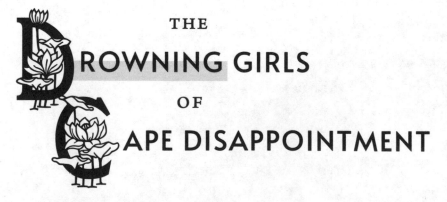

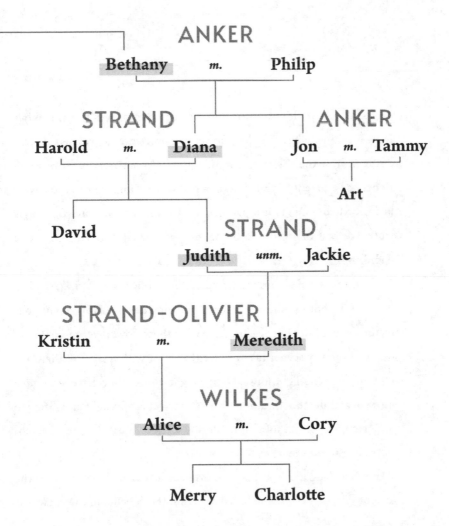

ANKER
Bethany   *m.*   Philip

STRAND   ANKER
Harold   *m.*   Diana   Jon   *m.*   Tammy

                                         Art

David

STRAND
Judith   *unm.*   Jackie

STRAND-OLIVIER
Kristin   *m.*   Meredith

WILKES
Alice   *m.*   Cory

Merry   Charlotte

1. Meredith and Judith's relationship is as complex as it is heartbreaking. How would you describe their power dynamic and the way secrets play a role in how their relationship developed? What are your own experiences as a parent or the child of a parent who might not have always been forthcoming? Is it a parent's job to shield their child from ugly truths, or is it their duty to be honest, even when the truth might be damaging?

2. Thalias are crucial within the world of *They Drown Our Daughters*. How does the author use them as a foreshadowing device? How might your reading experience change knowing what these flowers represent?

3. Many of the key scenes take place either in or within sight of the Cape Disappointment lighthouse. Why might the author have chosen a piece of architecture traditionally meant to represent light and safety to underscore dark and sometimes deadly scenes? What does that searching red light represent?

4. When her daughter is kidnapped, Meredith is keen to latch on to the idea of a curse, despite the fact that her mother's belief in the curse was

part of what soured their relationship. Why might she be so willing to believe in it now, at this critical juncture? What "truth" about her own ability as a mother is she trying to deny by embracing the idea of a curse?

5. Meredith struggles with the fear that, despite all her efforts, she isn't a "good" mother. What might be feeding that fear?

6. Though Regina is revealed to be a villain, she is often portrayed as a victim. How might her victimhood have contributed to her becoming villainous? Does she believe herself to be a villain or victim? Why?

7. As a parent, Diana's decision to pretend that the danger plaguing their family doesn't exist appears to have disastrous consequences. Can it be argued that Diana was acting in the best interest of her children? Or were her intentions selfish?

8. When Meredith first returns to the cape, she compares the French words for sea (la mer) and mother (la mère), noting how close they are to being the same. How might the setting for the novel be representative of motherhood? How might it be a parallel of Meredith and Judith's fraught relationship?

9. As a child, Judith had an incredibly vivid imagination. How was that used to build her character? How does she use stories to cope with upheaval and uncertainty?

10. Judith tries to both bargain with and fight back against Marina, leading to a couple of tragic deaths. Was Judith responsible for those deaths? Why did Marina drown her uncle and friend?

11. Meredith, Judith, and Alice all use the pink shell to communicate with Marina's ghost. Is there any significance to when the shell presents itself to each character? How might you compare their experiences?

12. The legend of the mermaid was once the backbone of Cape Disappointment. How might Marina's presence in the water have

inadvertently inspired the legend? What similarities are there between her spirit and a siren?

13. How does this book compare to other novels you've read that are set near the ocean? What similarities can you think of? What differences?

14. How does the book's title work in relation to its contents? What assumptions did you draw about the curse based on the title? Do Meredith's or Judith's assumptions about the curse mirror or oppose your own?

15. Is there any significance to Alice allowing the lighthouse to fall into complete disrepair? What are the possible implications of your interpretation of the ending?

16. What book or movie or story has scared you the most? How do the frightening aspects of this novel compare?

ACKNOWLEDGMENTS

First and foremost, thank you to my wife, Crystal. Thank you for letting me talk at you while I untangled plot snarls, for taking care of the house, the kids, the cat while I locked myself away in my office, but mostly for being proud of me and making sure I knew it. I love you.

Abby and Dillan—thank you for trying very hard not to make me crazy. You're good kids.

Big thanks to my incredible agent, Joanna MacKenzie. Your patience and support as I bounced between genres and age groups as I churned out manuscript after manuscript trying to find my place as a writer should all but guarantee sainthood. I will be forever grateful for the advice, the kindness, and the hard work you've put into this book and others.

To Mary Altman, editor extraordinaire, your encouragement has done wonders for my ego. Thank you for believing so passionately in this book, in me, and for helping me discover a genre I never would have imagined for myself.

Thank you to Kim for listening to me whine without complaint, and for being honest when I asked it of you. I am a better person and writer because of your friendship.

To Renee, Henry, Kate, Wendy, Carlos, Andrea, and everyone else from the OG On Fiction Writing group, but especially to Renee, who was never afraid to tell me when I sucked, and then stuck with me until I didn't.

Finally, thank you to friends and family who have shared in the excitement of this journey and given their unending support: Allison Keller, Emily Monroe, Raul (Oates) Fernandez, Kate Moretti, Erica Nohr, Bert and Amy Jones, and Kellie Gave.